HER KNIGHT'S DESIRE

CINDY KEEN REYNDERS

PRESS

Kenmore, WA

CAMEL
PRESS

A Camel Press book published by Epicenter Press

Epicenter Press
6524 NE 181st St.
Suite 2
Kenmore, WA 98028

For more information go to:
www.Camelpress.com
www.Coffeetownpress.com
www.Epicenterpress.com
www.cindykeenreynders.com

Cover design by Scott Book
Design Melissa Vail Coffman

Her Knight's Desire
Copyright © 2025 by Cindy Keen Reynders

Library of Congress Control Number: 2024952555

ISBN: 978-1-68492-328-1 (Trade Paper)
ISBN: 978-1-68492-329-8 (eBook)

*As always, thank you to my husband and my family
for their patience and understanding when
I go into my office and disappear for hours.
They appreciate my writing addiction
and for that I will be eternally grateful.*

ACKNOWLEDGMENTS

THANK YOU TO THE GREATER POWER that has blessed me to have my way with words. Also, I appreciate that Camel Press has allowed me to join the ranks of their authors.

ONE

The Southern Coast of Ireland, 1170 A.D.

T HE STEADY BEAT OF *BODHRAN* WAR drums rang in Rhiannon
O'Kelly's ears, the sound reverberating against her weary soul.
She stood atop Doon Hill where her father's troops had taken their
final stand, their life's blood staining the soil muddy red.

O'Kelly warriors lay around her, their corpses twisted into
gruesome poses. They'd fought to the death to defend their kingdom. This day, they met their glorious end. For such loyal bravery,
they were ripped and torn asunder, their insides strewn toward
Lough Corrib's vast blueness shimmering in the noonday sun.

Nostrils twitching with the smell of singed flesh and gore, she
glanced down at her tight-fitting leather leggings and tunic. Blood
spattered the outfit, her arms—her entire body.

Heartsick, she lifted her gaze with trepidation and watched,
sweat dotting her brow, as Tadgh Donovan marched his troops
steadily up the slope. She hated that son of Satan with every fiber
of her being, hated the dark pall of death his greed had caused.
Because of his false claim to her father's kingdom, many people's
lives had been shattered, including hers. For years, he'd battled
her father to steal Callinon. Now he would lay illegal claim to
her home.

As a chill breeze brushed her cheeks, she shivered, recalling the events that led to this fateful moment. It was not unusual for Irish princesses to be schooled in the art of war in order to protect their homeland. She had trained to be a warrior along with her brother, Seamus, though females weren't expected to participate in battle. However, when her father's army grew so weak, Rhiannon insisted upon joining the ranks. Before one particular melee, Moran had begged her to stay home, yet she'd stubbornly insisted upon going.

That was the skirmish in which her brother had been felled by Donovan's arrow—the one meant for her. Guilt lanced through her, sharp and painful. Seamus gave his life so that she might live, and the memory weighed heavily upon her. Especially since her mother had died shortly after Seamus—no doubt from a broken heart.

As if this double tragedy hadn't been enough, during that very same battle, Jamie O'Brien, her betrothed, had betrayed the O'Kelly clan. Fearing for his life, he'd deserted her father's army and joined Donovan's cause. Having known each other since they were little, the two had once been close, but his treachery had devastated Rhiannon.

Moran and the elders had appointed her the next in line to lead the clan. With no other sons, Moran's eldest daughter was a reasonable choice. Honored by her father's decision, she took her responsibilities seriously. She would fight to the death for her people—it was her duty.

The approaching army's chain mail clanked with brutal finality, drawing Rhiannon from her introspection. The men's voices grated against the smoky air. It was over for her, over for her kinsmen and women.

Throughout this unholy war, it seemed her efforts had all been for naught. She felt ineffective, powerless. By now, nearly all of Clan O'Kelly's members had fallen.

Rhiannon lived but couldn't be certain of her future. During the thick of the conflict, she'd been separated from her father. When she assumed her position on the hill, she watched several of

Moran's men help him limp from the battlefield. He survived, but where was he? Why did he not return to rescue them?

Her stomach wrenched with grief, and she fought bitter tears. She felt empty, numb. Her will to live, stripped. The brutality of war ached like a knife in her heart.

The villagers who fled to safety in the emerald, green highlands of Connemara were the lucky ones. Those left behind; the weak and the elderly, and those too young to travel, would be the ones to pay the price. Her eight-year-old sister, Ailleen, hidden away at Callinon Castle, was in grave danger.

Taking a shuddering breath, Rhiannon glanced down at Donovan's men approaching with sickening speed.

They're almost here.

Rhiannon plunged her sword into the earth, her fingers gripping the ring hilt as she knelt to pray. "I've failed you Holy Father," she muttered into the salty sea breeze that whipped her long red hair around her shoulders. "Take my life if you must but spare my people."

TWO

*T*HEY'RE COMING FOR ME.

Rhiannon lifted up from her hay pillow when she heard hollow footsteps in the hallway. She'd existed in this cramped, four-walled prison cell so long; she'd lost count of the days. By now, she wasn't even certain her brain functioned properly.

Have I taken leave of my senses? Am I hearing things?

She pressed back against the stone wall and rubbed her nose, trying to rid it of the permeating stench. Her thin woolen shift barely protected her from the cool dampness and she tried to quell her shivering. Staring into the darkness, she wondered again what had happened to her father.

She felt certain she'd seen him being helped from the battlefield. Why would he leave his daughters in the O'Kelly Clan's Fortress, Callinon Castle, in the clutches of his enemy? It made no sense, and it wasn't like him to abandon his loved ones. Family meant everything to Moran. Something must be preventing him from conducting a rescue. Had he died? No, she felt certain if he were dead, Donovan would have delighted in telling her so.

She feared for Ailleen and their maid, Glenna. How had everyone else in the castle fared under these conditions? The heavy cell door creaked open and she flinched with apprehension as two of Donovan's guards entered.

Flickering torchlight filtered into the dim, dusty confines of the dungeon and she squinted. *Are they going to beat me again?* Rhiannon shuddered at the thought. Hopefully they would simply leave more maggoty food, which she would promptly shove in a corner, and refuse to eat. Mayhap death by starvation would offer her sweet release, compared to this bleak existence.

To her disgust, the burly men grabbed her arms and hoisted her to her feet. "Leave me alone!" she demanded in a hoarse voice, trying to sound braver than she felt. Despite being weak from lack of decent food, she managed to shove away their grubby hands.

She spit in the heavyset fellow's face, her heart hammering with rage. *My body may be wounded; my mind fragile, but no one can steal my spirit.*

Grimacing, the guard wiped away the moisture with the back of his hand. His subsequent slap sent a sharp explosion through Rhiannon's cheek and jaw.

Agonizing pain rocked through her as she grabbed her face. She'd bitten her lip and tasted salty blood. Somehow, she managed to lift her chin and stare even harder at the brute. She refused to give either of Donovan's men the satisfaction of seeing her cry out.

"I ought to throttle ya," the heavyset guard snarled. "But there's no time. You've been summoned before his lordship; we must make haste."

Filthy swine, Rhiannon thought as outrage filled her soul. Donovan finally wanted to speak with her after leaving her to rot. She railed at the insult. He held her future, nay, her very life, in his hands, yet she could do naught to change the situation.

"Get a move on, girlie. Donovan's waitin." The heavyset guard swiped a meaty paw toward her, and she stumbled backward, repulsed.

"Don't touch me," she spat.

"Have it yer way," he grumbled, and lunged at her again. "I'll have to carry ya."

Enraged, Rhiannon fisted her hands. "May you rot in Hades!"

"That's where you'd go if I had my say." His scraggly brows drew together with irritation. "Since it's not my place to decide, you'd best get your scrawny backside over here and walk between the two of us. Don't try nuthin' funny."

Glaring at Donovan's guards, wishing she had her sword, she moved into position. As she plodded heavily from the depths of the castle's belly and up the stone steps, she wrinkled her nose at the guards' putrid breath.

The treatment she'd received during her captivity was outrageous. She was a princess. She deserved better, even as a prisoner.

"Clean yerself up, girlie." The heavyset guard shoved her into a room with a tub of water and a clean dress stretched across a chair. A brush sat nearby.

Rhiannon hesitated. "Must you watch?"

The two guards snorted with laughter as they turned their backs to her.

"She's a feisty 'un," the heavyset guard said to his partner. "No wonder Donovan's hot to bed her."

"There won't be much happenin' between the sheets, I'll vow," the other guard answered. "The poor man doesn't function properly. Otherwise, he'd have availed himself of this barmy wench long ago."

He made an obscene gesture, and both guards guffawed.

Rhiannon's face burned with indignation as she hastily bathed, dressed, and worked the knots out of her damp hair. "I'm ready, and I demand to know what's going on."

"You'll find out soon enough," the heavyset guard said as he turned around, licking his rotten teeth.

ABOARD LE BON NAVIRE

A CRISP WIND WHIPPED PAST SIR CORT Guyot's face as he watched his ship's bow slice through dark ocean waves. He shaded his eyes from the sun, observing as Ireland's sheer cliffs and misty hills came into view like a glorious emerald gem.

The warriors milling on the deck talked in low voices with each other. Their expressions were resolute, and Cort sensed they were ready for battle. Before long, he would march them ashore to engage yet another enemy. He had dressed in full body armor for the impending conflict and had ordered the men to do the same. Firm resolve built within him. This was his life—waging wars for King Henry II of England. It was all he'd known for the last decade.

Truthfully, he was tired of the constant conflict. After all this time, he no longer looked at upcoming battles with the eagerness of a bare-faced youth. He longed for his fighting days to end, longed to be able to settle down in one place, but it wasn't likely to happen any time soon.

For this mission, Cort's contingent of Norman soldiers had been ordered by King Henry to sail to Ireland with King Moran of Leinster to help him regain his kingdom. King Moran had appealed to King Henry, explaining his home had been seized unlawfully by a man named Tadgh Donovan, and that the blackguard held hostage his two daughters.

Cort would have no problem dispensing with such a man. To take hostage innocent women and children was loathsome.

Raoul D'Arcy, a fellow Norman who had served alongside Cort for years, shouldered his way through the men and approached him. Side by side, they watched the distant shores grow closer, moving to the deck's swaying motion.

"From what King Moran told us, we outnumber Donovan's forces two to one," Cort broke the silence, sensing Raoul's mind also dwelt upon their impending task. "I daresay this will be a precise strike."

"It would seem that way," Raoul returned, his jaw set with resolve.

To Cort, Raoul's service in the military seemed to be but an amusing adventure that would eventually end. Unlike Cort, the man had options regarding his future when he left His Majesty's military service.

As the legitimate son of a Norman nobleman, he'd been raised with the privileges of an upper-class citizen. Tutored by the finest scholars, he also had the benefit of a university education.

Upon his father's death, Raoul would inherit the D'Arcy family's vast estate. Eventually, he would marry a nobleman's daughter. A well-heeled wife would bring Raoul prestige in social circles, along with a fat dowry. When he left the army, his life would be one of luxury and ease.

In comparison, as the bastard son of a Norman nobleman, Cort stood to inherit nothing. No vast estates or wealthy wives lay in his future. His father, Searlas Guyot, had been ashamed of his illegitimate son, begotten from a lowly maid in his household. Searlas had a wife and legitimate sons; therefore, he couldn't publicly acknowledge Cort.

Soon after giving birth, Cort's mother left him with Searlas and disappeared. Anxious to be rid of the product of his illicit affair, Searlas sent Cort to be fostered by his brother, Fitz.

Cort's uncle had done the best he could for his nephew, but he didn't have the patience or time needed to raise a young boy. He soon learned to accept his uncle's shortcomings, learned to rely on himself, and rarely sought the company of others. Disappointed too many times to trust anyone, he spent most of his youth engaged in solitary pursuits.

"Why so pensive, my friend?" Raoul said.

Immersed in memories of his past, Cort drew himself back to the present. "I have a lot on my mind.

Raoul shoved his fists on his hips. "You know, I've been thinking, too. I wonder why King Henry agreed to help King Moran?

He's barely paid any attention to Ireland since it was claimed as English territory. Why does he give a whit about it now?"

"He's not made war upon anyone for a while; mayhap he grows bored." Cort shrugged. "Who knows how Henry's mind works."

"No doubt his wife, Queen Eleanor, wonders the same."

The two shared a hearty laugh.

"From what I've heard, the Irish are a warring lot," Cort said. "It seems men spend most of their time stealing each other's land."

Raoul playfully punched Cort's bicep. "It's good we lusty Norman men only steal each other's women, one of my favorite pursuits. We're young, now is the time to sow our wild oats, eh? We'll settle down with wives later."

Cort grunted. "I have no plans to marry, so I waste precious little time thinking of the fairer sex. They have their place, but females and war don't mix."

"Always the serious one." Raoul shook his head.

"It escapes me why Dublin's high king didn't help Moran when he requested assistance," Cort said.

"He felt my landholdings are too small to fret over," a deep voice said.

Cort and Raoul turned to see King Moran, his long cloak flapping in the breeze. His black hair, shot with streaks of silver, fell in shaggy disarray around his face. His jaw was set at a hard angle, and dark smudges rested beneath his eyes.

"Callinon Castle and the surrounding area is not the largest kingdom in Ireland," he added. "Donovan has enlisted so many of the clans to his cause, no one dares challenge him. When I presented my case to King Rory, he turned me down. Therefore, I sailed to England and appealed to King Henry."

"Sire, I apologize for what you overheard." Cort felt foolish that he'd been caught voicing his thoughts.

"No need for apologies, Guyot. Were I in your shoes, I would wonder the same thing." King Moran sat down wearily upon a crate and stretched out his long legs. "Please know that

I'll be forever indebted to your Norman troops for freeing my daughters."

"Of course." Cort studied Moran closer, determining that he seemed shaky, out of breath, and deeply troubled. No doubt he feared for his family.

"Are you well, sire?" he asked.

"I rarely sleep, Guyot," Moran admitted with a heavy sigh. "The last months have been difficult, knowing Donovan holds captive my daughters and my people. God help me, leaving them in his clutches was distressing. Alas, I had no choice. I had not the troop numbers to challenge him again."

"We'll reach land soon," Cort said. "My men will have him on the run in no time."

"That is my sincere hope," Moran said.

"Rest assured, sire, you will sup in your home this eve," Raoul added.

"Guyot, there's something I want to speak with you about." Moran folded his arms across his chest and stared pointedly at Raoul.

Apparently realizing Moran wished to be alone with Cort, Raoul cleared his throat, excused himself, and joined the other men.

"I haven't felt well during this voyage," Moran admitted. "I thought at first it was only the strain of being aboard this vessel for so long, but it has continued to plague me. I paid a visit to your ship's physician yesterday. He said my heart is failing. I don't have much longer to live."

"Sire . . ." Cort frowned. *What do I say to a dying man?* The proper words failed him.

"My daughters will in inherit my kingdom after I'm gone," Moran continued in a tired voice. "However, they'll not be able to hold it, considering my army is in a shambles. I fear for their futures."

"I'm sorry to hear of your illness," Cort said slowly. King Moran's revelation made him wary. Where would this conversation lead?

"I've watched you closely these last months as we journeyed to Ireland, Guyot. I admire how you manage your men; you're firm, but even handed. You're a good man, and I feel I can trust you. That is why I have come with a proposition for you."

Cort lifted a curious brow. "A proposition?"

"I'd like you to marry my oldest daughter, Rhiannon, and stay on in Ireland," Moran said firmly. "You'll inherit my kingdom when I'm gone."

Stunned, Cort stared at King Moran. "This is most unexpected. Isn't there someone else, perhaps another clan member you'd like her to marry?"

"None of the remaining clans have the strength, or the stomach, to stand up to Donovan. There would be nothing gained by Rhiannon marrying into one of those families."

"Your offer is . . . most unexpected." Cort felt hesitant, yet since he had no land to inherit, he felt tempted. "Are you certain you wish me to wed her, sire?"

"I know your father, Guyot, and I'm fully aware of your financial circumstances. By marrying Rhiannon, you'll gain land and wealth. As a commander of a Norman army contingent, you can offer my people military protection. They will no longer fear being burned out of their homes."

Cort contemplated the idea, giving it serious thought. If he married Moran's daughter, he would have a secure future. Could he truly trust what the Irish king offered? He looked directly into Moran's eyes and sensed the sincerity.

"What about your daughter, sire? I doubt she'll appreciate being wagered off to a Norman warrior. And don't you think it's unlikely your people will welcome a foreigner to take your place?"

Moran rose slowly. "All good questions, Guyot, but I've already considered them, and my offer still stands. However, you must know that Rhiannon is headstrong. Since I promised she would become clan leader upon my death, she'll no doubt believe me daft. Nevertheless, she's a well-educated woman, and has good sense. She'll eventually come around to my way of thinking. As for my people, it will be up to you to treat them fairly in order to earn their respect."

Another disconcerting thought crossed Cort's mind. "My orders from King Henry—"

Moran held up a hand. "I know what your orders are, Guyot. Nevertheless, even the King of England has no say in your choice of a wife."

Moran's reasoning seemed sound, even though the offer of his daughter's hand in marriage seemed sudden. Indeed, Cort had never imagined himself with a wife. The idea concerned yet intrigued him. In fact, he became so intrigued, his resistance began to fade.

"If she'll have me, I'll marry Rhiannon, sire," he said with conviction, although he felt that waver briefly.

What tangle might he be getting himself into?

"We'll hold the wedding in a fortnight," Moran announced heartily, his dark mood seemingly lifted, at least for the moment. "I know not when this heart of mine will give out, so it is propitious that we move forward quickly."

"I understand," Cort said, tamping down any doubts he may still be experiencing.

"Promise me this one thing, Guyot," Moran said. "Treat my daughter well. She may seem fierce and fiery, but she is a sweet girl. Never hurt her, or any of my people, or I swear, I'll arise from the grave to haunt you."

Cort bristled. "You have my word, sire. I'm an honorable man. I've never lifted a finger to harm a woman. And I never will."

"Aye, 'tis good to hear, and we have struck a bargain." Moran held out his hand, and Cort clasped it firmly.

DREAD FILLED RHIANNON AS THE GUARDS led her through the chapel doors. The bath and fresh clothing made her feel human again, but she remained apprehensive. Why would Donovan conduct a meeting with her in a place of worship? An unusual request, but he'd proven himself a lunatic on more than one occasion. She shouldn't be surprised by his actions now.

As the guards marched her up to the altar, Donovan emerged from a back room, along with a tall, cloaked man with a hawk-ish nose. Two more of Donovan's guards followed them, one drag-ging a reluctant Glenna by the upper arm, the other one bringing Ailleen in a similar fashion.

Rhiannon noted, with a small measure of relief, both her maid and sister appeared to be in good health, albeit distraught. Glenna's pale face was pinched with worry and fear shone in her eyes.

Ailleen met Rhiannon's gaze with a tear-stained face. She imme-diately cried out and struggled to twist free from the guard. The brute grasped her roughly by the shoulders and forced her to stand still.

Rhiannon started toward her sister, but a guard held her back. She tried to shove away his filthy hands, but he gripped harder.

"Don't you dare hurt her," Rhiannon shouted at the guard hold-ing Ailleen. "Or by God I'll . . . I'll . . ."

"You'll do what?" Donovan's scarred and pockmarked face broke into an evil grin as he sauntered arrogantly toward to her. "Methinks you're in no position to demand anything."

"You rotten beast," Rhiannon growled, feeling like a failure for not being able to protect her sister and her people from the likes of him.

"Perhaps that's so," Donovan said. "But I'm the beast you're about to marry."

Rhiannon's insides twisted with fury. "In a pig's eye! I'll never agree to wed you."

He absently flicked a piece of lint from his tunic and yawned. "I grow weary of your histrionics. As I said before, you're in no posi-tion to demand."

"But my father . . ."

"Face it, dear girl, your father has abandoned you." Donovan smirked at her. "After I took control of Callinon Castle, I had him followed. My spies say he escaped to Dublin, and I assume he's still there, hiding out like a cowardly dog."

"That . . . that can't be!" Rhiannon sputtered, her head swim-ming with disbelief.

"Oh, but it is," Donovan continued. "I sent a ransom demand that would secure your freedom to his residence in the city. He never responded."

"You're a filthy liar. And you can't force me to marry you against my will!" Rhiannon stomped her foot in irritation, certain there had to be a good reason for her father to ignore the ransom demand. "I won't stand for it."

"You will indeed stand for it," Donovan returned in a surly voice. "Otherwise, I'll slit someone's throat."

"You . . . you wouldn't dare do such a thing," Rhiannon said, fully aware that he could, indeed, be that malevolent. Among his many atrocities, Donovan had sent the arrow flying into her brother's chest. He had also lent support to Jamie when he'd deserted their clan. The last she'd heard, he was still with Donovan, fighting for the man's misguided cause.

Rhiannon's heart ached at the bitter memories.

Donovan lifted a black, shaggy brow. "Oh, but I would, my sweet. Now tell me, who will it be? Your pretty little sister or your maid?" He nodded at the guards holding Glenna and Ailleen. The men unsheathed wicked-looking knives, and pressed blades against their slender throats.

A sharp tip pierced Glenna's tender skin, and as blood dribbled down her neck, she swallowed convulsively. Ailleen began to whimper.

"I'll wed you since I have no choice." Rhiannon bristled with outrage, realizing the extent of Donovan's cruelty, and a sick feeling twisted through her. If marrying that beast was the price she must pay to save Glenna and Ailleen's lives, then by the saints, that's what she'd do, though she loathed the idea.

"That's much better, my dear." Donovan motioned to his guards, and they sheathed their knives.

Glenna and Ailleen relaxed, and while they still appeared upset, they didn't seem quite so panic-stricken.

"Just tell me," Rhiannon asked Donovan in a dry, cracking voice. "Why are you doing this?"

"Since I'll apparently get no ransom for you, I've decided you're valuable in other ways," he returned in a sardonic tone. "The villagers have been stealing from me and making my life hell. But they're worried about you, and they've been asking about your welfare. I believe they'll behave better with you at my side." Donovan turned to the tall man in the cloak. "Dyfed, will you do the honors?"

"Is he a Catholic priest?" Rhiannon eyed the hawk-nosed man warily.

"Dyfed?" Donovan gave a cynical chuckle. "He doesn't have a Catholic bone in his body. He practices the old religion. The *true* religion of Ireland."

Rhiannon shivered. Dyfed practiced the type of worship the Catholic Church warned them against. The ancient traditions were evil and revered dark, frightening deities. Surely this marriage wouldn't be recognized by the Church.

When scuffling noises and shouts rose outside, a guard glanced out a window, then turned to Donovan with a worried expression. "Sire, we are being attacked. Several warriors have swarmed into the bailey."

"That few? They'll be defeated quickly by our forces." Donovan nodded at Dyfed who began to chant.

Suddenly the chapel doors flew wide. A stream of warriors burst into the room and rushed toward Donovan's guards. Steel clashed loudly against steel; shouts echoed. Donovan fought his way toward the door where he and Dyfed managed to slip away, although several warriors gave chase.

Donovan's guards were overtaken so quickly, Rhiannon's head spun. She wished, once again, she held a weapon. Could she even heft one in her starved condition? After months of mistreatment, her physical condition was pitiful.

She, Glenna, and Ailleen huddled beside the chapel altar, watching in horror. Feeling useless, but not certain what to do, she hugged her sister and Glenna close to her sides.

As the tallest warrior lowered his sword and walked toward her, Rhiannon's heart pounded. It was a boon that the warriors had halted her marriage to Donovan. But had they driven him away, only to claim Callinon Castle as their own?

The glint of a sword, dropped by one of Donovan's guards, caught her eye. Impulsively, she lunged for the hilt and stood, attempting to handle its weight. She barely touched the object and her hands wobbled from the strain. Perspiration popped out on her brow. Muscles she hadn't used in months screamed at the exertion. Nevertheless, she managed to crouch into a fighting stance.

"Put down the sword, Rhiannon," the warrior commanded, his voice tinged with an unfamiliar accent. "You are King Moran's eldest daughter, are you not?"

Rhiannon circled him slowly, her breath hissing through her clenched teeth as she muttered, "Who are you? What do you want?"

He sheathed his bloody weapon and held up his gauntleted hands. "You need not fear me, *fille.*"

"Aye, like a mouse shouldn't fear a hawk," she snapped, then gripped the sword tighter, prepared to exchange blows. With each passing second, the weapon seemed to grow heavier.

The warrior lifted the visor on his helmet, revealing a strong chiseled face with a cleft chin. His dark, intense gaze bored into her. For a moment, something flickered in the bottomless depths of his eyes—admiration, perhaps? Nay, it couldn't be so. This man meant to steal her home.

He stiffened, holding back his broad shoulders. His hauberk stretched tightly across his muscular chest and a spark of annoyance flared in his gaze. "I've no intention of fighting you."

THREE

"**W**HY?" RHIANNON TAUNTED. "ARE YOU FRIGHTENED?"
"Nay, woman, I'm here to—"
When he reached out, Rhiannon slashed the blade at him, nicking his cheek. Blood oozed from the tiny cut, and she realized she'd attacked without considering the consequences.

He could easily strike her down, disarm her. No matter what happened, she must protect her sister and Glenna.

"*Sacre bleu!*" The warrior swiped away the blood droplets with the back of his gauntleted hand and glared at her.

"Rhiannon, stop! Guyot is with me. His army has defeated Donovan's forces. We're safe." Moran O'Kelly limped through the chapel's double doors toward Rhiannon.

Bloodied and bruised, he existed, unless Rhiannon's eyes played tricks on her. Joy and relief at seeing him flooded through her. She dropped the sword and ran over to hug him.

"Father!" Ailleen rushed toward Moran as well, clung to his leg, and began talking excitedly. "I've been so scared, and Donovan is an awful man! He locked me in my room, but Glenna took care of me. And poor Rhiannon, he kept her in the dungeon all these months."

"King Moran," Glenna's face filled with relief. "Praise be, you're alive."

Moran crushed Ailleen and Rhiannon against his chest and kissed the tops of their heads. "My girls—how I've missed you both."

Tears streaked down Ailleen's cheeks, and she brushed them away, leaving dirty smudges on her face. "We feared never to see you again."

"Lord knows I hated leaving you," Moran rasped, his voice filled with emotion. "After the battle with Donovan all those months ago, I had but a handful of men left alive. We had no more fight in us. We couldn't go back."

Rhiannon's eyes stung with grateful tears, yet she struggled with rising irritation. "Where . . . where have you been all this time, father?" she choked out. "Did you receive Donovan's ransom note?"

"I first went to Dublin to ask King Rory for assistance, but he refused. While there, I did indeed receive Donovan's bloody ransom note. I felt certain he would try to trick me into paying a high price, then continue to hold you hostage."

"Why wouldn't King Rory help you?" Rhiannon asked. "You're one of Ireland's high kings, and you've always been loyal."

Moran shrugged. "He doesn't think my landholdings significant enough. With no other options, I sailed to England, where I received King Henry's backing. He sent Sir Cort Guyot's contingent of Norman soldiers to help me secure Callinon."

Rhiannon fell silent, absorbing this information.

"We owe these Normans a debt of gratitude," she said, now humbled as she exchanged a glance with Guyot. "My apologies for injuring you, sir."

He nodded but remained silent.

"Aye, we're all grateful." Moran looked around at the bodies strewn in the chapel and turned to Guyot. "What has become of Donovan?"

"He escaped," Guyot answered. "I ordered five of my ablest men to go after him."

Disappointment filled Moran's voice. "I had hoped to be rid of that wretch once and for all. I want him to pay for what he's done."

"I believe he'll be captured. If not, I doubt he'll be back after the sound whipping we gave him." Guyot's voice contained a reassuring tone. "Excuse me, sire, I'll rejoin my troops."

"Of course," Moran said.

Guyot's assessing glance caused Rhiannon to squirm uncomfortably, and warmth tingled up her spine. Completely baffled by the unusual stirrings in her chest, she watched closely as he left with his men.

Moran pulled Rhiannon and Ailleen close again. "I ached every day, knowin' that Donovan held you."

As Rhiannon studied her father's face, she noted that he seemed older and grayer. The months of exile had taken a toll on him, as it had all of them.

"The brute intended to marry me today," Rhiannon said with a shiver of disgust. "He thought to control the villagers better with me at his side."

Moran narrowed his gaze. "Did you wed him child?"

"Nay." She shook her head. "Your arrival prevented that."

"Thanks be to the saints."

Rhiannon stiffened as an unsettling thought crossed her mind. "When Guyot's forces leave Callinon, how will we stand up to Donovan again?"

"Guyot's troops will not leave. They will continue to defend our kingdom."

Rhiannon frowned at Moran, knowing full well how men transacted their business. Nothing came about for free. "At what price did Guyot agree to help?"

"You have been betrothed to him, Rhiannon. The wedding will take place in a fortnight."

"You've gone daft!" Rhiannon blinked in amazement, unable to believe what her father had just uttered.

Ignoring Rhiannon's outrage, Moran held her chin in his hand and studied her face. "Is it true, what Ailleen said? Did Donovan hold you in the dungeon all these months? Did he abuse you?"

Tears burned at the back of her eyes. "Aye, father. He beat me and fed me terrible food. But he couldn't break my spirit."

"I'll draw and quarter that bastard for what he's done." Moran's face filled with dark rage.

"I'll do it myself if I ever see him again," she swore. "He's a disgusting brute not fit to walk this earth."

"It's good you'll have some time to heal before your nuptials."

"I still think you've lost your mind, father."

"I knew you'd feel that way." Moran met Rhiannon's gaze and held it steadily. "I assure you, I'm in full control of my faculties."

"I haven't seen you in ages, yet you've pledged me in marriage to a complete stranger." Hunger gnawed at her stomach, and she felt faint. " 'Tis madness. I'll have nothing to do with this wild scheme."

"Guyot's an honorable man." Moran's brows knitted with concern. "He's given his word that he'll protect you and our people from harm. Our kingdom needs his military strength."

"Have I escaped the clutches of one mercenary, only to be thrust into the arms of another?" Rhiannon cried, rage trickling through her. " 'Tis not right. If I marry him, how can I be clan leader? Guyot is a foreigner. Our people will never accept him."

"You will not assume leadership of the clan as we'd planned," Moran said slowly, his voice brittle.

"What?" Rhiannon's anger nearly choked her, and she stared at her father through a haze of frustration.

"I promised clan leadership to you a long time ago, when I still hoped to defeat Donovan. That's no longer possible. So, tell me daughter, what good is it to be leader of a defeated kingdom?"

Rhiannon lowered her gaze; aware her father spoke reasonably. She disliked his decision to marry her off to the Norman, yet he was only trying to do what he felt was right for their people.

Moran cupped Rhiannon's chin in his hand and gently tilted her head up. "You know full well my army no longer has the strength to fight Donovan, or another like him. That's why we need Guyot. 'Tis your duty to marry him."

"At least let me try to rally the clans one more time," Rhiannon suggested, grasping for an alternative solution other than wedding a stranger. She realized immediately her words were hastily spoken, for her father's countenance became stormy.

"Impossible," Moran snapped. "Most are already loyal to Donovan, and the others are afraid of him."

"But—"

"My decision stands." Moran withdrew his hand from her face. "I'll hear no further argument from you, my girl. Come now, 'tis not so bad. Guyot is a fine looking fellow."

Rhiannon sniffed. "Why must I marry him so soon?"

"I've not much time left, Rhiannon. I'm . . . I'm dying."

"No! I don't believe it." Sobs welled in Rhiannon's throat. One moment she'd been angry at her father, now she ached with sorrow.

"Father!" Ailleen started to sob and clung even tighter to Moran. "Promise me you'll not die like mother did."

"Shhh, little sprite," Moran soothed. "I promise, you're going to be all right."

"Have you even consulted with a physician?" Rhiannon asked as sadness made her voice waver.

"Aye, and he said my heart's failing me," Moran returned with resignation.

"Perhaps we can find a cure," Rhiannon suggested. "We can't give up hope."

"I appreciate your sentiment, daughter, but there's naught to be done. I've only months, perhaps less, left on this earth."

Glenna's eyes glittered with unshed tears, and she clasped her hands tightly together. "This is why you've decided Rhiannon should wed the Norman?"

"Aye, Glenna," Moran said. "These are dangerous and uncertain times. It would be irresponsible of me not to make provisions for my people's safety."

A buzzing sounded in Rhiannon's head, and she tried to make sense of her mixed emotions. How could she trust her life to the Norman? She could never rely on another man as long as she lived—they weren't to be trusted. Even now, the memory of Jamie's deceit filled her with shame. Shame that she hadn't seen through his subterfuge of caring for her.

Disbelief swept through Rhiannon. Her father was dying. She wasn't going to be installed as clan leader. Like autumn leaves tossed upon a chill breeze, her life had shifted direction yet again.

"When we marry, Guyot will inherit Callinon Castle and all O'Kelly land holdings," Rhiannon said, finally accepting what the Norman stood to gain by taking her to wife.

"Aye," Moran said. "Yet through your children, our home will stay secure in the O'Kelly family line."

Rhiannon swallowed hard, realizing she wouldn't only be expected to entrust her life, and those of her people, to the Norman. She would also be required to give him her body, as that would belong to him once they wed.

By the saints, why had it been her lot in life to be female? Whenever it behooved men's plans, women were handed off like chattels, without a thought to their own ideas. It seemed nearly inhuman, yet they were expected to comply.

"I still find this situation highly objectionable," she murmured, knowing full well her protests were futile.

"Please, Rhiannon. The matter is settled, and I'll discuss it no further." Moran rubbed his grime-streaked forehead. "I should like to live out the rest of my days in peace."

Rhiannon's cheeks stung, as if she'd been slapped. Too many had lost their lives in the constant wars they'd fought with Donovan over the years, Seamus, her mother, and many others. A sense of purpose filled her, and she reluctantly accepted her fate.

"You'll have your peace, father." Despite her anxiety, Rhiannon gave her father's leathery cheek a reassuring kiss.

He looked pleased, and for that, she was grateful.

She would hold up her end of this bargain. But would the Norman?

WHEN CORT JOINED HIS MEN IN the bailey, he observed their good spirits. This day brought them an easy victory with few injuries. As the troops attended to their horses, pitched tents, and went about the business of setting up camp, he climbed the steps to the castle walls and glanced over the parapets at the Irish landscape.

One side of Callinon Castle overlooked the sea. On the other side, rolling green hills, brushed golden by the sun, covered the landscape. A cluster of wattle and daub huts, encircled by a thick wall, lay at the base of the hill upon which the castle rested. A shining ribbon of river snaked lazily through the fields, and tall stone edifices that Moran had explained were ancient Viking watchtowers stood sentinel over the area.

Crops seemed thin this year, and the small herds of sheep and cattle appeared depleted, no doubt due to Donovan's greed and mismanagement. Autumn would bring a small harvest, and food would have to be carefully rationed. From now on, he would see to it that land and animals were cared for properly so the people would be well fed.

My people.

By marrying King Moran's daughter, all this would eventually belong to him. Thoughts of the Irish beauty filled him with a mixture of dread and anticipation. As her father had told him, she was indeed headstrong. He touched the scratch on his cheek and mulled over his decision.

A vision of Rhiannon's fiery red hair flying, and her challenging green eyes flashed through his mind. Even in her battered condition, no doubt from mistreatment at the hands of her captors, her spirit shone about her like a bright beacon. She'd been prepared to battle with him, even though she was bruised and thin as a rail. He couldn't help but admire her courage.

Cort never expected King Moran's daughter to be quite so formidable. She definitely had a mind of her own. She intrigued him. No doubt their sudden betrothal shocked her, and he realized Moran had been wise to suggest she take time to heal before they wed.

His thoughts of the Irish princess dissipated when he spotted Arch, his greyhound, walking amongst the men. Placing his fingers in his mouth, he whistled. The hound perked his ears and sprinted toward him.

IN HER ROOM, RHIANNON SAT IN a wooden tub full of steaming hot water. As she soaped herself, she felt more than grateful to be out of that filthy jail cell. So many things had changed in a short span of time. Most of all, Moran was dying. The thought of losing yet another family member tortured her thoughts.

At a time like this, she wanted nothing more than to be able to spend as much time with her father as she could. His last days should be spent with family and friends. Considering her impending marriage, she frowned.

Aye, she would marry Cort Guyot. However, that didn't mean she had to do so willingly.

When a knock sounded on the door, Rhiannon called out, "Yes?"

"Your father wants you down in the great hall for supper," Glenna said as she entered the room. "He's invited the villagers to attend his homecoming feast."

"Tell him I'm tired and I'm going to bed," Rhiannon said. "I had the cook send up a tray of bread and cheese, so I'm not hungry."

"King Moran insists," Glenna said. "He'd like you to bring a potion that will ease the ache in his joints. I'm afraid if you don't come down, he'll drag you from your chamber."

Rhiannon sighed. "Aye, Glenna."

Glenna handed Rhiannon a towel and she stepped from the tub. The maid helped her don a fresh gown and brushed her damp hair. After she collected a small chest that held her healing potions, she and Glenna hurried downstairs.

Rhiannon's mother had always helped the villagers with her knowledge of healing. Fiona had passed this talent on to her daughter, and after she died, Rhiannon had continued in her mother's stead. This was one of Rhiannon's favorite pursuits—healing people, for she gained satisfaction at easing their pain. She not only set bones and stitched cuts; she had also helped midwife. Nothing compared to the appreciation she received when her patients were finally on the mend.

The great hall, packed with villagers and Norman soldiers, rang with laughter and conversation. It was good to see the people in such a lighthearted mood after the months of agony they'd endured while Donovan held the castle. Rhiannon realized Moran's return had given them hope, something they'd had little of lately.

Moran had taken a seat in his favorite chair at the high table, his feet propped on a stool. Ailleen sat nearby. Glenna busied herself by putting out trenchers for everyone.

Though it was summer, it was chilly in the keep, and a low fire crackled in the fireplace. Amazed that she'd been locked up through the entire winter, Rhiannon now looked forward to this season. She'd had the chance to glance at the surrounding fields and realized they hadn't been tended to properly in the spring, no doubt a result of Donovan's mismanagement. Food would have to be carefully portioned until another growing season was upon them.

Moran smiled and held up his goblet of wine. "I know you have something that will help my old bones relax, daughter."

"Aye," Rhiannon said. She put the chest on a table and removed a small pouch, then walked over and poured the contents into Moran's goblet. Though she longed to discuss her troubling thoughts about the Norman, she remained silent.

Moran stirred the wine with a fingertip, then sipped slowly. He leaned his head against the back of his chair. "Ahhh, I believe I feel the effects already. And something smells delicious."

Servants emerged from the kitchen carrying large platters of food. Rich venison stew, roasted boar, quail pie, seafood dishes, and loaves of freshly baked bread offered variety. Plates of berries and small honey cakes provided a sweet touch.

Rhiannon sat down next to Ailleen, and despite her earlier meal, her stomach growled. When a servant handed her a trencher, she helped herself to berries and vegetables. After her ordeal, her stomach seemed to have shrunk, and she knew she could only handle small amounts of food at a time.

Moran's gaze sought the Norman, standing in a cluster of his soldiers. "Go fetch your betrothed, Rhiannon, so he can join us in the evening repast. Let him know I've had a room prepared for him."

Rhiannon frowned at Guyot. He'd cleaned up since the battle, and now wore a clean tunic and trousers, along with tall leather boots. Even without his chain mail and sword, strength seemed to emanate from his broad-shouldered, muscled physique.

She recalled his dark eyes when she'd challenged him, and a warm shiver rippled up her spine. What had he thought when she'd raised her sword against him? Surely, he understood she had only been trying to protect Ailleen and Glenna. If he didn't, he must not have a heart.

A gray, leggy hound with a long snout walked obediently at the Norman's side as he wandered among his men issuing orders. They nodded dutifully and appeared to have great respect for him despite his gruffness. The Norman seemed unyielding, but capable, and obviously shared a good rapport with his soldiers. His dealings with them must be fair, otherwise they wouldn't be so willing to comply.

Rhiannon decided that bode well in his favor. Regardless of what she sensed in watching him right now, she'd vowed never to suffer mistreatment again. By the saints, if Guyot even tried lifting a finger to hurt her, or any member of her family, she would make him regret it.

Recalling the nuptials would be held in a fortnight, heat flared in her cheeks. As though he sensed her stare, he looked up.

"What are you waiting for?" Moran growled, interrupting her introspection. "Show your future husband the proper respect."

AS CORT WORKED HIS WAY AROUND the great hall talking to his men, he stole glances at Rhiannon from the corner of his eye. *Sacre bleu*, she was beautiful. Beauty or not, he sensed there would be challenges between them. Considering her fiery spirit, they would not be easy ones to resolve.

Raoul walked up to Cort and jabbed him in the ribs with his elbow. "What's this I hear about you marrying King Moran's daughter? I thought you'd planned never to wed. Yet look at you now, betrothed to an Irish princess."

"I've been looking for you, Raoul. I wanted to tell you what's going on. Apparently, the rumor mill is at work."

"Indeed," Raoul confirmed. "So, explain this new development to me."

"King Moran told me he's dying," Cort said. "He fears that once he's gone, Donovan or another clan leader will try to seize his kingdom again. As Rhiannon's husband, I'll see to it that doesn't happen."

"It's too bad about King Moran. Nevertheless, this assignment has been profitable, eh?" Raoul grinned. "You've not only accomplished King Henry's mission, but you've also got a rich wife for yourself in the bargain."

"Wouldn't you have agreed, if King Moran had offered it to you?"

"In a second, my friend," Raoul said. "You'll gain land and wealth, and the Irish princess is not so long in the tooth, is she?"

A smile touched Cort's lips. "It appears not."

Raoul grabbed two tankards of ale from a passing serving wench's tray. He handed one to Cort and held up the other one.

"To your wedding night," he exclaimed. They clanked the vessels together then drank heartily.

Unfortunately, Cort didn't notice Rhiannon's approach until it was too late. She looked tired, no doubt from her ordeal in prison. The becoming rose color blossoming in her cheeks enhanced her visage, adding to her appeal. Her eyes flashed with green fire and distress.

He feared she'd overheard he and Raoul's ribald toast. Too bad it wasn't their wedding night. He'd do his best to douse that fire with his kisses; though he had a feeling she would not welcome his ardor.

Rhiannon gave a slight curtsy. "Good eve, Sir Cort," she said in her unique Irish brogue. Uncurling her palm, she offered meat scraps to Arch, who gobbled them down.

Cort reached down to pet his dog, and doing so, his hand brushed against hers. A shock went through him at the feel of her silken skin against his calloused flesh. The image of her hands and fingers touching him in other ways flashed through his mind. For some reason, all the air in the hall seemed to vanish.

He found it difficult to breathe.

Did he dare hope for her touch to fall softly upon him, considering their hasty nuptials? Incredible, that he would entertain such an idea. Yet, he couldn't help but wonder.

"*Bonjour*, my lady," he returned, fighting to maintain control of his voice. "You know you've made a friend for life."

A canny fellow, Raoul set aside his tankard and bowed to Rhiannon. He exchanged a knowing glance with Cort, called to Arch, then disappeared with the dog into the crowded hall.

Despite the polite greetings Cort and Rhiannon exchanged, he sensed, once again, that he had affronted her. Her lips, red and moist as berries, trembled slightly, and she clasped her hands so tightly the knuckles showed white. Unbidden, his gaze drifted toward the creamy flesh thrusting from the top of her gown. The thought of his wedding night caused him to fill with warmth.

He considered Rhiannon's current fate and realized it would no doubt be unsettling to have your future decided for you, but that was the way of things for women, and he could not change the facts. He decided that even if the idea of marrying him disturbed her; she would soon grow accustomed to it.

Rhiannon cleared her throat. "How is the wound I inflicted upon you?"

Cort patted his cheek. "'Tis only a scratch."

She nodded but offered no further apology. "My father wishes to invite you to sup with the family. He has also ordered the servants to prepare a room for you."

Cort observed her closely, watching for any sign of emotion. "What is your heart's desire?"

Rhiannon shook her head, her fiery, unbound locks, sweeping her small shoulders. "I would prefer for you to stay away. Actually sir, I would prefer that you leave this place and never return. However, I will honor the bargain my father struck with you as I realize the wisdom of it."

Cort raised his brows, studying the fine structure of Rhiannon's face and her high cheek bones. "I daresay you don't mince words."

"Donovan has nearly annihilated my father's army," she continued. "I realize I've no hope of holding our kingdom intact without assistance." Her eyes flashed, and her breasts rose and fell with uneven breaths. "Please understand how important my kinsmen and women are to me. They deserve to have their interests represented properly. I intended to do that as clan leader."

"Your father mentioned he had initially chosen you to succeed him." Cort watched closely for her reaction. Rewarded for his efforts, he noted the slight downturn of her mouth.

"Aye. As it stands, when my father passes on, the people will be looking to you for the leadership he once gave them. He has placed much trust in you, sir, and feels you will deal fairly with our people."

"He's correct. There will never come a time that he could doubt my sincerity."

"That is my hope. However . . ." She paused, as though to collect her thoughts and find the appropriate words. When it seemed she had, she lifted her chin higher. "However, you must be aware that if you ever behave unjustly with anyone; or if you ever hurt anyone, you will answer to me."

Cort stood ramrod straight, offended, yet amused, by her manner. Princess or not, her attitude could not be tolerated. "As much as I respect your position in the O'Kelly clan, Rhiannon, I will not bow to your dictates now or ever. Rest assured; I will work accordingly with your people. If at any point in time you feel I've made an incorrect decision, it is your right to discuss that with me in private."

Sparks practically flew from Rhiannon's emerald green eyes. "I pray that you will forgive me for my concerns. However, I don't know you well enough to place the kind of trust in you that my father has."

Cort deflected her insults as easily as she gave them and refused to allow them to sink past the thick exterior of his skin. Over the years, it had toughened. As a child, the village children had taunted him mercilessly about his parents' abandonment, and how his uncle ignored him, leaving him to be raised by servants.

Therefore, her attitude didn't bring him down. In fact, he found it amusing her Irish brogue grew more pronounced the angrier she became.

"Don't forget, King Henry gave me orders to assist your father in regaining this kingdom. I never planned on anything else. Since circumstances have changed, and I have agreed to help your father in his time of need, I expect you'll be respectful of not only me, but my men, for their efforts."

"Oh, I'll always remain respectful, and I do appreciate that you've made my father's final days peaceful," Rhiannon shot back. "But I am no stranger to men and their false promises. And I'm not certain my father is in his right mind, considering his illness. So, I'll be watching you, Norman. *Closely.*"

Lines of concern creased her brow. She was uncertain of her words; he was sure of it. Did she really mistrust him or someone else?

"I'm convinced that since I've never given you cause for concern regarding my intentions, your anger toward me must stem from other sources. Sources that have disappointed you in the past. A man perhaps?"

When Rhiannon pulled back, as though stung by a bee, he realized he'd hit a sore spot. "I thought as much. Do not deign to judge my character the same as his, my lady. I pride myself greatly in believing I am a just and reasonable man."

"I'm only judging what I've seen so far," Rhiannon said slowly. "And that is a man who landed in Ireland with much better prospects than when he sailed from his own country. Do not take advantage of your profit. We both know that by your marriage to me, you gain immeasurably."

"We also both know that by your marriage to me, you and your people gain immeasurably." Cort folded his arms across his chest and met her cold stare. "We're even, are we not?"

Her nostrils flared. "We will never be even."

Cort wanted something from her, but he couldn't quite put a finger on it, because he himself didn't understand. "*Sacre bleu*, woman! What type of impertinence do the Irish breed into their women? Where are your manners?"

The pink in Rhiannon's cheeks intensified, enhancing her lovely features. "I have thanked you for your help in freeing my kingdom, sir. I have agreed to this marriage. What else can I offer?"

Cort couldn't explain the strange feeling that wound its way through his gut because he didn't know what ailed him.

She tossed her hair over her shoulders, her gaze icy. "What shall I tell my father? Will you sup with the family, or not?"

"Nay." Cort tried to make sense of his mixed emotions. "I won't need the sleeping chamber, either. I intend to spend the night with my troops."

Her mouth twitched. "I'll tell my father of your decision."

With a swish of her skirts, Rhiannon made her way through the throngs of people and back to the high table. Cort did not waste his time watching her any longer. He strode past his men and stormed outside. Rhiannon O'Kelly must be the most vexing woman he'd ever met.

Not surprising since his previous experiences with women left him cold. As a bastard with no land or future to offer a wife, he wasn't considered marriageable material. Women at court had found him desirable enough; however, they'd toyed with him, always reminding him to never consider himself their equal. Cort had developed a disdain for high-born females and hadn't allowed any of them to touch his heart.

It appeared Rhiannon would have no more regard for him than the others. He'd freed her people, and though she had thanked him, he had tasted her bitterness.

Cort clenched and unclenched his fists as he stared up at the keep, desperately trying not to allow his thoughts to dwell on the wild cat living within. In fact, he was nearly of a mind to forget all of this and return to Normandy.

Instead, he walked the castle grounds, examining the gardens, the orchards, and numerous outbuildings. All of these elements were in poor shape and in desperate need of tending.

FOUR

Two weeks later, Rhiannon found herself preparing for nuptials to a man not of her choosing. A combination of fresh air, rest, and good food during the past days had boosted her health and she felt much better physically, nevertheless, her heart and mind remained in turmoil.

Glenna helped her don her mother's wedding gown. It seemed a travesty to wear it for this marriage, but she'd vowed to honor her father's request. Sadness twisted through her and she wished mother had lived so she could be with her now.

After Glenna brushed her hair and adorned it with a golden circlet, she escorted her to the castle chapel where relatives and acquaintances, who had been fetched from around the countryside to witness the wedding, awaited her arrival.

A musician in a corner played a flute, yet the merry tune contrasted with Rhiannon's dour mood. Amazing, she thought, that everyone around her should be so jovial, while she had a cold pit in her stomach.

Her heart squeezed with trepidation when Moran took her arm and led her down the aisle. It squeezed even more when she saw the expectant faces of people in the pews. Because of her marriage, they would remain safe from further attack, as the

Norman's army would protect them from this day forward.

One side of the chapel held a group of Norman soldiers, whose conversation faded as she and Moran arrived. Guyot waited for her at the altar, his expression firm and unrelenting. Her spine went stiff as her gaze met his. Did he want land and security so badly that he would marry a woman he didn't love? And what of affection? Would there ever be any between them, or would it always be a cold, political arrangement?

Most marriages between nobles were arranged for political gain. Had her parents' marriage been arranged or had it been for love? If their union had been political, they had eventually developed deep affection for one another. Would she and Cort ever share feelings for each other?

Shock rippled through Rhiannon, for her unexpected thoughts caught her off guard. Nay, she could never develop feelings for the Norman. It would be impossible to ever feel tenderness toward him. Why had that possibility even occurred to her?

When Jamie's face flashed in Rhiannon's mind, uneasiness wound its way through her. It seemed a lifetime ago that she had looked forward to their life together. Because of his betrayal, her dreams of a love-filled marriage had been doused like water poured over a flame.

Mayhap it's good my father arranged this marriage for political gain. Love is unreliable. An emotion like that can't be trusted.

She held even tighter onto her lavender bouquet. Never again would she allow herself to be so vulnerable with a man. Once was enough for her to have learned a good lesson—a lesson that had been branded into her soul.

A compelling urgency washed over her, and she met the Norman's intense perusal. Strangely enough, Rhiannon thought perhaps his countenance held regard for her. Of course, he would be courteous to his new bride—she was a princess. But was there something more, deep down, shining in the depths of his dark eyes?

Nay, she was fooling herself. Surely, he considered her nothing more than a reward for a job well done.

Moran's grip on her arm intensified, as if he sensed his daughter's thoughts. Father and daughter exchanged knowing looks, and he patted her hand reassuringly. Rhiannon, however, was not calmed by the gesture, and she couldn't help but feel she'd lost control of her life.

She sent up a small prayer to Saint Brigit.

Rhiannon glared at the Norman. Despite her concerns, his striking facial features, framed by dark hair, held her attention. For a moment, she allowed herself to study his tall, muscular form.

His finely woven black tunic, shot through with silver thread, stretched across his broad shoulders. Dark trousers encased his powerful thighs and once again, he wore tall leather boots. He was a handsome man, and exuded prowess.

In a few moments, he would be her husband, bound by the vows of the holy Catholic church. She met her father's gaze, aware of the pain in his eyes and the concern lining his face.

At least for his sake, she did her best to force a smile.

CORT WATCHED RHIANNON APPROACHING UP THE aisle toward him wearing a stunning blue gown that swept the floor, her long curls unbound, save for a golden circlet on her head. The gown hung loosely, and dark hollows resided beneath her eyes. She looked better than when he'd first arrived. Remembering Donovan's mistreatment of his bride-to-be, a jolt of anger surged through his chest. He clenched his fists, outraged that anyone could be so cruel to another human being.

Despite her fragile state, Rhiannon remained lovely, and she held her head high, as befitted her station. Cort admired her courage. Unexpectedly, his breath caught in his throat.

"*Sacre bleu,*" he muttered.

"You can't help but be enchanted by that vision, eh, Guyot?" Raoul, who stood beside him at the altar, whispered, "Lucky you."

Cort grunted. "Beneath that vision are sharp claws, well hidden from view."

"I take it she isn't overjoyed to become your wife?"

"She knows this marriage is for the good of her people, but she is far from pleased."

Raoul chuckled softly. "You'll have a temperamental female in your bed, eh? You've got your work cut out for you, my friend."

Both Cort and Raoul fell silent as Moran reached the altar and handed Rhiannon to her bridegroom. As Cort took her small hand, he noted her thin-lipped smile. He did not fool himself into thinking it was meant for his benefit. More than likely, it was meant for her father.

A board at his side would have been more comfortable than Rhiannon's stiff body. How could such a curvaceous maiden be so hard? Was she made of steel?

Cort understood how unexpected this marriage was for Rhiannon, yet her reluctance disturbed him. True, they had much to learn of each other. But he was no monster.

He shifted uncomfortably. Mayhap he gained a kingdom by marrying the princess, but what barbs awaited him within her silken arms? A sour taste rose in his mouth.

When the flute music ceased, a priest approached the couple, his ceremonial robes rustling as he withdrew a Bible from the folds of rich material. Speaking in Latin, he uttered the marriage rites, then performed Mass.

Finished, he held up a cushion with two gold bands, one small and the other much larger. Making the sign of the cross, he placed the pillow on the altar.

In English, he said, "Rhiannon Rose O'Kelly, do you take this man to be your lawfully wedded husband?"

Rhiannon looked into Cort's eyes, her expression a storm of emotions. She didn't say anything for what seemed like an eternity. Would she refuse to become his wife at the last minute?

Cort glanced at King Moran, questioning him with his gaze.

Moran frowned, as if he, too, was perplexed by his daughter's stubborn silence. He reached out and tapped her on her elbow. Rhiannon turned to look at her father and the two exchanged knowing glances. When she faced the priest again, Cort felt a shudder run through her small frame.

She held her head high, and said softly, "I . . . I d-do, if the Holy church will ordain it."

Whispered comments rippled through the audience. The priest looked unsure about performing the rest of the marriage ceremony. He cleared his throat and looked down at his Bible. No doubt he'd known Rhiannon and her family for years. Surely it bothered him to see a member of his flock in such distress.

Cort sensed the stares of everyone in the chapel. He clenched his jaw, feeling for a moment as though he'd indeed taken advantage of the situation. Then he grew irritated, recalling he'd risked his life and the welfare of his men to free Callinon Castle.

He had nothing to regret. King Moran had placed his trust in him to protect his kingdom after he was gone. Before long, Rhiannon and her people would realize he was a man of his word, and that he could be trusted. This land and people were now his, as he was theirs.

"Please proceed, Father," Moran said to the priest.

With a nod, the priest asked Cort, "Do you, Cort Lothair Guyot, take Rhiannon Rose O'Kelly as your wife?"

"I do, if the Holy church will ordain it," Cort responded without hesitation.

Father Murphy handed the small ring to Cort, who slid it onto Rhiannon's trembling left hand. The gleaming band fit perfectly on her third finger—the one closest to her heart. Cort couldn't help but wonder if he'd ever find a place there—or if he even wanted to.

The thought disturbed him. Love had no place in this arrangement. Obedience and respect were all he desired from his new bride.

Rhiannon placed the larger gold band on Cort's finger then the couple knelt at the altar so the priest could bless them.

"I now pronounce you man and wife," the priest said. "May God be with you in your daily lives."

Cort released the breath he'd been holding since Rhiannon had hesitated with her vows. The trembling of her lips concerned him, and he sensed she still struggled with her doubts. Yet her squared jaw told him she would carry out her duty to her kingdom.

Leaning down, he captured Rhiannon's mouth with his, sealing the bargain. His lips were met with his wife's cold ones. They felt like pieces of clay pressed against his flesh. He quickly pulled back, noting the angry green sparks flying from her eyes.

He would have his hands full dealing not only with the political unrest of his new home, but also in dealing with Rhiannon's fierce pride. Part of him quaked at the challenge, another part relished it.

THE BELLS IN THE CHAPEL PEALED loudly as Rhiannon walked down the aisle beside her new husband. Guyot's arm around her waist felt like a lead weight and her heart grew heavier with each step. It was hard to believe, but it was true. She was a married woman. The silent stranger at her side was her husband. She juggled feelings of wariness and guarded optimism.

At the arched doorway, people showered them with wheat kernels—a symbol of fertility. Of course, they wished the couple peace and prosperity because they wanted it for themselves—and they deserved it.

However, they needn't have bothered with the symbolic act. Cort Guyot and his troops, by their very presence in this kingdom, would be able to give them a bright future, the type of future her father had fought long and hard to win for them, the type of life she would have tried to bring about as clan leader, had she been given the opportunity.

Rhiannon hated to say she was jealous of Cort, because that had no place here, not after all the suffering her people had endured. No, she needed to put aside petty feelings and disappointment. In all actuality, this wedding wasn't for her; it was for her people.

She considered the night ahead, and heat rose in her cheeks. The Norman would expect her to perform as a wife. Though she would be required to give her body to him, she would never release her heart. Love wasn't a part of their bargain. For some reason, a wave of melancholy washed over her, and she grew confused at her peculiar reaction.

Isn't that what I want? Never to form attachments to any man?

Baffled by her mixed emotions, she moved with Cort into the great hall. Piles of green boughs decorated trestle tables, which had been covered with creamy white tablecloths. Flickering candles cast glowing light and vases of wildflowers gave off a heady fragrance. The servants toiled long and hard to embellish the room for the occasion on such short notice.

Despite the suffering they'd endured not so long ago under Donovan's control, they had put much effort into this occasion. Indeed, the smiles she saw on her people's faces were worth her sacrifice. The laughter and good cheer made her eyes grow warm with unshed tears.

Guests filtered into the room and their voices echoed throughout the chamber. Musicians began to play a merry tune and a lighthearted atmosphere infused the great hall. Years had passed since this room had heard such hearty laughter. Too bad it had to be her marriage to the Norman that brought it about.

Cort led Rhiannon to the high table where her family waited for them.

"Please be seated," Moran instructed the newlyweds. "'Tis a night for celebration."

Cort helped Rhiannon sit and lowered down next to her. She was acutely aware of his large warmth pressed up next to hers. Despite her determination to deny any feelings toward the Norman, her blood stirred. In another place and another time, mayhap she could have felt differently about him, but not now—not under these circumstances. He hadn't agreed to this marriage because of affection for her. This was another business transaction for him. He had won her, like a prize in a bloody joust.

Rhiannon fought disappointment. Her wedding day should have been full of joyous hopes for her future as she joined her life with that of her beloved. That beloved should have been Jamie O'Brien. She cursed the day that he'd been tempted by the devil and torn from her arms because of his cowardice.

She and Jamie had played together as children, and they'd grown up sharing youthful secrets and later, when they were older, kisses. They'd been betrothed from the time they were young, and she'd never expected to marry another. It didn't seem right that this was her wedding, and that Jamie wasn't here. After all this time, his betrayal still seemed like something from a bad dream. Alas, she knew it was real, as much as it pained her to realize it.

"You are disturbingly quiet, Rhiannon." The Norman's dark assessment begged her to reveal her thoughts. "Have you nothing to say to your bridegroom?"

What did he want her to say? *Thank you for trying to pick up the pieces of my shattered world?*

Rhiannon looked down and clasped her hands together. "We owe this merrymaking to you, sir. It has been a long time since the people had a reason to rejoice."

"It's good for people to be happy and secure. Don't you think?"

"Aye," she returned, knowing he was right, but still pained by the nightmares of the past.

He gently cupped her chin in his hand and lifted it. His gaze searched hers as he ran a thumb along her cheek. "Is that not what you want for yourself?"

"Perhaps someday." Rhiannon shivered at his touch and pulled away. But not before a flare of heat extended from her core, all the way to her toes. How could he have this effect on her?

Was that disappointment she saw on the Norman's face?

Nay, it couldn't be. He was Callinon's liberator, and that was the extent of his association with her. He surely wasn't worried about her lack of enthusiasm toward him. He was getting what he wanted—land and wealth. He would soon possess her body, but he surely did not seek her affection.

Her thoughts were interrupted when servants brought forth platters of roasted suckling pig, goose, venison, steaming vegetables, and bowls of strawberries. Loaves of bread were passed out as well, along with copious amounts of mead.

It smelled scrumptious, but Rhiannon doubted she would be able to eat much. Afflicted with a case of the jitters, she studied the food longingly. The physician had told her it would be months before her stomach returned to normal and that she would have to be patient in the meantime. Instead, she satisfied herself by enjoying the sight of others consuming the savory meal.

Every time Rhiannon and Cort's specially assigned goblets became empty, Moran signaled for them to be refilled. He and Cort discussed the disturbing news that Donovan had indeed escaped, and remained at large, despite every attempt by Cort's men to track him down. Both men were concerned, though the Norman firmly believed Donovan would not give them further trouble.

"You don't know Donovan as I do," Moran advised. "He's out of his mind with vengeance and blames me for the death of his wife and son who were killed in one of our clan raids. The man will never rest until he feels he's avenged their untimely deaths."

"I understand his blood lust," Cort returned. "However, I can't believe he'd be insane enough to try and go up against my army."

"He's a cagey old fox," Moran said. "He may not attack directly, but he'll find another weakness to take advantage of."

As the men continued to discuss war and politics, Rhiannon picked at morsels of food. She'd eaten all her stomach would allow and she also felt squeamish at the realization that she now belonged completely to her husband. The small gold band on her left hand felt heavy, like a wooden yolk around an oxen's neck.

She sipped the honeyed mead. The fermented brew settled nicely into her brain. With her senses dulled, Rhiannon's anxiety began to fade and items in the room became imbued with a misty haze. Her malice toward Cort began to abate. Her gaze roamed freely over him, and she realized he was indeed an interesting specimen of manhood.

Not in full control, her mind wandered. She recalled Jamie's looks. He'd been small and thin, not tall and muscular like the Norman. While she'd appreciated Jamie's hearty looks, Cort's had a more appealing edge.

His dark hair and chiseled face intrigued her and his eyes, full of mystery, drew her more than Jamie's ever had. Rhiannon's gaze lowered to the Norman's strong hands. They were well-formed, and their rough appearance revealed that he was a fighting man who had seen hard work.

What would it feel like to feel his touch lingering upon my face again? Or my body?

Rhiannon shivered. She noticed Cort watching her in a hungry fashion, his lips slightly parted, revealing strong white teeth. He'd kissed her at the church altar, a simple peck to seal their wedding bargain. What would it be like to have those lips of his placed upon her in full blown passion?

She recalled the kisses she and Jamie had exchanged. They'd been traded in a quick fashion and had always seemed awkward. What would the Norman's kisses be like? Considering the raw masculinity he exuded, she sensed he possessed great knowledge of how to please a woman . . . in all ways.

At some point in his conversation with her father, Cort must have noticed Rhiannon's stare. When he was done talking, he turned to her with a questioning gaze.

"Rhiannon," he said in a husky voice.

She leaned closer to him so she could hear over the noisy merrymaking. Their faces were close now, their mouths only inches apart.

"Yes, husband?" The word *husband* sounded strange on her tongue.

"You need to eat more. You'll need your strength for tonight." He winked at her, then transferred food from his trencher onto hers.

A coil of warmth spread through Rhiannon at the Norman's consideration. She appreciated his efforts to feed her, though she realized he only wanted her hale and hearty in his bed.

She patted her abdomen. "I honestly cannot eat another bite, or I'll burst."

Cort waved a hand toward the room. "Your people have gone out of their way to welcome me. I want you to know how much I appreciate it."

"They are grateful for your army, my lord. They can sleep well at night, knowing their homes and fields won't be raided by Donovan, or the likes of him." Rhiannon fought off a wave of hiccoughs brought on by the mead.

Apparently ignoring her insult that the people appreciated his military prowess, and not him, he gently lifted her hand. Flipping it over to examine the palm, he began stroking the flesh with his thumb. "What I want to know, my lady, is will you sleep well at night, now that I'm here?"

"That depends." Rhiannon drew in an uneven breath. Her heart pattered as he etched invisible circles on her skin and a shiver trailed down her spin. "You are my husband. Will you let me sleep?"

He cocked his head at her. "That depends as well. You are lovely beyond compare, Rhiannon. I look forward to bedding you."

Cort's words nearly took Rhiannon's breath away. He continued to rub her palm with his thumb, and the room began to spin. Between his rhythmic strokes and the heat rising between them, she felt suffocated, but in a pleasant way.

"No doubt I'll disappoint you, husband," she managed. "I d-don't plan to enjoy your lovemaking."

He lifted a brow. "Is that a fact, *ma cherie*?"

"Aye," she returned, feeling the hot stare he rested upon her, searing her flesh.

"No matter what I do, you're bound and determined not to find pleasure?"

His voice swept across Rhiannon like warm wine, melting her reluctance. Yet, she denied her secret longings. What part of this conversation did he find confusing? Her reluctance to bed him, or did he sense her reluctance to admit she might actually be looking forward to it?

"Aye," she said again, trying to convince him she disapproved of his gentle persuasion.

"Then I have my work cut out for me. But be forewarned, I've been told I possess some skills in the art of lovemaking."

"Mere flattery I'm certain. I'll not give in easily, I can assure you," Rhiannon warned. She couldn't prevent her heart's fluttering, or the dangerous excitement building within her. "This entire . . . situation is not to my liking."

"I'm a patient man, Rhiannon." His eyes glimmered with invitation. "Very patient."

He removed his thumb from her hand and placed it on her throat, tracing it down her neck to the hollow of her throat. The skin beneath the Norman's touch burned. In fact, every part of Rhiannon flared to life.

Something flew over Rhiannon's head, hit the wall, and exploded into pieces. A small wheat cake, symbolic of fertility, lay crumbled on the fireplace hearth. Rhiannon shook her head, drawn suddenly from the spell the Norman had begun to cast.

Chuckling, Raoul approached the couple, his fists shoved on his hips. "There'll be plenty of time for that on your honeymoon."

Mortified that she'd been so immersed in the Norman's seduction, a warning bell sounded in Rhiannon's mind. She admitted, albeit reluctantly, she had actually begun to enjoy his flirtation, no doubt due to the effects of the mead.

She realized, with a combination of dismay and unwelcome expectation, that the night ahead would be fraught with further seduction attempts until she could hold out no longer. It was inevitable.

"You're just jealous," Cort laughingly shot back.

"Hang onto your wife, Guyot." Raoul nodded at Rhiannon. "You don't want her bride-napped on your wedding night."

"It had better not happen or I'll skin your backside." Cort pitched a hunk of bread at Raoul.

Raoul easily ducked the missile then strode over to one of the lower tables where Cort's men greeted him enthusiastically and made room for him on a bench.

Rhiannon was still so flustered by Cort's attempts to woo her that she paid scant attention to the troupe of entertainers in bright clothing and colorful scarves who noisily entered the room. Some played flutes and harps, others began to dance and sing. Men and women in the hall joined in a traditional circle dance. One of the performers in a bright yellow costume walked forward and bowed deeply toward Rhiannon and Cort.

"The bride and groom are invited to participate," he said.

"We're honored." Cort took Rhiannon's small hand in his large one and led her out into the hall. Everyone smiled at the newlyweds, pleased they'd joined in. They scooted aside so Cort and Rhiannon could move into place.

Cort seemed to have a difficult time trying to duplicate Rhiannon's intricate steps, no matter how hard he tried. Before long, he was breathing heavily. Rhiannon laughed at his awkward movements. Lost in the moment, she began to clap in time to the music.

Suddenly the room began to spin, and she stumbled. She put a hand to her forehead and tried to dispel the lightheaded sensation, but to no avail. She stumbled, but before she could topple over, Cort caught her in his strong arms and carried her from the dance floor.

As they stood in a quiet hallway, Cort put her down, allowing her body to slide seductively against his.

"I feel as awkward as a donkey on ice, Rhiannon. Before I make myself look any more foolish, I think I should stop. Someday, I shall teach you a Norman dance."

Grateful for his strong arms around her, Rhiannon pressed her cheek against his broad chest and struggled to catch her breath. She wanted to give herself over to the comfort of his embrace, longed to do it. Instead, she held her body rigidly and tried to quash the desire that urged her to melt into him.

When she met his dark gaze, she wondered if he was truly being considerate of her light headedness. "Was your intention to save yourself further embarrassment or to save me if I fell flat on my face?"

He shrugged. "Both. I am not the most graceful dancer. And you're still recovering from your ordeal. I'm sure the mead added to the problem."

"Thank you."

Cort's laughter brought a sparkle to his dark, hypnotizing eyes. "You have the greenest eyes. They're like sparkling emeralds."

Rhiannon swallowed hard as his hungry gaze raked across her. She'd heard such talk before from Jamie, though not quite as eloquent. She tried not to let Cort's compliments affect her but found it difficult.

He moved closer to her, until his breath transformed into a whisper upon her face. Her senses chimed with alarm. This attraction must be denied. Duty, and duty only, brought her under his control. She'd been handed over to him like a prize cow at market.

Rhiannon's perilous fascination with the Norman evaporated like a snowflake exposed to sunlight. As his warm lips sought hers, she pressed her hands against his chest and pushed him away.

He stood up straight, his face etched with irritation, looking very much like an intimidating giant.

"Enough of this," he growled. "I tire of pretending to be the merry bridegroom. 'Tis time we retire. Make no mistake; *you will* fulfill your obligations in my bed."

"Aye," Rhiannon spat, cold threading through her stomach. "Obligation is a good word to describe the response you will get from me between the sheets."

She turned to leave but felt his restraining hand on her arm.

"Be ready in half an hour's time for my arrival, wife."

Rhiannon glared at him. "Of course, *husband*." Jerking free of his grasp, she stormed toward the staircase.

Glenna quickly caught up with her, ready to attend to her needs. "My lady, watch your steps, else you'll stumble," the maid warned.

"Mayhap that would be a good thing," she returned harshly.

"Surely you don't mean that." Glenna lowered her voice to a whisper. "Don't be talkin' foolish. One of the little people might hear you and grant your wish."

"Glenna, you are far too superstitious for your own good." Rhiannon realized her maid may have a valid point.

"Come now, a little salt thrown over the shoulder and candles lit to Saint Brigit can do a world of good, you know."

"I've never held with those superstitions, Glenna. I'll not start doing it now."

When she turned toward her room, Glenna stopped her. "Your father had the servants prepare another chamber for you and Sir Cort."

Rhiannon frowned. "I don't understand."

Glenna guided her down a different hallway. "Surely you didn't expect to stay in that tiny place of yours now that you're married, did you?"

"It suits me."

"Aye, but it wouldn't suit now that the Norman will share your bed."

Glenna opened a door and led her into a large, candlelit chamber usually reserved for guests. Several chests rested against the walls along with a couple of intricately carved chairs. A richly woven tapestry hung next to a curtained bed embellished with colorful ribbons and strewn with flowers. A fire crackled on the hearth and herbs had been sprinkled on the flames, filling the chamber with a spicy, inviting scent.

Rhiannon flushed, realizing the place had been carefully arranged in order for the Norman to seduce her. Blood thrummed anxiously in her veins. "This is a mistake."

"I convinced your father to let me prepare you for your wedding night rather than have all the guests herding up here to gawk." Glenna lifted a brow at her.

"That's not what I mean," she said. "The preparations are unnecessary. You see, the Norman . . ."

Rhiannon fell silent. How could she explain what she was feeling? The Norman would have his way with her, whether or not there were flowers and ribbons strewn about. He would take her without compunction, feeling it was his right, and not caring a whit about her feelings.

Glenna laughed softly and placed a light hand on her arm. "Have no fear, my lady. I know what distresses you. Men are lusty goats, the lot of them. I'm certain Sir Cort will be exercising his husbandly rights, regardless of the decorations. The pretty touches are for you."

"You are such a dear, Glenna." Rhiannon struggled to keep her emotions in check. "You've been a Godsend for Ailleen and me. I never thanked you for taking such good care of her while Donovan held the castle, did I?"

"It was my place to do so." Glenna smiled. "I've tried my best to be loyal to your family. Over the years, they've proven themselves generous benefactors to our people."

"We've all lost so much, haven't we Glenna?"

She nodded. "Aye, that is why we must appreciate the Norman for coming to our assistance. Even if it seems difficult at first. Because of him, we'll be able to learn what it's like to live in peace again."

In a roundabout way, Glenna referred to Rhiannon's reluctance to bed the Norman and encouraged her not to oppose carrying out her part of the bargain. She was right. Because of the Norman, they all had cause to give thanks.

Rhiannon clasped Glenna's hands in hers and squeezed. "You are most wise, Glenna."

Glenna bowed her head, revealing strands of gray. "I did not get this color of hair without learning a thing or two along the way."

After helping Rhiannon undress, Glenna prodded her toward the bed where she swept aside the flowers and helped her slip under the covers.

Used to wearing a nightgown, Rhiannon shivered at the coolness of the sheets as she pulled them up to her chin. The material brushing against her bare skin made her feel sinful. Something about this whole marriage didn't seem right. She leaned back against the feather pillows, plagued by doubt.

"If your mother could be here, she'd have a discussion with you, telling you what it's like to be with a man," Glenna began hesitantly. "Since she's not, are there any questions I can answer for you milady?"

Embarrassed heat prickled Rhiannon's cheeks. She didn't understand everything that went on between a man and a woman, but she had a good idea. The thought that she and the Norman would soon know each other intimately made her skin prickle.

"I've seen the farm animals, Glenna," she said, her mouth going dry.

Glenna smiled. "Aye, but you need to know it's not so rough an act as it seems with the beasts in the field. There will be some interlude of lovemaking beforehand. And there will be a mite bit of discomfort for you at the start. But it will get better, I assure you."

"I'm very much doubt that," Rhiannon said, absolutely certain this marriage would not improve. Warmth burned at the back of her eyes, but she refused to give into emotion. "The Norman doesn't want to be a caring husband to me, Glenna. This wedding was only a prerequisite for him to collect my dowry. He cares naught for my feelings."

"He gave his vows Rhiannon, as did you. That is no small thing. Remember, marriage is a sacred union between two people." Glenna's eyes misted. "When my Paddy was alive, we were nearly inseparable, God rest his soul. The good Lord allowed us fifteen years together and I recall every one of them with great fondness."

Rhiannon looked at Glenna with a different view—as a young woman in love, rather than just her maid and friend. "Did your parents arrange your marriage, too?"

"No. Our families lived close by each other in the village. As Paddy and I grew up, we came to love each other.

"How wonderful it must have been to fall in love and not be forced into a marriage." Rhiannon allowed herself a moment of reflection as she thought of Jamie, and what might have happened between them if things had turned out differently. Alas, her wishful thinking would not make her current predicament any easier to bear. "Did you have any children?

"We weren't so blessed. I've come to love you and your sister as though you were my own daughters. I hope you don't mind."

"Of course not. We're fortunate you care about us so much."

"I'll leave you to your husband now. No doubt the brawny man will be charging up here any minute now, wanting you all to himself."

Glenna hugged Rhiannon, then left, shutting the door softly behind her. Rhiannon wished she could leave as well. She would have rather been anywhere but here waiting for the Norman to come and claim her.

Moments ticked past, and finally she climbed out of the bed. She yanked off the top blanket, wrapped it around herself, and paced in front of the fireplace. As the flames coated her bare skin with warmth, she attempted to control her frustration.

"SHHH," CORT TOLD HIS MEN AS they prodded him up the stairs toward his chamber. "You sound like a pack of rutting animals."

Boisterous male laughter filled the hallway, echoing off the stone walls. Several of Cort's men thumped him on the back, encouraging him to go along with the fun.

"Mayhap we sound like a pack of animals, Guyot," Raoul added. "But I'd say you'll be the one doing the rutting this night."

Self-conscious, Cort glanced at his new father-in-law, hoping he wasn't insulted by the comment. Rhiannon was his daughter, after all, and he may not appreciate the men's ribald humor. Moran merely shrugged and grinned.

Without warning, the men started clawing at his clothes and tossing them aside. In short order, Cort stood unclothed in the hallway. One of them opened the chamber door and Raoul shoved him inside while the men shouted coarse taunts and made randy gestures.

Rhiannon stood in front of the fireplace wrapped in a blanket, her soft, creamy shoulders and back exposed. Cort caught his breath, then grabbed a tablecloth from a carved wooden chest and tucked it around his waist.

Unbidden, his gaze wandered back to his bride. The woman's magnificence nearly overwhelmed him. Her long, fiery red hair, backlit from the crackling flames, imbued her with the glory of a legendary goddess. Heat and desire raced through him; however, he tamped it down. He didn't want to frighten her.

Faded bruises marred her pale skin. At the sight of her injuries, the memory of Donovan's mistreatment sparked a flare of rage through his chest. He would never let that man lay a hand on Rhiannon again. Or for that matter, anyone. With every fiber of his being, he swore it.

Rhiannon turned to look at him and her gaze was far from warm and inviting. Her eyes pierced him like shards of ice; nevertheless, she appeared apprehensive and frightened. His heart filled with compassion, and shame coated him.

He wanted her, but he would not take her. Above all, she needed to desire him as much as he desired her.

"Leave us," he growled at the men. They shuffled away, their laughter and loud comments fading.

Raoul remained, his hand on the wooden frame. "I'll be right

outside, Cort. No one will get in." He tossed a glance at Rhiannon.
"Or out."

After the door closed, Cort walked slowly toward Rhiannon.
His new wife was lovely and desirable, and he counted himself
lucky. Aware how she'd been mistreated, he realized he would need
to be patient and kind. She would not easily accept her new position, and he didn't blame her for being nervous considering the
poor treatment she'd received from Donovan.

Hopefully in time she would come to trust him.

FIVE

RHIANNON WHIRLED AROUND TO LOOK AT the Norman, shivering beneath his intense perusal. Her heart fluttered like a trapped bird within her chest. She'd seen village men bare from the waist up when they participated in festival games, but she'd never seen a man unclothed.

During her sheltered existence, she'd had no experience with the opposite sex. Nevertheless, she'd overheard the female servants whisper of their intimate encounters. Her mouth went dry as she realized she may possibly soon have one of her own.

Perhaps he felt as apprehensive as she?

As Cort approached her, she recoiled, amazed by her mixed reaction of inquisitiveness and apprehension. She wanted to look anywhere else but upon his powerful form, yet her gaze was inexorably dawn toward it. Relief flooded her when he covered himself, although curiosity bubbled within her.

Stirring up her courage, she allowed herself to examine his appearance again. Muscles rippled in his biceps and upon his broad chest were whorls of dark hair that ran in a thin line down his abdomen. Blood raced like wildfire through her limbs, and she wondered if her reaction was normal.

"You have my dowry now, sir," she said, managing to find her voice. "Is that not enough? If it pleases you, mayhap you'd prefer to find somewhere else to sleep this eve."

"Did I hear you correctly, my lady?" He lifted a brow. "You don't care for the attentions of your groom this eve?"

Rhiannon nodded. "I realize that for political reasons, we've both tolerated this marriage charade. But I shan't hold it against you if you chose to spend your time elsewhere."

Cort frowned. "I didn't expect you to be so . . . displeased with me."

"I hope you haven't misunderstood my intentions." Rhiannon turned to concentrate on glowing embers of the fireplace, selecting her words carefully so as not to anger him. "I agreed only to wed you, Norman. I had no expectations that you would care to share my favors."

When she felt his arms encircle her, she stiffened. His lips pressed against the nape of her neck. Lower and lower his mouth moved, sweeping across her shoulders and the aching spots on her back where Donovan's fists had landed on more than one occasion.

"He'll never hurt you again, *ma cherie*. Now one will. I promise."

Rhiannon closed her eyes and shuddered, attempting to deny the pleasurable sensations that stirred in her abdomen.

"My army secured Callinon Castle as I promised your father," Cort continued as he gently spun her around. "Everyone expects me to take you as my wife in all ways."

Rhiannon managed to control her trembling lower lip. "It's truly unnecessary, my lord. There are ways to . . . ah, convince everyone that we are truly man and wife and have engaged in . . . the duties expected."

"Possibly," he said in a hoarse voice. "And if this is what you would like, I will honor your wishes."

"You may have my inheritance," Rhiannon said slowly. "But never my heart."

"I never asked for your heart, my lady." He pulled her so close she could feel his own heart beating. "Only your trust and perhaps someday, your respect."

Rhiannon held herself stiffly in Cort's embrace, trying to deny the effects his tender words had on her. Yet her flesh was weak, and her body betrayed her. Her anger toward him faded and her cheeks blossomed with warmth.

A voice deep inside told her to flee this room; get away, yet she dismissed it. This man from his faraway land of Normandy would not force her to be with him. Despite her trepidation, she realized Cort would behave as a gentleman, and her heart warmed toward him.

"*Sacre bleu*, you are more beautiful than I imagined. In fact, you're perfect." He studied her intensely but did not touch her further.

Rhiannon realized he was leaving it up to her to make the next move. She found she didn't want to shy away from him. Hesitantly, she looked up. To her delight, she found only acceptance in his gaze.

Cort smiled at Rhiannon, and she found herself captivated. She envisioned herself as a timid rose, opening its petals to the sun, soaking up its nourishing warmth. After the last months that had been wrought with uncertainty, she felt herself come alive and in charge of her fate.

Everything in the room became more vivid: the fiery-orange flames of the fire, the intoxicating scent of the flowers, the invigorating sight of the man before her.

Inhaling deeply, she drew the masculine, raw sent of him in her nostrils. A tremor of excitement rippled up her spine and her thoughts burst with dazzling possibilities. Dare she allow this man into her world?

"Rhiannon," he muttered, then claimed her lips in a deep kiss. Sensations swirled within her, sweeping her away on a cloud of passion.

Cort bowed low to her and said, "My wife, I shall leave you to your slumber, and I pray that it is sweet and restful."

He eased toward the door.

"Don't leave," she whispered, amazed by her boldness.

He turned back around to face her, his expression inquisitive. "My lady?"

"I, I don't know what to do," she stammered, her cheeks filling with heat. "Will you show me?"

He whispered to her in French, his native tongue, a language both beautiful and soothing to her ears.

"You are ready then, eh?" He moved quickly toward her and nuzzled the palm of her hand with his lips. "I will show you such wonders, my bride, and I daresay you will be pleased."

His words slipped over her like honeyed wine, heating her core and melting any resistance she had left.

"I'm afraid," she admitted.

"Never be afraid of me, *ma cherie*. Your body is made for loving. Your lips, your hair, your emerald eyes—all bewitch me."

"You truly desire me?" she asked, still surprised to find her new husband to be tolerant of her concerns. It wasn't at all how she expected him to behave.

"You're my wife, Rhiannon. I wish to have you this night with you, and many more to come. But if it's too soon for you to give yourself to me, I beg you, let me know and I will indeed leave."

What type of person was she? She could face an enemy on the field of battle and never flinch. Yet this man could reduce her to a mass of quivering flesh by allowing her to have her way.

Mayhap in time, love would grow between her and Cort. She would pray for that and have faith.

Rhiannon placed her hands on either side of his face and drew it close to hers. "I wish for you to stay with me this night and as many more as will please you."

Later, after they'd shared pleasures together, they exchanged stories about their lives and what was most important to them. Eventually, Cort fell asleep next to Rhiannon, and she was satisfied to see him so content. Understanding her husband much better now, and hearing of the difficulties he'd endured, Rhiannon smiled.

She leaned over and softly kissed his brow. Uttering a sigh, she reached over to the nightstand and snuffed out the candelabra. The room filled with darkness, save for the glowing embers in the fireplace. Listening to Cort's even breathing, she wondered what lay in store for the both of them.

When he reached out and pulled her toward his large body, she held herself stiffly in his embrace, unsure of how to react. She could feel his moist, warm breath on her neck and while it wasn't entirely unpleasant, it was unfamiliar.

This is what it's like to be married, she told herself, willing herself to relax.

After a bit, she allowed herself to enjoy the feeling of being protected. It was a new, unfamiliar feeling, especially after months of doubt. Sleep eluded her for what seemed like hours, and she considered what this change of circumstances would bring about. Eventually, she drifted off to sleep, comfortable with all that had passed.

By all that was holy, she wanted her marriage with Cort to be peaceful. In time, he may possibly grow to love her, and she may grow to love him. As God was her witness, she would learn to be a good wife to him. Meanwhile, she would pray for the two of them to develop genuine affection for each other.

FINGERS OF DAWN TRACED THE CHAMBER window when Cort opened his eyes. Immediately, he rolled over to look at his new wife lying next to him. She curled against his side, so small and warm, yet so fiery and full of spirit. He admired her creamy curves while touching her silken hair, feeling as though last night he'd held heaven in his arms.

It pleased him how they'd talked late into the night, discussing their childhoods, their homes, their hopes and desires. He'd explained his situation of being a bastard, yet how his father had sent him to be fostered by another family. Rhiannon seemed to appreciate how difficult Cort's upbringing had been, and he felt closer to her.

A surge of possessiveness washed over him, along with a fierce desire to protect her at all costs. Rhiannon was no meek and mild female. Nay, her fierce will matched his. Somehow, he had to convince her, as well as her people, that he meant no harm.

He pondered Rhiannon's dowry, the O'Kelly's vast, fertile Irish landholdings. There was much work to be accomplished to restore its former productivity, and he realized it would not behoove him to waste time.

It was unfortunate that the property had been depleted while Donovan held captive the fertile fields. Out of spite it seemed, he'd allowed everything to fall into ruin. The land needed to be healed of the scars heaped upon it during war. The people needed to feel encouraged to restore their homes and nurture their crops. Building their confidence and their skills would be his first order of business.

Rhiannon stirred in his arms, murmured something, and burrowed against his chest. Not wishing to disturb her slumber, Cort carefully lifted bright curls away from her face so that he could admire her rosy cheeks and the pout of her berry lips. He couldn't resist leaning down and kissing the soft curve of her neck, just below her ear.

Rhiannon moaned softly and reached up to touch the spot where his lips had been. Encouraged, he placed kisses from her ear to her mouth where he lingered briefly. Her lashes fluttered and she opened her eyes. She smiled up at him.

"*Bonjour,*" he said softly.

"Hello to you," Rhiannon said with a yawn. "Merciful heavens, I have much to do. An estate such as Callinon requires much tending."

"Sweet *Jesu,* I will not think you lazy if you set aside your work for this one day." Cort watched his wife closely.

She smiled. "It is no troublesome task to attend to my home. Besides, do you not expect me to behave as a good wife should?"

"Is that all you think I want from you? To be a good wife?" Cort rolled out of bed, towering over her. Had he been a fool to hope tenderness could grow between them?

She sat up, frowning. "What did I say that upset you?"

"No worries, lady wife. I'm simply anxious to be about my day." Stewing about something he couldn't explain, he shoved on his trousers and shirt and pulled on his boots.

Rhiannon sat up, her eyes wide with concern. "Where are you going?"

"To do my husbandly duties, of course," he said, instantly regretting the unkind edge in his voice.

"I must be up and about as well," she said quietly as she stood and draped herself in a robe.

"I'll have your maid send up bath water." A muscle twitched in his jaw as he studied her, confusion winding through him. What did he desire from her? He couldn't quite put his finger on it.

"I'm capable of ordering it myself," she said, sending a puzzled glance in his direction.

"Very well," he responded. "When you're ready, find me in the great hall."

Rhiannon arched her delicate brows. "What are we doing today, my lord?"

"Touring your lands and tenements," he said.

"My father is perfectly capable of handling his own estate."

Cort folded his arms across his chest. "I'm sure you understand the nature of your father's illness. He needs his rest and has requested that I assume these duties. In his absence, I'd like your opinion about the condition of O'Kelly landholdings."

Apparently, Rhiannon had forgotten her father's ailment. As realization that her father was dying came over her, her proud shoulders slumped. Tears glittered in her eyes, yet she held them back.

"I'll be down shortly."

"Rhiannon, I didn't mean to—"

"So much has changed," she said softly. "I'm unaccustomed to him not being in charge."

Cort disliked the direction of this conversation. It had quickly gone downhill and to his frustration, he didn't know how to change it. Rhiannon had suffered much, however he was far from perfect. Most of all, he did not know how to explain his concerns to her. Managing the estate did not worry him. Yet, this marriage business was troublesome to say the least. It took commitment to unlock the intricate machinations of the heart.

Turning on his heel, he strode from the bed chamber and closed the door. The creek running near the castle, nestled between rolling green hills, bushes and trees, called to him. He knew the water would be cold, but it might startle some sense into him.

AFTER CORT CLOSED THE DOOR BEHIND himself, Rhiannon began to pace. Confusion coursed through her, a measure for herself and a measure for Cort. Last night, she'd dared to hope that the two could learn to have affection for each other. She'd dared to believe he may want that, too.

Alas, had it only been her dream?

Rhiannon's world had suffered such upheaval recently. Everything had been fine one minute, then the next, she'd been held captive in the dungeon and nearly forced to marry that lunatic Donovan. Two weeks later, she'd been compelled to marry Sir Cort Guyot.

Aye, her people would benefit from his protection. She realized she was not the first woman who found herself married to someone not of her own choosing. It happened all too frequently among upper class women in the Irish kingdoms. Honestly, she hadn't expected any more for herself, considering how political alliances strengthened clans.

Although still a child, even her own mother had been promised to Moran in order to mend fences between warring factions. Her mother had grown to love him, yet she'd admitted to her daughters that at the beginning, she'd also been concerned for the future.

Despite her reservations about her hasty marriage, Rhiannon appreciated that she could still remain mistress of Callinon—the land she'd loved her entire life.

She glanced outside her bedroom window, watching as the sun rose higher in the pink and gold sky. Beneath, blue ocean waves rolled across the beach and seabirds wheeled above. Warmed by the rising sun, distant hills began to shed their mist, revealing rolling turf colored with intense blue green.

This was her home. She loved it more with every breath she took. She would not allow anyone to threaten it as Donovan had; with her new husband's military forces protecting the estate, it shouldn't happen again.

If not for Cort, she would be married to Donovan. The thought turned her stomach. He deserved her appreciation for what he'd done. He may never understand her, but she hoped to someday gain his respect. She felt ashamed for getting so emotional with him this morning. No wonder he'd been caught off guard—he probably had expected more mature behavior from his new wife.

Hearing a knock upon the door, she wondered if Cort had returned. Her mood brightened, and she hoped to clarify any misunderstandings they'd had earlier.

"Come in," she called, watching as the door swung open.

Glenna entered, followed by an assortment of man servants. Two of them hefted a wooden tub, which they placed on the floor near the hearth. Several others poured buckets of steaming water into the bath.

After they left, Glenna turned to Rhiannon. "Be you well my lady?"

"I'm fine." Rhiannon removed her robe. She stepped into the warm depths and sighed as every muscle in her body released tension. When Glenna handed her a cake of soap and a cloth, Rhiannon washed herself.

"The color's drained from your face and you've lines on your forehead," Glenna observed. "I'll skin the Norman if he's hurt you in any way. I know your father would lend me the knife to do it."

Rhiannon shook her head. "He was . . . very attentive. I'm more upset at myself than him."

Glenna raised a curious brow. "And why is that?"

"I need to be wiser about how to conduct myself, Glenna," Rhiannon said as rinsed off suds from her skin. "I've got more responsibilities now, and I must take things more seriously."

"Do you and your new husband not see eye to eye?" Glenna frowned. "Come to think of it, he did seem preoccupied earlier when he came down to break his fast."

Rhiannon shrugged. "I'm merely confused about how to act around him."

"'Tis only new bride jitters, child. The unknown can be frightening, but that doesn't mean it will be bad. We'll have to pay a visit to old Sybil. She'll tell the future for you."

"'Tis only foolish nonsense, Glenna. She can't know what's to be."

"The woman has foretold a lot of things for me that have come true. I think we can't discount her prophecies."

Rhiannon got out of the tub and Glenna handed her a towel. After she'd dried off, she removed a brown riding dress from her wardrobe, stretched it across her bed, and began to put on her underclothes.

"Your husband awaits you in the great hall," Glenna said as she assisted Rhiannon. "He's anxious to be off."

Rhiannon hastened her movements. "I'll be along shortly."

Glenna grinned. "The man doesn't realize he's got a handful with you, does he?"

"I don't want to be a handful, Glenna," Rhiannon said with a chuckle. "I want my husband and me to get along. We both have Callinon's interests at heart."

Glenna brushed Rhiannon's hair and pulled it into one thick braid that ran down her back. "Aye, with his army, he'll protect the entire province from invasion. At first, I believed he only cared for the land and wealth he would accumulate. However, after getting to know him better, I believe he looks for more than that."

"I've learned that he is a man without a family," Rhiannon said.

"It's my belief he truly wishes to make this place the home he's never had."

"What makes you believe that?"

"He told me as much last night. 'Tis a sad tale, about his illegitimate birth, and how his father had been ashamed of siring a bastard and shipped him off to be fostered by a strict and hardhearted uncle. However, he's done his best to make a good life by joining King Henry's army."

"So, it seems."

"He's so rigid though, Glenna. I think it may be hard for him to fit in and feel truly as though he belongs. I don't know what it will take to help him realize that he's found it here."

"Men hold their feelings deep inside, for fear people might consider them weak. He may be reluctant to admit what he feels. Did you expect anything more?"

"Perhaps not."

"From what I saw last night at the feast, he seemed ready to settle down. But since he has been a soldier for King Henry so long, without a home and attachments, do you think that will honestly please him in the end?"

Glenna had hit at the truth, and Rhiannon pondered if she, too, felt worried. "I hope so, but I, too, wonder how well he will adapt."

"You must be patient with him and with yourself. I promise, as soon as we can spare the time, we'll visit old Sybil. She'll put your mind at rest."

"I highly doubt that." Rhiannon nodded at the stained sheets, embarrassed heat rising in her cheeks. "Do we have to hang the bedding for all to see?"

"I spoke with your father about that heathenish custom. He will take my word of what I saw, rather than publicly humiliate you."

"Thank the saints for that," Rhiannon said. "I wasn't relishing the thought."

"There, you're finished." Glenna patted Rhiannon's shoulder. "Go and meet your husband before he bursts at the seams."

Rhiannon hugged Glenna then went downstairs to find the man who had taken up residence in her bedroom and in her thoughts. She didn't dare look him in the eye for fear he'd look into her very soul and see her fears about him.

Setting her jaw with firm resolve, she entered the great hall.

SIX

SEATED AT THE HIGH TABLE WHEN Rhiannon descended the staircase, Cort put down his bread and watched her graceful movements. Watching her move made his heart leap, and he couldn't believe his good fortune to not only have her as his wife, but also to become the landlord to her kingdom.

Though he didn't blame her for remaining guarded toward him, he longed for the day she no longer looked upon him with suspicion. It seemed last night that he'd begun to melt the wall of ice around her heart, by comforting her over the devastating loss of her mother and her brother, and now with the inevitable loss of her father, yet he still had a long way to go.

She'd been through a lot, there was no doubt in his mind about that. Being imprisoned by Donovan for months, worrying about her sister, her people and her father must have been excruciatingly painful. The emotional turmoil she'd endured had left its mark, and he realized she'd had to deal with the cruel reality of war.

Although some of her apprehensions had been lifted, she now had a new husband to learn about. The idea made him take pause. He'd only been considering what he could readily see. What if she cared for another man?

The idea made him smolder with jealousy. Eager not to consider it too deeply, he pushed it away. Even if that were true, the reality remained that he was now her husband.

He had never been a patient man, but he needed to exercise that virtue with the young woman he now called wife. Tolerance and understanding toward her would help him gain her trust, so he needed to keep that utmost in his mind.

Rhiannon sat down next to him and sent him a hesitant smile. He smiled back, but discovered he couldn't manage to make small talk. Silence, like a heavy curtain, hung between them. Neither spoke as they broke their fast with fruit, bread, porridge, and mugs of ale.

"You're flushed," Cort finally commented, studying her closely and hoping she hadn't become overly fatigued last night with their lovemaking. "Are you unwell?"

"I'm fine," she said softly. "Pray, tell me what you would like to see today, husband?"

Cort would have preferred for her to be more forthcoming, but he realized she had much more to learn about him before being comfortable. She seemed awkward and hesitant around him, nevertheless, he must remember that much had changed in her world and she needed time to process it.

"If you're ready, my lady, let's go to the stables and collect our mounts for the day. Will you help me choose a steady animal?"

"I'll leave that to one of the handlers, my lord," Rhiannon answered. "They will know much better than I."

"Of course," Cort acquiesced.

As they entered the central bailey, which was surrounded by tall, pointed stakes, castle workers shuffled in and out of buildings carrying bulging sacks or baskets heaped with food. Rhiannon pointed out the well where servants fetched water in a bucket, along with the small buildings such as the kitchen and the bakery, which had fragrant cookfire smoke rising from their chimneys. In a shaded corner stood the storehouse, where grain, dried meat, dried fruit, and other food supplies were kept.

Cort absorbed Rhiannon's information as she described her home's amenities. His mind worked overtime, however, as it whirred with ideas of how he would strengthen the fortifications. For his men to defend the castle to the best of their abilities, he would need to take immediate action so that any further intruders, such as Donovan, could be immediately and solidly repelled.

"Do you approve, my lord?" Rhiannon asked, studying his face intently.

Startled back into the present by her comment, Cort said, "Of course. There are, however, improvements to the castle design that I plan to make."

Consternation shone on Rhiannon's face. "Improvements?"

"Extra fortifications to safeguard Callinon, my lady."

"I see," she said. "These fortifications are utilized in Normandy at their strongholds?"

"Yes, and they will help us secure this kingdom," he explained. "I'm anxious to begin."

"That's good," she added. "The last thing I wish to see is yet another attack on my home and my people.

In the outer bailey, they passed by the barracks where Cort's soldiers were housed, along with Moran's remaining troops. As they entered the stables, Cort's nostrils twitched with the smell of hay and manure.

"Good morning, Quinn," Rhiannon called to boy wearing simple clothing comprised of a woolen tunic, trousers, and a cap over his shaggy hair.

"And too you, my lady," Quinn said as he looked up from the dun-colored stallion he was grooming.

Rhiannon introduced Cort to him, then said, "Quinn, my husband requires a sturdy mount for today's visit to our land holdings."

"To be sure," Quinn said, patting the flanks of the animal he ministered to. "Sid here be a great mount, and he'll be ready to ride once I saddle 'im."

As Quinn prepared Cort's mount, Rhiannon entered a stall and lead out a small mare a few minutes later. As she slid a foot into a stirrup, Cort stepped over to help her into the side saddle. She arranged her skirts carefully, then nudged the mare into the yard. Cort mounted the dun and rode up alongside his wife.

"She's a pretty little thing," Cort commented as he patted her horse's neck, admiring its equine features.

"Aye, Una's a fine horse indeed. I raised her from when she was a wee colt." Rhiannon met Cort's gaze. "She had some definite spirit at first, but soon settled into a gentle and loving girl once she realized I only meant well for her."

Was that a subtle hint that Rhiannon sent toward him, indicating that with time, she, too, would learn relax around him? He certainly hoped so.

As they trotted their mounts toward the gatehouse, she asked, "Where would you like to go first, my lord?"

He considered his options, then said, "I want to determine the state of the pastures and fields so I can assess how the spring planting is coming along. I also want to start visiting the tenants. I'd like to establish a rapport with them as soon as possible."

"Of course," she said as the horses clomped across the drawbridge.

The rolling green countryside rose in the distance. Dotted with farms and people tending the fallow fields, it appeared almost pastoral, although Cort had recently witnessed the devastation Donovan's troops had waged upon it.

Like a stone thrown across a lake, Arch, Cort's hound, darted toward them. His tongue lolled to one side as he raced alongside Sid.

"Hey, boy," Cort called, smiling down at the loyal hound. Reaching into a small leather pouch, he tossed a piece of jerked meat. Arch snapped it down, then padded patiently alongside of them. Before long, the dog ran off to sniff at bushes and bark at birds.

Both Cort and Rhiannon laughed at Arch's happy pursuit of outdoor delights and robust smells.

"How long have you had your dog?" Rhiannon asked, her gaze riveted toward where the hound now joyously romped.

"A few years now," Cort said. "Actually, he belongs not only to me but to all of my men. We found him wounded on a battlefield, and it was agreed that we needed to nurse him back to health."

"How wonderful you saved him." Rhiannon gazed at Cort with appreciation radiating from her eyes.

"Arch has proved his worth many a time," Cort said. "He'll bark to warn us of an enemy's approach, and he's attacked predators sneaking up on our camp. We are all happy to call him a comrade and companion."

Rhiannon took them along a dirt road that led them around the vast O'Kelly holdings that stretched as far as the eye could see. Sunlight fell upon her lovely face and a crisp breeze brought pink to her cheeks as she talked about one thing or another, enthusiastically describing the surroundings and the people who labored over the land.

Cort did his best not to stare overlong at her, however, it was most difficult. The more she spoke, the more animated she became. He realized he'd hit upon her passion, which was good to know. She had a deep and abiding love for the land, and the tenants who were loyal to the O'Kelly clan.

BEFORE LONG, RHIANNON BEGAN TO FEEL comfortable riding along with Cort. After recalling their intimacy last night, she'd initially felt shy and self-conscious. Fortunately, her husband had a way of making her feel comfortable and appreciated for her knowledge, so her confidence began to soar.

So far, it seemed, she'd initially been incorrect about this man she'd married, and she'd been worried for no good reason. She believed he would fit in here with her family, her people, and with her at his side.

Farmhouses, byres, and granaries stood out amidst the countryside. Surrounding paddocks held grazing horses, cattle, sheep, pigs, and other livestock. Chickens, ducks, and geese pecked at grain scattered in pens. Children and adults alike tended to their duties, whether it was hoeing weeds from their gardens or clearing brush from their property.

"How many people reside within O'Kelly landholdings?" Cort asked.

"We used to have close to five hundred or so. When Donovan attacked, many people fled to the heights of Connemara. I believe most have returned by now, but I can't be certain."

"The land appears fertile. What type of crops do the fields typically produce?"

"They are numerous. Barley, oats, grain, hay, wheat, and the like. You can talk with our castle steward, and he'll pull the records of the average gross yields. Our gardens typically grow peas and beans along with other vegetables and herbs."

"What do those trees and stands of bushes I see everywhere produce?"

"The fruit orchards provide apples, cherries, pears and peaches. Hazelnuts as well, which are a particular favorite. The bushes give us blackberries, strawberries, cranberries, rowanberries, elderberries and much more."

"Impressive," Cort said. "I do have a new type of crop rotation that I'd like the people to try next spring. Three fields are planted, leaving a fourth fallow until the next season so it doesn't get leeched of nutrients."

"Is this something you learned from the farmers in Normandy?"

He nodded. "There is also a method of producing fertilizer I want to introduce. We'll strip turfs from hillsides near the ocean shoreline and use them as animal bedding in the byres around the farmsteads. After it has aged, we'll cast the enriched animal manure onto the fields.

Rhiannon noticed how Cort's eyes gleamed bright with passion, the type she'd often seen in her father's eyes as he'd ridden through the plough land. He seemed quite knowledgeable about maintaining property, which was no doubt due to how he'd helped his uncle manage his land. He'd told her last night that it had been backbreaking work, and his uncle had been a stringent overseer, however, he'd learned much.

When Cort finally stopped to catch his breath, Rhiannon took the opportunity to speak.

"I see you've developed a keen interest in my land."

"Our land." He leveled a solemn gaze at her. "As husband and wife, we will develop it together."

Rhiannon hesitated a second, wondering if Cort believed her people had mismanaged O'Kelly landholdings.

"Are you unhappy with what you see, my lord?"

Cort gave a hearty laugh. "Indeed, I am not! Your clan has obviously coaxed much from the land. But production technologies constantly improve. With new procedures, we can cultivate the acreage further and improve harvests. Everyone will benefit."

Rhiannon quelled her anxiety. She couldn't deny there could always be room for improvement and appreciated that Cort would bring these new methods to Callinon. Not so long ago, she'd believed her people were finished. Because Cort's men had liberated them from Donovan, hope for their future glimmered. Her heart warmed toward him, and she appreciated that her father had seen the wisdom of she and Cort marrying, that she had not.

Cort turned in his saddle to watch farmers working in fields, while others repaired outbuildings or cut chunks of earth from peat bogs to use for fuel in fireplaces. Low stone fences crisscrossed swells of green landscape covered in heather and other wildflowers. Rhiannon's nostrils tingled with the rich earth smells.

Despite Cort's reassuring words about Callinon's future, she wondered if at some point he might prove himself unreliable. She prayed that would not occur, because currently, she held him in high esteem.

"Does your steward also keep records of livestock production?" Cort asked.

"Aye." Rhiannon raised an inquisitive brow, wondering about her husband's numerous accomplishments. "How is it that you know about husbandry? Did you learn that from your father's people or your uncle's?"

Cort's face darkened. "My father barely acknowledged my presence after I was born, and ere long, mayhap when I was about seven years, sent me to live with my uncle. It was he who taught me these things."

"Of course, that makes sense," Rhiannon said, wishing she hadn't mentioned his father, because he'd told her last night of the man's negligence.

"I realize he sent me away so that his wife and legitimate sons would not learn of my existence," Cort continued.

"Nevertheless, it was a cruel dismissal." Rhiannon's stomach twisted, and she realized she was sad for her husband's mistreatment. How difficult it would have been for the young boy to know he wasn't wanted in his sire's home.

"With such a vast knowledge of farming, why did you decide to become a soldier?"

"So many questions." His brow furrowed. "In my youth, I spent a lot of time on my uncle's landholdings, tending the animals and the land as he taught me. At a certain point, I realized how much they relied upon the army to protect their homes. I begged my uncle to allow me to become a page. Finally, he found a position for me, although I was older than most youths who serve the nobility."

"What else do pages do?" Rhiannon asked, now curious about this part of Cort's life.

"Along with learning to read, write, and work numbers, I also learned the art of combat. Eventually, I earned the right to be a squire. When I turned eighteen, I became a knight, and later joined the Norman army."

"Will you remain in the army?

"I haven't decided."

Rhiannon watched various emotions cross his face, all of them unreadable. She sensed that he didn't care to elaborate on the subject.

"My mother taught my siblings and me," Rhiannon said. "She also brought in tutors and other scholars to help us learn about art, geography, and history."

"It's good you are a learned woman," Cort said. "You are intelligent, and no doubt would have been bored if not allowed to study."

"Was your childhood terribly lonely?" Rhiannon asked, again feeling sorry for the boy who had never truly been accepted by the people who should have loved him.

His gaze lingered appreciatively on her and a smile touched his lips. "It was rich with experiences, and I regret nothing."

"That is good," Rhiannon said. The warm sunshine: the music of the wind in the trees, and her husband's full attention sent a tingle up her spine.

"You are beautiful, *ma cherie*. Have I told you that?"

Pleased by his words, warmth blossomed in her cheeks. "Many times," Rhiannon admitted. "But still, I cannot but appreciate hearing that you regard me so."

Pulling her gaze from his, she turned toward the mountain range covered in vivid yellow gorse.

Breathe, Rhiannon. Just breathe . . .

When the river appeared through a canopy of trees, she urged Una forward with her knees, and rode rapidly toward it.

Cort soon caught up with Rhiannon for her small mare was no match for his stallion. They weren't far from the river's edge when he overtook her.

As she glanced at him, she noticed how a sporting gleam lit his eyes. Doing her best to outrace him, she kneed her mount into a faster gallop, but to no avail. He rode up alongside her, grabbed her reins and pulled back. Eventually the two horses slowed and came to a stop.

"Wife, I'm afraid you'll fall and crack open your pretty head," he called out, laughing. "Let us halt here and catch our breath."

She joined in his laughter and dismounted. "I believe you have a good point, but I've ridden like that since I was a child. I would have been fine."

"So, you say," he said, dismounting beside her. "But what if your mount had tripped?"

"Una does not trip."

"Mayhap you wish to kill yourself, but must you take the innocent beast with you?"

"Una loves the chase, my lord. She is sure footed, and no harm would come to either of us."

Cort pulled her against him, and Rhiannon enjoyed the sensation of his muscular body pressed against hers. Mesmerized, she watched as he lowered his shaggy head down to claim her lips.

God's breath, who was this husband of hers? His gentle attention caused her to tingle all over with desire.

"I mean to protect what is mine," he told her in a husky voice when he pulled back.

"And I as well," she told him.

Laughing, she swung onto her horse and rode up to the river's edge. A frothy waterfall tumbled over a rock ledge, roaring its way toward the blue depths. Cort rode up to her and studied the serene spot, his lips curved in a smile.

"A beautiful place," he commented.

""*Fionnbhair* Falls is one of my favorite destinations," she said. "I come here often to contemplate and consider my life."

Rhiannon dismounted and tethered Una where she could drink her fill. Next, she plopped down on the mossy bank and arranged her skirts. Removing her shoes, she dangled her feet in the river.

When Arch loped toward them, Cort picked up a stick and tossed it. They played fetch for a brief period of time before the dog grew tired of the game and bounded off to explore the shrubbery.

"*Fionnbhair*," Cort pronounced awkwardly. "What does that mean, Rhiannon?"

"White ghost." She glanced at him again then turned toward

the foamy water cascading over rock shelves. "The villagers have a legend about this place, which they believe is haunted."

"More superstitions." He sat beside her. "Enlighten me, please."

Her features softened and her eyes took on a dreamy quality. "Centuries ago, there were two lovers who had secret trysts here in the dead of night. Their families were from rival clans who would never allow them to marry. Alas, they were exposed by a traitor. Brokenhearted, they still refused to let anything keep them apart. One evening, they jumped from the top of the falls so they could spend eternity together. People who come here at night swear they see the lovers' white, ghostly forms flitting about."

"Do you believe it?"

Rhiannon shrugged. "I don't *disbelieve* it. I simply don't know. But my soul can entertain the idea."

"While I cling to the here and now, I realize things exist beyond what we can see with our eyes," Cort added.

"I wouldn't be afraid if I actually saw the wraiths. The lovers were never evil, just star crossed." She leaned down and scooped a hand full of water from the river and sipped at the refreshment.

Cort knelt down beside her and cupped her chin in his hand. "I feel fortunate to be here with you, *ma cherie*."

"And I feel blessed to have you here. Your protection is a boon for my people."

"Is it a boon for you?" he asked.

"I am pleased—"

"Lady Rhiannon! Where are you? Sir Cort? Where are you?"

"We're over here," Cort called out in an uneven voice. He grasped Rhiannon's elbow and helped her rise along with him.

She smoothed her hair, her flesh still tingling at his touch. A moment later, a horse and rider crashed through the trees. Quinn, the stable boy, rode toward them and reined in. Urgency gleamed in his eyes.

Between heavy breaths, he said, "King Moran . . . sent me to find you . . . my lady. I've been looking everywhere."

Rhiannon clasped her hands anxiously. "Is he all, right? Did something happen to Ailleen or Glenna?"

Quinn shook his head. "'Tis Carleen McCarthy. Her babe is coming, and she sent her husband to the castle to fetch you."

"Where is the midwife?"

"In the next village. She's too far away to make it in time."

A sense of urgency rushed through Rhiannon. Along with other healing arts, she had also been taught how to deliver babies, though she'd only attended a few birthing's. "Did you bring my bag?"

"Yes." Quinn handed her the small leather case which she kept stocked with ointments, balms, teas and other healing powders.

"How long has she labored?" Rhiannon hurried to Una and hooked the bag's handles over the saddle horn. She climbed onto the mare's back, eager to be off.

"Dwyer said she's been this way for quite a while."

"God bless her," Rhiannon said.

Cort swung onto his horse and whistled for Arch, who darted through the bushes and loped toward them. Wheeling their mounts around, they rode from the river and headed toward the village.

RHIANNON, CORT, AND QUINN'S HORSES TROTTED through the cobbled streets of the village, stopping when they reached the McCarthy's thatched cottage. Rhiannon dismounted and handed Una's reins to their oldest son, Luke. His younger brother, John, stood behind him, his face tear stained. Rhiannon smiled at the youngsters, trying to reassure them.

"Luke, please take care of Una while I attend to your mother," she told the older boy as Cort and Quinn dismounted from their horses.

Fear etched his dirt-smudged face. "Ma is very sick. Something's not right with the babe, I think."

Rhiannon patted his shoulder. "I'll see to her. Don't worry."

Luke gathered Una's reins while Rhiannon hurried inside and

entered the small bedroom. Three women surrounded the bed, including Carleen's sister, Nainsi. Carleen huddled on the blankets; her face dotted with sweat.

Dwyer clasped her hand tightly, his expression pinched with fear. He glanced up at Rhiannon when she entered. "Things went easier when Luke and John were born."

"I'll do everything I can, Dwyer. You can be assured of that."

Dwyer nodded; his lips pressed into a grim line.

Rhiannon noticed the pool of blood between Carleen's thighs. *This isn't good,* she thought as she made the sign of the cross and offered a silent prayer to Saint Brigit. Any help that came her way would be appreciated. She sensed it wasn't going to be easy to bring the babe safely into the world.

Nainsi pulled Rhiannon aside and spoke in a low voice. "We've done everything we can think of. But the child . . . it refuses to come."

"I've seen this before," Rhiannon said. "I have a good idea what to do."

"I'll gather whatever you need," Nainsi said.

Rhiannon thought a moment then said, "I need a kettle of water, a teacup and a spoon. Also, clean towels."

Nainsi gathered the items while the other two women stroked Carleen's brow and muttered encouraging words.

"I'm afraid," Carleen told Rhiannon breathlessly. "I don't . . . want to lose the baby."

Rhiannon tried to keep her own nervousness from seeping into her voice. "I'll do everything I can, Carleen."

Some of the distress in Carleen's face receded, though she still looked troubled. Rhiannon didn't blame her. She'd seen enough birthing's to know sometimes women didn't survive. Her own mother had nearly died giving birth to Ailleen.

Cort appeared in the doorway. "Can I help with anything?" he asked solemnly.

"No." Rhiannon turned to Dwyer. "You might as well wait outside," she said softly. "This is going to take a while."

"Take care of Carleen," he said in an uneven voice. "Me'n the boys . . . we need her."

"I'll do my best." Rhiannon watched as Dwyer and Cort left.

When Nainsi brought the items, Rhiannon poured water from the tea kettle onto a towel and washed her hands thoroughly. Then she dug through her bag and removed dried mint, fennel and marjoram, which she mixed into a cup of hot water.

"What is that for?" Nainsi narrowed her gaze suspiciously. "Don't be giving her some witch's concoction."

Rhiannon sent the woman an irritated glance, though she understood her apprehension. "This will help Carleen relax. It will also staunch the bleeding and lower any fevers she may develop."

"Hmmph." Nainsi's response held a note of skepticism.

The women helped Carleen sit up and Rhiannon held the tea to her lips so she could drink. When she was finished, Rhiannon removed a jar of rose balm from her bag and put some on her hands. As she rubbed it onto Carleen's swollen abdomen, she felt the babe's limbs beneath the skin.

"The babe is in a breech position," she said.

The women gasped.

"Dear Lord," Carleen sobbed.

"You have to cooperate if you want your child to live," Rhiannon told her. "Will you do as I ask?"

"Y-yes," Carleen returned, nodding wearily.

Rhiannon retrieved a wooden spoon from the stove and had Carleen put it between her teeth. "This won't be easy. When the pain's more than you can bear, bite down. Hard."

Carleen's eyes widened with fear, but she didn't protest.

"We need to keep Carleen still," Rhiannon told the women.

"What are you doing now?" Nainsi asked.

Rhiannon met the woman's gaze. "Saving your sister and her baby's life."

"How?"

Nainsi was only trying to protect her sister. Rhiannon realized she would have felt the same concern if Ailleen were in danger.

"The babe needs to be turned."

Nainsi's brows arched. "You can do that?"

"I'm going to try." Rhiannon had done this with mares when they were ready to foal, and the birth was breech. Mayhap the same technique would work for Carleen and her child. Hopefully the powers above would guide her hands.

Nainsi called over the other women and they clustered around Carleen, holding her arms.

"Be as still as you can," she told Carleen. "Don't bear down and don't fight me. Most of all, you've got to trust me."

Carleen nodded, her eyes wide with fear.

Rhiannon patted her shoulder reassuringly then began the procedure.

Dwyer paced back and forth in the yard, no doubt worried about his wife. The anxious father raked his hand through his sandy-colored hair and muttered to himself while his boys' skipped pebbles in a mud puddle. They battered their father with questions about their mother. Dwyer answered patiently.

Cort paced nearby, hoping Rhiannon would be able to deliver Dwyer's wife of the babe safely. He realized he'd married a woman who was as capable as she was beautiful.

Carleen began moaning again and Cort noticed a difference in the tone.

Dwyer glanced anxiously at the cottage, an expectant expression on his face. "This is the hardest thing I've ever done in my life. My wife's in agony and I'm the cause of it."

Cort wanted to point out that since they had two sons already, Carleen knew the risks of pregnancy and childbirth. However, he realized that wasn't what Dwyer needed to hear.

"I can imagine how you feel," Cort said. "I'm sure it's difficult to see your loved ones in pain."

He had never lost anyone close to him, but he'd held comrades dying from battle wounds. No matter how many times he offered comfort to mortally wounded soldiers, it never got any easier.

"Aye." Dwyer clenched his fists at his sides. "I feel so helpless."

"Trust Rhiannon. She knows what she's doing." An unexpected sense of pride rushed through Cort. The woman possessed great talents and he appreciated that their relationship seemed to be progressing in a positive direction.

When an infant's mewling cry filled the air, Dwyer grinned with relief.

Cort clapped him on the shoulder. "Congratulations."

A short while later Rhiannon came out with a small bundle tucked in her arms.

"You have a daughter," she announced.

Relief flooded Dwyer's expression. "Carleen?"

"She'll need a lot of rest, but she's a strong woman. She'll be back to herself in no time."

Luke and John ran over to stand beside Rhiannon. She pulled back the blanket so the boys could see their little sister's wrinkled pink face and tiny, curled fists. The boys immediately began to argue about who would be the first to hold her.

Cort watched Rhiannon cradling the infant. What would it be like to see her belly swell with his child? What would their sons and daughters look like? A strange sensation washed over him.

He'd never seriously considered having a child before, considering his lack of stability. All that had changed.

Dwyer stroked the baby's cheek with his finger. "Carleen and I expected we'd have another boy. We were going to call him Daniel. I don't know what we'll name a little girl."

"How about Sarah?" Rhiannon suggested.

"'Tis a nice Bible name." Dwyer raised his brows. "Sarah McCarthy . . . I like it." Can I go in and see Carleen now?"

"Give the women a little more time to get her settled. Then you can go in." Rhiannon handed the baby to Dwyer. "For now, get acquainted with your daughter. She's a tough little lady, just like her mama."

Dwyer beamed as he looked down at the swaddled infant. "We owe you so much, Lady Rhiannon."

"I'm relieved I got here in time."

Nainsi came to the door. "Carleen's asking for you Dwyer."

He disappeared inside with the baby. Luke and John followed close on his heels.

"Every time I hold a wee one in my arms, I realize that life is a miracle." Rhiannon folded her arms across her chest. "'Tis truly amazing."

Cort couldn't resist drawing Rhiannon against his chest and holding her close. A ripple of lightning shot through him when her body melted against his. It felt good holding her.

"I know I had divine help in there," Rhiannon whispered.

Cort lifted tendrils of hair from her face. "You look exhausted. I need to take you home so you can rest."

Quinn sauntered toward them with Arch. Apparently the dog had taken an instant liking to the boy.

"It grows late," Quinn warned. "If we wish to return to the castle by nightfall, we must take our leave."

"Aye," Rhiannon said as she walked toward the cottage. "I'll have a brief word with Carleen then we'll be on our way."

SEVEN

B Y THE TIME THE SUN SANK lower on the horizon, paint-
ing the sky with a blaze of orange, they reached Callinon
Castle. At the stable they dismounted, handing the horses over
to Quinn.

Gently, Cort took Rhiannon's elbow and led her upstairs to
their chamber, drew her drew her inside, and closed the door.
The covers were already down on the bed, a fire blazed on the
hearth, and a tub of hot bath water sat beside it.

Rhiannon's cheeks suffused with warmth as she concluded
a servant must have seen their arrival and prepared the room.
When her stomach rumbled, she pressed a hand against her
abdomen.

"Breakfast was our only meal, Cort. Are you as hungry as I?"

He chuckled. "We had a busy day, so I asked Quinn to have our
supper brought up here."

"Thank the saints," Rhiannon said as she sank into a chair and
propped her feet on a stool. She studied Cort's broad back and
shoulders, appreciating the strength she noted in how he carried
himself.

When a knock sounded on the door, Cort opened it and servants brought in a tray and two trenchers, along with a bottle of

wine and goblets, arranging everything on a table. After they left, Cort approached the food and inhaled deeply. "*Sentir bon,* your cook is very talented."

"Leila has been with us for a long time," Rhiannon said. "She works hard to prepare the best meals."

Cort piled fruit; cheese and steaming meat on two trenchers, then carried them to the bed and sat down. He patted the sheets. "Sit beside me, *ma cherie.*"

The meal smelled tantalizing, so Rhiannon did not hesitate to go and sit beside him. Cort handed over a plate then began munching on his food, licking his fingers. She wasted no time eating her fill. Although preoccupied, she appreciated how his sensuous mouth nibbled the morsels.

After pouring two goblets of wine, he handed one to her. "This will relax you."

"We usually save our wine for special occasions."

"This is a special occasion. It is our honeymoon."

Honeymoon. The concept seemed strange. Sipping at the contents, tingling warmth filled her, right down to her fingertips, Cort had been telling the truth; the tenseness in her limbs began to dissolve and she became woozy.

When she sipped the last drop, he took the cup from her and set it on a bedside table, along with his own. He nodded toward the wooden tub. "Your bath awaits. Since your maid isn't here, I'll attend you."

She raised a questioning brow. "You will tend to my needs?"

"It would please me very much to do so," he answered.

Too tired to question further, she made no protest has he peeled away her clothing. She shivered as cool air caressed her skin. Hesitation rose up within her, but she realized he had seen her without clothes before, so she had no reason to be ashamed—and truth be told, she appreciated his kind ministrations.

Taking his hand, she stepped into the tub and sank into the silken depths, glad of the warmth. Curious, she watched as he picked up the soap. He knelt beside her, immersed the cake in the water, then gently rubbed it over her limbs.

She closed her eyes as slow pleasure wound its way through her. Moments later, after he finished tending to her, he reached for the towel on a chair.

"Stand and I'll dry you off."

She stepped from the tub, appreciating when he wrapped her in the fire-warmed material, rubbing her limbs.

He picked her up and carried her to the bed, then began massaging her feet and her legs, working lose the kinks. Like a balm, his touch soothed her. She sank deeper and deeper into a state of contentment.

He climbed onto the bed next to her, his weight sagging the mattress. She thrilled to his touch as he massaged her buttocks, her lower back, then her shoulders and neck. He moved carefully past her healing bruises, careful not to re-injure her, but kissing her flesh instead. Soon, his fingertips were replaced entirely with his lips as he blazed a trail of kisses across her skin.

A shiver of delight rippled through her. How could such a large, powerful man be so gentle? This was a new side of him that pleased her.

When his touch lifted, she rolled over to look at him. He had begun drawing the coverlet up, tucking it around her.

"What are you doing?"

"You need your rest, *ma cherie.*"

"But—"

"But what?" He raised a dark brow, his lips upturned slightly.

"Where will you sleep?"

He shrugged. "I need to have a word with my men about making preparations for the castle improvements. My apologies, my lady. Duty calls."

In a heartbeat, he left.

Disappointed, Rhiannon grabbed a pillow and threw it at the door. It fell to the floor with a soft thump.

"I hope you're coming back," she said under her breath.

CORT LEFT HIS TENT AND STOOD in the bright morning light, yawning and stretching. He congratulated himself on the way he'd handled Rhiannon the other night. After he'd brought her to a state of full-blown yearning, he knew she'd have easily given in to his lovemaking. It had taken all his willpower not to take her, but the look of unfulfilled desire on her face had been priceless.

Hopefully he'd taught her a good lesson. If she tried to gain the upper hand with him, he would outsmart her. If she considered this marriage nothing more than a chess game, he was bound to win. From a young age, he'd learned how to best his opponents at any contest.

For the past few days, he'd been polite, but had kept his distance from his young wife. He'd spent his time with Uther, the castle steward, either reviewing accounts or riding throughout the O'Kelly landholdings in order to become familiar with them.

Everyone he'd met welcomed him with surprising warmth. It occurred to him that these people had grown so accustomed to war and strife; they worshipped the idea of peace, even if a stranger from a foreign land brought it about. At the end of each day, he supped with the family then retired to his tent in the bailey.

Rhiannon would quietly take her place beside him at the high table, watching him with guarded interest. No doubt she wondered why he never retired with her. As much as he wanted to sweep her into his arms, carry her to their bed chamber, and make love to her, he resisted the urge. Until she came to him of her own volition, he would leave her alone, no matter how difficult it became.

He decided it was just as well they didn't spend too much time together, as her presence would be a distraction and he had much to learn of his new home. Still, it went against his nature not to claim what had been given to him.

After leaving the great hall, he went outside and walked up a hill toward an outcropping of land overlooking the ocean. The air seemed thinner and fresher here, for it was higher up the slope than Callinon castle. With the ocean on one side, the Irish countryside on the other, the area provided a spectacular view. This is where he would build his new castle—a military fortification as fine as any that could be found in Normandy.

Believing this would be a good move, King Moran had eagerly lent his support. Cort wasted no time in dispatching a runner to Dublin to gather the finest surveyors available. They had arrived last night, and he'd visited with them at length, impressed by their knowledge.

Skilled in the latest triangulation methods, they'd demonstrated their precise instruments which they would use to make detailed maps. These instructions would assist the masons and carpenters in making the most accurate measurements in designing the castle.

Spotting the builders up ahead, he hurried toward them. It seemed they were just as anxious as he to start this project. After exchanging pleasantries and shaking hands, the men discussed the features, such as the deeper moat and the reinforced foundation.

"May I suggest a concentric castle structure my lord." Herr Volkner adjusted his brown woolen cap. "This will incorporate a square keep with protective stone curtains. Enemy attackers will find it extremely difficult to wage an assault. Especially since the only way to enter the keep will be through a gatehouse in the outer wall."

As Volkner explained further details, Cort became intrigued. Such a structure would make it nearly impossible for Donovan or another warring clan to threaten Callinon.

"It will take years to complete, Sir Cort," Herr Volkner warned.

"But it would be well worth the wait," Cort said. "Let's get to work laying it out. I'm authorizing you to hire whatever workers are needed to begin the construction."

The surveyors began to pace out the dimensions and placed rocks at well-measured distances. Cort worked alongside them, proud to help provide a safer environment for Callinon's people.

THERE WAS NO DOUBT ABOUT IT. Rhiannon felt certain the Norman had decided to play a game with her. And that game entailed trying to drive her crazy. He seemed to be doing a good job of it, too.

Ever since he'd taunted her into a breathless frenzy the other night with his sensual massage and hot, searching lips, he'd left her alone. He'd been coolly polite to her during the daylight hours, but every night after supper he disappeared. His maddening aloofness had driven her to the brink.

Her annoyance built daily, but why did she allow him to get to ruffle her confidence? What possessed her to feel this way? The fact that she couldn't figure it out maddened her further.

Pride wouldn't allow her to speak with him about the matter and she fought hard to maintain her composure each time they were together. He could never know how much his aloof attitude affected her. Otherwise, he might believe himself the winner in the battle between their wills.

Each night she retired alone, feeling strangely lost in the large, empty bed that still emitted his unique scent. As she caressed Cort's moonlight-covered pillow, shivering at its cool linen surface, she insisted it didn't matter a whit that he ignored her.

Although she attempted to deny it, she was dying to know what he did with himself each eve. Where did he sleep? Did he share his sexual favors with another woman? Did he think of her at all?

Why she felt such a maddening loss, she didn't know. It made no sense to her why she had developed such tangled emotions.

In an attempt to keep her mind off the Norman, she spent a lot of time with her father, heartbroken to see him failing each day. Despite giving him as many herbal remedies and cures as she knew of, he continued to fail. The physician visited him regularly, but he, too, could not allay the symptoms her father suffered.

When it became too taxing to see her father's condition worsen, she occupied herself by getting the castle in order. It kept her mind from dwelling on what the future would inevitably bring. As for her home's condition, a cleaning was definitely needed. While

Donovan held it captive, he'd obviously not bothered to have any housekeeping done. Everything had fallen into a state of disrepair and filth.

She directed the servants to take down the tapestries and have them aired. The chores she assigned included having them sweep floors, wipe down benches, and lay fresh rushes. The scullery maids were tasked with scrubbing the kitchen from top to bottom along with polishing pots and pans. Sheets and blankets were washed, mattresses cleaned and even the accumulated clutter in the bailey was cleared away. As a final touch, she ordered the outer castle walls to be repaired after the battering they'd received during Donovan's siege.

The distraction of returning her home to normal, while tiring, didn't completely banish Cort from her mind. To her frustration, she seemed to run into him everywhere she went. His tall, commanding presence always brought a fresh reminder that he held her emotions captive.

She couldn't help but wonder; did he find it difficult to control his emotions around her as well?

One morning she decided to visit the garden and see how it had fared during Donovan's occupation. She found Glenna on her knees pulling weeds while two sturdy men worked nearby, hacking the hard-packed ground with hoes.

Despite months of neglect, her mother's red and pink roses grew in a glorious blaze along a wooden arbor. Fruit trees and berry bushes also thrived, despite a similar lack of attention.

A few persistent vegetables had taken root from seed which would produce a small harvest. Several herbs had grown back from seed—enough for some stew flavorings, salves, ointments, teas, and other health remedies.

After visiting with Glenna for a while, she heard distant voices. Climbing onto a tree stump, she glanced over the stone wall. Cort barked orders to a swarm of village men as they unloaded large rocks from carts and placed them along a grassy knoll. Several other men in long, brightly colored robes and caps fiddled with strange instruments on tripods.

Curious, she left the garden and headed up the slope toward her husband. What could he possibly be doing? The fact that he felt a constant need to change things around here made her uneasy. Even though he intended to reinforce the castle's battlements in order to provide more effective defenses, it bothered her. He seemed to find fault with everything she and her family had done up until now.

"What are you doing?" she asked him.

At the sensation of his dark, caressing gaze, she sucked in a breath. It had been days since they'd stood this close to one another. When his musky scent assailed her nostrils, a warm sensation laced through her. All of her nerve endings tingled.

Stop it, she warned herself. She forced her breaths to come steadily and focused on things other than the man's overwhelmingly masculine presence.

"I'm building a fortress." His voice rumbled with the accent that had become so familiar by now.

Insult welled. "Is there something wrong with my home?"

"No."

"I hope you don't plan to tear it down. I grew up there and it means a lot to me."

"You're jumping to conclusions."

"Why are you doing this?" She clenched her hands into fists.

"My reasoning is sound. I don't intend to overrun your father's home, Rhiannon."

"In other words, you don't think it is good enough." She struggled to quell the unsteady tone that crept into her voice. "Perhaps it's too crude, too unsophisticated for your well-heeled boots?"

His expression darkened. "That's not it at all. Think, woman. While Callinon is lovely, it doesn't provide the military protection we need."

"Is that so?" While she disliked his penchant for making changes, she recognized the validity of his words.

"Be reasonable woman."

"I refuse to leave Callinon." She pressed her lips together. She didn't like the idea of abandoning her childhood home. She'd lost so much already, and it hurt deep down to think of losing yet another part of herself.

He lifted a brow. "I'm sure there'll eventually be little ones filling the rooms with their loud antics. God willing, if your father is still with us, he won't want to live with such ruckus on a daily basis."

Exasperation tingled throughout her, right down to fingertips. Of course she wanted children, but she needed to adjust to being married first. Another puzzling piece: if he planned to have a family with her, why didn't he ever retire to their bed chamber? The last she'd heard, a man needed to sleep with his wife to beget children. Her mind thrummed with confusion.

"Does my father know of your plans?"

"Come now. Do you think I would have village men out here marking dimensions for a new castle if he didn't? He is in full agreement."

"I see." Even her father had known of this, yet Cort hadn't bothered to consult her. Hating to be left out of such an important decision regarding her home, she spun on her heel and stormed back down the hill. Cort called her name, but she ignored him.

Glenna pushed to her feet when she entered the rose garden. "You're lookin' pale, my lady."

"No wonder." She took several ragged breaths, her lungs burning. "The Norman is plotting dimensions on his new castle. Apparently, our home isn't good enough for him."

Glenna patted her shoulder. "'Tis not all so bad. The man means to protect us. Would you expect less of him?"

"He could have at least let me know."

"He is your husband, Rhiannon. He has the right to make decisions without your consent. Now don't pine away over something so insignificant. Show him what backbone we Irish possesses."

Rhiannon still felt left out of an important decision governing her future, but she accepted Glenna's counsel. "No doubt that's the advice my mother would have given me."

"Your mother was a wise woman, so in her absence, I'll offer it. The Norman is not so bad, is he? You could do worse for a husband, you know. Had your father not arrived when he did, you'd be married to Donovan."

"Aye, you're right." Rhiannon tried to stop worrying. "I'm just feeling sorry for myself, which is sinful."

"Everyone's allowed self-pity now and then. But it's time to stop wallowing. The talk I hear from the villagers is all favorable toward Sir Cort. They say he is fair, kind, and intelligent."

"Of course they would. They feel safer with him around. Hopefully, they're not placing too much confidence in him."

Glenna chuckled. "I think it's time we pay a visit to old Sybil. For a coin, she'll give you your fortune. Will that make you feel better?"

"What if she sees my fortune darkly?"

"I can't believe she will. 'Tis a bright one I see for you. Surely, she'll see one as well."

Glenna and Rhiannon retrieved horses from the stable and rode over the lush green hills to Sybil's cottage nestled beside a silvery blue lake. Gray smoke curled from the chimney and drifted over the thatched roof.

They picketed the horses and Glenna knocked on the front door. A wrinkled old woman in ragged clothing with long white hair opened up. She leaned heavily on a cane, her hazy gray eyes staring vacantly.

"Who goes there?"

"'Tis Glenna Connor. And I've brought Rhiannon O'Kelly with me."

"Ah, Fiona's oldest girl—little Rhiannon." Sybil touched her face, running gnarled fingers over her cheeks and shoulders. "My sight's gone, but I can tell you're a young woman now."

"You remember me?"

"Aye. Fiona visited me frequently and sometimes brought you. A wild one, you were, and I sensed back then you were meant for great things."

Rhiannon felt a pang of regret at her mother's passing. It seemed the ache of her death would never subside. Not a single day passed when she didn't miss her.

"Come in, rest yourselves." Sybil gestured for them to enter.

The small cottage held comfortable warmth but contained a sparse amount of furniture—a table, four chairs and a bed.

Sybil pointed at a table with a knobby, age-spotted finger. "Sit down and be rid of your shoes."

Rhiannon slipped out of her shoes, wondering why Sybil had asked them to do such a strange thing. It wasn't wise to question the old crone. She apparently had a reason for everything she asked of them.

Sybil felt her way over to a shelf where she located two cups and placed them in front of her guests. She shuffled toward a fireplace and removed a heavy kettle. With well practiced movements, she poured hot, steaming brew for both of them.

"Drink," she insisted.

Glenna sipped, as did Rhiannon, who noticed the brew had a spicy, sweet taste.

Sybil replaced the kettle, returned to the table and sat down. She shifted her body toward Rhiannon. "I've been expecting your visit, child."

"H-how did you know I would come?" Trembling, Rhiannon put down her cup. Hair on the nape of her neck prickled.

"I know things." Sybil gave a slow, broken-toothed smile. "I always have. Now, what concerns you? No wait, I see your thoughts swirling around your head like bees buzzing about a hive."

She could *see* her thoughts. Rhiannon cleared her throat, uncomfortable, but curious.

"You've come to me about the Norman warrior." Sybil blinked her sightless eyes. "Your husband."

"Aye." Goose bumps erupted on Rhiannon's flesh, and a chill shot through her. "The villagers say he is a good man. So why are you in a dither, child?"

"I fear my father's lost his mind. To give me away to a man he barely knows seems rash and foolish. How can we really trust this Norman to protect us?"

Sybil smacked her thin lips together. "Moran is wise. He sees what many don't. He plans for the future."

"You think he's done the right thing?"

"You don't see it now, but you need not fear your husband. Do not be dismayed by his manner. He will usher in a peace Ireland hasn't known for centuries."

"I fear the clans will resent his marrying into the O'Kelly family. They'll consider him an invader."

"There are some who are not pleased." Sybil nodded. "They are of no consequence and should not concern you. This land is one of unrest with a long history of violence. The Norman's influence will unite us all. It is foreordained that you would become his wife."

Rhiannon thought, once again, of how Jamie had betrayed them. He had promised to fight for her father's army, then had turned around and gone over to Donovan's side when they began to weaken. The idea that he could so easily fight against the O'Kellys, after he'd sworn fealty to them, enraged her.

He'd also promised to love her until the day he died. She'd given him her heart and they'd spent many pleasurable moments planning their wedding and their lives together. How could his conscience have allowed him to forget the feelings they had for each other? What would have caused him to become so desperate that he'd joined forces with Donovan, which she considered in essence selling his soul to the devil?

She recalled when they were children and how he'd pouted and carried on when he didn't get his way. At the time, she'd decided he behaved in such a way because as an only child, he'd received everything he'd ever wanted. Since he made her laugh and had such an entertaining way of looking at life, she'd loved him anyway.

At the time, she hadn't been concerned by his behavior. Obviously, that had been a mistake. To this day, Jamie's deceit continued to fill her with pain. She'd learned from that experience it wasn't wise to trust anyone too completely.

"It troubles me to think he may not be entirely truthful with us," she told Sybil. "What if we regret allowing him in our midst?"

Sybil cackled with laughter. "You, my child, have much passion in your blood. The fire in your soul will light Ireland with hope. Rest assured—all will be well."

Rhiannon's confusion tangled with her common sense. She didn't know if her concern about the Norman was unreasonable or if she was simply being vigilant. "Are you suggesting that I meekly bow to this man and allow him to dictate my life?"

"Don't worry, young one. He will soon learn that you cannot be controlled, nor will he try to do so. Fate has other things in mind for the two of you. You see, there is a storm coming. The young lion's father will lay claim to these lands. Many will perish and a great darkness will fall. You will face numerous trials, young Rhiannon. But take heart. By marrying the Norman, you are fulfilling your destiny."

What in the world could old Sybil be talking about? She frowned. "Marriage seems more like a convenience for the Norman, than a great destiny for me."

For entertaining such rebellious thoughts, she felt instantly guilty. After all, her father felt this marriage, this alliance, to be of great importance for her people. If it brought about peace, was that not a small sacrifice to pay for the happiness of her kin?

Sybil stood and rested on her cane. "It is done. Take your leave now, for I am weary."

Rhiannon slipped on her shoes and deposited several coins into the old woman's outstretched hand. "Thank you."

Glenna, who had also donned her shoes, patted Sybil's shoulder. "We are most appreciative of your time.

Outside, Rhiannon blinked in the bright sunlight. She climbed onto Una and sighed heavily. "Sybil spoke in riddles, Glenna. I don't understand most of what she said."

Glenna settled into her saddle and arranged her skirts. "Heed her advice well. In time, you will know what she meant. Don't you feel a wee bit better now?"

"No."

"Hard-headed girl. But 'tis no surprise, for you've always been that way."

As they rode home, despite old Sybil's predictions, she remained uneasy.

EIGHT

LEATHENACH CASTLE

"**D**AMN IT!"
     Tadgh Donovan read the scrawled writing on the note his messenger had delivered earlier. He shoved his trencher of roasted mutton and vegetables across the table. It clattered to the floor. Several hound's dove for the food, snarling and snapping. Servants scrambled to clear the mess.

Why were his plans to kill Moran O'Kelly foiled at every turn?

Snatching up the note, he shoved to his feet and began to pace. He kicked a dog gnawing on a haunch of meat in front of the hearth. The dog yelped, snatched the bone and curled up in a distant corner.

Seated at the other end of the table, Dyfed set his goblet aside. "What is it? What's happened?"

"'Tis a message from Tulley. He has information on Moran." Donovan tossed the parchment into the fireplace and watched the edges crinkle and burn. "He says the Normans have secured Callinon Castle so well, it's virtually impenetrable."

"Why are they still there?" Dyfed's face clouded over. "I thought by now they would have sailed back to Normandy."

"As did I. But Tulley said they still remain."

"No doubt the Norman commander's marriage to Moran's

daughter keeps him and his men here." Donovan thought of the Norman availing himself of Rhiannon's voluptuous charms, something he hadn't been able to do because of an old war injury. "Damn it to hell."

"This is disturbing." Dyfed chewed thoughtfully on his bread. "Mayhap if I sacrifice another beast to the gods, we'll be given a sign that will help us."

Donovan spit on the floor and wiped his mouth with the back of his hand. "I'll not be launching a full-scale attack any time soon. Blast it all! I had everything in my grasp, and I lost it. I've got to get it back."

The oaken doors to the great hall swung open and a servant rushed toward Donovan.

"Jamie O'Brien is here to see you, my lord."

"Send him in," Donovan growled.

Tall and wiry, his dark hair in disarray, Jamie strode confidently into the room dragging a sobbing wench at his side.

"You'd better have useful news about what's going on at Callinon Castle. I must defeat Moran O'Kelly." Donovan glared at Jamie. "I pay you well enough; I'd better see a decent return on my investment."

"Aye, my lord." Jamie cleared his throat. "Moran married off his oldest daughter to the Norman commander, so his men have become a permanent fixture. I doubt they'll go anywhere unless King Henry gives them another assignment. Even then, I'm sure they'll leave a contingent of soldiers to guard the castle."

Jamie fought off his anguish at repeating the news that had driven a knife through his heart. Rhiannon was married. He'd loved her for so long; it had nearly killed him to hear it. But he didn't blame her for moving on with her life. Surely, she considered him nothing more than a Judas. He'd betrayed both her and her family, but felt he'd had no choice.

Since his father had spent most of his family's fortune on gambling debts, he needed money to pay his mother's physician when shed fallen ill. His friends had given what funds they could, and hed been too proud to ask Rhiannon's father for a loan. Two years ago, when Donovan spread the word he would pay well for spies, the lure of the money had been too great for Jamie. Against his better judgment, hed hired on with the bastard.

Originally, hed thought hed only give away a few military secrets in order to pay for his mother's care. He'd mistakenly hoped a physician would be able to cure her straightaway. He hadn't counted on her lingering illness. His mother had suffered quite a while before she passed away.

By then, hed become deeply indebted to Donovan. O'Kelly people were beginning to suspect him, and hed grown anxious. So, he left Callinon and went to Leathanach Castle, asking for permission join forces with the Donovan clan.

He and Donovan had grown extremely close over the years. Since the man had no children to inherit his landholdings, hed told Jamie that when he died, he would pass on his castle and property to him. Moran's kingdom would have been passed to Jamie as well, but now that the Norman had seized it, that wouldn't happen, unless the Donovan clan could get it back.

Donovan slammed a fist into the table, jolting Jamie back into the here and now. "Are you here to tell me it's impossible to gain entrance to Callinon Castle?"

"On the contrary." Jamie shoved the wench toward Donovan so forcefully she fell hard against the stone floor. "Moran's serving maid has been quite talkative since I bedded her. I found out something that should prove useful to us. Tell him Ena."

"Speak up, girl. Or else I'll cut out your tongue." Donovan drew a knife and twisted the blade in front a torch in a wall sconce. It gleamed wickedly.

"There is a s-secret entrance to Callinon Castle," she babbled, her eyes wide with fear. "King Moran only uses it if he has to evacuate his people quickly."

"Do you know where it is?" Donovan fired a glance at Jamie.

"Aye my lord."

"I knew there had to be a way we could gain entrance." Donovan threw back his head and roared with laughter. He jerked Ena to her feet, crushed her against his chest and squeezed one her breasts.

"Ouch, that hurts!" Ena wriggled in his grip, squawking with pain as he fondled her further. At last, he shoved her toward Jamie.

"Use the bitch however you like, Jamie. Then kill her. I don't want her mouthing off to anyone."

Ena gave a bloodcurdling scream as Jamie dragged her from the room. He'd become so numb to the vile acts he'd had to perform for Donovan over the years, he didn't even cringe. Ena's sobs reached a remote corner of his soul. He'd taken a liking to having the wench in his bed, so it might be a while before he ended her life.

WORK ON THE NEW CASTLE HAD consumed most of Cort's time during the last days. After another tiring day of setting the foundation, he looked forward to nice meal and a relaxing evening back at Callinon—especially after his disturbing confrontation with Rhiannon about the new fortress.

Why did she feel threatened? It made no sense.

He tried to push away his disturbing thoughts but had no success. Whenever Rhiannon was unhappy, he found it made him unhappy as well. In such a short time, she had managed to entwine herself into his brain and he could do naught to extract her. Good or bad, thoughts of her traveled with him everywhere he went.

In the bailey, he decided to observe the new foundation from a distance. Despite his fatigue, he climbed the steps that led atop Callinon's thick outer wall. With his mind on other things, he didn't see Rhiannon until too late. As he made his way around an outcropping, she ran into him. Automatically, he caught her in his arms.

She stiffened and turned a disillusioned glance on him. He gritted his teeth and prepared for verbal warfare. He didn't like this encounter and obviously neither did she.

Unfortunately, his manhood wasn't afflicted with the same sensibilities as his head, and at the brush of her thigh against his, it jumped into action. He fought to control his body's traitorous reaction but found it extremely difficult.

The memory of burying himself deep in her velvety sheath came back and he grew so hard, his groin ached. There would be no stopping the appendage between his legs. It wanted Rhiannon.

There goes my relaxing evening.

Rhiannon tried to escape his embrace, but he refused to let her go, basking in the warmth her soft curves emitted. He recalled her response to him on their wedding night. While she'd seemed hesitant about making love with him, it hadn't been long before he had her writhing with passion in his arms. If only she would give herself over to her desire again.

She'd tasted of the pleasure he could give her, and he could tell by her body's reaction she'd enjoyed it. Why did she so vehemently deny herself any further sexual delights? His groin began to throb with need.

Sacre bleu how he wanted her!

"Excuse me."

She tried once again to escape from his grasp, only to find herself still locked in his firm embrace.

"Why are you in such a hurry?"

"I have much to do." She wet her lips, and they glistened like precious rubies. Her breath came in tiny pants.

He lifted a brow. "Do you ever rest?"

"Aye, when my work is done."

Determination wound through Cort. "Damnation woman, why are you frightened of me?"

"I'm not frightened." Her voice came out sharp. Too sharp.

"We're husband and wife, yet it seems you spend more time running from me than toward me. Why is that?"

She shrugged.

"Look at me, Rhiannon." Cort cupped her face between his

palms and lifted her face toward his. The feel of her luxuriant red hair against his skin sent a thrill of excitement through him. Rose-scented sachet drifted from her tresses and into his nostrils, filling him with unexplainable need. "You're the most desirable woman I've ever known."

"I'm sure you've said that exact same thing to other females."

"No, I haven't. I want you to know I'm glad you're my wife."

"Aye, I'm sure you are. My dowry has changed your life, has it not?"

He bristled at her insinuation that her dowry was the only reason he wanted her. Pride made it difficult enough for him to accept he'd become a rich man the day he married her. Must she also taunt him with the fact?

"That's not the only reason I am attracted to you."

"How can I believe that?"

"How can you not?"

"King Henry only ordered you to roust Donovan from my home. You did your duty to the crown—you didn't come to Ireland out of regard for me or even my father."

He shook his head. "Would you rather that I had turned down your father's offer? It would have left Callinon vulnerable to attack after I left."

"Nay." Rhiannon shivered at the knowledge of how things could have turned out under different circumstances. She knew full well Cort had rescued her home. Her gaze drifted toward the men and women in the bailey, scurrying about, laughing and smiling. "You have brought hope to my people. They are no longer in fear for their homes and families."

He pulled her closer, looking deep into her eyes, as if the answer resided in those deep pools. "Then what do you want?"

"I want . . . I need, oh I don't know. Never mind."

"Why aren't you satisfied, woman? What eats away at you?"

She reflected on her inner thoughts. Jamie's betrayal had taught her never to trust men too completely, especially when it involved affairs of the heart. Her father's withdrawn offer of clan leadership had taught her that political events and the winds of war often changed men's promises.

How could she explain all of that to him? Something else bothered her, something she couldn't discern at this moment.

"Rhiannon . . ." His voice became unusually hoarse. "You know how much I want you, don't you? I sense you want me too, yet you hold yourself back."

"No, I don't want you. I *can't* want you." She realized she'd just lied outright to not only him, but to herself. How could she admit that being with him like that drove her to the edge of reason and frightened the wits out of her?

"What can it hurt to let me love you? Love is healing, *ma cherie.* I can take away your pain."

He lowered his head and claimed her lips with his. At the touch of his flesh upon hers, a surge of heat plunged through Rhiannon, instantly consuming her. She whimpered with the sweetness of his kiss and the overwhelming possessiveness with which he held her. She'd wrestled against her desires for so long she hated to acknowledge how much she enjoyed this.

It seemed right. She felt safe and secure.

Unable to resist, she melted into his big, strong arms. His powerful need enveloped her, and she felt the hardness thrusting through his trousers. The embodiment of his desire pressed into her thigh.

His musky scent filled her nostrils, driving her to giddy heights. Recklessly, she opened her mouth, allowing him further access. All of her reluctance discarded, she worshipped this sweet assault on her senses.

He groaned insistently, deepening his kiss and drawing her tongue into his mouth. His earlier vow to leave Rhiannon alone until she sought him out had been quickly abandoned. Usually, he exercised strict control over his emotions; important discipline to survive a soldier's life.

Yet night after night of burning for her consumed him. He couldn't think straight. Didn't want to think straight. He wanted only her.

He sucked her sweet tongue softly at first, then with more enthusiasm. As his passion mounted, he imagined himself inside of her tight, moist warmth. It was almost too much even to fantasize about, and he felt near to bursting.

He backed her up against the castle wall and bucked his hips into her abdomen, thrusting in a desperate attempt to breach her clothing. "I want you Rhiannon," he gasped. "I need you. Let me take you. Now."

"Cort I . . . I . . ."

"No more holding back. We both want this, do we not?" He undid the lacings at the top of her gown and dipped his hands inside. Cupping her breasts, he thumb-stroked the nipples. Then he took the rosy peaks in his mouth, one at a time, and traced circles on them with his tongue. She arched back her slim white neck and moaned with pleasure. Her mouth parted and her chest rose and fell erratically.

Encouraged by her response, he lifted her skirts, gathering them up about her thighs. At last, he found bare skin and caressed her firm buttocks.

"Ahhh," she moaned.

"You like this, no?" He grinned. "Your body tells me it does. I have so much more for you *ma cherie*. Don't deny our mutual pleasure any longer. We need each other."

Footsteps sounded on the castle wall. "Rhiannon where are you?"

She jerked away from him at the sound of her sister's voice.

"Over here," she managed.

"Sweet *Jesu*." Breathing heavily, he leaned against the jagged parapet. He attempted to focus on the countryside, trying to control his raging desire.

Rhiannon straightened her skirts, her thoughts jumbled. With the crook of his finger, she'd found herself under the Norman's spell again. Strange discontent laced through her at the idea she and Cort hadn't been able to finish what they'd started.

How could she feel that way? She'd nearly given herself to him, despite her promise to resist his charms. Thank goodness Ailleen had shown up to prevent their tryst from progressing.

For some reason, she still didn't feel so happy about it.

Ailleen came around the outcropping. "There you are Rhiannon. Glenna sent me to fetch you. She said you'd taken a walk along the wall to get some fresh air."

"What do you need?" As she struggled to regain her composure, Rhiannon noted the concern in Ailleen's small face.

"There's been an accident in the kitchen and Fagan needs his burns attended to. 'Tis not bad, but he'll need some salve and bandages."

Rhiannon pressed hands against her chest. "Saint Brigit preserve us, what happened?"

"Fagan bumped into Leila accidentally and she dropped a pot of water on his arm. Ever since her daughter Ena disappeared, she's been distracted in her cooking. She feels terrible that she hurt Fagan."

Cort sent Rhiannon a pointed look. "We can talk another time."

Relieved to be gone from the man who had such an unusual hold on her, she took Ailleen's hand and hurried from the wall.

"Damn it." Cort stared at the spot where Rhiannon had just stood. Her scent still lingered in the air, causing his loins to ache. Unrequited need made him burn at hot as the summer sun.

The stream winding its way around the castle called to him, as it had often of late. He hoped the cold depths could work their magic yet again and douse his yearning.

Maybe for the time being.

What about later, when thoughts of bedding her rose unbidden to tease him?

RHIANNON WAITED ANXIOUSLY FOR CORT TO join her at the supper table. He never put in an appearance, so she pretended, for her family's sake, that it didn't bother her when in fact it very much did. It felt strange to eat without her husband, but she supposed that after this afternoon, he didn't want to see her.

In all truth, she would have been uncomfortable around him.

"Where is your husband this eve?" Moran put down his goblet and slanted a concerned gaze at her.

Rhiannon finished chewing her meat and swallowed with difficulty. "He spent the day working on his new castle. I suppose he's tired."

"What's this? You *suppose*? He's your husband Rhiannon. You should know."

Moran shoved aside his nearly full plate. It seemed that as his appetite dwindled and he grew frailer, Rhiannon's appetite increased and her health improved. It wasn't fair. At the idea of losing her father, a sad ache twisted through her.

Moran continued to watch her closely, the dark circles under his eyes seemingly more pronounced of late. Shame rose at his intense stare. Her father had tasked her with only one dying request. While she'd fulfilled it by marrying the Norman, she found it increasingly difficult to relate to her new husband.

Why couldn't she manage to do that one simple thing?

Finished with her meal, she blotted her lips with a napkin and rose. "I'm weary, father. May I be excused?"

"Aye."

Rhiannon hurried to the stairs and climbed to her bed chamber. She couldn't stand to see her father's distressed face any longer. In her room, she paced back and forth in front of the fireplace. The flames did little to warm her.

She felt numb and confused by her inability to dispel Cort Guyot from her thoughts. His strong, muscled body tempted her, and she fought against her urge to give in and make love with him again. One part of her wondered what it would hurt to surrender to the need he'd awakened in her. Another part of her, the more reasonable side, warned that it was dangerous. Mistrust of the Norman still ran rampant in her soul.

Trying to think of some distraction, she finally fetched her embroidery bag and withdrew her work. Seating herself in a chair, she threaded her needle with a crimson-colored fiber and began to poke it in and out of the flowered design. Unfortunately, her hands trembled and she pricked herself.

Sucking on her finger, she put aside the cloth. It wouldn't do to have her work covered in blood. She rose and crossed to the window, watching the luminous moon on the rise. Her thoughts immediately turned to Cort. Where had he gone this eve? Did he think of her at all?

She'd overheard some of the servants talking the other day that he slept in a tent in the bailey along with his men. In addition to wondering why he didn't spend his nights with his wife in their bed chamber, they also discussed what willing maidens he might have taken to bed to service his needs.

The idea made her stomach turn sour. It occurred to her that while she still entertained suspicions of the Norman, she also didn't want any other woman to enjoy his lovemaking skills. Though she'd sent him away and asked him to leave her alone, she now realized her folly. He'd introduced her to an entirely different side of herself, a sensual nature that longed to be satisfied.

Baffled by her mixed emotions, she finally threw on her night-gown and crawled in bed. Snuffing out her candelabra, she leaned back onto the pillows and tried to sleep. What a fool she must be to wish for a restful evening. Cort's musky scent still clung to the bedding and thoughts of his hard warrior's body rose in her mind, despite her reluctance to receive them. She recalled their encounter on the castle wall earlier in the day.

His lips had infused her body with aching need. Waves of pleasure had washed over her like waves on the ocean, insistent and all consuming. Lord help her, she wanted him. How could she continue to deny herself?

Hearing heavy footsteps in the hallway, her heart skipped a beat. Could it be Cort? Her family and the servants would all be abed by now. It couldn't be anyone else but him.

By now she was so hot for the Norman, she could hardly contain herself. Sitting up, she ripped her gown from her body and tossed it aside. Then she burrowed down under the covers, shivering. Her body tingled in anticipation of his touch and her breath turned ragged.

The footsteps stopped at her door, and she drew in her lower lip, praying he would enter and satisfy this burning desire. But when the steps continued on down the hall, she gasped in dismay. Jumping from the bed, she hurried to the door, opening it a crack.

Holding a candle aloft, Cort walked away from her chamber door. His large form overwhelmed the small corridor and she longed to call out to him. Something prevented her from doing so. Instead, she watched as he hesitated at the end of the hall.

"*Sacre bleu*," he muttered then turned in the direction of the servants' quarters.

With trembling hands, she closed her door and hurried back to bed. Miserable, she crawled under the covers. She stared into the darkness for a while, unsure of what to think. Disappointment wound through her. More than she wished to admit.

Tears filled her eyes and spilled down her cheeks. She turned her face into the pillow that still contained Cort's enticing male scent, hoping her sobs would be muffled.

CORT AWAKENED ABRUPTLY. HIS SLEEPING COT seemed unnaturally hard, and he pushed impatiently to his feet. He poured himself a drink of water and swallowed it, but realized he wouldn't be able to quench the ache in his loins.

He wanted Rhiannon.

His patience had nearly reached a breaking point. He refused to cool his ardor in the stream again. Their time together on the castle wall this afternoon made him realize that she desired him.

Surely, she would not turn him away. He'd tried earlier this eve to visit her but had lost the courage. So, he'd wandered the castle grounds, trying to talk himself down. That wouldn't work now. He had his mind on one thing, and one thing only.

Donning his trousers and boots, he headed out into the cool evening air. Staring up at the castle, his gaze immediately focused on Rhiannon's window, and he noted the flickering candlelight.

Was she thinking of him, as he was thinking of her?

With long strides, he entered the castle and found himself at her door once again. He reached out to open it then hesitated and drew back.

What am I doing?

He could usually contain himself when it came to women. Over the years, he'd learned to hold himself aloof and limited his emotional entanglements. He let sex remain what it was, *just sex*. It went against his personal code of conduct to form attachments. No woman had ever wanted him because he had no lands, no wealth.

This situation was different. Though their marriage had been arranged, Rhiannon was his wife and he missed her. She haunted his thoughts and consumed his dreams. The sweet fulfillment that lay between her silken thighs drew him, as well as the fact that he'd become quite attached to her. He knew he would never underestimate her abilities in or out of the bedroom.

Stop, a voice said as he moved forward. *Do you really want to want to risk outright rejection again? Is it worth it?*

The burgeoning desire thrumming in his veins provided his answer.

Heart hammering like a drum, he entered the chamber. His gaze swept the area and he saw Rhiannon asleep on the bed, her hair splayed like wildfire across the pillow. Bathed in silvery moonlight, her curvaceous body presented him with a heavenly sight.

Like a thirsty man, he drank in the sight of her creamy-skinned, supple form as though it quenched his parched throat. From her red tresses down to her small feet, the woman presented a portrait of perfection. She looked healthier than when he'd last seen her naked, and he rejoiced in her recovery. Her body had lost its angular qualities and had filled out nicely. Her breasts, tipped with rosy peaks, rose and fell with her breathing and her legs were spread ever so slightly.

Raking a hand through his hair, he wondered what to do next. Awaken her and risk her annoyance? Damn it, she was his wife. He had a right to sleep with her.

Suddenly she cried out in her sleep and began to whimper, flailing her hands against an unseen attacker. His hesitation faded and he became angry at what she'd suffered prior to his arrival. No doubt she still had lingering nightmares from her ordeal. Sitting next to her, he lifted stray hair from her forehead and cupped one side of her face.

"Rhiannon," he whispered.

She slowly awakened, blinking in recognition.

He flinched, awaiting her barb-tongued reaction to his presence.

"Wh-what are you doing in here?"

She drew the covers up over her nakedness, wondering how long he'd watched her sleep. Remembering she'd seen him go down the hall earlier toward the servants' quarters stabbed her with unexplainable hurt and she pushed away his hand.

His lips turned down. "I was in the hallway when I heard you cry out. Are you all, right?"

"I'm fine." She glared at him, sensing a note of falsehood to his words. "What were you doing outside my room?"

"*Our* room."

"No doubt you were on your way back to your tent after slaking your lust on one of the female servants." She couldn't believe she'd just said that and watched as his he drew back from her, as though she'd struck him.

"I've not had a woman in my bed since we were together last time."

"But I saw you in the hallway . . ." She fell silent, noting the light of understanding in his eyes.

"So, you did hear me outside your door earlier this eve."

"Aye."

"I stopped by our chamber but lost my nerve and returned to my tent. I can't sleep Rhiannon." His jaw slanted with determination. "I saw the light in your window and decided to come up again."

"You didn't go to the servants' quarters?"

He shook his head. "The guards can vouch for me. They saw me wandering about the castle grounds."

Relief poured through Rhiannon. The guards posted along the wall were loyal O'Kelly men. They would not lie to her.

"Why didn't you come in earlier? As my husband, you have a right to enter this bed chamber at any time. You have the right to claim my body at any time, too."

He stroked the side of her face. "I don't want to simply *claim* you, Rhiannon."

"I don't understand."

He drew in a deep breath. "I can't abide the thought of you lying stiffly beneath me as I thrust inside you like some wild rutting beast. Sweet *Jesu*, I want you to want me."

She swallowed hard and returned in a whisper, "I want to want you. But I'm . . . I'm scared."

"I would never hurt you *ma cherie*. From the moment I met you I've been intrigued. You are an amazing woman. A woman I'd like fighting beside me, not against me."

Rhiannon's resistance faded and she nuzzled his calloused palm. A curl of warmth grew in her belly, and she felt her body responding to the invitation she saw in his eyes. No longer could she push away what she felt for him. His touch was irresistible, her need undeniable.

Emboldened by her gesture, Cort moved aside the covers. He drew her close and said huskily into her ear, "Let me stay with you, *ma cherie*. I promise, I can make your heart sing and your body soar."

She recognized the burning need in his eyes. The time for refusing to admit what she wanted from him had passed. Her body demanded his intimate caresses.

"Kiss me, Cort." she whispered, feeling herself melt into his comforting embrace. "Make love to me."

NINE

Blood rushed through Rhiannon's veins like warm, honeyed mead as he drew her close, his lips pressed against hers. The expanse of his broad chest pressed against her sensitive nipples, and they tightened in response.

She wrapped her arms around his neck, drawing him closer, unwilling to let him go. As he cradled her in his arms, her lower body throbbed with desire. Wild, wanton thoughts flew through her mind as she felt the beat of his heart against hers.

I want him.

The idea that she desired him perplexed her. She'd fought against these treacherous feelings for weeks. She didn't know exactly how it had come about, but at some point, she'd begun to think highly of him. The aspects of honor and duty ingrained in his soul, along with reasonable nature, drew her. His splendid male body ignited a fire in her soul, and she found herself fascinated. Her feelings for him coursed raw and uncontrollable through her blood.

Do I love him?

As their kiss deepened, she considered that, but realized she hadn't known him long enough to be certain. Her feelings were also much different from those she'd had for Jamie, which added to her indecision. She and Jamie were betrothed, but she'd never been intimate with him beyond kissing. Her affection for him stemmed from the fact she'd known him her entire life.

Cort had taken her virginity and introduced her to the sensual world of lovemaking. He fulfilled not only her sensual needs, but it seemed he understood her inner self and accepted who she really was. She felt herself unexplainably drawn to him.

Over the weeks, she'd found his male charisma held a certain allure, which is why she'd tried desperately to avoid him. To welcome his lovemaking represented a big step, for it allowed the two of them to grow closer. Yet such intimacy could leave her vulnerable.

She prayed he wouldn't be reckless with her heart.

He pulled away, never taking his dark, mesmerizing gaze from her as he stood. Pulling off his boots and tossing them aside, he crawled up beside her on the bed.

"*Sacre bleu,*" he murmured as he combed his fingers slowly through her long hair.

He said nothing else. He didn't need to. His eyes spoke of his raw need.

Her fears having vanished, Rhiannon shivered with delight. Her limbs tingled and her heart fluttered as though filled with a million tiny dragonflies. Breathing grew difficult, concentration impossible.

"Are you still afraid of me, *ma cherie?*" He pressed his lips to the palm on one of her hands, nuzzling the soft flesh.

"No," she responded in an uneven voice then licked her dry lips.

"Why do you tremble?"

"It's chilly in here."

"I can take care of that. Let me warm you." His lips found hers again. His hot, thrusting tongue delved into her mouth where he explored every inch of the soft cavern.

Rhiannon wound her fingers in his thick hair, pulling him closer. Her thoughts flew recklessly. An inner voice still rebelled, warning her that by trusting him she took a great chance. Her body took no heed of the voice and behaved of its own accord, responding enthusiastically to him.

Primal urges overcame her senses; she became a willing slave to his captive touch.

"Enough of this." He sat up and removed his trousers.

With nothing existing between them but the warm air, he softly kissed the juncture between her neck and shoulder, sending shivers up her spine. In response, her body swelled with yearning and a sharp, pleasurable ache developed in the sensitive spot between her thighs.

As he showered her skin with hot, urgent kisses, she clung to him like a woman possessed. A whirlwind of sensation nearly carried her away. She could wait no longer.

"Take me," she begged. "Now—before I burst."

His eyes flashed with heated urgency, and she knew he felt the same. He nudged her legs open with one of his knees and mounted her. When he entered her in one swift movement, she arched her back and received him completely.

His large girth filled her, and she gasped when he began to move in and out with mighty strokes. She instinctively wrapped her legs around his waist so he could enter her more deeply. He burrowed himself in her moistness, holding her buttocks firmly.

His thrusts came faster, his brow glistening until he finally exploded. Arching his neck, he groaned and shuddered. Afterward, he collapsed atop her drawing in ragged breaths.

Despite the weight of Cort's large, muscled form, Rhiannon felt no discomfort. Her mind still reeled with his sweet lovemaking, and she welcomed his nearness.

She needed to start trusting the man she'd married. Though she'd been anxious about his motives at first, he'd done nothing to earn her distrust and everything to make a place in her world. She enjoyed being his lover. Mayhap she should learn to be his wife.

He smiled down at her. "You intend to kill me with your insatiable sexual appetite, don't you woman?"

She smiled back. "Actually, I've decided to keep you around."

"Have you now?"

"Indeed." She laughed softly. "You have ways of pleasuring me that I would miss."

He began to stroke her eager flesh. "Are you hungry, *ma cherie?*"

"Yes," she gasped. "But not for food."

"I see I shall have to feed you. Are you ready?"

Once again, she felt ready to burst. "Yes!"

As they made love again, the world fell away. Only the two of them mattered and nothing else.

CORT AWAKENED SEVERAL HOURS LATER AS the stars and moon shone brightly outside the window. Amusing, how the heavenly bodies cast a blanket of soft light across their nakedness. The feel of Rhiannon's warm sleeping body pressed closely against his, her leg thrown casually over his, enthralled him.

He drank in her unique scent—roses and a spicy aroma. It filled his senses with poignant memory as he recalled how eagerly she'd made love with him. Hopefully tonight had been a positive step toward her trusting him; hopefully her fears had been scattered to the four winds.

He kissed her forehead, her scent filling his nostrils. She made soft noises and squirmed at his touch, a smile curving her berry-colored lips. Her even-paced breathing and her very presence comforted him.

Not many marriages transacted for political gain turned out successfully. However, he now felt more encouraged than ever by the possibility that theirs may.

As a bastard son, he'd always wondered what it would be like to be part of a family. Now he had the opportunity to experience it. He and Rhiannon would surely produce sons and daughters that he could bounce on his knees and rock to sleep. After years of waging wars for King Henry, returning battle-scarred and weary, he welcomed this change.

Sweet Jesu. He longed to make love to her again, but felt she needed her rest, so he resisted the urge to wake her. Instead, he endured the agonizing, wonderful torture of waiting.

Does she know what she's doing to me?

It must have been hours that he held her close, appreciating her beauty and enjoying the brush of her silken skin against his. Sometime later, when he felt he could hold back no longer, he nibbled her ear lobe.

"Mmm," she murmured and her eyes blinked open.

"You're a stunning woman, Rhiannon. Your eyes, they sparkle like the finest gems and your hair is the color of a blazing fire at midnight."

"Are you trying to flatter me, hoping that I might shower you with more of my favors, sir?" Her lips turned up with a knowing smile.

"Absolutely."

"Mayhap, if you behave yourself," she teased, "I shall entertain the idea of pleasuring you again."

He nearly rolled off the bed. This was a woman made for the bed chamber. She may not realize it, and it may be blasphemous of him to think it, but her sensual nature was much better served by a virile husband than a man who didn't appreciate her sexual appetite. The image of her writhing naked beneath him in bed spurred him on to kiss her deeply.

They made slow, sweet love again. The idea that she welcomed his advances heartened him and he increased the tempo of his thrusts inside of her. He reveled in the fact that Rhiannon belonged to him now and forever.

Once they were fully sated, they curled together, exhausted, in each other's arms. Satisfaction consumed him like a slow burning fire, and he pulled her closer, knowing he could never let her go. This was his home now and the Irish were his people. He drifted into a serene sleep,

When he awakened again, dawn had begun to stretch ribbons

of rosy color across the horizon, signaling the beginning of a new day. As much as he disliked the idea of leaving the warm covers and Rhiannon, he realized he had a lot of work to do today.

Reluctantly, he shifted her sleeping body from his embrace and rolled out of bed.

ON THE VERGE OF WAKING, RHIANNON became aware of Cort sliding her gently from his arms and pulling the blankets up over her shoulders. Yet she continued to lie still, observing her husband silently from beneath her lashes.

He washed his strong, muscled body with a sponge dipped in a bowl of soapy water. Finished, he retrieved a towel from a chest and patted himself dry. He withdrew fresh clothing from a wardrobe then dressed quickly in trousers and leather boots. After donning a shirt and a black tunic, he drew a belt around his trim hips.

She filled with warmth, recalling the time they'd spent in each other's arms last night. Truly, she was a woman now fulfilled and . . . *in love?*

Not entirely certain what love really entailed, she dismissed the idea. If it meant she wanted to be near Cort every minute of the day, wanted to touch him, smell him and make love with him, she supposed she was afflicted.

In many ways, he still remained a stranger. She realized that knowledge of her husband would come in time. Until then, she would be patient and bask in the glow of their blossoming relationship.

Casting a glance her way, Cort grinned. "Have you enjoyed watching me dress, *ma cherie?*"

The blankets fell away from Rhiannon's breasts as she sat up and hugged her knees. "How did you know I was awake?"

"I have eyes in the back of my head."

She laughed. "Watching you has been pleasant."

He leaned down and brushed her lips with his. "I'll have Glenna send up bath water for you."

This time, she didn't become angry. She judged his offer generous, not controlling. "Will you break your fast with me when I come downstairs?"

"I've made arrangements to ride out with my men to review fortifications along the city wall."

She quelled disappointment, but she appreciated that he had taken a special interest in keeping the castle, the village, and the surrounding lands less vulnerable from enemy attack.

"*Au revoire.*"

He kissed the back of her hand and gave it a warm squeeze, then left. She buried her head in his pillow, breathing deeply of his distinctive musky scent.

After the servants delivered her bath water and left, she sank into the luxurious warmth of the tub. She considered the events yesterday and last night. Something important had changed between her and Cort. No longer did she feel ashamed of giving herself to him and enjoying it. It seemed as though a giant weight had been lifted from her shoulders.

Finished, she toweled off then dressed in her chemise and a flowing green velvet gown that she belted into place with a gold kirtle. Seated at a table in front of a small mirror, she hummed to herself and brushed her hair, when a knock sounded at the door.

"Enter," she called out.

Glenna walked inside and shut the door. "Oh, you've already bathed and dressed my lady."

She instantly noted her maid's concerned expression. "Is everything all right? Is my father ill?"

"He's fine," she said. "But we have visitors. They arrived a short while ago."

"Who?"

"Sir Cort's father, Searlas Guyot, and King Henry. Also, a woman who purports herself with much authority, but I have no idea who she is."

"Mayhap she's the king's mistress." Rhiannon remembered Cort telling her that his father barely acknowledged him while he grew up. Why would he bother to pay him a visit now? And who could this mystery woman be?

"Possibly. Either way, I sense she's up to no good. She's got a baby with her. Your father had me settle her into a room so she and the child can rest."

"I suppose we'll find out later." Rhiannon didn't like the feeling of trepidation that crept over her. "It will be interesting to meet Cort's father. But why is King Henry here?"

"From what I gather, the trip was unexpected," Glenna said. "Nevertheless, King Henry has brought a full staff of servants, cooks, and guards. He's moved his followers into the great hall and intends to hold court."

She tapped her toe as she considered what all of this meant. "I wonder what he wants, Glenna. I don't like that he's come here."

"Aye, I agree with you. He gazes around with a gleam in his eyes, as though summing up the worth of everything."

Though her maid tended to be overly superstitious, she'd learned long ago to trust the woman's instincts.

"There's no sense in sitting here fretting," Glenna announced. "King Henry has requested your presence downstairs."

"Saints above." Reaching for her brush, Rhiannon ran it through her hair with trembling fingers.

Glenna took it from her. "Let me help you. You're as nervous as a chicken sensing the axe and woodblock."

"Wouldn't you be troubled too?"

"Aye," Glenna said. "But you must never show your fear. It gives your power away."

Glenna divided strands of her hair and worked them into two braids. She pinned them atop her head and wove in a strand of pearls that had belonged to her mother and stood back to admire her work.

"There, you look most presentable. Go to your husband so you can properly greet your guests."

"You're not coming?"

"I need to calm the servants. Like you and I, they're uneasy."

Rhiannon hesitated, contemplating the best way for her to make an appearance.

Glenna patted her arm reassuringly. "You'll be fine. You're an O'Kelly, after all. None of your clan is faint of heart, to be sure."

"Thank you, Glenna." Confidence bolstered; Rhiannon made her way down the stairs. Pausing at the entrance to the great hall, she listened to the voices and soft music. It was impossible to understand what anyone was saying, so she built up her courage and walked toward the high table where a cluster of people stood. She couldn't exactly discern her father's expression but could tell he wasn't pleased.

"Good morning my dear," he said tiredly. "I'd like to introduce you to King Henry."

Moran gestured toward a man seated in a carved wooden chair. His rich blue and red robes trimmed in fur indicated great wealth and prestige. A gilded and bejeweled crown rested atop his red hair, and he held a gold scepter topped with an orb and cross. Almost all of his fingers bore heavy gold, bejeweled rings.

"Welcome to Ireland your majesty." Rhiannon curtseyed deeply to the king of England and rose again.

"We are pleased to be here." King Henry glanced arrogantly at Rhiannon. Then his gaze raked over the scores of people who had crowded into the great hall.

Cort appeared at Rhiannon's side. He bowed to the king, his large presence nearly overpowering the short, stocky man. "Welcome to Callinon, your majesty."

King Henry nodded. "Guyot, it's a boon to see you again."

An unfamiliar man separated himself from the crowd near King Henry and stood beside Cort. No doubt this must be Cort's father, for he looked nearly identical—dark haired, dark eyed and tall. His well-made clothing indicated modest wealth. His face, lined with age, bespoke his advanced years.

The king's gaze once again came to rest on Rhiannon, and he stroked his short beard. Rhiannon blushed at the way he stared as if he were slowly removing her clothing. She'd heard of King Henry's many mistresses and knew he had a fondness for pursuing women, single or married.

Cort apparently saw the king's direct stare at her. His dark brows drew together, and his expression took on an even harder edge. His hands clenched into fists, but he remained silent.

Could he be jealous? Rhiannon found the idea amusing. She did not, however, find any humor in the king's unexpected visit. Up until now he'd only had a passing interest in Ireland and had never stepped foot in the country. Yet here he was, and like Glenna had said, he had a certain gleam in his eye as he assessed his surroundings—including her.

"Your daughter's quite lovely O'Kelly," King Henry said to Moran, as though she couldn't hear. "We approve."

"Thank you sire," Moran returned uneasily.

Cort gripped Rhiannon's hand possessively and turned to the man standing next to him. "Rhiannon, this is my father, Searlas Guyot."

She gave another curtsey.

Searlas nodded. "'Tis good to meet you, young Rhiannon."

Curiosity filled Rhiannon and she wondered why Searlas had come to Ireland. Cort hadn't said much about him, but she knew he'd been raised by his uncle. What could possibly bring Searlas to meet his son now?

"'Tis good to meet you too, sir." She noted Cort's father had a strange glint in his eye. His manner seemed stilted, and she remained wary.

When everyone took a seat at the high table, servants brought forth a light repast of fruit, bread and ale. As people began to break their fast, musicians played soft music in one corner of the room. Servants constantly attended to King Henry's every need.

Rhiannon picked at her food, silently observing Cort seated at her side. She could feel the tension coursing through his body and his expression remained uneasy. When he glanced at her, her face filled with heat as she recalled her hungry response to his pleasant lovemaking.

As the meal wore on, conversation became stilted. Rhiannon feared it would never end. At last, when everyone had finished, the servants cleared the table. King Henry motioned to one of his guards and spoke in a low voice.

"King Henry requests the room be cleared except for those at the high table," the guard announced.

Not typically included in men's discussions, Rhiannon picked up her skirts, intending to leave.

Cort put a restraining hand on her arm and whispered, "Stay."

She sat back down, uncomfortable, but curious.

King Henry stroked his beard slowly. His gaze could have bored holes in stone. "Since your arrival here, Guyot, your men-at-arms have taken control of a large portion of Ireland. You have begun to acquire a great new colony for England. For your years of devoted service to the crown, and for what you've accomplished here, you will be well rewarded."

Her heart dropped to her feet, and she shot Cort an incredulous look. Her doubts about him rushed back full force, souring her stomach.

"Have you been in league with King Henry all along? Did you know of his plans to come here?"

Cort's eyes flashed. "No."

"Rhiannon," Moran said warningly. "You must stop . . ."

"I don't believe you." She turned her glare from Cort to King Henry. "Tell me truthfully, do you mean to enslave my people?"

The rings on King Henry's hand flashed as he waved dismissively at her. "I don't intend to *enslave* anyone my dear. Ireland's people will, however, become loyal subjects and pay homage to the English crown. Or suffer the consequences."

"Sire, I thought . . ."

"Don't be modest, Guyot." King Henry silenced him with a hard look. "You know we agreed to this. Why else would I have spared the troops to come here? Ireland has much to offer, and we're pleased to claim her as English territory. So pleased that I sailed here with an entire fleet."

"Sire?" Cort gripped the edge of the table.

"I know this is unexpected Guyot. But you've been so successful on this quest; I brought ten thousand English soldiers to assist your men in the task of securing the rest of the country. I understand there's a lot of clan unrest that must be quelled."

Moran's face darkened. "I thought you only intended to help me liberate my kingdom, not actually set up an English colony in Ireland."

King Henry shook his head. "By order of the Pope, Ireland has belonged to England for many years. We believe it's time to see what this country has to offer us."

Rhiannon angrily shot to her feet. "It's not right that you show up like this and try to take control."

King Henry burst out laughing then lifted a haughty brow. "You're a feisty one, aren't you?"

Cort increased his grip on Rhiannon's arm and pulled her back down beside him. He glared at her, as if she'd grown two heads. Heart palpitating wildly, she glared right back then met King Henry's gaze. "I refuse to sit idly by if you intend to harm my people."

Moran sent her a silencing glance. "Hush, child. You don't understand the way of things."

"Aye, I understand full well. King Henry means to steal our livelihood from us."

Cort turned white. "I apologize sire. My wife is merely trying to defend her people's interests—"

King Henry held up a silencing hand. "I admire her passion for her people, which is befitting a true princess. However, in the future, I expect you to restrain your wife, Guyot. Otherwise, I'll have no choice but to consider her outbursts an insult to my sovereignty."

Rhiannon's insides twisted. She felt tricked, betrayed. No wonder Cort had worked so hard to get his new castle started. He'd only wanted to demonstrate to King Henry how entrenched Norman troops had become in Ireland. All of his explanations about needing the fortification to defend Callinon's people had been a ruse. His hints at needing a larger home for their growing family, a lie.

He had no consideration for her people, and he certainly didn't respect her.

Why didn't I listen to my reason? Why did I allow myself to fall under his spell?

King Henry interrupted Rhiannon's distressed thoughts. "Being a good Roman Catholic, you surely recognize and honor the Pope's dictates. Pope Adrian, in his infinite wisdom, has given me clearance to claim Ireland as England's province."

"Rhiannon realizes that," Cort said.

"You don't need to speak for me *husband*. I'm capable of doing that myself." She jutted her chin at a defiant angle.

King Henry smiled, obviously amused at her distress. "Was it not Ireland's Saint Patrick who taught the people to believe in the Holy Church and its dictates? All things sanctioned through that religious entity are directed by God himself. Therefore, you will obey Pope Adrian's decree, or be deemed a heretic. You realize we burn heretics at the stake."

She bit her lower lip until she tasted blood, forcing herself to be quiet even though she wanted to rail with the injustice of this situation. How could the Pope just hand over Ireland to King Henry like a shiny trinket? She recalled her father mentioning the Church's declaration long ago, but since nothing had come of it, she'd dismissed it from her mind.

King Henry gave a mighty sigh, as though bored. "As I said before, you will be well rewarded for your services Guyot."

A muscle in Cort's jaw twitched. "How so, your majesty?"

"I shall grant you the lordship of Leinster and you may maintain control of the lands held within by my decree, which includes the village of Callinon and those serfs and freemen tilling the soil. You will rule the people in my name, and they shall forever recognize me as their overlord." King Henry handed a rolled parchment to Cort.

Cort accepted the paper, broke the wax seal with his thumb and opened it. As he read it aloud, Moran and Searlas listened intently. After Cort finished, the men discussed the various declarations.

Rhiannon listened to all of it, outraged. She felt certain she and her father had been duped. Blood thrummed angrily through her veins. What had originally been a simple promise of support to keep Callinon safe from marauders had turned into a full-blown invasion by the English crown.

Cort lowered the document and bowed to King Henry. "Thank you for your generosity, your highness."

Rhiannon bristled. What did this mean for her people? Were they to be subjugated and downtrodden by England just like so many other countries they'd invaded? She knew how England treated the territories they defeated, and it sickened her to think her people would be relegated to the same punishment.

King Henry rubbed his hands together. "I should like to take a ride and see some of the countryside. In the morning, you gentlemen shall accompany me on the visit so my people will become acquainted with me."

His people?

Rhiannon quelled her outrage. What nerve he had, demanding that Ireland pay homage to him. Despite her anger, she knew there was nothing she could do. Nothing right now, anyway. She needed to go somewhere and think.

She pushed quickly to her feet and curtseyed quickly to King Henry. Turning on her heel, she hurried away.

Moran's disappointed voice reached her ears. "I apologize for my daughter's impudence, your majesty. She's usually not this impetuous. I don't know what's gotten into her."

"No worries," King Henry returned laughingly. "She's young. She'll soon learn how the world is and her part in it."

Overwhelmed by the idea that her husband hadn't disclosed the actual nature of his involvement with King Henry, Rhiannon rushed from the room. Her heart wrenched painfully. Why hadn't he told her?

England had waged so many atrocities in other countries. What if they did the same to Ireland? How would she ever be able to protect her kinsmen and women?

Unbidden, thoughts of Jamie's betrayal rose to haunt her, lancing her with fresh agony. His disloyalty would haunt her forever. Now her husband's deceitful actions would add to her nightmares. Considering all the disappointment she'd experienced of late, she felt broken, like a child's toy thrown against the wall and dashed to pieces.

She'd played the fool far too often. Alas, she had done so again.

TEN

As Cort listened to the king drone on, he tapped his fingers on the table, anxious to find Rhiannon so he could explain that King Henry lied whenever it benefited him, as he'd done in this case. At no point had the king of England disclosed his intent to bring his army to Ireland and stake a claim. In fact, he'd seemed almost flippant when he'd assigned Cort and his men to help Moran.

Also, he needed to warn Rhiannon to be very careful around King Henry. Though he'd laughed off her outburst, Cort knew he'd be watching her closely. If she gave him any cause to brand her disloyal to the English crown, he'd put her to death. The man had no compunction about getting rid of anything, or anyone, he deemed contentious.

An additional worry ate at him. Why had his father decided to come to Ireland with King Henry? Searlas had barely visited Cort as he grew up. Once Cort had reached adulthood, Searlas's contact had completely stopped.

Finally, King Henry sat back in his chair. "We would like to rest," he announced. "It has been a long voyage."

Moran nodded. "You'll be shown to your chamber."

"We thank you, O'Kelly. Guyot, be prepared to take me on a tour of Leinster starting tomorrow." An entourage of bodyguards scurried to assist King Henry as he rose and followed one of Moran's servants up the stairs.

Cort shoved to his feet, but Moran caught his sleeve, a knowing look in his eye. "Give yourself a minute to think of what you're going to say to my daughter. She's high-spirited, as I'm sure you know by now. She'll be worried for our people, considering what has just transpired."

"I want you to know that I had no idea King Henry planned to show up here with his army." Cort narrowed his gaze at Moran. "This has come as a complete shock to me."

"I believe you." Moran patted Cort's arm. "I'm afraid I'm to blame since I begged for his help in regaining my kingdom."

"I thought his intention was only to send my army to assist with that," Cort said.

"I know King Henry well. Nothing gets past him. When you married Rhiannon and stayed on in Ireland with your troops, no doubt his advisors warned him of the possibility that your Normans may decide to build up defenses that could pose a threat to England."

Cort frowned. "I would never do such a thing."

"I'm certain you wouldn't, but King Henry doesn't trust anyone. I'd hoped your marriage to Rhiannon would escape King Henry's notice, but I realized there was a chance he might find out."

"You only wanted to protect your people."

"Aye, that I did. But there's no fool like an old fool." Moran nodded tiredly. "You have a large responsibility on your shoulders, Guyot. As King Henry's emissary, you can convince him to deal reasonably with the Irish."

"I hope he'll listen to me."

Moran nodded encouragingly. "I see how you work with your men and how my people respect you. Your judgment is sound. I'm sure that's why King Henry chose you to do this."

"I appreciate your confidence in me, sire. I just wish your daughter felt the same way."

"Rhiannon?" Moran chuckled. "She'll eventually come around. Be patient."

"I'll try." Cort decided he'd have to have exercise extreme endurance to deal with Rhiannon's temperament.

"I'll have a word with her, too," Moran added. "She's not always happy about what I have to say, but she listens."

Searlas, who had been speaking with one of King Henry's servants, excused himself and approached them. He introduced himself to Moran and the men shook hands.

"You created quite a stir back home by marrying King Moran's daughter," he said to Cort. "Everyone's talking about the Norman commander who took his troops to Ireland to settle clan unrest and wound up marrying a princess."

Cort scratched his chin, watching his father with a wary eye. "How does that concern you?"

Searlas lifted a dark brow. "I'd like to congratulate you on your marriage. I feel safe that with you over here in Ireland, my wife and family will continue to remain ignorant of our true relationship. They still think you're my brother's ill-gotten son."

The barb of Searlas's words seemed as cruel as ever. No matter how much time passed, his father's dismissal remained difficult to swallow.

"Why are you here Searlas? Please enlighten me. I don't have all day."

Searlas cleared his throat. "A delicate matter has arisen that I need to bring to your attention. Do you know a young woman named Josette Portier?"

Cort fought uneasiness. He'd met her at court when she'd traveled there with her father, a wealthy merchant, to deliver a shipment of wine. They had conducted a brief love affair and when she left, that had been the end of it.

"It has been almost two years since I made her acquaintance."

"I'm assuming the two of you are more than simply *acquainted*. She has a child, Cort." Searlas squinted accusingly at him. "A son she claims you fathered."

"She never told me anything." Cort narrowed his gaze, sensing something amiss. He couldn't believe Josette wouldn't have told him about a child.

Searlas shrugged. "Whatever her reason for keeping it to herself, she has discovered you are my son. She threatened to tell my family unless I either paid her off or helped her find you. When I found out King Henry was sailing to Ireland, I secured passage for myself and Josette. Now she's your problem to deal with."

Blackmailing wench. Cort struggled against rising frustration as he realized what trickery Josette was up to. It seemed hard to believe he'd fathered a child after such a simple affair. Yet he realized it could be possible.

"Have you seen this child Searlas? Does he even look like me?"

"It's difficult—he's a baby. But she named him Fitz after your uncle. And she brought him here so you can see him yourself."

Cort drew in a shocked breath. "Where is he?"

"Resting. The boy became quite cranky during the voyage."

"How old is he?"

"Josette said he recently had his first birthday."

Cort mentally calculated nine months of pregnancy and the time that had passed since then. Unfortunately, it all added up to indicate he could be the father.

"Let's not jump to conclusions." Moran clapped Cort on the shoulder. "We can't be certain the child is yours."

Cort raked a hand through his hair and began to pace in front of the hearth. Just when it seemed he and Rhiannon were getting along, things had become complicated. He glanced around to see that Moran and Searlas had gone, leaving him to sort through this mess on his own.

"Why are you so morose my friend?"

Cort heard footsteps and looked up to see Raoul standing next to him. He hadn't even heard him enter. Relieved to unburden his thoughts, he explained the situation.

"You need to find people who can verify her story."

"There's a problem. King Henry expects me to give him a tour of Leinster and that's going to take a while." An idea occurred to Cort, and he snapped his fingers. "You will go in my stead. Check out Josette's family. Her father, Gaston Portier, is a rich merchant and is well known."

Raoul's lips twitched. "So, I'm being enlisted as a spy?"

"Does it matter what I need you to do?"

Raoul grinned. "I'll prepare *Le Bon Navire* for the trip."

After Raoul left, he went in search of Rhiannon. The idea of confronting his temperamental wife didn't appeal to him, but he needed to talk to her. He wanted to help her see things his way.

As time went on, other events in their marriage may occur that she would need to accept. This was as good a time as any to make it clear that he refused to spend the rest of his life putting up with her impetuousness.

"YOU ARE CORT GUYOT'S WIFE?"

Rhiannon spun around. She'd been pruning the roses in the garden with such a vengeance; she hadn't heard the woman's approach. Ever since her audience with King Henry, she'd been outside, doing her best to settle her frazzled mind.

"Yes. I'm Rhiannon." She studied the dark-haired woman in the gold brocade gown, taking note of her exotic beauty and her accent, so similar to Cort's. Assuming she must be King Henry's mistress, she smiled, deciding it best to greet her with respect. "Welcome to Callinon Castle."

"It's a lovely little place." She sniffed arrogantly. "Quaint but comfortable."

Ignoring the insult, Rhiannon continued to stare at the woman. "And you are?"

"Josette Portier, the mother of your husband's son."

She nearly dropped the small knife in her gloved hand, unable to ascertain she'd heard the woman correctly. "Excuse me?"

Josette strode over to a red blossom and inhaled deeply. "Obviously he never told you about me."

Making no comment, Rhiannon removed her gloves and placed them and the small knife on a stone garden bench. The day's revelations had begun to wear on her nerves. First King Henry's arrival had turned her world upside down, and now this. What else had her husband forgotten to tell her?

"How long have you known Cort?" Rhiannon's heart twisted with distress, aware how quickly she'd become attached to him. That's why she felt so unsettled to discover all the things he'd never told her. Could she ever really trust him?

"Long enough to know his heart belongs to me," Josette said, batting her eyelashes. "I'd lost touch with him since he's been busy on military assignments for King Henry. Now that I've found him, I plan to stay in his life. A child needs his father, as I'm certain you can understand."

Josette's words stabbed into Rhiannon's skin, as though someone tortured her with sharp steel barbs. "And the boy? Where is he?"

"He's here with me. It's time for him to meet his father."

"I see."

"Listen well, Rhiannon. Cort is mine. If he had never come here, we would have gotten married. I love him and he loves me." Josette fluffed her artfully coiffed hair. "Don't attempt to meddle in my affairs or you'll pay a price."

Something akin to jealousy shot through Rhiannon and she realized Josette would stop at nothing to get her way. Sensing the woman to be capable of vile acts, she decided to be cautious when dealing with her. She would not allow Cort's mistress to run slipshod over her life or those of her family.

"Don't threaten me, Josette. You won't like the consequences."

"Oh really?"

"Really."

"Rhiannon are you out here?"

Hearing Cort's voice, Rhiannon filled with anger, then calmed herself down. Marriage was about compromise, and she needed to learn how to handle it—like it or not.

Josette plucked a blossom and disappeared from the garden, laughter trailing behind her.

Cort entered the garden a few moments later. "I've been looking everywhere for you."

Rhiannon folded her arms across her chest, irritated beyond belief at her truth-challenged husband. "Why?"

Despite her frustration, an ache lanced through Rhiannon when she saw her handsome husband approach. She had awakened this morning fulfilled and content after a night of lovemaking, but after everything that had happened today, her ease had vanished. Any feelings she'd developed for him had been squashed.

Long ago, Jamie's betrayal had eroded her ability to trust. Cort had started to build it in her, but now it had disappeared, like a water droplet in the sunshine.

"We need to talk," he said in a serious tone.

"About what? I know all I need to," Rhiannon responded. "You transacted some sort of a deal with King Henry so that he felt free to come here and exploit my people. Now your mistress has arrived to warm your bed. You must be very pleased with yourself."

His face drained of color. "You've met Josette?"

"She just left here a few minutes ago. We had quite an enlightening conversation. I must compliment your taste in women. She's quite lovely."

"*Sacre bleu!* What did she say?"

"She intends to claim your affections at any cost. And introduce you to your son."

"I swear I didn't know about him. Josette and I had a brief affair that didn't really mean anything."

Rhiannon's pride flared and she fought the tears burning at the back of her eyes. "I can't believe you had the nerve to speak such sweet words to me when we made love. All along you had a woman back in Normandy you cared deeply about. She's been searching for you to let you know about her child."

"I have suspicions about why she didn't try harder." He pressed his lips into a firm, disapproving line. "Namely that the child isn't mine and this is some sort of scheme she concocted now that she realizes I've got better financial prospects."

"She claims the two of you would have gotten married. That you love each other."

His expression clouded. "We were never that serious. She was a mere dalliance; I can assure you."

Rhiannon stiffened her spine, refusing to believe him. "Mayhap I, too, am a mere dalliance. Of course, the deal with my father required you to marry me in order to inherit my dowry."

"Rhiannon—"

Her vision blurred. "Are you toying with me, Cort Guyot? Am I simply a pawn or do I mean anything to you?"

Cort sorted through his emotions. He wasn't certain what he felt about Rhiannon right now. Making love to her was like drinking the sweetest wine on earth. Spending time with her pleased him.

Yet, when she became upset and angry, he wanted to toss her over his knee and spank her. He found her the most maddening, exciting woman he'd ever met. However, he refused to let her lead him around on a chain, teasing him into submission.

Her hands began to shake, and she clasped them together. "Your refusal to answer tells me everything."

Exasperation surged through Cort. "Why must you be so stubborn? Of course you're important to me."

"Aye, I understand just how important. Because of your marriage to me, you are now in great favor with the king of England. If he plans to cause problems here, I swear I'll—"

"Be careful what you say about Henry." Cort glanced around; certain they were alone but wanting to make sure. "He won't hesitate to strike out at anyone he deems disloyal. He's fond of putting to death people who challenge him."

Rhiannon's face drained of color. "In the future keep your lunatic mistress away from me."

Cort pulled her against chest and felt the racing of her heart,
heard her ragged breaths. If only there were a way he could calm
her fears. "Understand me well, woman. Josette is *not* my mistress.
Unfortunately, I don't have any control over her. I do, however,
have control over you."

"Oh, are you my master now?"

"Of course I'm not," he growled. "I am your husband, your
protector and . . ." He kissed her, claiming her mouth with fierce-
ness. She didn't pull away, but neither was she responsive. When he
lifted up, she studied him closely.

Her lips, still moist from his kiss, trembled as she spoke. "Did
you know King Henry was coming here to flaunt his lordship over
Ireland?"

"We only discussed my mission to help your father reclaim
Callinon."

"Convenient, this lack of memory you've developed." She jutted
her chin defiantly. "How can I believe you?"

He frowned. "I thought we'd grown close these last few weeks.
Don't you trust me?"

She didn't answer.

"You're thinking of him, aren't you?" A flare of jealousy lanced
his insides.

"Who?" Her eyes flared brightly.

He looked into those limpid green depths. Pain and confusion
lived there. "The man who broke your heart."

"Jamie O'Brien didn't break my heart," she blurted. "He betrayed
my people."

"He broke your heart *ma cherie*. I see it in your eyes, and I hear
it in your voice."

She extricated herself from his embrace. "Do you love *her*?"

"Josette?"

She nodded.

"I barely know her."

"Apparently you know her well enough."

She thought of the child Josette had brought with her. Did the boy look like Cort? Did he have his father's dark eyes and dark hair? Unconsciously, she pressed a hand to her abdomen. She'd never considered the idea seriously until now, but she felt disappointment at not being the woman to bear Cort's first child.

Straightening her back, she dismissed the foolish notion. The man's affections were fickle. He wouldn't care about such a thing, and she shouldn't either.

"I'm not going to apologize for being with her. I hadn't met you yet."

"Are you going to let her stay?"

"I can't turn her and the boy out. I have sent Raoul back to Normandy to investigate her claims, however. Hopefully it won't take long for him to find the truth."

"What if the child is actually yours?"

"I'll do the right thing by him. My father treated me like the bottom of his shoes my entire life. If Fitz is my son, I plan to acknowledge him and see that he has a decent upbringing."

"And Josette? What will you do with her? She'll stop at nothing to get you."

"I'll deal with her."

"She's a witch. I fear for the child."

"He'll be fine. I'll hire a nursemaid in the village and pay her extra to keep an eye on Josette."

When he tried to gather Rhiannon in his arms again, she scooted away, unable to bear his touch. His sincerity was in question, and she didn't want to reward him by giving into his needs.

His expression darkened. "See that the kitchen staff prepares a special feast this eve. King Henry is used to rich fare, and I'd like to make a good impression on our other guests."

"Of course, *husband*. I'll take care of it straightaway. You won't be disappointed. Do you have any other orders for me?"

"Not at the moment."

Rhiannon spun away from Cort's steely gaze and hurried inside. If she could have her way, she'd serve King Henry and Josette poisonous eel.

THE AFTERNOON SKY FILLED WITH DARK purple clouds and rain began to patter across the countryside. Mighty gusts of wind whipped and wailed around the castle walls like banshees howling for vengeance.

Though Rhiannon had managed to quell her irritation at Cort, she still stewed at the maddening revelations of this morning. Keeping her frustrations at bay, she'd arranged with Leila to prepare a bountiful feast and had sent a servant into the village to hire a troupe of performers for this eve's entertainment.

Glenna helped Rhiannon bathe and dress in a burgundy-colored silk gown reserved for special occasions. After the maid had helped her twist her hair atop her head in an artful style, she went to the great hall and took her place at the high table.

Cort acknowledged her presence with a brief nod. She nodded back, sensing his cool reserve. Her skin prickled, as if brushed by an icy breeze. Apparently, he was still upset at her. Too bad.

Josette, who sat across the table next to Searlas, shot her a haughty glance which Rhiannon promptly ignored.

After the servants presented the rich dishes on gleaming platters, she helped herself to several portions, but ate sparingly. Josette's heated glares made it difficult for her to even swallow. That witch could go jump in the moat for all she cared. In the meanwhile, she would have to tolerate her cutting presence.

Painfully aware of Cort's warmth next to her, she tried to avoid looking at him, but found her gaze straying toward him more often than not. Then she chastised herself for her weakness. She didn't want him to sense her inner torment.

For his part, Cort continued to steal glances at her, his gaze hard and unrelenting. Nostrils flared, he seemed to be imparting his disapproval of the way she'd comported herself earlier.

Josette spoke louder than necessary and laughed at a great volume. She continually flipped her dark brown hair over her shoulders, drawing attention to herself. Men at the table seemed mesmerized by her every move.

She stared at Cort like a starving hound desperate for a scrap of meat. To anyone who noticed, it would be obvious how much the woman coveted Rhiannon's husband. Did she have no shame?

To his credit, Cort didn't seem to be amused by anything Josette said or did. He seemed too engaged discussing politics with King Henry and her father.

During a lull in the conversation, King Henry addressed Josette. "We had no idea Norman women were quite so charming. Visit my castle the next time you're in London, my dear. I'd like to give you a personal tour."

"Oh, I should like that very much," Josette purred. "Unfortunately, I find myself far too busy for entertainment these days." She sent Cort a knowing glance and bubbled with laughter. "My son is a demanding young man and occupies vast amounts of my time."

King Henry grinned, and he held up a goblet of wine. "To motherhood."

"Here, here," everyone called, holding up their drinking vessels in a toast.

Rhiannon's thoughts were filled, once again, with the idea of what it would be like to have Cort's child. Her face suffused with warmth, and she found the idea appealing. Her sons or daughters with Cort would have a legitimate claim to O'Kelly lands. If for some reason they never had children, and Cort allowed Josette's son to lay claim to her father's holdings, her blood wouldn't inherit. She absolutely couldn't let that happen.

Her gaze at Josette could have melted a rock and she realized she could never let the woman sink her sharp talons into her husband. In her mind, she launched a full-scale war against Cort's former mistress.

As the servants cleared away the remains of supper, Earc O'Crowley, the hunch-backed storyteller, began spinning another of his fantastic yarns full of Irish myth and lore. Rhiannon could barely follow his tale. Cort's unsettling presence diverted her attention and Josette's endless prattling made her head ache.

She longed to retire to her chamber. *Alone.* Humiliation at being forced to sit here watching Josette's coquettish behavior toward the male guests made her queasy. The little tart deserved to have her mouth washed out with soap. But the men, so easily swayed by a pretty face and curvaceous hips, were taken in.

Rhiannon noticed her father hugging Ailleen as they listened to the entertainment. Such a tender scene, yet it pained her to see how slowly he moved around these days and how his face had taken on a blue tinge.

She recalled earlier when she'd met him in the hallway outside her room. He'd defended Cort, explaining that neither of them had been aware of King Henry's intentions to show up in Ireland. Rhiannon believed her father completely. However, she still felt unsure of Cort's innocence.

Arch snored contentedly beneath the table, his belly full of scraps. She leaned down to scratch between the dog's pointed ears, trying to get her mind of her problems. A pleasure-loving hound, Arch groaned and stretched out, thumping his long whip of a tail on the stone floor.

"What a giant beggar you are." Cort grinned at his dog.

When her gaze collided with Cort's, her heart wrenched painfully. Every fiber of her being shouted that she should look away, but she still felt unexplainably drawn to him.

She tried to force his tender and provocative kisses from her mind but found it difficult. Never would she have envisioned feeling this way for him. It would be impossible to deny this fascination he held for her. The man had only to touch her, and every shred of her willpower dissolved.

Once again, she tried to concentrate on Earc, but couldn't

manage to do it. Despite her frustration at Cort, she still burned for him. When his arm brushed against hers, a sizzling sensation exploded across her skin. She started to scoot down the bench away from his large warmth, but he pulled her back.

"Don't," he said in a low voice. "Stay here and behave as a proper wife."

"Why should I worry about you saving face?" she whispered, nearly intoxicated by his male scent.

"Because like it or not, you're married to me. My reputation reflects on you."

"Wonderful."

Cort leaned closer to whisper in her ear, his breath hot and moist, "Once upon a time, not so long ago, you writhed with pleasure in my arms as we made love. What happened to change all of that?"

A shiver of pleasant remembrance trickled down her spine. "Did you forget what happened today?"

"There are some problems I need to work out. What's that got to do with us?"

"Everything."

"Are you going to sit here and tell me you never enjoyed the passion between us?"

She tapped her toe impatiently, feeling like a bug trapped beneath a rock. "Very well. I admit I've enjoyed our time together. That doesn't mean anything."

He lifted a brow. "Ah ha. Now I know you've only been using me for your pleasure. I'm wounded. Do I mean naught to you?"

"You're incorrigible." Rhiannon's cheeks filled with burning heat. He'd tricked her into saying that. Clever man. How had he turned this conversation around so easily?

At the sound of King Henry's jovial laugh, they both turned to watch him. He leaned forward, elbows propped on his knees, watching Earc.

Earc's vivid hand gestures regaled a tale of the legendary

seer-warrior Fionn Mac Cumhaill. As the story progressed, Earc explained how Fionn gained his wisdom as a boy by tasting the salmon of knowledge. This had helped him triumph over ancient giants and evil magicians. Earc talked of the Lugh next; a Celtic god who slew his grandfather because of his gruesome eye that destroyed everything it gazed upon.

As King Henry's laughter boomed across the room, he beckoned with a curled finger to a woman in a low-cut red gown. When she approached, he pulled her into his lap, slapping her ample backside.

Rhiannon wrinkled her nose with disapproval. Apparently, the rumors of King Henry's extramarital exploits were true. He was a man with a roving eye, to be sure. His gaze sought not only women, but new countries to conquer.

Josette tossed another arrogant glance at Rhiannon, and she sent one back, full of equal venom. That woman may think she had the upper hand by coming here and swearing Cort had fathered her child. But Rhiannon would never let her take what was hers. Cort was her husband. He belonged to her. They would have children and rule this land together.

She blinked hard several times as bewilderment wound its way through her. Where had that thought come from? One minute, she was irritated at him, now she found herself ready to do battle with the hussy across the table if she threatened her marriage.

What's gotten into me?

"And that, ladies and gents, is how Ireland gained its fightin' warrior spirit." Earc thumped his fist against his chest, signaling the end to his story. He bowed before the crowd, unashamed of the hump that bulged at the back of his tunic.

Rather than letting his deformity hinder him, he had capitalized on his differences. He told people that his hump was where he stored the knowledge of his tales. Others, too superstitious to know otherwise, rubbed the hump for luck. Earc encouraged their curiosity, charging people a few coins for the privilege of touching his misshapen form.

At the sound of a child's cry, Rhiannon glanced around to see a servant carrying a babe, not more than a year old, into the room. She handed the child to Josette, who made a huge fuss about arranging the blankets over his chubby legs.

Rhiannon watched, nearly torn in two, as the woman walked around the table. Cort rose as she handed the child to him. With awkward gestures, he held the boy in his arms. Gurgling happily, the baby reached up and played with his nose. Cort grinned.

"This is your son, Cort. I named him Fitz after your uncle." A catty expression crossed Josette's face. "Aren't you pleased?"

A pain exploded in Rhiannon, as if someone had thrown a knife into her heart. While she had no ill will toward the child, she couldn't stand by and watch the tender scene unfolding.

Feeling as though she were the outsider who didn't belong, she shrank away from the sight. She hurried toward the stairs, eager to be gone. In her room, she bolted the door and leaned against it, attempting to catch her breath.

Outside the window, lightning sliced through the sky, illuminating the heavens with an eerie glow. Could the nasty weather be a bad omen of things to come? Shaking off her silly fears, she lay down on the bed, trying to make sense of the thoughts racing through her mind.

Sobs threatened, but she stifled them by stuffing a fist in her mouth.

ELEVEN

CORT STUDIED THE CHILD IN HIS arms, deciding he bore no resemblance to either himself or Josette. The little boy had a tuft of soft yellow hair and bright blue eyes. Both he and Josette had dark wavy hair and brown eyes. He'd observed many infants who didn't reflect the looks of their parents. Nevertheless, he couldn't shake off the idea that Josette had somehow concocted this scheme to try and deceive him.

She had much to gain if he decided to acknowledge her child. On the other hand, he could always send her and the boy away. But if Fitz was his son, he wanted to have a say in his upbringing. He wouldn't be like his own father and not give a damn about the offspring he'd sired, legitimate or not.

He wouldn't know for certain if Josette told the truth until Raoul returned. Hopefully, his friend would be swift in providing answers. Until then, Cort refused to turn out Josette and the child into the streets.

"Isn't he adorable?" Josette smiled fetchingly.

"He's a baby," Cort commented. "All babies are endearing."

He handed the child back to Josette and her mouth drew into a pout. "Don't you want to hold him longer?"

"Not right now."

"He has your chin, don't you think?"

"If you say so."

Josette reached out to take Cort's hand and he brushed it away.

"I assume you'll be needing help with Fitz, so I've hired a nursemaid. She'll be here on the morrow."

"How thoughtful." Josette jounced the child on her hip. "I knew you'd be pleased to see us. Is there somewhere private where we could talk?"

He ignored her wheedling tone. "Don't get the idea that we're going to start up our affair again, Josette. You and the child will be provided for, and that's as far things between us will go."

Glancing around, he noticed Rhiannon's absence. When had she left? Ignoring Josette's angry red face, he excused himself and went in search of his wife. He looked a couple of places before he headed to their bed chamber. To his surprise, the lock had been secured. Aggravation fired his senses.

"Rhiannon, let me in. Right now. We need to talk."

"There's nothing we need to discuss," she called out.

"Yes, there is," he growled. "There are things you don't understand. Now open up before I force my way in." When she didn't respond, he rammed the heavy oak with his shoulder until the wood cracked and gave way.

Rhiannon stood there with her arms crossed over her chest. Despite the proud set of her jaw, he could tell by her mottled face that she'd been crying. Her defiant nature also couldn't hide the pain reflected in her emerald eyes.

"Never lock the door on me, woman. It will not go well for you if you do."

"Don't threaten me, Norman. What are you going to do? Whip me?"

"I should punish you somehow." Cort scowled, refusing to allow his wife's infuriating attitude to make him behave like an animal. He wanted to win her love with kindness and understanding—not brute force.

"Why are you here, Norman?" Rhiannon pointed toward the

door, now hanging awkwardly on its hinges. "Go take care of Josette and your son. Leave me alone."

"Rhiannon, what's gotten into you?"

"I may have longed for your touch at one time, but no longer," she spat. "You mean nothing to me now."

It occurred to him that she was suffering. At what point had she begun giving a damn about him? Her change of heart struck a chord within him, and he wondered about his own feelings toward her.

To fulfill his bargain with Moran, he'd taken Rhiannon to wife. He'd never considered his relationship with her beyond duty and honor. But as time passed, his feelings about her had gone beyond simply fulfilling a promise to a dying man.

Had her feelings for him bypassed mere duty as well?

"*Sacre bleu*, woman, you're jealous. Aren't you?"

"Nay. Absolutely not. I couldn't care less if you and Josette resume your affair. In fact . . ." She faked a yawn. "I could use some rest. Your demands of late have completely worn me out."

His lips trembled with a smile, but he resisted the urge. He did not want to make light of her emotions and perhaps embarrass her.

"As far as I can tell, you have been enjoying yourself, my lady wife," he pointed out. "If I recall correctly, you begged for more."

When Rhiannon reached out to slap him, he caught her small, soft hand.

Uncurling it, he pressed his lips to the soft flesh if her palm and heard her sharp inhale of breath. Closing her eyes, she shuddered as his lips trailed up her arm. He paused at her face and looked deeply into her eyes so that she could see his sincerity.

"Never, *ever* try to strike me again," he warned. "I am a fair man, Rhiannon, but I will only tolerate so much. Treat me as your husband please, not as a cur dog that has come begging on your doorstep."

He pulled her against him and lowered his mouth onto hers. He stroked her back and her supple, inviting curves. She was his for the taking, and he felt confident he could break down her resistance.

At first, she squirmed in his embrace, but the more ardent he became, the more she relaxed. Her whimpers of protest quickly turned into breathless moans.

When she lay quietly in his arms, his blood ran like molten lava through his veins. Sweet *Jesu* how he wanted her! Enjoying her sweet surrender, he deepened his kiss.

He pulled away and stared down at her. "I know you want me, beautiful lady. Will you lie and tell me otherwise?"

She shook her head. "No. But I don't like being manipulated like a puppet."

"I know things are confusing right now," Cort said. Believe me, I never expected Josette to show up with a child or King Henry to lay claim to this property. But I promise, I will work it all out in a way that you agree with."

Tears spiked the end of Rhiannon's lashes and Cort felt his heart squeeze.

"Thank you," she said quietly.

"I need something from you," Cort insisted. "Be my wife and honor our marital vows. Will you do that?"

Emotions crossed her face like storm clouds. Distress and fear combined with something that seemed like admiration for him. Did she understand what he needed?

"Cort? Where are you?" Josette's voice echoed in the hallway.

Rhiannon instantly stiffened. "Mayhap it's best you go to her. She obviously needs you."

"Damn her hide. I hate that I ever took her into my bed," Cort admitted.

"I told you she doesn't intend to leave you alone."

"I'll just have to be more convincing the next time I tell her we're through. You remember that I'll be leaving with King Henry at first light to take him on a tour of Leinster, right?"

She nodded.

"We'll talk more when I return. I promise."

"Cort darling? I saw you come up here." Josette's whiny voice had become louder as it echoed down the hall.

"Don't worry," Rhiannon said coldly. "I won't embarrass you in front of King Henry or anyone else. I'll behave as a proper wife should. Just don't expect me to welcome you into my bed with that woman cavorting around."

In one quick movement, she slid back into the bed chamber and shut the door. Something scraped across the floor, then *thunked* against the wood. Cort frowned. He could have easily dislodged the furniture she'd obviously placed there, but he decided it wasn't worth the effort. It would be best to leave Rhiannon alone for now to nurse her bruised feelings.

Fists clenched, he stormed down the hall and nearly collided with Josette.

"What do you need?" He gritted his teeth, barely able to stand the sight of her. "Aren't your accommodations sufficient?"

"I'm not in a mood to be toyed with, Guyot." Plucking his sleeve, she studied him with a pout. "You dumped me like a sack of wheat once you were done with me. There are consequences from our affair that you must acknowledge. Namely your son."

"Rest assured, I intend to do the right thing by you and the child. If he is my child." He shook off her grip.

She arched a thin brow. "You have my word."

"Your word isn't worth a cobbler's nail," he shot back. "I need proof."

"You can't turn me out. It would be cruel and heartless, and your father wouldn't allow it."

"No one's turning you out, Josette. I do intend to find out what you're up to. So be prepared to explain yourself."

Josette jutted out her chin. "I've only told the truth."

"We'll see," he growled.

"Hmmph." Josette strutted back down the hall.

Cort regretted every minute he'd ever spent with that woman.

She was a liar and a troublemaker. He should have known better than to involve himself with her.

Now it had come to this.

He slammed his fist against the wall, bloodying his knuckles. Cursing under his breath, he went outside and strode toward his men's tents. Sleeping on the cold ground would serve as a good reminder that he had a difficult time ahead. Dealing with both Rhiannon and Josette would be a full-time occupation.

RHIANNON AWAKENED THE NEXT MORNING, YAWNING as light slanted across her bed. Her stomach felt as though it had begun to gnaw itself in two. She rose and stretched, then crossed over to the window and stared out at the undulating, sapphire sea.

Yesterday had been awful. From the moment the day started, it seemed like nothing but calamity had befallen.

King Henry's and Josette's arrival were upsetting. Yet there was nothing she could do but stand by and let the situation play itself out . . . and behave as a proper wife should. For some reason, the idea didn't disturb her as much as before, and her irritation at Cort had lessened.

Her stomach growled and pitched, reminding her she needed to eat. She removed her nightgown and sponged off, then scrubbed her teeth with a clean cloth. After donning undergarments, she dressed in a simple gown and hurried downstairs, wondering if Cort had left yet.

No doubt he'd spent the night in his men's tents, or perhaps he'd slept in Josette's bed, though she doubted it. He'd seemed none too pleased with the woman's presence. Part of her had become convinced that Cort never expected his previous mistress to come calling.

Opening the front doors, she glanced out into the bailey where several horses snorted and stomped. She waved at her father who sat astride his mount. When he lifted a gauntleted hand in farewell, she noted the crinkles around his eyes and sensed his weariness.

Why did he push himself so hard these days, knowing they were numbered?

Her heart wrenched at the idea of losing her father and she didn't know how she could bear it.

Searlas sat near Moran atop his horse. King Henry rode at his side, his English soldiers armed with shields and iron-tipped lances.

Her breath caught in her throat when she saw Cort lead his horse from the stable, his strong bearing filling her with pride. He wore his hauberk today, along with tight chausses and tall leather boots. Like a raven's wing, his dark hair gleamed in the sun as he sheathed his sword at his side.

It surprised her to realize that at one time, not that long ago, she'd been afraid of him. Unease still lived in her, but she realized it stemmed from the idea that he stirred sensual, wild thoughts.

Also, she disliked the idea that he could ride away from here and never return. Once she had wanted that. Now she had a hard time even considering the possibility.

As though sensing her intense perusal, he looked over at her. Their gazes locked and though unspoken, a million questions glimmered between them.

What about Josette and the child? What about King Henry and his claim to Ireland? Rhiannon wanted desperately to discuss these things with Cort.

However, it would be impossible for them to have any time together this morning. Cort's duty to King Henry beckoned. She brightened, thinking that at least she could give him a favor to send him on his way.

Sprinting down the castle steps, she approached him. Her hands trembled as she undid the clasp on her necklace—a golden cross her father had given her long ago. She handed it to him, feeling almost shy.

"Travel in safety, husband," she told him in a trembling voice.

Cort slid the chain around his neck, then caught her fingers in his large, gauntleted hand. He kissed them, his lips a whisper upon her skin, sending a thrill up her spine.

"I will return, I promise," he told her in a sincere tone. "And all will be well."

He slid on his helmet and their gazes held for another breathless second. Then he lowered his visor and swung onto his mount. Gripping his shield, which bore a red griffon, he cantered over to the mounted party. A moment later they rode from Callinon.

Rhiannon hurried through the bailey and climbed the steps to the castle wall. At the sight of the mounted troops and foot soldiers swarming over the hills as far as the eye could see, her mouth parted in awe. Campfires from the English army, located a distance from the castle, had been visible up until now, yet she'd never imagined the troops would cover such a vast amount of land.

Watching the party march north, King Henry's colorful pennants flying, her gaze sought Cort. She thought she spotted him, but couldn't be certain. *I wish he wouldn't go.* Surprised at the strength of her feelings, she realized the concern welling in her chest couldn't be denied.

She must admit she cared for him, even though recent developments made it difficult for her to understand him. Lord knows she wanted to, but frustration tugged at her heart.

When the army disappeared from sight, taking her husband with it, she felt strangely empty. She already missed Cort's steady, assuring presence. The day ahead seemed overwhelming.

She did not look forward to an encounter with Josette and potentially having to listen to her steady whining. The very idea put a bad taste in her mouth. Hoping that breakfast would help dispel the sourness in her belly; she went to the kitchen where she found Glenna discussing the day's meals with the Leila, the cook.

"Both you and your sister are quite the sleepyheads this morning," Glenna said. "King Henry just spirited off your husband and father on his grand tour."

"I know, I saw them leave." Rhiannon sat down at a wooden table. Reaching into a bowl of apples, removed one and bit into the crisp, tart fruit. "No doubt King Henry will take stock of the villages so he can decide which to plunder first."

"None of us like it, child," Glenna said. "But we've no choice in the matter, especially since the Church of England backs him."

"The man is a monster." Rhiannon took another bite of apple and chewed, feeling the gnawing in her stomach abate.

"Rhiannon, it does no good to defy fate and complain about events that are beyond our control," Glenna said.

"I hate feeling so helpless." Rhiannon set the apple core aside, licking the juice from her fingers. She stopped when a thought crossed her mind. "What of Josette and the child? Did Cort say anything about what's to be done with them?"

"Just that they're to stay here for the time being."

"Great."

"Don't be petty," Glenna warned. "What else could he do?"

"I know. But while King Henry drags him across the countryside, we'll be tending to her and the child. It's humiliating."

"It's the right thing to do."

Rhiannon sighed. "Of course. And I promised Cort that I'd tolerate her. I don't have to like it though."

"I don't blame you, Rhiannon," Glenna admitted. "This can't be easy."

"I need to get away from here for a while, so I don't have to put up with her catty comments." Rhiannon tapped her fingers on the table. "I think I'll go for a ride."

"That's a good idea. Perhaps Ailleen would like to go with you."

"I'll go rouse her lazy bones out of bed."

Looking forward to spending time with her little sister, Rhiannon climbed the stairs to the little girl's room and knocked. When Ailleen didn't answer, she frowned with concern. Opening the door, she looked around. Her sister wasn't in bed and twisted covers were piled at the end of the mattress.

Rhiannon searched in the hallway next, then the great hall. Growing more concerned by the minute, she continued to search. Ailleen wasn't in the garden or any of the grassy outdoor areas where she often played with servant children.

By now, nearly consumed with worry, Rhiannon climbed the stairs to the castle steward's office. Fortunately, she found Uther poring over a registry instead of out in the fields. When she told him Ailleen had gone missing, he gathered everyone in the great hall and instructed them to start searching.

Josette, who had wandered into the room to see what was going on, raised a haughty brow. "Has the girl wandered off before?"

"No," Rhiannon told her, her patience nearly at a breaking point.

"I am merely trying to help," she said petulantly. "I thought mayhap she had a tendency to do this sort of thing. I'd hate to think she's fallen down a well or off a cliff."

Rhiannon inhaled sharply. "Did you do something to hurt Ailleen out of spite for me? By Saint Briget, if you've hurt my little sister—"

"Don't be ridiculous," Josette shot back. "I've been taking care of Fitz all night. How could I have had the time to do anything to her?"

Uther glared at Josette. "Ladies let's focus on the task at hand. We must find Lady Ailleen."

"I believe I know where she is." Leila crossed herself. "The same place my Ena has been taken."

"Where?" Rhiannon asked anxiously.

"I fear the *si*-people carried them both away to their secret kingdom."

"You think the fairies took my sister?" She struggled with rising frustration. "That's nonsense."

"Little Ailleen's been seein' spirits, I tell you," the cook continued. "I think they took her away because she's a sensitive. The *si*-people worship humans who have special abilities and use them as familiars."

"As much as I believe in our local tales, I think that's utter blarney," Glenna said.

"I agree." Uther nodded. "I'll gather some of the local boys and we'll search around the castle. It shouldn't take long to find her."

The staff wandered off, muttering in low voices. Rhiannon hated that Leila had planted in everyone's minds the idea that the little people might be involved. They may not look as thoroughly, believing they couldn't outwit dark magical forces.

Father Murphy approached her, his long robes brushing the floor. He patted her hand comfortingly. "I'll pray for your sister's safe return my lady. Surely the Lord wouldn't let such an innocent be harmed."

"Thank you, Father," Rhiannon said.

"I'm going to search the chapel from top to bottom," Father Murphy promised. "Maybe she went there to pray."

As he left, she and Glenna went upstairs for a thorough search of the castle. They checked the spinning room and all the empty chambers, including the storeroom. Despite their efforts, they still didn't find her.

Something nagged at Rhiannon, urging her to return to Ailleen's room.

Glenna followed close on her heels. "I thought you'd already checked here."

"I have a strange feeling I missed something."

Inside Ailleen's room, she ran her hands across the tops of chests and sorted through toys. She paced back and forth, studying every nook and cranny, but still saw nothing out of place.

Something on the bed flashed in the sunlight pouring in through the window, and Rhiannon rushed toward it, shaking out the blankets. An object thudded onto the floor. *A dagger, carved with ancient runes.* As her hand closed around the hilt of the knife, she trembled with rage.

She recognized the blade immediately. It belonged to Donovan.

TWELVE

"**E**NGLISH BASTARD!" A TALL, STRAPPING MAN with wavy black hair spit on the ground in front of King Henry's horse. King Henry's royal guards bristled and reached for their weapons. Searlas and Moran both backed up their horses, their faces creased with alarm.

Cort's mount pranced skittishly, and he gave it a calming pat. He didn't have a doubt in his mind this irate villager could snap the pampered king in two if given the opportunity. He'd never get the opportunity. If he lifted another finger, King Henry's guards would cleave him in two.

Several days had passed since they he'd begun escorting the English king throughout Leinster and the surrounding countryside. Up until now, they'd only been met with curiosity and bold stares. But here in the village of Bradaigh, they'd run up against troublemakers.

He realized King Henry and his troops could easily take on the poorly armed men, but it would result in a total bloodbath. After all of Cort's strides to gain the people's trust, that type of incident would destroy their faith in him.

"If ya think to conquer the Irish," the man continued, "yer in fer one helluva fight."

His followers shook their crude weapons threateningly and shouted taunts.

King Henry held up his hand, restraining his guards. "How dare you show such disrespect to your liege lord? I should have you whipped."

"Try it. You'll have us breathing down your neck."

"You fool," King Henry growled. "What is your name?"

"Jamie O'Brien. And I won't back down from some blue blood English king who thinks he owns Ireland." A fire of indignation burned in his eyes.

Anger flared in Cort. So, this was the man Rhiannon had cared for. He envisioned this filth kissing her, and a knife of pain lanced his heart. How could she ever have loved him? The thought of how O'Brien had hurt and betrayed his wife, and the O'Kelly's, made Cort want to punch him.

"King Henry's not here to start trouble," Moran explained. "He's goin' to help us join our clans so we can live in peace and rebuild our country."

"Aye," O'Brien barked. "I've heard how the English rebuild countries. They rape, ransack and pillage. They're nothing more than greedy sots!"

"Seize him," King Henry growled. "We'll allow none of this insolence."

In a heartbeat, two men-at-arms dismounted, grabbed O'Brien's shoulders, and jerked his hands behind his back.

Cort felt like letting King Henry's guards give O'Brien what he deserved. But if things got ugly and Irishmen were killed, other rebellious factions might feel it necessary to avenge their deaths. Ireland already dealt with enough political unrest. There didn't need to be more—not if he had anything to say about it.

He swung down from his horse and approached the man, surprised at the vehemence of his own manner. "Stop acting like a lunatic, O'Brien. Apologize to King Henry."

He struggled in the guards' grasp, his gaze fiery. "I will not."

"Then you'll be jailed. Your choice."

King Henry waved a hand at him. "What are you doing, Guyot?"

"You've given me Lordship of this province. Allow me to handle this recalcitrant subject. That is unless he wishes to rot in prison."

O'Brien scuffed the dirt with a cracked boot, but finally said, "I'm sorry, *your highness*. I was rude."

King Henry pierced him with a hard stare. "Very well—you've been spared this day. But mark my word, Jamie O'Brien, I'll remember your name. If you dare show such lack of respect in the future, you will not be so fortunate."

Cort couldn't help but notice the defiant gleam in O'Brien's eyes. A sense of foreboding washed over him as he mounted his horse. Hopefully they wouldn't run into any other disgruntled people or King Henry may not be so easily persuaded to let them live.

"Let us continue our excursion," King Henry declared. "We wish to see more of this wild country with its undisciplined people."

O'Brien grunted and stormed away with his followers. Grumbling to each other, they disappeared inside a pub.

Cort frowned. If Jamie were seen as a martyr by his comrades, there could be trouble brewing. As they rode to the next village, he contemplated the disturbing possibility of an Irish uprising.

When he'd first arrived with his troops, it had been a relatively simple and non-violent blending of Norman and Irish objectives as he'd traveled the countryside. Because of his marriage to Rhiannon, the people soon accepted that his troops meant to assimilate into their way of life; not change it.

King Henry, however, demanded they swear fealty to him and insisted they respect English customs and laws. Cort realized if O'Brien or another headstrong leader like him instigated unrest, there would be a mass slaughter of Irishmen.

Rhiannon and her impulsive ways drifted through his mind. No wonder she had such a fiery personality; she came by it naturally. She hailed from a long line of proud Irish ancestors. Having pride was a good thing, if it didn't become misplaced.

He'd strive to help the Irish avert disaster, but there was only so much he could do. As far as his willful wife was concerned, if she got out of hand, he would have his father take her to Normandy where she would be out of harm's way. Only when things settled down would he allow her to return.

Cort knew Rhiannon would argue against that idea, but he had a responsibility to keep her safe. The intense protectiveness he had for his wive surged through him, catching him off guard. He gripped his horse's reins tighter, realizing he'd never felt that way about a woman before.

Did it have to do with the fact that Moran had made him promise to take care of her? Deep down, he sensed it stemmed from something of a different nature. That opened a whole new realm of possibilities he didn't feel prepared to deal with right now.

Josette and Fitz came next in his thoughts. Hopefully there would be no more trouble with that state of affairs. He counted on Raoul to find out what sort of mischief the woman had stirred up. Once it had been resolved, he and Rhiannon could focus on their marriage and their duties to Ireland.

A sense of satisfaction washed over him. That's how he liked to take care of problems; attack them head on and get them resolved before they bubbled over into a huge mess.

He spurred his horse onward, watching the lush green countryside pass. The sooner they finished with King Henry's expedition, the sooner Cort could focus on the business of running Leinster and his new landholdings.

Rhiannon's face flashed in his mind, and he allowed himself to dwell on thoughts of his lady wife. He looked forward to returning to her, which he found very interesting. Most men would shrink from the duty of dealing with a woman who had an astute mind of her own.

Yet he found it challenging.

He enjoyed the spirited dialogue they often shared, for none of the women he'd ever known had such a lively way of conversing as Rhiannon did. Mayhap the pleasant task of teaching her the various methods of lovemaking intrigued him the most. He sighed.

His wife's disturbing disregard for danger and her impulsive nature sat on the top of his list of items to be dealt with. Helping her curb her enthusiasm could prove to be the biggest test of all.

His mind drifted back to the time they had spent in each other's arms. It occurred to him despite the difficulty he faced in dealing with her, there would be many perks along the way. Taking her to bed being the most important of all.

Sweet *Jesu*, making love to her was something he could definitely get used to.

"MY LADY, 'TIS LATE AND THE men are bone weary," Uther told Rhiannon as they rode through the forest. "We must stop."

Rhiannon realized she'd pushed them hard today, as well for the past several days. She, Uther and ten of her father's men had been following a trail that led toward Donovan's land. It still amazed her he'd managed to get into Callinon Castle, but she decided he must have found a way in through their secret escape route. It hadn't been used in ages and Moran held it a strictly guarded secret in case his people had to escape during a siege. She felt certain Donovan had discovered it.

But how?

Glenna had begged her not to go off searching for Ailleen; had pleaded with her to wait for Cort and her father to return. Yet Rhiannon raged against the idea, refusing to leave her sister with Donovan any longer than she had to. There could be no telling what that monster had in mind.

With every breath she possessed, she vowed to find Ailleen. No doubt the little girl would be scared witless. Every moment she spent in Donovan's clutches was one too many.

"I'm sorry Uther. It's just that I'm so worried about my sister." She sighed as exhaustion sifted into her bones.

"Aye, my lady," Uther said, his horses' reins threaded through his fingers. "We all are."

Lavender twilight had begun to draw a blanket of darkness over the horizon. Uther had a point—night would be upon them before long. The men's faces were lined with exhaustion and they all must be starved.

"Let's make camp," Rhiannon said with reluctance. "But we leave at first light."

Uther nodded grimly.

They found a grassy clearing with a stream where the horses could be picketed. Rhiannon dug out a cauldron and food supplies. Before long, she had a hearty stew bubbling over a fire. The men settled down to eat, murmuring their approval.

She sat on a fallen log with her supper. After only a few bites, nausea rippled through her and she put down her bowl. The queasiness had increased lately, and she fought it constantly. Even certain smells made her dizzy and her stomach lurched at the most inopportune moments.

Counting backward, she realized several weeks had passed since she should have had her woman's flow. *I must be carrying Cort's child.* The idea both frightened and intrigued her. Many women died in childbirth, but many lived. She was young and strong—she should be fine.

What would Cort think about her condition? She sensed he would be happy, as was she. She'd always wanted to be a mother. Marriage bound her to the Norman forever, but a child would create a more powerful link between them.

Additionally, this child, son or daughter, would stand to inherit Callinon. The idea encouraged her even further. As Moran had predicted, their kingdom would stay in the O'Kelly line. Once again, she could see the sense in her father's decision that she marry the Norman.

Warmth, that had nothing to do with the crackling campfire, filled her. Her affection had grown for Cort, despite her initial reluctance to join with him. Did he feel the same way? She admonished herself for her silly thoughts. There wasn't time to dwell on them.

Putting her feelings for Cort aside, along with the realization that she carried his child, she thought of the task at hand. Pregnancy wouldn't stop her from searching for Ailleen. She vowed Donovan would rue the day he ever dared to step on O'Kelly land, let alone kidnap one of their own.

"Did we find any more wee bits of cloth today?" Uther settled at her side with his supper.

Drawn from her introspection, she fished out a piece of red material that she'd put in her pants pocket. "Aye."

"Your sister is surely a clever girl for leaving clues in tree branches." He scooped stew from his bowl with a chunk of bread and stuffed it in his mouth.

"Aye. The pieces of cloth belong to the skirt of Ailleen's favorite doll. They're helpful as they mark the trail we must follow."

"It worries me, though." Uther squinted into the dark forest. "Mayhap the trail is too well marked. This could be a trap."

The men muttered amongst themselves, voicing the same concerns she had entertained.

"We need to be especially careful. Watch for anything suspicious." She nibbled on her bread, ignoring her queasiness. She needed her strength for the battle she knew loomed ahead. Especially carrying a child, she couldn't starve herself. She'd make both herself and the babe ill.

A shiver of uneasiness crawled up her spine as she thought of something she hadn't before. Cort already had a son with Josette, so what would her child be to him? Though illegitimate, he'd made it clear Fitz would always hold a place in his heart. However, their child would be his legal heir.

Though she still suspected Cort hadn't been entirely truthful with her, she had strong feelings for him. One look at his face and her heart pattered like a trapped dragonfly's wings. One touch, one magical kiss, and her spirit soared.

Could such simple things make up for his lack of candor? She didn't think straight when it came to him. What kind of life would she have if she tolerated his disloyalty? How much disappointment would the man eventually cause her?

Pressing a palm against her abdomen, she reminded herself no one could know the future, except perhaps old Sybil. Even the prophetess's methods of divining events still remained suspect. Rhiannon recalled her visit to the crone and what she'd said.

In the end, all will be well. But there will be trouble along the way.

So far, the trouble part had come true. She wished they would get to the part where everything would work out. Rising from the log and stretching, she decided her choice to wear boy's attire had been a good one. The shirt, tunic and sturdy trousers were more practical for a long journey.

"I'm going to lie down now," she told Uther.

"Sleep well my lady," Uther said with a nod. "We'll all be taking turns with the watch."

"Wake me when it's mine."

Gathering her blankets, she spread them near the campfire. Making sure her sword sat within reach, she crawled under the covers, feeling the warmth of the flames on her cheeks. Anxiety stifled her ability to relax, and she stared, transfixed, at the stars.

Thoughts of Ailleen assailed her, and she wondered what she might have done better to prevent her from being kidnapped. Why hadn't she watched the little girl closer?

It's all my fault.

At last, she drifted into a troubled sleep.

MORNING LIGHT SLANTED ACROSS THE SPRAWLING military camp as Cort emerged from his tent. He glanced around at the soldiers preparing for the day's ride and watched King Henry milling outside of his tent, conversing with his guards.

After the confrontation with O'Brien several days ago, no one else had challenged the English soldiers' presence. Hopefully that would be the end of the Irish unrest, but Cort had a sneaking suspicion it wouldn't be.

He walked to his horse and plopped the saddle on its back. As he tightened the straps, a rider crashed through the trees. Guards rushed to subdue him, but recognizing Callinon's stable boy, Cort shouted to let him through.

Quinn jumped down and led his horse toward him. "Sir Cort . . . I must talk to you. 'Tis urgent."

He frowned. "Catch your breath, boy. What is it?"

Moran emerged from his tent and hurried toward Quinn, lines of concern etching his face.

"Ailleen has been taken." Quinn rested his hands on his knees and gulped at the air.

"My little sprite." Moran's face fell. "What's being done to find her?"

"Uther took a contingent . . . of castle guards . . . to search. Lady Rhiannon . . . she went with."

"*Sacre bleu.*" Cort shoved his hands on his hips. "Where did they go?"

"Lady Rhiannon found Donovan's dagger in Ailleen's bedroom. We figure he got in through our secret escape route and kidnapped her. They've gone after him."

Moran pressed his lips together in a thin line, his drawn expression revealing his concern. As a father, he no doubt placed blame on himself that the girl had gone missing.

Cort knew full well Rhiannon could handle herself in practically any situation, but that still didn't prevent him from worrying.

"Glenna tried to stop Lady Rhiannon from going, but she refused to listen," Quinn added. "She's out for blood."

Moran shook his head. "What did she say?"

"She's sworn to kill Donovan. That's why Glenna sent me to find you. She's afraid."

"How long ago did all this happen?" Cort raked a hand through his unruly hair and began to pace. Mixed emotions raced through him as he thought of Rhiannon in danger. Alarm and irritation swirled in a morass of thoughts, along with his fears for her safety.

"I had a difficult time finding you," Quinn admitted. "It's been a couple of weeks."

"Once again, I've failed to protect my girls. I've got to find them." Moran started to walk away, then pressed a hand against his chest and winced.

Cort laid a hand on Moran's shoulder. "I'll go. You stay with King Henry."

Moran examined him and nodded slowly. "I'm afraid I'm in no shape to argue with you. Don't disappoint me, Guyot."

"I won't." Cort turned to Quinn. "Go fetch yourself some breakfast, boy. I'm sure there's bread and ale still available."

"Yes sir." Quinn headed over to where the food was spread out on a small trestle table.

Moran spoke again, his voice punctuated with pain and disappointment. "I fear I've botched things badly. I'm a failure as a ruler and as a father. Now, my daughters are in danger again."

"You couldn't have seen this coming." Cort noted the dark circles spreading beneath Moran's eyes. He'd seen the man's health growing steadily worse over the last days and felt powerless to help him.

"I know Rhiannon was confused and hurt by my insistence that you two marry, but I still believe it was the right thing," Moran said to Cort. "You're a good man."

They shook hands and Cort could feel the weakness in Moran's grip. He knew he would do everything in his power to maintain the man's trust. He'd never had a true father, and in the short space of time he'd known Moran, the Irish king taken that place in Cort's heart.

"I'll find your daughters and bring them back sir. You have my word."

RHIANNON CAME AWAKE QUICKLY IN THE silvery light of pre-dawn. Something didn't seem right; she could feel it in her bones. Eerie forest sounds echoed—an owl's hooting, wild creatures calling to each other. A heavy mist drifted inland from the sea, swirling around bushes and trees and swathing them in a pale shroud of mystery.

Anxious, she stood and rubbed her tingling arms. The fine hair on the nape of her neck stood on end and she shivered. She glanced around, acutely sensing danger, but not seeing anything amiss.

The men were still sleeping, their weapons within reach. Artur had taken the watch and sat upon a hill, which gave him a bird's eye view of the countryside. Suddenly, the bushes behind him parted and several warriors emerged.

"Donovan," she gritted out, alarmed, but not surprised he'd found them.

She cried out a warning to Artur, but the warriors cut him down before he had a chance to hear her. Uther and the other men instantly sprang awake and seized their swords, battle axes, and war hatchets, as the warriors attacked.

"Flee my lady," Uther shouted at Rhiannon.

"I will not!" She hefted her shorter, broader sword—a weapon that was easier for her to handle. Releasing a bitter cry, she joined in the defense.

With a start, she realized they were outnumbered three to one. Fatigue crept through her, yet she continued to fight, encouraged each time a man crumpled at the tip of her sword.

One after another her father's men fell, yet she refused to admit defeat. Releasing an outraged cry, she fought with renewed vigor.

Being small, it was easy for her to dodge the enemy's sword thrusts. Nevertheless, their blades nicked her over and over, like one thousand bee stings. Warm blood dripped on her skin, but fortunately her wounds were only superficial.

Hearing thundering hooves, she glanced toward the break in the trees. Riders on horseback crashed toward them. For a moment she feared them to be enemy reinforcements, then she recognized Cort astride his black stallion. The men with him carried banners bearing King Henry's colors.

Relief washed over her, then a mighty thrust knocked the sword from her hand. A glancing blow sliced her arm and sharp agony rocked through her. Grabbing her wounded limb, she swirled to see one of Donovan's men aim for her again, but she managed to elude his next blow.

Seeing that she was now defenseless, the brute grinned broadly. He swiped at her with one meaty fist, and she tried to scramble away, but not before it smashed against her temple. Dazed, she slumped to the ground.

Agony tore through her and it felt as though she'd been trampled by a herd of horses. She struggled to maintain consciousness, but darkness teased the fringes of her mind. Her body trembled and she fought the shadowy wave threatening to overcome her.

A man with crooked, broken teeth leaned over her, his foul breath raking across her face. She tried to slap him away, but he sent another glancing blow to her temples.

As his laughter filled her ears, everything faded to black.

THIRTEEN

Cort and his soldiers engaged Donovan's warriors, easily cutting them down. Those that weren't mortally wounded ran off into the forest. Cursing the time it had taken his men to get here, he looked around. Judging by the bodies strewn across the glen, they'd nearly arrived too late.

Rhiannon.

A flash of long red hair caught his eye and he and turned toward it. One of Donovan's men carried her limp body.

"Put her down." Cort charged toward him, aware of nothing but the raw anger consuming him. His blade quickly found a home in the man's midsection. Grimacing, he toppled to the ground.

Cort withdrew his sword and knelt beside Rhiannon, gently rolling her over. Thank God she still breathed, for he could see her chest gently rising and falling. He lifted strands of matted hair from her bloody face, fearful of the wounds she'd sustained.

Upon examination, he discovered most of the blood wasn't hers. Except for the nasty gash on her arm and the swelling red bump on her forehead, she seemed unharmed. Relief filtered over him, along with admiration for his wife. She'd fought courageously.

"Rhiannon," he said softly. When she didn't respond, he removed his helmet so he could kiss her.

Her eyelids fluttered open. She cried out and began to pummel his chain mail with her small fists. Sharp words flew from her tongue as she began to curse at him in a language he'd come to know as Gaelic.

"Rhiannon, stop! It's me." Cort grabbed her wrists so she wouldn't bloody her knuckles any worse.

Her glazed eyes stared at him for a moment, transfixed, as though she didn't know who he was. Finally, as if a veil had been lifted, she released a small cry of recognition.

Cort gathered her in his arms. "Mad woman—you nearly got yourself killed."

"My father's men?" she muttered.

Cort silently shook his head.

"I led them into a trap," she sobbed. "It's my fault. I rushed in headlong to find Ailleen."

"Have you found her?"

"No, she's still with Donovan."

"We'll get her back." He stroked her hair, trying to calm her. When she fell silent, he realized she'd lost consciousness again. Scooping her into his arms he carried her over by his men.

"I need a pallet, blankets and hot water. And clean dressings."

"Yes, my lord." A page hurried to do his bidding.

"We'll make camp here." He winced at the carnage and turned to one of his men. "Help those you can and bury the others."

"Right away sir." The soldier hurried to carry out his orders.

Several hours later, Cort sat in a hastily assembled tent where he'd been maintaining a vigil beside Rhiannon's pallet. She'd never regained consciousness, though he'd cleansed her wounds and wrapped them in fresh bandages. Unfortunately, a fever had settled in.

"*Sheelin siofra orthanach adare . . .*" She writhed and twisted, flailing her arms and whimpering.

He gently pressed a cool, wet cloth against her forehead and bare limbs, fearful of the delirium she'd fallen into. Despite his ministrations, heat continued to rise from her skin. Her face had taken on a gray, ashen color and her lips had lost their moist luster. He could barely stand to watch her suffering and he ached for her discomfort.

What if she didn't survive?

He'd promised Moran to protect his daughters and bring them both home. What if he broke the dying man's heart by not fulfilling his vow? What if she died? What if he couldn't find Ailleen?

Filled with a strange realization, it occurred to him how much he actually cared for Rhiannon, as well as her little sister and father. He'd never had the luxury of knowing what it felt like to have loved ones. Now he had a wife. Her family had become his, and he couldn't bear the thought of losing any of them.

Drawing the covers up around Rhiannon, he blinked the mist from his eyes. Warriors were trained not to allow emotion to rule over reason. It could knock a man off his guard and potentially kill him. Sweet *Jesu*, he couldn't stop himself. Rhiannon hung on a thread between life and death, and it troubled him.

Uther parted the tent flaps and strode inside, his brow furrowed. "How is she?"

"Restless."

"She fought like a little wild cat today my lord. She saved many a life."

"She's a determined woman."

"You should be proud."

"I am," he said unsteadily. "I just can't believe she would put herself in harm's way like this."

"She loves her sister. There was no stopping her."

"Her emotions are fierce," Cort admitted. "Fiercer than any woman I've ever known."

"Aye. Rhiannon's always been like that. There's no gray area with her, only black and white."

"I've come to realize how strong her resolve is." Cort stroked his wife's cheek with his thumb. "She's made of stern stuff."

"Mayhap I can help her." Uther lifted up a leather pouch and a jar.

"How?" He eyed the contents of the jar—a brown, muddy paste. It didn't look so special to him.

"I've got a healing salve for the lady's wounds and a special tea."

"I doubt tea will help."

"This be no ordinary brew," Uther said with a chuckle. "It came from an old hag hawking her wares at the village market. She swore it be made of secret spices and healing herbs that come all the way from Asia. My wife, God rest her soul, purchased some. I thought she'd gone daft and had wasted our hard-earned coins. But praise the saints, the stuff really works."

Cort narrowed his gaze, wary of old wives' tales. "Are you sure? If we were back in Normandy, I'd fetch a physician to bleed her and rid her blood of impurities."

"Nay, bloodletting 'tis a foul and obscene practice," Uther insisted. "Mark my words, Sir Cort. My wife's medicines will heal Rhiannon in short order."

He considered Uther's offer, anxious to do anything and everything in his power to help Rhiannon. The castle steward had known her a long time and Cort recognized the affection shining in the old man's eyes. Instinctively, he knew Uther wouldn't do anything to hurt her.

"Go ahead."

Uther set down his things and went back outside. He returned with a kettle and a mug and poured hot water into the drinking receptacle. Whistling a merry tune, he pinched a bit of the dark tea into it and stirred it with a twig.

Cort lifted a brow. "Does the whistling help her, too?"

"Mayhap, my lord. Mayhap." Uther nodded at the jar. "Rub the salve into her wounds."

Cort removed bandages and applied the sticky brown substance. As soon as he touched Rhiannon's skin, she began her tossing and turning anew, muttering the same phrase in Gaelic.

"Sheelin siofra orthanach adare . . ."

He shook his head. "Do you know what she's saying, Uther?"

"'Tis nonsense, mostly." Uther reached up to scratch a hairy ear. "Something about a lake of the fairies and a sprite changeling. She talks about prayers and charms and an oak tree grove. Things from the old religion the Irish practiced, back before the coming of Christianity."

"Hasn't Rhiannon been a Christian all her life?"

"Aye, but her mother taught her the old language and the old ways through the tellin' of bedtime stories. Fiona believed since it was their heritage, both her daughters should be well schooled in Irish myth and lore as well as religion."

"That seems blasphemous to me," Cort said.

Uther shrugged. "Father Murphy didn't like it and told Fiona she was being disobedient, but she never listened to him. She insisted her girls should learn about their ancestors' beliefs as well as the Catholic religion so they could understand their people better."

Trying to conjure up an image of Rhiannon's mother in his mind, he decided she must have been as beautiful and spirited as her daughter. A wry grin touched his lips and he wished he'd been able to meet her.

"Hold Rhiannon up so I can get some of this down her gullet," Uther instructed.

As Cort lifted her head, Uther pressed the mug to her lips. When liquid dribbled into her mouth, she began to cough and sputter.

"There, there, my girl," the old man said soothingly. "You need to drink it all so ye can feel better."

She spit out a good amount of the strong-smelling liquid, but fortunately much of it had trickled down her throat.

When Uther finished, Cort laid Rhiannon back down and dabbed tea from her chin and neck with a towel.

"That ought to put her on the mend." Uther gathered up his things. "Keep watchin' over her as ye have been my lord. By tomorrow, she ought to be better."

"I hope so."

Uther squeezed his shoulder. "Rhiannon's always been a stalwart soul. Her mother didn't name her after an ancient Irish warrior goddess for nuthin'. She had a strong, healthy wail and a fightin' spirit from the day she came into this world."

Whistling his merry tune once again, Uther left the tent.

Cort kissed Rhiannon's forehead. Did her skin seem cooler? Did she seem to be resting easier? He didn't believe the tea could work this quickly, but she had stopped tossing and turning.

Dipping a cloth in the bucket of cool water, he wrung it out and pulled down the blankets so he could sponge her skin again. He dabbed the cloth gently over her flushed face, her neck and then down lower to her breasts.

He remembered the first time he'd seen her, her hair flying about her like wildfire, sparks of outrage in her green eyes. A smile touched his lips as he recalled how she'd threatened him, even though she'd been so weak from starvation she could barely hold a sword.

After a rocky start, it seemed they'd begun to sift through the confusion and build on their relationship. He found their challenging mental banter enjoyable, and her unique personality constantly intrigued him.

It surprised him how much he'd begun to look forward to seeing her each day; how much it brightened his world. The pleasure Rhiannon's body gave him wasn't the only thing he enjoyed about her. He wanted to know what made her happy, what made her sad, what she wanted for her future. She amazed and humbled him. He hungered to discover everything he could about her.

Recalling recent events, his insides clenched. King Henry's arrival had planted the seeds of doubt in her again. Josette's presence made her wonder about his true feelings for her. It seemed that whatever attachment they had begun to form had been blasted into a million pieces.

Only by being patient could Cort rebuild Rhiannon's trust.

Gritting his teeth, he realized how lousy his attempts were at doing that. It had been ingrained in his nature to bark orders and commands in order to accomplish goals. That would not work with Rhiannon.

Nothing else could be done but give her time to accept the way things were now. Not insurmountable tasks, but also not easy ones.

He kissed her cheek, his lips tingling as they touched her warm flesh. Hating to see her pride and her body crushed like this, he lifted her hand and held it firmly against his chest. He knew she not only hurt physically, but from mental anguish at the idea others had lost their lives today.

Over the years, he'd become hardened to war. Seeing men die in battle had never been easy to bear. But he had developed a way to deal with it and knew he could handle the pain better than her. If only he could take away her troubles right now and place them upon himself, he would do it in a heartbeat.

With a bolt of realization, he finally accepted what she meant to him. How in the world had he become so captivated by her in such a brief time?

Heart squeezing, he whispered in her ear, "Come back to me Rhiannon. Come back now . . ."

MISTS SWIRLED AROUND RHIANNON AS SHE walked through a shimmering white landscape filled with light. She squinted, trying to see better. After a few seconds, her vision cleared and she saw tall trees, rolling hills and grass shrouded in pale, wispy clouds.

Where am I?

She called out, but her voice seemed muffled, as though she spoke into a feather pillow. A peaceful sense of calm washed over her, and she had an overwhelming urge to rest. Just as she was about to sit on a blanket of fragrant pine needles, a cloaked figure emerged from behind a bush, whistling an old Irish lullaby.

Familiarity sparked in her and she approached the character, searching her memory. Then she recalled her mother singing the tune to her as a little girl.

"Mother? Is that you?"

The figure slid the hood down, revealing flaming red hair the color of Rhiannon's. "Yes, daughter. 'Tis me."

Overjoyed, she hurried to her mother, and they hugged. "What are you doing here? What is this place? I thought you were . . . aren't you . . ."

"Aye, lass, I've crossed over," she said with a nod.

Disbelief rippled through her. "How can it be that we're together then? Unless . . . unless I've passed over as well."

"Nay, you're in the land of shadows," Fiona explained. "'Tis a place of transition and deep contemplation."

Rhiannon frowned. "Do you mean I'm not quite dead? I'm *dying*?"

"Possibly," Fiona said. "'Tis your choice whether to remain here or return."

"I don't understand." She struggled to remember what had happened.

Fiona took her hands in hers and squeezed. "Think hard, child. What brought you here? What is the last thing that happened to you?"

Rhiannon's thoughts wheeled like seagulls on gusts of wind. At last, her muddled brain cleared and she recalled recent events and finally the kidnapping.

"Someone's taken Ailleen," she blurted. "Donovan—it was him, I'm sure of it."

"What else?" Fiona prompted.

"Uther and several of father's men were riding with me to Donovan's castle to rescue her. We were ambushed and I fought alongside the men. I got hurt and after that I can't remember much."

"You're lingering on the brink between life and death." Fiona nodded sagely. "You must make a choice."

She shook her head. "How can I? I would miss everyone back

home if I stayed, but I haven't seen you in so long. I want to be with you, mother."

Fiona smiled. "I'm not going anywhere, Rhiannon. I'll always be here waiting for you."

She thought of Ailleen, still in need of being rescued. She thought of her father and the preciously few days he still had left. She also thought of Glenna, who always managed to have the perfect advice when she needed it.

When the image of Cort's strong face took shape in her mind's eye, her heart lurched. Warmth infused her at the memory of being with him. Though she felt frustrated by his actions, and much between them still needed to be resolved, she had hopes for their future.

Rhiannon rested a hand against her aching forehead. "Why is it so hard to decide?"

"Because you love all of us. Just remember, you have left things unfinished in your life. Do you feel ready to leave that yet?"

She pondered her mother's words for a moment, then Cort's voice rose in the surrounding stillness.

"Don't leave me, Rhiannon. Come back."

The sincerity in his plea made her throat tighten and her heart pattered like the sound of falling rain. Closing her eyes, she shivered. If she stayed, she'd have no cares and no worries ever again. She could be at peace.

"Rhiannon," Cort pleaded.

"Are you truly ready to leave him behind?" Fiona locked gazes with her.

Though she felt torn in two, Rhiannon made up her mind. "Nay, I can't come here with you yet. 'Tis not my time."

Fiona smiled. "You are a wise young woman. I'm proud of you, daughter. Go now and return to the people waiting for you."

Rhiannon closed her eyes and the air whooshed around her with dizzying speed. She arrived at a place where her body throbbed with pain. Opening her eyes, she blinked several times and glanced around at the tent. Wounds on her arms had been carefully bandaged, but her mouth was as dry as dirt.

As she smacked her lips, she noticed Cort stretched out next to her on a pallet, a frown on his whiskered face. Her breath trembled at the sight. He seemed so intense, so *worried*. Had he stayed beside her the entire time she'd been ill?

He'd probably heard her stirring, for his eyes opened. He lifted up on an elbow and studied her closely, then spoke in a hoarse voice.

"I feared I'd lost you." Taking her hand, he nuzzled the palm with his warm lips.

Though she ached from every pore in her body and her head pounded, a bolt of sizzling heat shot from head to toe. Her need for him rose, unbidden, and she realized that for better or worse, he had become a natural part of her.

"I thought I'd lost myself," she returned in a thin voice. "What happened?"

"Your cuts became infected, but Uther had you drink an herbal potion that helped you heal."

"Good old Uther. He's always taking care of people." Her thoughts turned toward the babe she carried, but she felt certain the herbs would not harm it. She'd used Uther's special cure before on people and had discussed the contents with him, so she knew exactly what it contained. Also, if she had lost the babe, Cort would surely have mentioned it.

Wondering what his reaction would be upon hearing he was to be a father, she decided to tell him straight out. "Cort, there's something you need to know . . ."

"We'll talk later, when you're feeling better." He pulled her close and stroked her hair. "Right now, you need to rest."

"But it's important. And Ailleen . . ."

"I've sent some men to search Donovan's castle. If she's there, they'll find her."

"Sir Cort?"

He jumped to his feet and parted the tent flaps. One of his soldiers stood there, his face lined with concern. "What did you find out, John?"

"Donovan's castle is located a few days travel to the north. He is holding Lady Rhiannon's sister for we saw her on the castle wall as we scouted the area."

Rhiannon's heart leapt. "Is she all, right?"

"She appears to be fine, my lady."

"How difficult will it be to lay siege to the castle?" Cort stroked his whiskered chin, a thoughtful look on his face.

"I think it should prove easy enough. It's not very big and we didn't see many guards on duty. Perhaps Donovan feels his fortress is so well hidden he'll never be attacked."

"You're wrong," Rhiannon said. "My father's troops waged plenty of assaults on his home. I even went on some of them. He knows full well he could be challenged at any time."

"I only know what I saw my lady." John shrugged and met Cort's gaze.

"Prepare another detachment to ride. I'll be out shortly."

"Certainly, my lord."

After John left, Cort allowed the tent flaps to fall back into place. He grabbed his clothing and began to dress, then shoved on his boots. He donned his hauberk, then sheathed his sword at his side and lifted up his helmet.

Rhiannon watched his activities with rising agitation. "I want to go with."

He grunted a response.

She tried to sit up. Unfortunately, her body refused to cooperate, and she flopped back down on her blankets, weak as a newborn kitten.

"You stay here," he ordered, his glance pinning her into place.

"I'll go crazy."

"Don't be foolish Rhiannon. You're still recuperating. You're in no condition to ride."

Though she knew he spoke the truth, she still didn't like being left behind. She threw the covers off of her legs. "If you help me get up and dress, I'm sure I'll be all right."

"Sweet *Jesu*, woman! For once in your life, listen to me."

"You can't order me about, Cort Guyot." Indignation burned in her gut. "You might be my husband, but you don't *own* me."

His dark eyes flashed with determination. "I may not own you, but I am in charge of your welfare. Now lie back down. I'll return with your sister as soon as I can."

"You're the one who is out of your mind," she shot back. "You don't understand the lay of the forest like I do. And you don't understand Donovan like I do either. He's shrewd and bloodthirsty. He'll stop at nothing to get what he wants."

"I've waged too many wars and battled with too many enemies to back down from one of your inefficient clan leaders. Because Donovan's so full of vengeance, he's not thinking straight. I'm sure my men and I can handle him with no problems. Now stop worrying."

A second later, he'd rushed from the tent.

She pounded a fist on the blankets. Damn him for being such a know-it-all. Did he think she knew nothing about her country and the politics that ruled it? By the saints, she believed herself as knowledgeable as him about wars and men's treacherous ways—especially Irishmen, and especially Donovan.

How could she lay here quietly while her sister languished at Donovan's castle? It was due to her mistake that the little girl had fallen into his grips. Her gaze drifted to the wedding band gleaming on her left hand. Cort Guyot may be her husband, but she still had a mind of her own and she resented that he constantly thwarted her decisions. It should have been her choice whether or not she wanted to stay.

And so, it shall be.

As an idea formed in her mind, she smiled to herself. Cort may think he had become her lord and master and that he could order her about like a puppet, but she would prove him wrong.

FOURTEEN

BEING BEDRIDDEN DID NOT SUIT RHIANNON one bit. Several days had passed since Cort left to find Ailleen, during which her health had steadily improved, her appetite returned, and her restlessness increased. She prayed he'd found her sister, but lying around waiting to hear threatened to drive her out of her mind.

She wanted desperately to know what had happened. The longer she waited, the more she wanted to go after Cort. As soon as she could, she got up and moved around camp. She practiced with her sword and found she could wield it fairly well, despite her stiff movements.

After several days passed without any word, she became more anxious than ever. When night fell on the eve of the third one, Cort and his men still hadn't returned. Her pallet felt like a bed of nails, and she tossed and turned throughout the dark hours, unable to sleep. Something instinctively told her things weren't right. She knew if they didn't return on the morrow, she would go after him.

Her mind fought with her decision, and she recalled her insistence upon going to the battle where her brother had lost his life. Both he and her father had begged her not to go, but she'd been too stubborn to listen. In her mind's eye, she saw Seamus block the arrow that had been meant for her. When it struck her brother's chest, she closed her eyes, feeling as sick now as the day it had happened.

Were it not for her hasty decision to join the battle, he would still be alive. She would have to live with that fierce reality the rest of her life.

Her hasty decision to go after Ailleen had also been made without thought to the consequences and look what had come of it. Several men had lost their lives due to her rushed choice. Should she trust her judgment in this case? Or would her doggedness cause more grief?

When the sun finally rose, washing the sky with glimmering gold light, she got up, rinsed her face and dressed. Despite all of her questions about what she'd decided to do, she'd made up her mind. Even if no one else would go with her, for which she wouldn't blame them, she would go alone. Emerging from the tent, she stopped.

The castle guards stood in a cluster beside their saddled horses. The camp had been torn down and packed and even the fire had been covered with dirt. A couple of the men began to quickly dismantle her tent and put it away.

"We're ready to go after Sir Cort." Uther sent her a grim look and handed her Una's reins.

As Rhiannon's horse tossed its head and nickered, she asked, "How did you know I'd want to go after him?"

"We all do my lady. If his rescue had been successful, he would have returned with Ailleen by now. None of us could sleep a wink last night. It's time we take action."

The men grunted their agreement.

"Bless you Uther. Bless all of you." She swung onto her mare's back and they rode from the glen into the thick spruce and pine covering the hills.

EARLY MORNING LIGHT FILTERED THROUGH THE air as Cort and his men emerged from the forest and onto a bluff that overlooked

Donovan's castle. Assessing the structure, he determined John had been right. Made of a simple construction, it seemed to be merely functional, rather than a fierce stronghold.

Built mostly of wood, with small amounts of stone, it seemed much less formidable than other keeps he'd stormed. The slopes leading up to it shouldn't be difficult to navigate and the walls themselves looked easy enough to climb.

His horsemen, his foot soldiers, and pikemen were finely trained. They wore the finest armor and carried the best weapons, which included scaling ladders and a battering ram.

They were well prepared.

Raising his sword, he issued a command to the archers who aimed their arrows toward the battlements. When he lowered his weapon, they released a flurry of the sharply barbed missiles. In the distance, guttural shouts filled the air, indicating castle guards posted along the walls, caught unaware by the surprise attack, had been wounded.

Releasing a battle cry, Cort led the soldiers up the slope.

Slashing their way through the thorn and weed-filled water surrounding the castle, they moved forward, fending off enemy arrows and rocks with their shields. They'd begun to gain ground when he heard bloodthirsty howls on their flanks.

Whipping around, he watched as naked, barbaric-looking men with crude weaponry bore down upon them, screaming and yelling like demons from hell. A fearsome sight, their bodies had been painted with stripes of blue, green and white.

A trap.

Cort's horse reared back and whinnied with fright. He gripped his sword and prepared to fight for his life and the lives of his men.

RHIANNON CURSED THE TIME IT TOOK to reach Donovan's stronghold. If only horses could fly, she thought. However, they could only travel so fast or else risk wearing out both man and beast.

Early one morning, they came upon a forest trail she

remembered from her childhood. "We're close," she said to Uther.

"Aye," he returned.

"I remember the raids my father took me on."

"I thought him insane for allowing such a wee lass to accompany his men. How old were you?"

"No more than ten when he allowed me to ride along. Seamus and I would get so excited, and we'd boast bravely with each other." Rhiannon shook her head sadly as she nudged Una forward, thinking of those long summer days. "We were much too young to understand how serious warfare really was, how much it changes lives, how devastating it can be."

"That is the way of children. They don't quite ken the true nature of what's going on around them." Uther stared thoughtfully into the distance and a bittersweet smile touched his lips. "The fat cattle and sheep your raids brought in fed our people for months."

"Aye. And then Donovan would raid us back, stealing livestock to feed his people. It all seems so silly now. We should have joined forces instead of fighting over land. That would have made both of our clans stronger."

"I agree." Uther set his mouth in a harsh line. "But when Donovan's wife and son were killed in one of the raids, there was no chance of that happening."

"Even though their deaths were an accident, Donovan never forgave my father," Rhiannon said.

"Now look at what it's all come too," Uther said. "Bloodlust is never a good thing. It only leads to tragedy."

"One good thing's come of it," Rhiannon decided. "At least during all those years of raiding we learned an alternate route to Donovan's castle. We'll be able to approach the stronghold without revealing our presence."

"For that we can be thankful."

She gripped her reins tighter. "Blast Cort for not waiting for me to heal before he went after Ailleen. I know Donovan better than he does."

"You may have intimate knowledge of the countryside and how Donovan behaves, but Cort's got the strength of his army. He doesn't feel threatened by him."

"I think it was more a case of not being able to admit I may know a thing or two he doesn't," Rhiannon complained. "He's judged me based on the women he's known in the past who can only embroider and sew. Their brains have been reduced to nothing but mush from lack of use."

Uther chuckled. "I'm sure it's come as a surprise to him that you can do those things as well as heal the sick and make war on those who would threaten your home and family."

"See? Even you know I'm made of sterner stuff."

"He's a man, Rhiannon, and he's got fierce pride. It might prove a wee bit intimidating for him to realize that even though you're a woman, a warrior's heart beats within your breast. And you're definitely not one to shrink from a fight."

When the spires of Leathenach Castle appeared through the trees, she reined up on Una. Uther stopped his horse as well and held up his hand so the men would halt.

"Listen," he said softly.

Sounds of a fierce battle drifted toward them and men's shouts punctuated the air.

Rhiannon slid down from Una's back and hurried over to a rocky outcropping. Uther and the men came up behind her as she parted gnarled tree branches to observe the skirmish. Burly warriors smeared with colored paint were ruthlessly attacking Cort's soldiers.

Stuffing a fist in her mouth, she struggled to keep from crying out, and stared hard at the unfolding scene. Her gaze desperately sought Cort in the melee.

Saint Brigit keep him safe!

"Holy mother of Christ," one of the men muttered then crossed himself. "I've heard of barbarian tribes hiding in remote mountain areas who still practice the old religion."

"It would be just like Donovan to pay them to fight for him." At last, she found Cort atop his horse, slashing away. He shouted something to his men and the soldiers began to retreat, hacking their way toward the dark fringe of forest.

Helplessness shot through her. She felt like a fool standing here doing nothing. But they were in no position to take action; they didn't have enough men. Anxious, she watched as the last of Cort's soldiers finally made it clear of the battlefield.

He'd nearly made it to the forest when one of the barbarians knocked him from his horse. She bit her lip, tasting blood. Instinctively, she reached for the dagger strapped to her thigh, watching as two incredibly large men dragged Cort away and dropped him beside the castle gate.

The drawbridge lowered and Donovan sauntered out, shouting orders. He pointed at Cort and two of his guards grabbed his arms and hauled him inside.

Panic twisted through her and she struggled to think of what to do.

THE WHIP CRACKED THROUGH THE AIR above Cort, came down and slapped his back. He gritted his teeth, tasting blood.

Chained to the dungeon wall, his arms ached from the strain. Sweat dripped down his face, coating it with a heavy sheen. His mind fought to slip away from the agony, like a snake slithering through the grass. The throbbing ached with such intensity, he wished desperately for it to end.

Pain ripped through him—agonizing, blinding torture. Each time the whip lashed against his back, thin leather strips sliced through his skin, leaving welts that bled and dripped hotly down his back.

Why the hell hadn't he finished off Donovan when he'd had the chance all those months ago? The mission to track him down should have taken priority in his mind and he shouldn't have rested until the man had been located.

Moran had warned him that Donovan had proven on more than one occasion to be a cagey old fox. Rhiannon had warned him as well and he hadn't listened. This is where his cockiness had landed him . . . in the clutches of a mad man.

How long have I been here? Days or weeks?

Thwak . . .

How much more of this can I stand?

Thwak . . .

I think I'm going to die.

Thwak . . .

God, please let me die.

Thwak . . .

"Enough," Donovan finally shouted in a gritty voice.

Surely his back must be torn to shreds. Cort tried to calm his ragged breathing. He had to get a hold of himself. When Donovan's guard unshackled him, he sank to the cold, filthy floor. Pain pressed him down, as though his body had become nothing more than a bag of bones. Moving even his little finger would be too much.

Donovan chuckled. "I'll bet you never thought to see King Henry's men whipped like puppy dogs, did you?"

Cort didn't respond.

Donovan kicked him in the ribs. He grabbed his midsection, groaning.

"Tell me where he's hidden the rest of his troops." Donovan grabbed his head and yanked it up, so they were eye to eye. "Mayhap I'll spare the whip. If you tell me where Rhiannon is, I'll even let you go free."

Rhiannon.

He closed his swollen eyes and swallowed hard. His throat ached. He hurt all over. *If only I could have a drink of water.* Conjuring up a mental vision of his wife, he felt a moment of heaven slip through.

Rhiannon stood beside a pool of water in a forest glen with a waterfall cascading down the rocky slope behind her. Her naked curves stunned him, her long red hair swirled around her shoulders like wildfire and her green eyes sparkled like the most precious emer-alds . . .

A weak smile touched his lips and darkness edged toward him invitingly. He began to fade into blissful unconsciousness.

Donovan kicked him in the ribs again. "Wake up you stupid Norman bastard. I asked you a question."

The jolt of Donovan's foot rattled his brain back to harsh reality. He smacked his dry, cracked lips together. "Where's Ailleen?"

"She's none of your concern."

"Mark my words," Cort managed in an uneven voice. "You'll wake up one morning and discover King Henry's army scaling your castle walls."

Donovan smiled. "They'll find a surprise if they try it. I've gathered most of the clans together. They'll fight to their deaths to defend this country against England's suppression."

"They don't stand a chance."

"They proved themselves capable today."

"They laid an ambush and my men walked into it. They won't be so lucky next time."

"Don't fool yourself. King Henry's not invincible."

Cort chuckled then winced at the ache lancing his side. "You don't know him like I do."

"I know him well enough."

"You don't know anything."

Donovan snorted with disdain. "Chew on this, Norman. Once you're dead I intend to find your wife and have some fun with her. Then I'll finish her off. She's ruined since she's been with you. I'll marry her sister now."

Rage tore through Coert and he shoved to his feet, stumbling for a moment before he regained his balance. The anger coursing through him dulled the sharp ache of his wounds. "You touch either of them Donovan, and I'll kill you. I swear by all that's holy."

Donovan's guards bristled and they both moved closer to their master, weapons at the ready.

"Who is locked in whose dungeon?" He snickered. "You took Rhiannon and Callinon from me. You'll pay for that."

"Where is Ailleen?" Cort blinked as blood dripped down his brow and into his eyes. "What have you done with her?"

"Oh, don't worry. Your wife's sister is in a safe place. In fact, so safe she's being guarded by the ancient kings of Tara. On the *fomhar* equinox, she will become my bride."

"What are you thinking? She's just . . . a little girl."

"She is somewhat on the young side right now, but in a few years, she'll be old enough to consummate the marriage. When people see two of the strongest clans unite in marriage, it will reassure them that I should be High King of Ireland. And I have this." Donovan held up an oddly shaped yellow gem. "Once I fit this into the keystone at Tara, I'll be given the ability to banish England from these shores."

"You're insane," Cort muttered.

"I never imagined you'd understand. You see, Ireland began to fall away from her true heritage centuries ago. We weakened ourselves. Our true roots need to be established and our country will be strong again."

"King Henry's troops will crush you and your barbarian mercenaries."

"Methinks, you overestimate the English ruler and his powers," Donovan mocked. "He's a fool and a philandering peacock. I, on the other hand, have an intimate knowledge of this country. Every nook and cranny and hiding place is known to me. I have the advantage."

"God help me, I'll send you to hell," Cort threatened.

"I don't believe in your god. And unfortunately for you, you'll never get the chance to lay a hand on me." Donovan turned to the guard holding the whip. "Leave the prisoner for now and resume his torture after you've supped. The Norman will have time to think about what it will be like to die. Mayhap then he'll decide to tell me what I want to know."

The guard nodded.

Laughing, Donovan left the room. As his voice faded, the guard reshackled Cort so that he hung by his arms, gritting his teeth against the pain.

WHEN DARKNESS FELL, RHIANNON EMERGED FROM her hiding place. Assuming Donovan would be holding Cort in the dungeon, she'd finally thought of a way to get inside Leathenach Castle to free him. Uther hadn't wanted her to go, but she knew her way around Donovan's castle, which qualified her as the one to carry out the plan. Also, she didn't want to risk detection if too many of their men accompanied her.

The moon's brightness lit her path as she stealthily approached Leathenach Castle. After wading through the moat at a spot she knew wasn't very deep, she emerged with her trouser legs dripping and wrung them out as best she could.

Carefully she navigated around boulders and bushes until she reached the base of the massive guard tower, moving as quietly as possible. At first, she thought her memory was faulty and it took several moments for her to find what she was looking for—an old drainage tunnel that hadn't been used in years. It had been large enough for her to crawl through as a child and she hoped she could still fit inside.

Hearing voices, she looked up and saw guards marching back and forth on the wall near the gate, their torches illuminating the night. Undaunted, she took a deep breath then began to crawl up the rocky slope, dragging her body through the dirt.

Sharp pebbles dug painfully into her palms, but she ignored them. Finding Cort and Ailleen as quickly as possible were the only things on her mind. When her foot slipped and a large stone bounced noisily down the incline, one of the guards leaned over the wall and waved his torch.

"Who goes there?"

Rhiannon froze. She pressed herself flat against the ground, hoping her dark clothing would blend in well with her surroundings. As she prayed silently, pleading for divine assistance, she heard the guards muttering.

As if her prayers for help had been answered, a rabbit shot past her and hopped down the slope. The guards saw it as well and concluded the noise they'd heard had been caused by the small animal.

Thank you, she said silently.

Drawing her lower lip into her mouth, she continued crawling toward the drainage tunnel. Reaching the opening she heaved herself inside the dark, dank passageway filled with leaves, dirt, and other foul-smelling debris. As children, she and Seamus had used this long-forgotten passage to sneak into Leathenach Castle. Their goal had been to find small valuables to steal such as pieces of jewelry, trinkets or coins. This time her goal was much more crucial.

Things in here were barely visible, but she pressed on, crawling on her hands and knees, relying on memory to guide her. Before long, the dimness grew lighter, and she knew she'd reached the dungeon. Hearing men's voices and occasional male guffaws, she cautiously peered out from the edges. Seeing no one around, she slid from the filth and stepped down onto the stone floor, blending into the shadows.

Covered in dirt, twigs and leaves, she made her way to the area where Donovan held his prisoners. As she peered around the corner of the dirt wall, flickering torches revealed two rough-looking guards seated on stools, tossing marked stones on the floor and exchanging coins.

"Aye, don't ya be cheatin' me now," one of them said, then took a swig of ale from his cup. He wiped his lips with the back of his hand, sloshing amber liquid across the dirt floor.

"On me mother's grave, I'd ne'er do such a thing," the other one declared with feigned innocence. He reached for his cup and downed his ale in short order, then snorted with laughter, spraying liquid through his nose.

"Pig!" the other one roared as ale splashed everywhere.

They both began to guffaw and sway on their stools.

Rhiannon drew herself back into the shadows and caught her breath. A few seconds later, she leaned further around the corner. Cort dangled unconscious, his arms stretched above his head and secured by iron cuffs, his back bloody and the skin shredded. She bit her lower lip, stifling the scream that rose to her lips.

Please God, don't let him be dead!

FIFTEEN

RHIANNON STRUGGLED TO GET A GRIP on her senses, wishing desperately she had her sword. She'd have run it through the guards without compunction. But she only had the dagger strapped to her thigh, thinking it less awkward to carry.

Do something!

Her raging soul grew quiet as a course of action became clear. Reaching for the dagger, she stabbed it into the dirt wall, loosened a small rock and tossed it down a passageway. As it skittered noisily across the dirt floor, she shrank back into the subterranean darkness.

One of the guards rumbled, "What was that?"

"I can't tell," the other one said. "It's best we find out; else Donovan will string us up and have us flogged like that poor bastard over there."

When the guards stumbled down the passageway to investigate, she slipped from her hiding place. Reaching into the leather pouch at her waist, she withdrew a pinch of Uther's sleeping powder that she'd thought might come in handy. It should knock the guards on their fat arses.

She dropped a measure of the substance into the drinking mugs and a larger portion into the pitcher of ale sitting on a table.

Glancing at Cort, her heart wrenched. She needed to get him out of this place of sadness and death. *Have patience*, a small voice whispered. Hearing the guards' laughing as they returned, she shrank back into the shadows and pressed herself flat against the dirt wall.

"Must've been a rat," one of the guards declared.

"Aye, mayhap it skittered away when it heard us comin.'"

The men resumed their game. Their boastful laughter echoed as they gambled and drank, gambled and drank. Finally, they began to yawn and their boisterous voices grew quieter.

Waiting for them to pass out nearly drove Rhiannon crazy. Cramps shot through her legs. She flexed and unflexed the muscles, trying to alleviate the ache.

Thump, thump.

When snores filled the air, she peered around the corner. The men stretched across the earthen floor in awkward positions, sleeping like babies. Their cups and the pitcher lay discarded in the dirt.

At last.

She hurried to the guard who had a fat ring of keys clipped to his waist. Using her dagger, she sliced through his belt and gripped the keys so they wouldn't clank together.

A hand closed around her ankle, and she looked down in horror at the guard's meaty paw clutching it. Leaning over, she tickled his nose with her fingernails.

He snorted and mumbled, then reached up to rub his whiskered face. As he rolled onto his back, she stepped away from him. A moment later he erupted into louder snores and a line of drool dribbled down his chin.

She crossed herself, thanking the saints that luck had been on her side. Moving a chair over by Cort, she climbed on it. At the sight of his bruised and bloodied face, his shredded trousers and bare, bleeding feet, her heart ached.

Holding his head in her hands, she whispered, "Cort, wake up . . ."

"Go to hell," he gritted out, trying to shake free of her.

"It's Rhiannon. We must flee this place." She glanced at the guards to make sure they hadn't been alerted. They looked like two lumpy sacks of wheat.

His brows knitted. "Wha . . . what? How? *Rhiannon*? Are you an angel? Am I dead?"

"We must make haste. Can you stand?"

He wet his dry, cracked lips with his tongue and nodded. "Why did you come for me? Too dangerous . . ."

Ignoring his comment, she tried fitting one key after another into the manacles. Fearing she'd never find the right one, she began to tremble, making it even more difficult to test the keys.

Finally, the lock came apart and he stumbled away from the chains. He spat at the guards and rubbed his bruised arms. "What happened to them?"

"A double dose of Uther's sleeping potion." She stepped down from the stool. "Where's Ailleen?"

"Donovan sent her away."

Her stomach knotted. "Where?"

"Donovan rambled off something about ancient kings of Tara watching over her." His brow furrowed. "He also said he will marry her on the *fomhar* equinox, whatever that is."

She filled with outrage. "I'll kill him."

"Not if I get to him first. He may be cunning, but he's not invincible."

"Were any other of your men captured?"

He shook his head. "When I ordered the retreat, I told them to make their way back to you and Uther."

She took his large hand and pulled him toward the tunnel entrance, nearly concealed by overhanging tree roots.

"What's this?"

"A long-forgotten air shaft."

His surprised gaze met hers. "How did you know about this?"

"My father took Seamus and me on numerous raids to Leathenach Castle. We found this passageway one time." She studied at his tall, broad-shouldered frame. "I hope it's big enough for you."

He eyed the dark tunnel. "Me too."

She crawled into it and helped him up. As he squeezed in behind her, dirt sifted from the ceiling.

"Can you fit?"

"Barely," he admitted.

Gradually Rhiannon's eyes adjusted to the inky darkness as she moved along. Cort scooted along behind her, breathing heavily. She tossed several glances over her shoulder and when she noticed he'd stopped moving, she stopped.

"Are you stuck?"

"Pain . . . the pain is . . . bad."

"Can you make it?"

"I'll try," he returned in an agonized voice.

This had to be another form of torture for Cort to drag himself, raw and bleeding, through the tunnel full of rocks and dirt.

"We're almost there," she said encouragingly.

Debris scraped her palms as she resumed her progress. Inch by inch, they made their way. At last, a rush of cool night air caressed her face and a splash of moonlight faintly illuminated the passageway.

She glanced at Cort. He had slumped over in the dirt and his breaths wrenched raggedly from his lungs.

"We can't stop now, we're so close."

He raised himself up and met her gaze with pain-filled eyes. "I . . . I'm not going . . . to make it."

"You have to." She fought to keep panic from entering her voice.

"Go without me. I'm tired, so tired . . ." He collapsed again.

"Cort look at me."

He clawed the ground with one hand but didn't say anything.

She scooted back to him, lifted his head and cradled it in her lap, stroking his matted hair. "Wake up soldier. That's an order."

His eyes shot open.

"You're strong. You're going to make it. And your son needs you."

"Josette . . . will take care of . . . him." He swallowed hard.

"No Cort, *our* son. *Our* child." Tears spilled onto her cheeks. "He'll need you to teach him how to be a man."

He reached up to feel the wetness on her face. "You're crying. For me?"

"Yes, you big lout. Now get up. Our child needs you."

"We don't . . . have a child." He began to cough.

"We will soon. And I sense it's a boy."

"You're going . . . to have my babe?"

"Yes." She kissed his forehead. "Now let's go."

She helped him up onto his elbows and crawled beside him, eager to escape this awful place. Her heart increased its hammering tempo as the patch of moonlight at the end of the passageway grew larger, beckoning with silvery freedom. At the edge, she slid out and turned to help him.

He clambered from the darkness and stood unsteadily, so she slipped her arm around his waist. As he leaned heavily on her, she braced herself and they made their way from the castle.

His unsteady gait made it slow going, but they made it down the rocky slope and slipped quietly into the inky forest. As the branches and leaves enfolded them in a cloak of invisibility, she sighed with relief.

"Thank the saints, we escaped without detection."

He sent her a weak smile then collapsed.

A RAGING INFERNO CONSUMED CORT; THE FLAMES licked wildly at his skin.

God had deemed him an unrepentant sinner and had cast him into the fiery pits of hell. Satan touched his skin with fiery fingertips, setting him ablaze and locking him in a burning cage.

Moaning, he licked his dry, cracked lips. He called for help, but no one answered. That didn't surprise him. He'd always been alone. His mother had abandoned him; his father sent him away. He'd lived his life as an outsider, seeing families daily, but never belonging to one. Children taunted him as a youngster, people refused to acknowledge him as an adult.

Born a bastard, he lived with the sins of his father.

Years of waging wars for King Henry came flooding back in full force. All the blood, all the crying, all the suffering. He'd taken part in it to further England's glory. Now he would pay the horrible price.

Make it stop.

He tossed and turned, like a haunch of venison over the fire pit.

His punishment—to burn in hell as strokes of flesh-melting fire seared his soul. His immortal soul—lost.

SEVERAL DAYS HAD PASSED SINCE RHIANNON and Cort escaped from Leathenach Castle's dungeon. Uther and the men had been waiting for them in the woods and they'd quickly whisked them away from danger. They'd ridden for a while before stopping to rest in this area—a glade where the thick foliage formed a protective barrier from prying eyes.

Even though Cort's men had eventually located them, they would still be outnumbered if Donovan discovered their whereabouts. She pushed the thought away, unable to deal with that possibility right now.

A latticework of branches arched overhead as Rhiannon sat on the ground next to Cort's makeshift pallet of leaves. Carefully she pressed a cool compress to his bruised forehead.

His ashen face worried her, and she longed to see it full of robust color again. Until now, she'd never realized how his handsome visage and broad smile brightened her day. She told herself she'd soon see it again.

The cross she'd given him still hung on the chain around his neck and she touched it reverently, offering a silent prayer to Saint Brigit for his speedy recovery.

Fennel plants growing nearby had been a boon, for she'd been able to brew a mixture to lower his fever. He seemed better, but delirium gripped him occasionally.

She'd meticulously cleaned the wounds on his back. Thanks to a good slathering of Uther's salve, they were healing nicely. Her careful bandaging had served its purpose and the oozing on his sores had stopped.

Why doesn't he wake up?

"No father don't leave me again," he mumbled in his sleep. "Don't call me a bastard. Don't . . ."

The anguish in his voice caused her heart to wrench. Awake, he acted as though his troubled youth hadn't bothered him. Yet his fevered mumbling told her otherwise. As a fatherless child, he wouldn't have been accepted easily into society. As a man, he was driven to prove himself as equal as any other. It had been ingrained in his nature to perform over and above what others achieved.

No wonder he jumped at the chance to marry her and stay on in Ireland where people didn't know him. Here, he could start fresh without his past to taint him. Here, he could build up a kingdom and a solid future; something he would never have had the opportunity to do in Normandy. Here, he could have a wife—something denied to him as a moneyless, landless soldier.

While she didn't like the idea that marriage to her had resolved his dilemma, she had to admit her home seemed all the better for his presence. People felt safe and for the first time in as long as she could remember, they smiled and laughed and went about their business with general ease. Until now, they'd never felt comfortable enough to do that.

However, King Henry's arrival had put everyone on their guard. His greed for new countries and the wealth they could provide was legendary. A part of her still suspected Cort had known of his plans to come here.

If he had, what could she do? She truly wanted to believe him, but mistrust prevented her from giving him the benefit of doubt. Yet she found herself in an awkward position. The Holy Church had ordained her marriage to the Norman. She was dutybound to honor and obey him.

"Don't call me a bastard," he muttered again.

She picked up his hand and held it against her cheek. "You're safe. You must rest now."

It occurred to her that it wasn't just duty that kept her at his side. Her feelings for him ran much deeper.

CORT SLOWLY OPENED HIS EYES. AN angel with a halo of glowing red hair held his hand against her silken cheek. No one could save him. No one except her.

"Rhiannon," he muttered.

"Praise be, you're awake."

He gritted his teeth. "Don't leave me."

"I won't. I'll stay by your side until you're better."

"And after?" he croaked.

"Aye, I'll be here then."

Those were the sweetest words he'd ever heard, spoken in a voice that touched him somewhere deep in his soul. *My angel*, he thought, as she continued to whisper soothingly to him. A cool cloth swiped across his fevered brow, taking the wicked heat away.

She smiled and his heart smiled with her.

"Rhiannon."

"Save your strength, man. Rest easy now."

As he relaxed, the nightmares of his past faded. Everything since he'd come to Ireland came flooding back. He recalled the first time he'd seen Rhiannon, her bright red hair flying about her as she'd hefted a sword to protect her family. The weapon had been far too heavy for her in her malnourished and abused condition, yet that hadn't stopped her from brandishing it.

He recalled their wedding day and how she'd come to him with green fire in her eyes, ready to take him on if he dared threaten her people. The first time they'd made love she'd been so hesitant, yet her passion had grown for him throughout the passing weeks.

Whether locked in a lover's embrace or quarreling, they were evenly matched. A spark of excitement constantly burned between them, like a flash of lightning during a raging thunderstorm. He'd never felt this close to a woman before; he'd never allowed himself to.

Rhiannon had entered his life during a point where he had become a stoic war machine—not thinking or feeling, just fighting for God and country. Doing his job had taken precedence overall.

She'd changed all of that. Together, they had formed an alliance between two countries. Soon their child would seal their union and form a family. He wanted to be there to hear his son's first cry.

The devil couldn't take him now—he would fight off the fire.

He would survive for his flame-haired woman who healed him with her touch and seduced him with her eyes. A giver of hope, a redeeming angel; she had become his reason for living.

She is my life.

Would she be kind with his heart if he gave it to her?

"Rhiannon," he muttered.

His angel leaned over him and pressed soft lips against his forehead. "I'm here."

The flames of hell dissipated, and he felt her cool touch stroking the molten skin of his brow. A healing breeze swept across his body and at last he slept deeply on a pillow of feathers, soft as clouds.

The angel would take care of him.

He felt safe.

He would live.

THE MEN SAT ON FALLEN LOGS in the clearing, speaking in quiet voices as they sharpened their swords. Uther separated himself from them and approached Rhiannon in the tent, the flaps open.

"We can't stay here much longer my lady," Uther told her. "If Donovan finds us . . ."

"I know. But Cort's still in no condition to leave."

"No wonder," he said, studying the Norman. "The boy took a solid thrashin'."

She inhaled an uneven breath and tried to dispel her unease. "Hopefully we're hidden well from prying eyes."

"For a bit anyway."

When Cort muttered something unintelligible, she took one of his large, calloused hands in hers and kissed it, noting the thin white scars and tight, healed flesh.

Battle scars from a life spent fighting.

This man had fought many skirmishes and lived through them. He'd cheated death more than once. Surely, he could survive this.

He must have sensed her touch because when she pulled back, his eyes flickered open. His smile lit her entire world. With a sigh, he fell back asleep.

"You love him, don't you?"

She shot Uther a look of surprise. "What?"

"The Norman." Uther gave a perceptive smile. "You love him."

"I don't know . . ."

"I see how you look at him. You've got a glimmer of tenderness in your eyes, lass."

Is that why I have a hard time breathing around him? Is that why my heart takes flight when he touches me?

She'd only had feelings for one other man—Jamie O'Brien. But he'd always seemed so involved with himself that she'd never felt that important to him—even after they'd become engaged.

Despite their rocky beginning, she felt a full-blown passion for the Norman that reached deep inside of her soul and drew out the mature woman. Not only had he become an integral part of her life, but they also both wanted the same thing—peace and safety for her people. Now, they would share a child.

Yet still she hesitated to label what she felt for him. To do so would make her vulnerable. "I don't really know what love is, Uther."

"No one does," he acknowledged. "It's something we feel when we're with the right person. Everything falls into place, and we experience that magic of feeling needed. I might be old, but I remember what it's like."

"Cort is so difficult to understand."

Uther hunkered down at her side. "When we rode through your father's lands together, I learned a lot about him. His mother abandoned him as a wee babe and left him with his father. Not wanting his wife to find out about his affair, Searlas sent young Cort to live with his cold-hearted uncle."

She studied her husband's face for a moment, trying to imagine him as a heartbroken boy. It wasn't difficult to do, for he seemed so powerless right now, just like a child.

"Sir Cort's been alone most of his life," Uther continued. "He purposely doesn't get too close to people for fear they'll leave him. Can you blame him for being standoffish?"

She studied her husband in a new light. He'd been even handed in his dealings with her; he'd saved her life. In her stubbornness, had she judged him too harshly? Yet she hesitated to place complete trust in him.

"I still wonder if he had prior knowledge of King Henry's trip to Ireland," Rhiannon said.

Uther ran a hand through his gray hair. "Aye, I suppose we can't know that for certain. Yet think of if my lady; he hasn't given us a reason not to place our confidence in him."

Uther's right, she thought. Except for Cort's penchant for bossing her around, which as her husband he had the right to do, he'd done naught to garner her suspicions. Even Josette's irritating presence in their lives hadn't diminished his honorable conduct toward her.

Regardless of all that had happened, she felt unexplainably drawn to him. His presence offered a much-needed peace between her clans and he'd become important to her. It wasn't just because he was the father of her unborn babe. Her feelings stemmed from a deeper attachment that plucked at her heart strings.

Confused by the true nature of her feelings for Cort, she pushed them aside. Right now, she just wanted him to get better. The longer Ailleen remained with Donovan, the longer she remained in danger.

"What have you and the men decided about going after my sister?"

"As soon as Sir Cort can ride, we'll be on our way." Uther patted her back in a comforting gesture, then sauntered over to talk to the men.

At suppertime, Uther brought Rhiannon a plate with dried meat and a sliced apple. Her nausea had begun to decrease lately, and she managed to eat a healthy amount, washing it down with a leather drinking flask filled with fresh stream water.

As a luminous moon rose over the hills and stars twinkled in the heavens, the men began to bed down. Fatigue sifted through Rhiannon and she curled up beside Cort on the blanket, snuggling her head against his shoulder. Pressing a hand against her stomach, she thought of the child growing inside of her.

Soon enough she could dream about what it would be like to swell with her husband's babe, nurturing it with her body. Also, what it would be like to hold it in her arms and let it suckle at her breast.

Right now, worry for Ailleen prevented her from thinking that far into the future. She drifted into a light sleep, mindful of every movement Cort made beside her.

SMACKING HIS DRY MOUTH TOGETHER, CORT awakened to the star-lit darkness. He lifted onto his elbows, wincing from the tight ache in his back. Rhiannon lay at his side sleeping, her hair splayed across her shoulders like an explosion of fire.

A second later, she pushed up and stared at him with wide eyes. "You're awake. How do you feel?"

"I'm parched."

She quickly handed him a drinking flask. He dribbled cool water into his mouth and down his throat, thoroughly enjoying the cool refreshment. Finished, he swiped his hand across his mouth.

"How long have we been here?" His voice sounded ragged and worn.

"Two days."

"I've got to get going. I need to find your sister." He started to rise, but she gently urged him back down.

"You don't even know where Tara is."

He frowned, irritated that she had pointed out a valid fact. "I promised your father—"

"We can leave in the morning. The men are ready to go."

He glanced at their sleeping forms under blankets and nodded. "Good. My men found you. They can go with me, and I'll have Uther take you back to Callinon."

She shook her head. "I have to go with. I'm the only one who knows the way to Tara."

His brows knitted. "Give me directions."

"It's been a while since I visited the place. I couldn't give them clearly."

"Damn it." He narrowed his gaze at her, not entirely certain why anger seethed within him. "You take too many risks, woman. It was crazy for you to come after me. What about our babe? Did you think of the danger?"

Her face, which had been so full of concern, now pinched with hurt. She pulled away from him, her attitude frosting over with cool disdain.

"I knew something had gone wrong."

"How?"

"It was strange, but I could *feel* it. Right here." She crossed her hands over her chest.

He cupped the side of her face in his palm, unsure of whether to spank her or hug her. "You could have gotten yourself killed."

She glanced at her hands and her lower lip trembled. "I couldn't leave you to rot in that dungeon."

"You could have sent one of the men to get me."

"I'm the only one small enough to fit through the tunnel."

He remembered the trouble he'd had squeezing past the rocks and dirt and realized she was probably right. "I still don't like that you risked your life and that of our unborn babe."

Anger suffused her features. "You forget, Norman. I'm no simpering maiden. I'm able to handle much more than other women you've known."

"I've witnessed that." His heart warmed toward her, and he found that despite her penchant for never listening to him, he couldn't remain upset with her for long. He suddenly wondered what their baby would look like.

Would it have dark hair like his or fiery red hair like Rhiannon? Whose eyes would it have?

He felt his lips lift with an unexpected smile. "Once the babe is born, we'll always have a bond between us."

"Aye, there's no denying that."

"Our blood will rule over this land long after we're gone. This child is our legacy to the future."

Drawing her close, he kissed her. She held herself stiffly then finally softened beneath his touch. Her rose petal lips gave him the type of healing no potions or balm could ever provide. He realized she'd saved him in more ways than one, body and soul. To his disappointment, she pulled away, leaving cool air between them.

Her eyes misted with green sadness. "I'll be glad when we find Ailleen. I won't relax until then."

He thought about her risking herself yet again and his voice took on an uneven quality. "I want you to go home. My men and I will find her."

She pierced him with a fiery stare. "Are you really worried about my safety? Or are you worried that if I'm killed, you will lose Callinon?"

It felt as though she'd physically struck him, and resentment tinged his words. "Do you think I'm that callous?"

"No, I believe you think I'm incapable of protecting myself."

He considered that, then admitted to himself he still considered her in the category of other women he'd known. By now, he'd come to realize she was not. "You possess great strength and fortitude, Rhiannon. I know you can take care of yourself. I'm just . . . just worried."

A smile touched her lips, and she reached out to stroke his cheek. "I possess warrior's training far beyond your ken. So, stop fussing over me, husband. Do we have a deal? Will you let me go with?"

He gave a reluctant nod.

Their conversation was interrupted when Uther, who had been on the night watch, slid through the bushes and hurried toward them. Cort pushed painfully to his feet and Rhiannon rose beside him.

"A group of Donovan's men approaches." Uther's voice filled with urgency. He motioned to his guards and Cort's soldiers, and they scrambled to their feet. "We must leave."

Cort shoved on the boots someone had rounded up for him, gritting his teeth against the pain lancing through his back. He and Rhiannon joined the others and as soon as the horses were ready, the group rode from clearing and galloped toward the mountains.

SIXTEEN

As they approached a mountain pass, Rhiannon pulled up on Una's reins. Shading her eyes from the rays of the setting sun, she observed the distant peaks. A lazy river meandered around the base of Mount Erin, coiled like a cool green serpent.

A hint of autumn cooled the nights, and she knew the *fomhar* equinox drew close. They must find Ailleen before that happened.

"We're almost there." She pointed toward the mountain pass. "Tara and the ring of stones lie in that valley."

Uther and the men talked animatedly about what they would do to Donovan once they found him. All were eager to give him the sound whipping he deserved.

Seated on his stallion beside her, Cort stroked his raspy chin. "How long until we reach it?"

"I'd say it's about a day's ride."

"We're running low on supplies," Uther said.

"There's a village up ahead where we can purchase more. But we can't tarry too long." She studied the gathering shadows, a sense of apprehension washing over her. "The moon increases its march into the heavens each night and the equinox is nearly upon us."

Cort frowned. "It'll be dark soon. We should spend the night."

"But—"

"The men are tired," he said firmly. "And hungry. We'll find somewhere to stay and leave first thing in the morning.

She sensed he wouldn't budge on this and reluctantly admitted he was right. Though she longed to find Ailleen, it would be difficult to locate Tara in the dark. A hot meal and a good night's rest would give the men the strength they'd need for a confrontation with Donovan.

Thinking of food, her stomach growled, and she placed a hand on her abdomen. Apparently, the rumbling had been audible and the men chuckled.

A hint of pride edged Cort's voice as he spoke. "Apparently my son needs solid nourishment."

She liked the way his eyes danced when he spoke about their child. In her mind's eye, she pictured him bouncing the wee one on his knee. A smile touched her lips.

"It's decided then," Rhiannon said. "We'll stay at the Red Stag Inn. 'Tis where my father took Seamus and me many a time."

THEY RODE THROUGH THE ROCKY HILLS until they reached cultivated fields dotted with herds of livestock and haystacks. In the village, thatched-roof dwellings lined the streets, smoke rising from their chimneys.

Drivers steered their wagons past people who stood elbow to elbow, pawing through merchandise loaded on tables. Several children looked up from their marble game, watching with curiosity as the riders dismounted.

Rhiannon leaned down and smiled at them. "Hello."

None of them said a word until she reached into her pocket and handed them each a coin. Wide eyes shone in their dirt-lined faces.

"Thank you, kindly mum," a boy with a snaggle-toothed grin muttered.

The little ones scampered excitedly toward a stall where a man in a white apron sold pastries and sweetmeats. Money exchanged hands and before long they each munched on a sticky bun.

"I think you made some friends," Cort observed.

They took the horses to a stable then walked down the street toward the inn. Once inside, they filled the room to near capacity. A man playing the fiddle stopped abruptly, bow held in midair.

"Ah, stop yer starin' boys and put your eyeballs back in your heads." A plump woman stepped out from behind the bar, her skirts and apron swishing as she approached. "'Tis only Rhiannon O'Kelly come for a visit."

Though it had been several years, Rhiannon immediately recognized Katie. The woman threw her plump arms around her in a friendly hug.

"Ignore those fools over there," Katie said. "They aren't used to seeing new folks. This neck of the woods is pretty isolated."

Grinning, Rhiannon introduced Cort and the others.

"Pleased to make your acquaintance, madam." Cort took Katie's hand and kissed the top.

Katie blushed. "So little Rhiannon's all grown up and even has a husband now." She narrowed her gaze at Cort. "'Tis an interestin' accent you got yourself, mister. Don't think I've ever heard it before."

"I'm from Normandy."

Her eyes opened wide. "That's a far piece from here. What brings you to our fair village?"

Rhiannon quickly explained about Ailleen.

Katie shook her head. "I'm so sorry. Come and sit. Forgive my rudeness." She motioned toward several empty trestle tables. "I'm sure you could all use a hot meal."

CORT FINISHED HIS LAST BITE OF mutton stew and washed it all down with a swig of mead. "This was truly a meal fit for a king."

"I agree," Rhiannon said. "I've eaten so much I fear I'll burst."

He smiled at her. "You've got the roses back in your cheeks. I think it was best we stopped here."

"I can hardly sit still, though," she admitted as tears filled her eyes. "Every minute that passes I grow more anxious about Ailleen.

She's so sweet and innocent. Surely, she doesn't understand everything that's going on and wonders why no one's come to rescue her yet. I'm her big sister and she relies on me. I feel I've failed her."

The fear in her eyes ran deep and he heard the sincerity in her voice. Something inside of him stirred that he recognized as compassion. He understood how much she loved the little girl. Since he'd never had a true family, he had never experienced that type of emotion. No wonder she would risk life and limb to rescue her.

Just as she come back to rescue me.

Does she love me as well? Sacre bleu, do I love her?

Warmth coursed through him at the idea, but he didn't allow himself to dwell on it overlong. Emotional attachments made a person susceptible to making mistakes, yet he still took her hand in his. "We'll get her back, *ma cherie*. I promise."

Surprise lit her eyes. "You said *we*. Have you finally given up on trying to get me to go home?"

"As much as I hate the idea of you in harm's way Rhiannon, I think it's time for us to work together." He cupped her cheek in his hand, thrilling to the silken feel of her flesh against his. "We need to learn to do that, don't you think?"

She swallowed hard and nodded.

"You must promise me one thing."

"What?"

"I'll allow you to go tomorrow, but you must let the men and I do the heavy fighting."

She hesitated briefly before speaking. "All right."

He could hardly believe his ears. For some time now, he'd questioned his sanity in marrying Rhiannon and taking on the responsibility of her headstrong ways. Even the lure of her inheritance had paled considering the trouble she brought.

But now, as he looked into her emerald green eyes and saw the shining trust in them, he realized it was all worthwhile.

Katie, ever attentive to her guests, bustled toward them. "Did you find the supper satisfying or shall I bring you anything else?"

"I can't eat another bite." Cort patted his stomach.

"I'm full to bursting," Rhiannon assured her.

"So where are you all off to in the morning?" Katie shoved her hands on her hips and studied them closely.

"We're certain Donovan's holding Ailleen at Tara," Rhiannon said. "We're leaving for the ring of stones at first light."

Her face drained of color. "Father Flannagan has forbidden us to go anywhere near the place. He said it's full of heathen symbols that will possess us with evil thoughts."

A tall, brawny man separated himself from the crowd and approached them. "She's right. Nobody decent goes there."

Rhiannon smiled up at him. "Dermot Sullivan, how are you?"

"Not fine enough till I get a proper greeting from you, young lady."

They embraced and Cort stood up beside Rhiannon, fighting back a twinge of possessiveness at the sight of his wife hugging another man.

She must have noticed his alarm because she quickly told him, "Dermot is Katie's husband. They own The Red Stag."

He relaxed but remained unsettled. It occurred to him that Rhiannon had become more than just the woman he'd married to gain an inheritance and landholdings. After all this time, she'd come to mean much more to him, but exactly how much he couldn't say for certain.

Unused to dealing with such feelings, he shifted anxiously from foot to foot, feeling like a bare-faced youth facing his first good fist fight.

"So you plan to visit Tara," Dermot said. "People around here claim the ring of stones is haunted. We stay clear of them. Otherwise, trouble is sure to follow."

Katie and Dermot exchanged dark glances.

Rhiannon's voice wavered. "Unfortunately, since we fear Donovan's holding Ailleen there, we have to go."

"What's this?" Dermot's shaggy brows drew together in concern. "You say Donovan's kidnapped your sister?"

Katie explained the situation to him, and his face turned red. "By God and all that's holy, I'll tear that bastard apart with my bare hands."

"Not if I can get to him first," Cort growled.

"You've got a mighty task ahead," Dermot pointed out. "I'm sure you wouldn't mind a few extra hands to help rescue the lass."

"We appreciate it, but I think my men and Rhiannon's can handle it."

"Most of the men in this tavern are my cousins, brothers, or nephews," Dermot explained. "All eight of my sons are here today, too. We wouldn't mind pitching in."

"I'd hate for you to go against your priest's wishes," Rhiannon said. "It's not right."

"You let us be the judge of that." Dermot called out at the crowd, gaining their attention. He explained that Donovan had kidnapped Rhiannon's sister and held her at Tara. "Will you lads join me in helping to rescue her?"

The men held up their tankards and roared with hearty agreement.

Dermot called out to a young man leaning against the bar. "Hurley, get your lazy backside over here."

Katie smiled. "Hurley is our youngest. I always wished for a girl, but God saw fit to give me a brood of strapping sons instead."

The young man strode over to Dermot. "Yes, Da? What are ya wantin'?"

"Show these nice folks your back."

"Ah, do I have to?" His face drained of color.

Dermot furrowed his thick brows. "I won't ask you twice, boy."

With a frustrated breath, Hurley lifted his shirt and turned around. His back showed the deep, healed scars of a solid whipping.

Rhiannon drew in a sharp breath. "Holy mother of Mary."

"Who did this?" Cort frowned.

"That bastard Donovan." Hurley lowered his shirt. "He and his men rampage through our village like thieves. Raping our women and stealing the food we've worked hard to harvest. He might be our overlord, but he's greedy and selfish. The bastard's not fit to live if ye ask me."

"Be off with you now, Hurley," Dermot growled.

Running a hand through his thick, unruly hair, the young man shuffled back to his friends at the bar.

Katie smiled sadly. "Hurley's wounds have healed nicely, but he's not the same since Donovan had him lashed. He's got blood lust in his heart and revenge in his soul."

"What happened?" Rhiannon asked.

"Donovan claimed the boy was poaching." Dermot's voice trembled with hatred. "It was a lie. Hurley wouldn't have stepped foot on his land. There is plenty of game hereabouts. He wouldn't risk such a foolish venture."

Cort shook his head, enraged that Donovan continued to get away with these atrocities. It was monstrous. "Why do you think Donovan would have him lashed like that?"

Katie's face clouded. "During a raid, Donovan spirited away one of our village girls and hauled her off to his keep. Hurley had been sweet on her for years. He tried to rescue her, but Donovan caught him. We're certain he made up the poaching charge in order to punish Hurley."

"Donovan is the devil's own." Dermot rubbed his hands together. "All I needed was an excuse to go after the son of a bitch. Now I've got one. He's gone too far this time."

Katie laid a hand on Dermot's shoulder. "Don't ya be haulin' my boys off to battle with his lordship again. I've nearly lost them all to that brute at least one time or another."

"'Tis a man's lot in life, Katie. To fight for what's his and show the world he's not a coward."

Katie sighed heavily; her face was lined with concern.

"You don't have to take on our fight," Cort insisted.

"Too late, my man. If Donovan's left his armed fortress, he's fair game for all of us."

RHIANNON RETIRED BEFORE CORT, INITIALLY THRILLED at the idea of sleeping in a real bed with a soft mattress. She'd spent so many nights on the rocky ground that her backside felt covered with bruises. However, she tossed and turned and found rest impossible. After Cort came to bed, she lay wide awake for hours. In her fear for Ailleen, she could think of nothing else.

She rose and walked toward the window. Parting the curtains, she watched the moon casting silvery light across thatch rooftops and cobblestone streets. In the distance, mists crept over the bogs, bringing them to life with haunting beauty.

A hollow feeling washed over Rhiannon as she thought about her little sister out there somewhere, alone and afraid. God forgive her, why hadn't she paid more attention to the girl? Why hadn't she thought to check on her? Instead, she'd been selfishly involved in her own life and her own needs.

The shame of it made her tremble. She hated to think this was the Lord's way of punishing her for being self-absorbed. Yet how could he allow Ailleen to be hurt in order to get her attention? It didn't make sense and it wasn't fair.

Blasphemous girl, how dare you question the Lord's infinite wisdom?

Rhiannon made the sign of the cross. Silently, she said a prayer asking for the courage of David as he faced Goliath. She begged forgiveness for her sins and promised to participate in confession more often when she returned to Callinon Castle.

"Please Lord, help us find Ailleen and bring her home safely," she muttered. "We implore you for strength in the face of our enemies."

As she said, "Amen," Cort's deep voice echoed hers. She turned to see he had risen and was standing behind her. The sight of his naked male body, powerful and corded with muscles, made her blush.

He strode over and knelt at her feet. Pressing a protective hand against the gentle swell of her belly, he kissed it.

Since her pregnancy wasn't visible yet, it was easy to forget she truly carried a babe—the tiny soul she and Cort had created through their lovemaking. She shivered with wonder and trepidation. He must have noticed because he pulled her against his broad chest.

Rubbing her back, he said, "You've taken a chill standing here. Come back to bed, *ma cherie.*"

"But . . ."

He placed two calloused fingers to her lips. "Shhh, wife. Let me warm you for a while."

She intended to protest, but he insisted. Sweeping her into his arms he carried her back to their bed and gently laid her down. After he stretched out beside her, he leaned over and kissed her.

Filled with longing and needing comfort, Rhiannon enjoyed making love with her husband. Feeling warm and protected, she finally fell asleep in her husband's arms.

In her dreams, she saw Ailleen, her small, pale face awash in a sea of darkness. She zig-zagged her way through numerous tall stones, as though lost. Rhiannon gave chase, but the little girl darted through the maze of monolithic rocks and disappeared.

Rhiannon cried out, but her voice caught in her throat. No sound came issued forth. Frustrated, she began to shove away the rocks, overturning them with each sweep of her arms.

Nothing will stop me. I'll find Ailleen and take her home.

"Rhiannon."

Rhiannon's eyes fluttered open. She realized that in her sleep, she had been swinging her arms. Cort sat next to her; her fists captured in his large hands.

"I am not the enemy," he reassured her. "Save your strength for Donovan and his men."

She sat up beside him and hugged herself. "I was dreaming."

"Either that, or you've decided to take me to task for some reason." Dimples showed in his whiskered cheeks.

She rubbed her eyes and looked around. "How late grows the hour?"

"We'll soon be leaving. I hear Katie rattling pans downstairs, hopefully preparing a good meal to break our fast. I'm starved."

Her stomach growled. "As am I."

He gave her backside a playful pat. "Then let's be up and about. I'm sure Dermot and the others will be ready to leave soon."

She went over to a pitcher of water and a bowl and performed simple ablutions. "How many men did Dermot finally rally to our cause?"

"At last count, he had around fifty."

"That many?"

He nodded. "There may possibly be more. Most of the men in the tavern vowed to return to their homes and encourage others to join. We'll see this morning how many more they've enlisted."

She understood the villagers were willing to fight Donovan because of the suffering they had experienced at his hands. Whatever their reason for doing so, it was a stroke of luck.

Cort splashed water on his face and arms and quickly dressed. Parting the curtains, he glanced outside.

"*Sacre bleu*, there must be an army downstairs," he said in an awestruck voice. "The tavern entrance is awash in horses and battle carts. I believe we've awakened a sleeping dragon."

SEVENTEEN

RHIANNON CROSSED TO THE WINDOW AND stood beside Cort, thrilling to the feel of his large warmth next to her, but anxious about the task ahead. It seemed a hundred-plus horsemen crowded the courtyard; their forms bathed in the early morning light. Their mounts anxiously tossed their heads and snorted, creating billows of steam in the cool air.

"You're right." She glanced at Cort, excitement spiraling through her. "'Tis a virtual army. I felt confident the men we already had would be enough. Now I'm positive we'll be able to defeat Donovan and free Ailleen."

He gave her a stern look. "Remember your promise to me. No heavy fighting. With this many men, you don't need to risk yourself."

She nodded. "Aye, but I'll be watching closely. I've decided to borrow a crossbow from Uther. It won't be as strenuous as hefting a sword."

"It goes against my better judgment to allow you to go along." He frowned. "But I realize I can't change your mind."

"I'll be careful."

"I saw you hurt once. I won't let that happen again."

He drew her into his arms and kissed her gently, running his fingers through her hair. He stole her breath, replacing it with his own. In that moment, she wanted him more than she could say. His touch filled her with desire and a trembling need that trailed throughout her entire body.

Cort's heart hammered with love for Rhiannon and he realized exactly how much he'd become attached to the woman he held in his arms. He wanted nothing more than to carry her to the bed and be with her. But he held himself back, aware they had a mission to complete.

Nevertheless, he allowed himself a moment to bask in this sensual embrace and to wonder at the woman he'd married. Once upon a time, she'd been an aloof stranger that he'd chosen to marry to enhance his future. Now she shone like a bright star in his heavens and the inheritance she had provided him with paled in comparison to her presence in his life.

Whenever they were together, she kindled a fire deep down in his soul; a fire that consumed him with sweet yearning. This discovery, though daunting and new, encouraged him about the future.

After spending so many years on his own, he'd never thought to find a woman he would feel this deeply about and be so evenly matched with. As the years passed, not only would he and Rhiannon share spirited conversations, but they would also always be able to seek refuge in each other's arms.

She would give him sons and daughters and stand beside him as they grew old. He would be her champion and she would always be his sweet angel. The idea filled him with such a sense of fulfillment that an ache spread throughout his chest.

He hated that Rhiannon insisted upon riding with the men today, and he'd be beside himself if something happened to her. But he understood her need to be there for her Ailleen.

Before they departed, he would speak privately with Uther and have him assign some of his men to keep her at a safe distance from the battle. He intended to do everything in his power not only to rescue Ailleen, but to keep his wife out of harm's way. Reluctantly, he withdrew his lips from hers and cleared his throat. "I'll meet you downstairs."

She picked up her shirt, her eyes dancing with eagerness, and began to put it on. "I won't be long."

RHIANNON HOOKED THE CROSSBOW AND QUIVER onto her saddle and swung onto Una's back. When the men started to leave, she nudged the mare into a gallop alongside them.

Riding near her, Cort sent concerned glances her way. Instead of being irritated at him, she became amused. Ever since he'd found out she carried his babe; he'd fussed about her more than ever before.

Did he simply worry for the child's sake, or did he also worry about her welfare? The idea made her briefly uneasy. Surely, he cared for her as well as the heir she would give him. Her disappointment would know no end if he only wanted to keep her safe because of the babe she carried.

She wanted, no *needed* to be important to him.

As the hills grew steeper and the forest denser, the dirt trail became increasingly difficult to follow. The sky darkened and dark gray clouds mounded like lumpy haystacks. Wind rushed through the trees, causing their branches to rattle, and leaves to skitter. She shivered, glad for the cloak Katie had loaned her.

"Are you all, right?" Cort's expression filled with worry lines.

"Aye. I'm just anxious to find my sister."

Cort seemed satisfied but continued to shoot concerned glances in her direction.

As the day wore on, the countryside took on a barren, rocky appearance. They stopped a few times to rest then continued on. The trees grew sparse; shrubs thrust gnarled branches into the air.

As they rode past four large upright stones balancing upon a capstone, Cort stared at them.

"We call them dolmens," she told Cort. "They're all over Ireland.

Some people think they were used for ancient ceremonies, and some think they were used for human burials."

"They're definitely unusual." He tilted his head back and forth studying the formation.

"Some people believe fairies built them."

He pressed his lips into a firm line. "The little people again."

She laughed softly. "Aye."

The sun began to descend in the sky and twilight gradually dulled the countryside. As the luminous full moon took its place among twinkling stars, long purple shadows etched weird shapes across the ground. Night creatures and birds called to each other, causing strange sounds to echo throughout the hills.

The wind began to shift and dark clouds mounded, shrouding the moon's luminescence. The region took on a menacing quality as jagged lightning lanced the sky.

The fine hair on the back of Rhiannon's neck prickled and she recalled Donovan's chilling prediction.

On the fomhar equinox she will become my bride.

When they reached the crest of a hill, she sucked in a breath. The ring of stones was close. So close, her stomach wrenched and her nostrils twitched at the evil permeating the air.

Dermot raised his hand and the men halted. He rode up beside her and Cort. "We're almost there."

As thunder rumbled, they tethered their horses on the bushes near a small creek. The men drew on long hooded cloaks, concealing their weapons beneath fabric folds.

When Cort handed one to her, she put it on, then slid the quiver of arrows over her back and collected the crossbow. As they walked quietly up the trail, Uther and several of her father's men closed in protectively around her. She looked curiously at the steward, and he nodded at Cort.

Obviously, Cort had assigned Uther and some of her father's men to stay close to her. She warmed at the idea of the lengths he'd gone to keep her safe, while at the same time she hated being hemmed in. Yet she knew he'd done it for her own good.

More lightning arched through the sky and the earth rocked with thunder. She sensed the men's anticipation and realized Dermot and his people had been waiting for an opportunity like this.

An eye for an eye, a tooth for a tooth.

In the cleft between two hills, the sky glowed with an eerie light. Low chanting reverberated, filling the air with a primitive rhythm. At the top of a ridge, she looked down and saw the ring of stones; exactly as she remembered it. People in hooded robes milled around, engaged in some sort of ceremony.

She tensed, her gaze searching the area. *Ailleen, where are you?*

CORT GAVE THE SIGNAL TO UTHER, and his men escorted Rhiannon to a large boulder that overlooked the clearing. He knew she wouldn't like being removed from the main activity, but he refused to let her get caught up in this. If something went wrong, Uther and the men would whisk her away.

Satisfied that he'd seen to her safety, Cort lowered his head and peered out from underneath his dark hood. There were probably close to twenty gigantic, upright boulders inside of which a large bonfire raged, casting menacing shadows. People had gathered around them, swaying and chanting.

He nodded to the men, and they emerged slowly from the fringe of trees, hopefully appearing like worshippers who had come to join the ceremony. They spread out in the crowd, moving at an unhurried pace so as not to raise alarm. Fortunately, they weren't noticed and blended in easily.

The multitude writhed, almost as one entity—like a serpent. Men and women in dark robes flailed their arms and prostrated themselves. Drums pounded as people muttered intonations, no doubt to ancient gods and goddesses.

Feeling someone pushing him, he looked down to see a young woman working her way to the front of the crowd. When she reached her destination, she stood beside a stone altar. As someone fed another piece of wood to the leaping orange flames, the woman's face glowed. She removed her hood and waited patiently.

A tall man moved forward in one fluid motion, the folds of his dark robe swishing. He leaned and patronizingly patted the woman's hair, kissed her cheek and sent her on her way. He immediately recognized Donovan.

"Bastard," Cort muttered under his breath.

It was all he could do to keep from attacking right now, but the time wasn't right. At some point, the man would bring out Ailleen. That's when he and the men would make their move.

One by one, people approached the platform and Donovan offered his bizarre benediction. At last, he stood back and motioned to another man who came forward and took a place beside the stone altar. Donovan disappeared into the shadows momentarily then returned carrying a little girl with long red hair.

Ailleen!

She appeared to be unconscious as he gently laid her limp form across the altar, her bright hair cascading over the gray stone. As a large flash of lightning ripped through the sky, the man beside the altar raised his arms and began to chant.

RHIANNON'S HEART NEARLY LEAPT FROM HER chest when she saw Donovan place Ailleen on the altar. She wanted to go to her, but she knew it wasn't time to do that yet. Her heart pounded anxiously as she stared longingly at her little sister.

Ailleen's pale, quiet form alarmed her, but she realized Donovan had probably drugged the girl. That son of Satan deserved to rot in hell. She narrowed her gaze at Donovan's priest standing next to Ailleen and her skin crawled with disgust.

Dyfed raised his arms and began to utter words from what must be a bonding ceremony. Immediately Cort, Dermot and the village men threw off their robes and drew their swords. The frightened worshippers ran screaming into the dark forest.

"Get the girl," Donovan shouted to Dyfed.

Before the priest could reach her sister, Rhiannon loaded her crossbow and aimed an arrow at him, letting the missile fly. As it buried itself in Dyfed's chest, he stumbled away from Ailleen and fell heavily to the ground.

CORT GLANCED UP TO SEE RHIANNON standing beside the boulder, the crossbow held expertly in her grasp. Glad of her steady hand, he hurried toward the ring of stones.

At the altar, he glanced down at Ailleen, quickly determining she bore no wounds. He decided her deep sleep had no doubt been drug-induced.

Donovan tore off his robe when he saw Cort. Growling, he reached behind the altar and grabbed a sword.

"It's not very noble to kidnap little girls." Cort held up his blade, blocking Donovan's blow.

"You dare speak of nobility?" Donovan sneered. "You, the unholy spawn of your father's whore? You're no man."

"You're wrong, Donovan. Dead wrong."

When Donovan turned and ran like a coward into the forest, Cort thundered after him.

RHIANNON, UTHER AND THE GUARDS HURRIED down to the altar. Kneeling beside Ailleen, she spoke softly.

"Wake up, sweetheart." She rubbed the little girl's cheeks, trying to bring color back to them. "I'm here; I'm taking you home."

Ailleen's eyes fluttered open and she threw her arms around Rhiannon's neck, speaking groggily. "The gray lady ghost said you would come . . . she told me not to be afraid."

After a large yawn, she released her grasp and drifted back to sleep.

Rhiannon took off her cloak and placed it over Ailleen's thin nightgown. Overcome with thankfulness to find her at last, she blinked back hot tears.

When a firm hand squeezed her shoulder, she looked up to see

Cort. He had scratches on his arms and face from running through the brambles. "Did you find Donovan?"

He shook his head, and his expression could have melted stone. "He got away again. If it's the last thing I do, I'm going to hunt him down."

"At least we got Ailleen away from him."

Without a saying a word, Cort opened his arms and she allowed herself to be pulled into his warm embrace. It felt so good, so right. The emotion in her heart right now couldn't be put into words.

After they pulled apart, he wrapped his cloak around Ailleen and swept the little girl into his arms. Cuddling the sleepy child against his broad chest, he spoke to the men who had crowded around.

"Let's go. At the very least, we've put the fear of God into Donovan."

"But we wanted the bastard dead," Hurley snarled, his face etched with disappointment.

"He'll meet the tip of a sword soon enough, my friend," Cort told him. "Believe me; I won't stop until he's brought to justice."

AFTER RESTING FOR A DAY AT The Red Stag Inn, Cort insisted on going back to Callinon. He was anxious not only to get Rhiannon and Ailleen home safely, but he also knew he and his troops needed to rejoin King Henry. He'd only been given leave to find his wife and her sister. Once that had been accomplished, his orders were to meet the king at Dublin Castle.

As they rode through the autumn-tinged countryside early one morning, the walls of Rhiannon's village took shape in the distance. Callinon Castle rose on the sea cliff above, weathered from the elements, but sturdy and protective. Further up the slope, walls of the new castle jutted into the air. Pride surged through him, and he made a mental note to reward his craftsmen for their skill. They'd made remarkable progress.

"There it is!" So small atop her horse, Ailleen pointed at Callinon Castle. "We're home! I'm so excited to see father!"

Gripping his reins tighter, Cort glanced at Rhiannon. Her smile filled him with a sweet ache. Her beauty took his breath away and his heart, though heavy at the idea of leaving her, skipped several beats. She'd come to mean more to him than he'd ever imagined possible, and his chest welled with emotion. He did not want to go away, especially since she carried his child.

But he had to.

As a soldier in His Majesty's army, duty took precedence over leisure. Before, whenever duty called, he'd been eager to pursue whatever new adventure awaited him. This time, he left behind his woman and unborn baby, and he disliked the idea.

Get a grip on yourself man.

Now, more than ever, it was vital that he remain in King Henry's good graces. With one simple decree, he could withdraw Cort's appointment as Lord of Leinster. Cort couldn't allow that to happen.

Upon reaching the castle gates, he shouted to the guards to lower the drawbridge. As they rode their horses inside the bailey, servants swarmed toward them. After dismounting, he helped Ailleen from her saddle, then Rhiannon. Shouts echoed throughout the courtyard and a flurry of activity ensued. Cort's men and Uther's guards led the horses to the stable.

Moran appeared in the doorway and a smile broke out on his face. Though it had only been several weeks, he looked older and wearier. His hair seemed even grayer than before and the lines around his eyes were craggier.

As the elder man embraced his girls, tears spilled down his leathery cheeks. He looked up at Cort and spoke in an emotion-filled voice. "Thank you, Guyot. You are indeed a man of your word."

JOY FILLED RHIANNON AS SHE FELT her father's comforting arms around her. There had been a few tense moments when she thought she may never see him again. She rested her cheek against his chest and heard the steady beat of his heart, afraid for his worn and weary appearance.

Her own heart lurched and she wondered how much longer he would be with them. The idea filled her with such sadness.

"I'm so glad to be home, father," she told him.

Moran held her at arms length and frowned. "You were very brave to go after your sister like you did, but you had me worried sick."

"You know I can handle myself."

"Aye, but I imagine you welcomed Cort's help."

She glanced at him and blushed. "He saved my life."

"As she did mine," Cort joined in. "I've never seen a woman with the fighting skills to match your daughter's."

Moran nodded. "She was taught by the best."

Barking wildly, Arch raced toward Cort, and he knelt down to scratch the greyhound's ears. "Did you miss me, boy? Or did the servants spoil you rotten and break all your training?"

Moran smiled at his daughters. "No harm has come to either of you?"

"No father," both Rhiannon and Ailleen said at the same time.

"I missed everyone terribly," Ailleen added. "Donovan is a very bad man. I hate him."

"He got away after we rescued Ailleen." Frustration shot through Cort. "We weren't in a position to give chase. He won't be so lucky the next time I meet him though. I intend to end his reign of terror once and for all."

"I've tried all these years and failed. I hope you'll be able to." Moran ruffled Ailleen's fiery red curls. "You're safe now, little sprite."

"I'll double the guard postings." Cort rose up and hugged Rhiannon. "No one's going to get in or out of Callinon without detection."

Rhiannon leaned into Cort's warm embrace, enjoying his protective strength.

Moran gripped the doorway. "Let's go inside and celebrate your safe return. I'm sure you're hungry after your long journey."

Sensing movement above, Rhiannon looked up and saw Josette glowering at them from the parapets. Her gown flapped in the breeze and her glare nearly devoured them, like a vulture shredding carrion.

Rhiannon's skin crawled at the woman's unpleasant perusal. If that shrew dared to start whining and complaining, she'd put her in her place straightaway. She was not in a mood to deal with her petty attitude.

AFTER THEY'D EATEN, CORT TOOK RHIANNON's hand, led her outside into the garden and sat beside her on the stone bench. He pulled her into his arms and kissed her with urgency. She responded in kind which suffused him with sweet longing.

"Rhiannon." Cort heard the grating edge in his words and cleared his voice. "My men and I must be on our way."

"So soon? We've just returned." Disappointment filled her voice and she moved away from him. The coldness coming from her could have frozen the ground like a hard winter snowfall.

"As long as King Henry is in Ireland, I'm at his command," he told her. "I can't disobey orders unless I'm prepared to deal with the consequences, which I'm not."

She lowered her gaze. "Of course."

"I don't like this any more than you do." His temples began to throb and he reached for her hand, but she pulled away. "I made my commitment to be a soldier long before I met you. King Henry will not release me from service now."

"I still fear for my people," Rhiannon admitted.

"After what we've just been through you still mistrust me?"

"Not you. *Him.* King Henry will deal with Ireland however he wants and we're all powerless to stop him."

"I'll do my best to help the Irish," Cort said. "After all, this island is my home now. But I'm only one man."

"Aye, I understand the dilemma." After a long pause, she spoke again. "How long will you be gone?"

"Until King Henry feels that clan unrest has been quelled and returns to England."

"That could take a long time, considering Donovan and others like him still oppose King Henry's overlordship." She sighed heavily.

He took her hands in his. "I hate leaving you, especially knowing we have a babe on the way."

"I hate it as well," Rhiannon added.

When Cort pulled her against his chest and kissed her again, an unusual pain lanced her heart. She couldn't know the future and it loomed before her like a dark, unknown entity. What if the unrest wasn't quelled for years? What if Cort never returned?

Once she'd been afraid of marrying him, now she dreaded for the future if she lost him. Terrified she couldn't bear the agony, she allowed a calm aloofness to sift over her. If she remained void of emotion, mayhap she could deal with the potential loss of her husband before it happened.

When he pulled back, she bit her lower lip to keep it from trembling. She understood Cort's duty to King Henry, but what about his duty to her? She needed him too. Lifting her chin higher, she tried to put on a brave face.

"When will you leave?"

"The men are waiting for me right now. I told them earlier we would only be resting here briefly before we began our journey to Dublin Castle."

"I see."

Her voice remained steady as she held her emotions in check. He would leave her and see to King Henry's needs. Yet she longed to have him at her side as she grew large with his child. And what about the birthing? Would he be home in time for that? It seemed doubtful.

"Don't be angry."

She shook her head and heard the lie as it escaped her lips. "I'm not angry."

"I'm no fool, Rhiannon. I can tell you're upset. But I promise, I'll do my best to encourage King Henry to deal fairly with the

Irish. When it's all over, I'll come home to you as soon as I can."

Despite her best efforts, her lower lip trembled, which didn't go unnoticed by Cort. Sparkling warmth filled his dark eyes.

"Remember, Ireland has become my country now; your people are my people." He lifted her left hand and kissed the ring he'd placed there nearly a year ago during their wedding ceremony. "You are my wife. My place is at your side."

Watching as he took long strides from the garden, her breath caught in her throat. She fought the tears burning at the back of her eyes, refusing to let them spill. So much uncertainty existed, not only for her country but for herself and Cort. Her affection for him had grown to great proportions, especially now that she would bear his child.

"Damn you for making me feel this way Cort Guyot," she whispered to the wind.

Despite her harsh words, tenderness toward him welled in her chest and she realized that wherever he went, now and in the future, a piece of her heart would follow—yet so much lay between them and true happiness.

Could she be patient until then?

EIGHTEEN

JOSETTE HID IN THE SHADOWS BESIDE the stable, watching as Cort saddled his horse. Once he led the stallion outside, she stepped in front of him, blocking his movement toward his military troops gathered in the bailey.

His eyes snapped with impatience and his voice grated. "What in the hell are you doing here?"

"I can hardly stand this ruse any longer, Cort. I want to be with you."

Before he could utter another word, she drew his head down toward hers and kissed him deeply, enjoying the feel of his full lips against hers once again.

Pushing her away, he wiped his mouth on his sleeve, as though repulsed. "*Sacre bleu*, woman, what are you doing?"

Damn that little Rhiannon. What had she done to Cort? It would take her a while to work her way back into his good graces, but she was determined to do it. She refused to allow anyone to cross her—especially not some simpering, spoiled Irish princess.

"Admit it. You still desire me, don't you? You know how I can please you. I can make you . . ."

"Enough!" Cort glowered at her. "I am a married man, Josette."

She sniffed. "Since when did the sanctity of marriage prevent you from conducting an affair?"

His countenance darkened.

She smiled. "Don't tell me you think you love that Irish wench as much as you once loved me."

"I never claimed to love you," Cort growled. "And you never loved me. We both know our relationship was only for pleasure."

Anger swirled in her, but she managed to quell it. "But now I love you. And we have little Fitz."

He shook his head. "I'll see to it that the boy has a decent upbringing. But that is the end of it. There is nothing between us now and there never will be."

"Don't say that," Josette said, stomping her foot. "I want to be with you. Why can't you understand?"

He chuckled. "Come now. We both know you only want what I can *give* you. You don't give a tinker's damn about me."

She blinked several times, pretending not to understand. Deep down, she had to admit that his new position as the Lord of Leinster made him much more of a catch in her eyes. As his mistress, she had much to gain. She just had to convince him to take her to his bed again.

"I have no idea what you're talking about."

"Don't play the coy maiden with me, Josette. Until now, you only desired how I could satisfy you in bed. I had no lands, no long-term prospects and no title. As a bastard son, I had nothing to my name. Now you're desperate to renew our relationship because you stand to profit from it."

"Such cruel words. You can't really mean them."

When she reached for him, he pushed her hands away. "I'm not amused by these feeble attempts to profess your love. Go back to the castle and take care of Fitz. That's where you belong."

She'd done dangerous things to be near him and had even traveled the ocean to be at his side. Sea sickness had made her miserable and Fitz had cried during a large majority of the voyage. How dare he turn her away like this? With great difficulty, she tried to silence the rage flaring in her mind.

"Think about what I said, Cort. I'll be patient."

Grunting, he shoved past her and led his stallion toward his men. She watched as he and his troops mounted and rode away, trying to think of what she could do to gain his attentions again. Then it all became clear to her, as if she'd received a vision from beyond.

Her lips upturned with a satisfied grin. She had to get rid of Rhiannon. That bitch had somehow managed to wrap Cort around her little finger. With her out of the picture, he would turn to her for comfort.

Laughing at how clever she'd become, she picked up her skirts and went for a walk along the ocean cliffs. Her feet as light as air, she made plans. As the wind whipped her hair about her shoulders, her mind whirred with ideas.

She would dispense of the wench who had dared to steal her man. Fortunately, to pass the time these last months, she'd thoroughly questioned the servants about Rhiannon. By now, she knew quite a bit about the Irish princess and her family.

All she needed to do was find a way to get rid of her. She knew if she watched and waited, an opportunity would make itself clear.

THE TIME PASSED WITH EXCRUCIATINGLY SLOWNESS. By December, Rhiannon still hadn't heard from Cort. She continued to stew about him and barely had an appetite. In order to keep up her strength for the child, she made herself eat regularly and tried to remain optimistic. It would do no good to brood about things she couldn't change.

She tried to keep her mind occupied by preparing for the birth. The babe wouldn't arrive until spring, but there were swaddling cloths, diapers, nightgowns, bonnets, bibs, and booties to be sewn. Moran, despite his ill health, spent hours building an oaken cradle, which she knew she would cherish forever.

She had even visited Sybil, who predicted the birth of a healthy son. The old prophetess said she would live through the birth and would go on to give Cort many more children. That encouraged her, but she still she worried.

Sybil had only read her tea leaves—how could she truly predict the future? She faced her mortality with uncertainty, as she did her father's. Most of all, she missed Cort's presence. If he were here, he would have calmed her fears.

Cort.

Every day she wondered how he fared and how the situation with her countrymen was being resolved. Her people were at a crossroads politically and she wished she could do something to help achieve peace. Ireland's destiny hung in the balance. Hopefully it would be a good one.

One day she awakened with a surge of energy she hadn't felt in quite a while. She decided to keep herself busy in order to take her mind off her concerns. After bathing and dressing, she went downstairs to the great hall and sat at the high table to break her fast with the family.

Moran was already there, picking at his meal. Though his face had taken on a gaunt quality and his eyes were large in his face. Rhiannon kissed his sunken cheek, feeling the parchment thin quality of his skin.

"How are you feeling?" she asked him.

"As well as can be expected. I fear I'm not long for this world, but I'm happy for the time I've had. I've had a good life."

She had no answer for him, except one simple declaration. "I love you, father."

He smiled. "As I love you, Rhiannon."

When Glenna appeared and began to clear away the dishes, she put a hand on the maid's arm.

"No, Glenna. I'll see to things."

Her brow furrowed. "Really my lady, that's not necessary."

"I insist. I need to stay busy. Otherwise, I fear I'll lose my mind."

After finishing her meal, Rhiannon went to the kitchen to discuss the day's meals with the cook. She and the pantler also discussed ordering more supplies.

Though Glenna had seen to it that the kitchen and the great hall remained orderly, Rhiannon ordered a thorough scrubbing. Her mother had always believed that cleanliness warded off illness and she had inherited that belief.

Next, she directed the servants as they decorated the great hall with pine boughs and bowls of pinecones to celebrate the impending holidays. She also gave the cook a list of savory foods to be prepared for the merriment that would occur during the season. Perhaps filling the halls with holiday joy would lift her mood.

After the day's activities, she went upstairs and passed through the solar in order to reach the castle's small chapel. Seated on the family pews, she concentrated on the candlelit altar. Standing in the highest niche was a large statue of Mother Mary cradling the infant Jesus. Flickering torches cast shadows that seemed to infuse the stone effigy with life.

Rhiannon crossed herself and began to pray softly for her father, asking for the Lord to ease his passing. She prayed the discontent in Ireland would soon be resolved and she also asked for Cort's safe return.

"Are you praying for your beloved?"

Surprised by the voice, she looked up to see Josette standing in the doorway, a smirk on her sharp features.

"What are you doing here?"

"Mayhap I wished to pray as well."

"These pews are for family," Rhiannon shot back. "Other guests are welcome on the lower level."

"Guests?" Josette snorted with contempt. "I'm the mother of Cort's son. How dare you relegate me to the servants' entrance."

Rhiannon didn't answer.

"You will soon find your husband doesn't think of me as such a lowly individual." Josette's nostrils flared. "In fact, before he left, he told me of his plans to have special quarters built for me in his new castle. He wants to keep me nearby."

Infuriated, Rhiannon held her hands tightly in her lap to keep them from trembling. "You're lying."

"Don't you wish."

"I refuse to listen to this nonsense."

With an arrogant toss of her dark curls, Josette continued. "Cort merely tolerates you, but he loves me. Always has. He had to be chivalrous toward you, otherwise your father would be displeased with him."

"Leave now," Rhiannon snapped. "Before I summon the guards and have you forcibly tossed out."

"Has Cort ever professed his love for you?" Josette lifted a finely arched brow.

"That is none of your business," Rhiannon shot back.

Now that Josette had brought up the subject, she realized it unsettled her that Cort hadn't declared his love. He obviously felt protective of her, but what exactly did she mean to him? Raw, vulnerable thoughts coursed through her and her chest filled with a hollow ache.

She reminded herself she hadn't told Cort she loved him, either. But did she? And if she did, would he ever return the sentiment?

"Ah ha. I thought not." Josette grinned. "Look at the bright side. Fitz and your child will be playmates. They'll grow up like brothers, yet since my son is older, I wonder if someday Cort will want him to inherit Callinon?"

Unable to stand the woman any longer, Rhiannon stood. "Guards!"

"You are a nervous little thing, aren't you?" Laughing, Josette flounced away.

The guards appeared in the doorway. One of them asked, "Is anything the matter, my lady?"

Pressing a hand against her heart, which had finally begun to ease its frantic beating, Rhiannon shook her head. "Thank you for coming so quickly, but everything's fine now."

When the guards left, she returned to her prayers, but a permanent knot had formed in her stomach. She wished she could kick Josette out of Callinon Castle. But for Cort and Fitz's sake, she would tolerate her.

THROUGHOUT THE NEXT WEEKS, RHIANNON MADE a point of avoiding Josette as much as possible. On Christmas Eve, Earc O'Crawley, the hunchback storyteller, arrived at the castle. He entertained everyone with his typical tales of humor and morality. Then he shared news of King Henry and his dealings with the Irish uprising. There had been several clashes of the king's troops against the rebels to the north. The Irishmen, poorly armed and outmanned by trained English soldiers, had suffered great losses.

When he began to recite details about the battles, Rhiannon clutched the arms of her chair so tightly her knuckles turned white. Everyone at the high table also wore tightly drawn expressions. Why must the blood of innocents be shed in order to restore peace?

Her thoughts were drawn immediately to Cort. Was he all right?

"Have you heard news of my husband?" she finally asked Earc.

Earc shook his head. "Sadly, my lady, I have not."

Glenna reached over to pat her arm. "Take heart," she said. "I'm sure he's very busy."

"Aye, I'm sure he is."

Another week went by and at last she received a letter from Cort. He'd filled it with interesting details about his duties, but he never mentioned his affection for her. Did he care for her as she'd begun to care for him? Or did he hold back as she did, for fear of rejection?

I love you, Cort.

The intensity of the thought sent a shock wave through her. She knew if he never returned her life would feel adrift and without meaning. Her heart squeezed as she thought of him lying hurt somewhere. The uncertainty of her people's future also weighed heavily on her mind.

Whenever unpleasant thoughts threatened to overwhelm her, Rhiannon struggled to banish them from her mind and concentrate on good things. For example, her growing child who had begun to kick firmly within her womb.

Christmas and the New Year came and went. The cold months lingered far past their usual season. Icy surfs pounded the beach below the castle and strong winds mercilessly lambasted the stone walls. The lingering cold weather added to her unease.

Despite the miserable weather, she clung to the hope that Cort would be home soon and all would be well, though she realized life never played out that simply. Most heartbreaking of all was watching her father fade from the robust man he'd once been into a bedridden old man gasping for air.

At last spring arrived, showering the countryside with warm rains that brought forth tender green shoots of grass and colorful flowers. The babe had grown large and her back ached more with each passing day. Her ankles swelled to great proportions and she found she could barely move about, let alone catch her breath.

One sunny afternoon, she and Glenna and Ailleen were in the garden preparing the soil for planting. Resting on her hands and knees in the dirt, Rhiannon gasped when a severe pain lanced her abdomen.

Groaning, she pushed to her feet and stretched, placing her hands on the small of her back.

Glenna looked up at Rhiannon with concern. "Are you all right?"

"I believe this child is anxious to born soon."

A scullery maid entered the garden and curtseyed before Rhiannon. Her voice shook when she spoke. "King Moran is calling for you and Ailleen. The physician says he's taken a turn for the worse."

She bit back a cry and hurried into the castle as fast as her unwieldy form could manage. In Moran's chambers, the women huddled at his bedside. His frail body stretched under the blankets and his labored breaths filled the chamber with a rasping sound as Father Murphy finished giving him the last rites.

The priest hugged both Rhiannon and Ailleen then stood aside.

When he opened his eyes and saw them, Moran managed a faint smile. "My girls," he muttered. "You must all be brave and strong . . . after I'm gone."

He began to cough and Rhiannon clasped one of his hands while Ailleen grabbed the other.

"I love you father." Warm tears spilled down Rhiannon's cheeks. "I always will."

"God's calling me home," he muttered. "Don't be sad. He's got a place . . . waiting for me."

Ailleen sobbed inconsolably and she wiped her small damp face on her sleeve.

"Cort promised me . . ." He coughed again and cleared his throat. "He promised me . . . he will take care of my daughters."

Rhiannon's heart felt as though it would break in two. The world would lose a good and honest man when her father passed. Life would not be the same without him.

He closed his eyes and his breathing became erratic, then finally stopped. The physician, who had been standing quietly in a corner, stepped forward and laid an ear on his chest. A moment later he straightened and shook his head.

Rhiannon couldn't hold back her own flood of tears as she rested her cheek against her father's. When Ailleen ran from the room crying, Glenna followed her.

She kissed her father's barely warm cheek and whispered, "I'll keep you in my heart until we meet again on that distant shore."

She ached all over, realizing she would never hear his voice again, never hear his laughter or benefit from his wisdom. Only memories of him would remain, as did those of her mother.

Pain ripped through her abdomen and she felt a gush of water running down her legs. Looking at her feet, she saw the pool of liquid between them. Her heart lurched, realizing the babe would make his way into the world on the same day her father had left it.

RHIANNON BORE DOWN AS EXCRUCIATING AGONY tore through her. It seemed like a thousand horses tore at her with their sharp hooves, but she gritted her teeth against the pain. Before long, she would hold her child in her arms. The child she and Cort had created with their lovemaking, the future heir of Callinon.

Glenna sat on the bed beside her, wiping the perspiration from her forehead with a cloth she dipped frequently in a bowl of cool water. "You're doing fine. It won't be much longer now."

The midwife at her feet lifted the blankets and peered between her legs. "Aye, the babe's nearly here."

She groaned as yet more torture ripped through her body. Weariness gnawed, like a hungry animal, but she refused to give into it.

The midwife's brows arched expectantly. "I see the wee one's head. It's time to bear down, my lady."

When an extreme pressure unlike anything she'd ever experienced filled her lower extremities, she summoned her remaining strength and pushed.

"Harder," the midwife encouraged.

Gritting her teeth again, Rhiannon gave another firm push. Something wet and warm slipped from her body. At last, the throbbing subsided to a dull ache.

Glenna clapped her hands. "Sybil predicted accurately. 'Tis a fine healthy son for you and Sir Cort."

An infant's wails filled the chamber and Rhiannon leaned back, exhausted. After the midwife cleaned him off, she handed her the squirming, red-faced baby. Immediately placing him at her breast, she watched as he nuzzled her nipple and began to suckle hungrily.

Gently stroking the dark tuft of hair on his tiny head, she noted that he had Cort's chin and his dark eyes. "I'll name you Moran, for my father."

"'Tis a good name." Glenna smiled down at the babe.

When little Moran had finished suckling and fell asleep in her arms, Rhiannon handed him to Glenna who laid him gently in his cradle. After a wide yawn, the child drifted into a contented slumber. As did Rhiannon.

Later, the midwife nudged Rhiannon awake. She handed her the whimpering child, who once more nuzzled greedily at her breast. Smiling down at her son, she gained a sense of satisfaction that the tiny boy would grow healthy from the nourishment her body provided.

A sense of overwhelming protectiveness rippled through her. No matter what the future held, she would defend her child and keep him safe from all harm. She just hoped that Cort would soon return home. She'd known when he left that she would miss him, but hadn't realized exactly how much.

When the babe had finished suckling, Rhiannon handed him to the midwife, who placed him gently in his cradle. Slowly, she rose from the bed and shuffled over to her writing desk. Seating herself carefully, she reached for quill and parchment then began to write another letter to Cort.

Dublin Castle, one month later

Sunshine slanted on Cort and his men as he practiced marching drills with them in the bailey. It had been weeks since they'd been engaged in any skirmishes and it seemed the Irish rebels had lost their taste for battle. Hopefully by now they had realized it was useless for them to try and challenge King Henry. The English were here to stay. The ragtag forces the locals had tried to pit against Henry's well-disciplined soldiers had quickly been disbanded.

Being a commander who insisted on accuracy and skill on the battlefield, Cort felt it important to keep his Norman contingent well practiced. He wanted them always at the ready for whenever King Henry called them to action.

Loud voices issued from the guard tower and he glanced over as the spiked gate slowly lifted up, allowing in a lone horse and rider. Cort recognized Quinn as he rode toward him and dismounted.

He smiled at the maturing adolescent who had carried messages between himself and Rhiannon these past months. "Have you another missive?"

"Aye, Sir Cort." Quinn withdrew a piece of folded parchment from his saddlebags.

After dismissing his troops, Cort took the letter. "Thank you, Quinn. How is everyone at Callinon?"

"Well, my lord."

"It's good to hear. Go inside and let the cook know I've sent you to get refreshment. Use the same chamber as before to stay the night before you return to Callinon."

"Will you have a letter for me to take back to Lady Rhiannon?"

"Yes. Visit my chamber before you leave in the morning." Cort handed Quinn some extra coins for his dependable service.

Quinn strode toward the castle, a confident grin on his lips. No doubt he enjoyed his promotion from mere stable boy to important messenger who bore letters between the lord and the lady of the manor.

Leaning against a stone wall, Cort broke open the wax seal. Eagerly he read the words, written in Rhiannon's fine penmanship.

Dear husband,

I hope this missive will find you in good health. I'm certain you would want to know that my father has passed, but we now have a healthy son. I named him Moran, after my father. He has your eyes . . .

Sadness struck him at the news that Moran had died, then was instantly replaced with joy when he read that Rhiannon had given birth to their son and how well her recovery had been coming along.

"Sweet *Jesu*, I hate that I couldn't be there with her," he exclaimed. He felt like he'd failed her on that account. Nevertheless, if relations between King Henry and the Irish continued to improve, he believed he would soon be returning to Callinon. Nothing would please him more than seeing his wife and newborn son.

Thinking about Callinon and the people there made him not only dwell on his wife and child, but he also wondered about Raoul and his investigation of Josette. He didn't find it surprising that he hadn't heard from his friend in all these months.

No doubt Raoul had chosen not to cross the Irish Sea during the winter months because the waters were choppier and more dangerous. That's what he would have done were he in the same position. Now that the weather had warmed up, Raoul would surely be arriving soon to report his findings.

Whistling, Cort went inside the castle and climbed the stairs to his chamber. He placed fresh parchment on his desk, dipped the tip of his quill pen into an inkwell and began to compose a message for Quinn to carry back to Rhiannon.

NINTEEN

WHEN JOSETTE ROLLED OUT OF JAMIE O'Brien's bed and pulled aside the curtains on his window, the sun warmed her bare skin. As she paced back and forth, she watched villagers bustling through the market square, going about their business.

A week ago, when she'd overheard servants mention that O'Brien was in the village outside of Callinon Castle enlisting O'Kelly clan members into his rebel army, she'd decided to make contact with him. If even a remote chance existed that he could help her get rid of Rhiannon, she felt willing to take the risk.

She'd slipped away from the castle one evening and found him in the local tavern, deep into his cups. Pretending to be a prostitute, she'd easily gotten him into bed. Thinking her nothing more than a common whore, he'd drunkenly told her everything he and Donovan had planned. He'd been so fascinated by her sexual abilities that he'd asked her to visit him each day, which she'd agreed to do.

"Come back here, woman." Jamie lifted the blankets, giving her a flash of his naked body. "I'm not finished with you."

"I can't dally with you all afternoon, Jamie. I've got to get back out on the street so I can pay my bills."

Her patience had worn thin. By now, it seemed her plan wouldn't be productive and she decided she'd been overly optimistic. Jamie hadn't mentioned anything that would help her. After she left here today, she decided not to return. She'd have to try and find another way to accomplish her goal.

Jamie pierced her with a hard stare. "If you service me well enough wench, I might consider taking you back with me to Leathenach Castle. Then you won't have to walk the streets anymore."

"At least as long as I keep you satisfied, right?"

He grunted a response and patted the mattress impatiently.

"How much longer will you be here?" Bored, Josette watched as a scruffy dog chased a cat into an alley, knocking over a barrel and spilling the contents.

"I hope not too much longer. The Clan O'Kelly men aren't eager to join our cause, so I might as well give it up."

She turned to him and lifted a brow. "Why?"

"There's not a single one who dares to go against that Norman bastard who's taken over Callinon Castle and considers himself Lord of Leinster. They're all loyal to him." His nostrils flared. "Donovan won't like this at all."

Josette paced a while longer, deep in thought. She knew Rhiannon and O'Brien had been betrothed at one time. Since a romantic history existed between them, mayhap she could use it to her advantage. When a possible solution to her predicament suddenly occurred, excitement gushed through her and she crawled back into bed.

Reaching for Jamie, she grinned and began to stroke his leg. "I have an idea that might help you."

"Wh-what?" He arched his back and groaned.

"I visit some of the guards at Callinon Castle on a regular basis. The other day, I overheard a servant mention that Princess Rhiannon planned to go shopping in the village tomorrow. If I create a distraction, when no one's looking, you could kidnap her."

"Why would I do that?"

Thinking him somewhat of a dullard, she continued patiently. "Even though she's married to the Norman, she's still an O'Kelly. Force her to join your cause. Then you'll have your Clan O'Kelly representation."

"Guyot would kill me."

"He's in Dublin. By the time he realizes his wife's gone, you'll have already waged the assault against King Henry."

He narrowed his gaze at her. "How do you know where Guyot is?"

"Like I said before, the servants talk. I listen." Josette laughed. If things worked according to plan, Rhiannon might either die in battle or King Henry would execute her as a traitor. Having her reputation besmirched would be perfect.

After Cort found out his wife had betrayed him, he would be livid. When he returned to Callinon, he would be raw and vulnerable. At that point, she felt certain she could convince him to take her as his lover again or possibly even marry her.

Josette imagined herself as the mistress of the keep and found it quite pleasing indeed. A fire of determination consumed her. She intended to see this through.

"Hmmm, it's an idea worth considering," Jamie admitted.

"It's brilliant, Jamie. After you've taken Princess Rhiannon, tell her that if she doesn't cooperate, you'll attack Callinon Castle. The Norman's taken most of his troops with him and it would be an easy target right now. She'll be so worried for her sister and child that she'll go along with whatever you want."

He chuckled. "Clever, clever woman."

Once, a long time ago, Jamie had believed himself in love with Rhiannon. What a young fool he'd been. If he had married her, he wouldn't hold his current prestigious position with Donovan.

Nevertheless, the idea of having Rhiannon under his control tempted him greatly. By forcing her to join their cause, it would mean they had representation from all the clans. Never in the history of Ireland had all of them joined together to fight off an enemy.

The men would be more encouraged than ever. He and Donovan would drive King Henry and his troops from Ireland once and for all. Afterward, Donovan would take over as Ireland's high king.

Most attractive of all; Donovan had promised to promote Jamie from captain to the commander of his army regiments. In that position, he'd have the world at his fingertips. Everything he'd ever wanted would fall into his lap.

IT HAD BEEN A MONTH SINCE Rhiannon had given birth to little Moran. To her delight, he seemed to grow bigger each day. Since he had such a demanding appetite, she'd hired a wet nurse. She hated to turn over the experience of nursing him to someone else, but unfortunately, she didn't have enough milk to keep him satisfied.

She wished Cort were here to see him. Every day she saw something new in her son and she hated that his father was missing so much. It would have been wonderful to share the experience of watching their son grow together.

Cort.

Did she have a place in his thoughts? He seemed to be on her mind every minute of every day. She hated to think it was only her who felt this way about their relationship.

One morning she had a servant carry Moran's cradle out into the sunny garden and set it in the shade. After placing the babe in his in his wooden bed, she rocked him gently, humming a soft tune.

Once he'd fallen asleep, she turned to the arbor and began to trim pink and red roses with a small knife. Inhaling their sweet fragrance, she smiled, recalling how much her mother had loved them.

"Lady Rhiannon?"

She dropped the blossoms into a basket and turned to see Quinn striding toward her with a letter in his hand. "'Tis a note from Sir Cort."

"Thank you, Quinn. Go to the kitchen and get yourself some

breakfast from Leila. When you're finished, will you drive me into the village? I'd like to do some shopping in the marketplace."

"Of course, my lady."

After dismissing the stable boy, she sank onto a stone bench and tore open the sealed parchment. Eagerly she read Cort's words, his sadness at her father's passing and joy at little Moran's birth. Warmth filled her cheeks as he talked about how he wished he'd been with her when she gave birth. He also wrote of how much he missed her and longed to hold her in his arms.

Hopefully King Henry will return to England soon and I'll return to you . . .

She filled with anticipation at the thought. No longer could she deny her feelings for Cort. She thought of him constantly— his magical kisses, his sensual touch, and his large, comforting warmth beside her as they slept. Most of all, she recalled the tenderness with which he always made love to her. She shivered as she recalled each of the treasured memories and looked forward to the time when they could be together again.

Though she'd been hesitant to accept him as her husband at first, he'd shown himself as a true champion of Ireland. Earc had visited several times that spring, bringing more news of small uprisings throughout the country. All had been quickly put down by the English army. True to his word, Cort had encouraged King Henry to be lenient in his dealings with the rebels. She dared to hope that the trouble would end soon and that peace with England might be at hand.

Glenna entered the garden. "Quinn wanted me to fetch you, my lady. He's ready to drive you into the village."

She put Cort's letter into a pocket of her gown and stood. "Moran's growing so fast, I'm going to shop for material to stitch him larger clothing."

"He'll be a brawny man someday, just like his father." Smiling, Glenna moved toward the cradle and glanced down at the sleeping child.

"Will you watch him for me?"

"Aye. That's one duty I'll never grow tired of."

"Thank you, Glenna." After kissing her son's petal soft cheek, she hurried into the bailey where Quinn stood waiting beside a wagon. He helped her into the seat then drove toward the village.

Loud voices rang throughout the marketplace brimming with stalls displaying furniture, trinkets, and pastries. Quinn parked the wagon and as she got down, she spotted a table loaded with bolts of bright material.

She pointed at it. "I'm going over there, Quinn."

"I'll wait for you here, my lady."

At the table, she fingered the different textures. As she chose her favorites, she imagined the tiny clothing she would create. When a scream pierced the air, she looked up to see a plume of smoke rising from a bale of hay in the middle of the market square.

A tall man pushed his way through the crowd shouting, "Fire, fire!"

More cries of alarm rose his as people ran in all directions. Others gathered buckets, dipped them in horse troughs, and quickly doused the smoldering straw.

When a large hand clamped on Rhiannon's mouth, she struggled to free herself. Her strength couldn't match her attacker's and she felt herself being hauled into the dark shadows of the alley.

She twisted this way and that, trying to break loose. Nothing worked. Whoever held her had the strength of an ox and she couldn't budge an inch. Panicked, she bit down hard on the meaty flesh of her attacker's palm. A man's hoarse growl filled her ear and the hand fell away from her mouth.

She tried to shout, but a blunt crack to her temples rendered her speechless. Stunned, she fell to the ground. Red agony tore through her as she saw Josette's face swimming before her eyes, a chunk of wood in her hands. Then Jamie O'Brien leaned over her and grinned.

"Wh-what's going on?"

Josette's laughter echoed in her brain as a vortex of swirling blackness claimed her.

WHEN THE DRAWBRIDGE LIFTED, CORT RODE with his men into Callinon Castle's bailey. After nine long months in Dublin helping the English army put down unrest among the Irish, King Henry believed the threat had subsided enough that Cort and his Norman contingent could be released from duty. After Searlas sailed back to Normandy, Cort and his men had left.

Home at last. After a lifetime of never belonging anywhere, the idea of having a place to hang his armor filled him with contentment. His chest swelled with anticipation as he thought of his little family waiting for him. He looked forward to seeing his new son for the first time, but the thought of seeing Rhiannon again made his heart race.

Ever since he'd left, she'd been constantly on his mind. Not a day had gone by when he didn't think of her. Everywhere he went, she'd been there with him in spirit and in thought. Never in his wildest imagination had he believed he could ever miss a woman as much as he did her.

His dreams had been filled with images of her fiery red hair and his loins had burned at the memory of her ardent passion. The fact that he wanted to be with her as much as possible filled him with awe.

Back when Moran offered marriage to his daughter in return for military protection of Callinon, Cort had planned only on a political match that would enhance his future. It had never occurred to him that he would become this fond of his wife.

Does she think about me as much as I think about her?

He believed he'd sensed traces of affection flowing from the words in her letters. Hopefully, he hadn't been mistaken. He'd feel like a fool if he had let his emotions rule over his common sense.

As his men dismounted and began to get settled, he climbed down eagerly from his saddle. A boy emerged from the stable and took the stallion's reins.

Cort glanced at the front steps of castle, wondering why Rhiannon hadn't come out to greet him yet. He frowned as an anxious moment cast a shadow over his mood, but he forced it aside and turned to the boy.

"Where is everyone?"

"Inside, my lord."

"Lady Rhiannon as well?"

The stable boy lowered his gaze to study the ground and shuffled his feet, as though uncomfortable. "Glenna is in the great hall. She'll want to tell you about Lady Rhiannon."

Puzzled, Cort hurried inside and found Rhiannon's maid. Seated in a chair, she bounced a baby on her lap as several servants set out a light repast on trestle tables.

"Thank the saints you're home." She rose to greet him. "I've ordered a meal for your troops. I'm sure they're hungry."

"Yes, they're famished." Cort had noticed the tightness in her voice and dreaded the cause. A hunch that things weren't right hit him. Studying the child, he asked, "Is this my son?"

She nodded. "I'm sure you'd like to hold him."

When he held out his arms, she placed the infant in them. His heart melted at the feel of his son's small warm body pressed against his chest. When the babe looked up at him and began to gurgle, he smiled.

"Rhiannon was right. He does take after me, but I see her features in him as well." He heard the anxiety in his voice and for some reason, dreaded hearing the answer to his next question. "Speaking of my wife, where is she?"

Glenna's countenance paled. "We're not entirely certain. Quinn drove her to the marketplace one day and neither of them returned. We fear Donovan's taken her, but no one knows for certain."

Disbelief shot through him. "I can't believe it. She's gone?"

"We've looked everywhere for them, my lord, but so far—"

"I know what happened." Josette flounced into the room, her skirts swishing importantly. "She ran off with Jamie O'Brien."

"We don't know that," Glenna scoffed.

"Yes, we do." A haughty smile spread across Josette's face.

Cort wanted to pound a fist on the table or slam it into the wall, but for his son's sake, he held back his temper. He didn't want to frighten the child. Still, he could hardly believe Rhiannon had left him. All this time, he'd thought they were growing closer. *Has she been planning to leave me all along?* Even though the idea occurred to him, it didn't seem right. Rhiannon had great common sense. This didn't seem like something she'd do.

He held the babe closer, wanting to study him for hours on end. But he couldn't relax and enjoy the miracle he and Rhiannon had brought into the world. His heart was deeply troubled.

A part of him couldn't imagine she would abandon their child, even if she had been upset about something. She'd expressed sympathy to him about his own mother leaving him with his father when he had been a babe. How could she be so heartless that she would do it to her own son?

A small voice taunted him with further questions. Had her acceptance of their marriage been merely a ruse so that as soon as she could make her escape, she could go to O'Brien?

It didn't seem rational. She'd had more than one opportunity to go to him before. The man worked for Donovan, a man she swore to be her family's worst enemy. Sweet *Jesu,* the dilemma tore at him. Why would she do such a thing?

At last, he managed to get a grip on his wandering mind. Uneasiness continued to wash over him, but he had to gather all the facts. "How long has she been gone?"

Worry lines creased Glenna's forehead. "She disappeared about a week ago. Uther and the castle guards have searched everywhere, but so far, they haven't had any luck. There are many rumors floating around about what happened, but I fear she's been taken."

"Have people in the village been questioned?"

Glenna nodded. "No one saw a thing. I feel so responsible. I should have left little Moran with his wet nurse and gone with her and Quinn to the market that day . . ."

He placed a hand on her shoulder. "You couldn't have known this would happen."

"I told you I saw Rhiannon with my own two eyes," Josette snapped. "She was betrothed to O'Brien once, wasn't she? Mayhap she grew bored waiting for Cort's return and took him as her lover. And she hates King Henry. It's no wonder she's joined the rebellion."

Glenna shook her head in disbelief.

How had Josette known of Rhiannon's past with Jamie? Cort began to fume. She'd obviously been snooping around asking questions about her. Why? What was that she-devil up to now?

He didn't blame Glenna for her skepticism, especially since he didn't put much weight in Josette's ideas either. Nevertheless, he decided to hear her version, though he doubted she would speak the truth.

"All right, Josette. Why are you so convinced my wife left?"

"On the day she disappeared, I was in town. When people around me began to whisper about seeing Jamie O'Brien, I turned to look. That's when I saw her with him."

"And?"

"They were . . . well . . ." Her face went blank.

He detected the uncertainty in her story, but wanted to hear what lie she had concocted. "Go on. I'm waiting. What were they doing?"

She licked her lips and seemed to struggle for words. "Kissing. That's right. They were kissing. They were in an alley with a couple of horses. And men. Lots of them. They all rode off together. I swear it didn't look like he was forcing her to do anything."

A cloud of doubt hung over her details. Could Rhiannon really have done such a thing? She may have been anxious at first to accept Cort into her life, but she'd never deceived him. On the other hand, Josette had proven herself a scheming wench. He knew he couldn't trust a word she said.

The rational part of his mind told him not to believe Josette. But what if Rhiannon *had* left of her own accord? He'd look like a complete idiot chasing after her if she'd rejected him.

Yet the fact remained that they were man and wife and it was known far and wide. He would not allow her to make a laughing-stock of him if she had indeed been cavorting about the country-side with the rebels. A muscle ticked in his jaw as he contemplated his conflicting emotions, still in shock and disbelief that Rhiannon would do this to him.

"Is it that difficult to believe that your wife would leave you? Women are fickle creatures." Josette trailed her fingers up and down his arm. "You've said so yourself."

"Not Rhiannon."

"It's sad, but true." With a nonchalant shrug, she continued. "You think you know someone, then *poof,* they go and do some-thing that completely catches you off guard."

He handed the baby back to Glenna and when Josette tried to take his arm, he shook it off. "Leave me alone, woman. I don't have time for your nonsense."

"I only wanted to comfort you."

"I don't need comfort from the likes of you. I'm going to look for my wife."

When Josette flounced away in a huff, he stormed to the sleep-ing chamber he and Rhiannon had shared. He went to a large chest and threw it open. He lifted a gown and buried his face in the soft material. Rhiannon's scent still lingered and he envisioned his fiery-tempered, beautiful woman. At what point in time had he come to care for her so much? It didn't matter. He wanted her back at his side where she belonged.

It drove a lance of pain his heart to even think of her being gone. Raw jealousy coursed through him. Never had he experi-enced that dark emotion and he didn't like the way it felt. Stepping back, he eyed the clothing. Nothing seemed out of place.

That puzzled him. Had she been in such a hurry to leave him

she hadn't bothered to pack? Or had she been taken against her will as Glenna suggested?

He stormed outside and whistled for Arch. The dog darted from the stable where he'd no doubt been stalking cats and loped toward his master.

Cort hunkered down to scratch between the greyhound's ears, deciding what course of action to take. In his dog's trusting eyes, he found his answer. "We need to go after Rhiannon, don't we?"

Arch began to lick his hand and whine.

"You're right. There's no time to waste. I'll gather my best men to scour the village for any clues Uther's men may have missed."

Arch trotted eagerly alongside him as he headed to the barracks he'd ordered his men to build. Since his troops would now reside at Callinon, he'd decided they needed more permanent quarters than tents.

Approaching the door, he stopped to glance up the hill where the walls of his new castle jutted gracefully. He'd looked forward to living in it with Rhiannon. Without her at his side, it no longer held the same appeal.

I have to find her.

After he'd enlisted fifty of his finest troops, they saddled their horses and rode into town. Once there, he had the soldiers spread out to search every nook and cranny. He ordered that each man, woman, and child be questioned about the day of the fire. An event like that wasn't likely to be forgotten. Even the slightest spark could prove devastating to a roof made of thatch, and the villagers lived in fear of flames reducing their homes to rubble.

The villagers were more than cooperative. They, too, loved Rhiannon for the kindness she'd shown them over the years. Unfortunately, even after he and the men had conducted a thorough search, they still hadn't turned up any traces of what happened to her.

Even more troubled than when they'd arrived, Cort mounted his stallion and prepared to ride back to the castle with the other men. Arch suddenly pricked his ears and began to bark wildly at something.

"What's wrong, boy?" Cort wheeled his horse around so he could see what had alerted his dog. Someone in disheveled clothing had staggered into the village. Covered in bruises and bloody cuts, he held out a hand toward him.

"Sir Cort . . ."

When Arch gave a short, happy yip and ran toward the figure, Cort instantly knew who he was. Swinging down from his horse, he hurried up to the youth. "Quinn!"

"I'm so sorry," he said in a strangled voice, then collapsed in Cort's arms.

CORT AND HIS MEN RODE BACK to the castle as quickly as they could. He called for Glenna who insisted Quinn be placed in one of the chambers where she could take care of his wounds and watch over him.

During the last couple of days, she'd conducted a bedside vigil, tending to his injuries. The boy had been unconscious during the entire time, and no wonder. He'd been beaten nearly beyond recognition.

Cort wanted to hunt down and squeeze the life out of whoever had done this to the boy. Sleep eluded him and he could barely eat. He worried about Quinn's health and he pondered Rhiannon's fate. The idea that she might be lying somewhere in this condition, or worse, haunted him constantly.

Until now, he'd never realized how much losing her would impact his life. It had finally become clear to him what it meant to love someone. For as surely as the sun rose each morning and set each evening, he knew now he loved her.

On several occasions, Josette sidled up to him to offer her version of comfort. Each time, he dismissed her curtly. He couldn't stand the sight of the witch, for he felt certain she knew what had happened to his wife.

Glenna had nearly worn herself to a frazzle taking care of Quinn. Even though she'd done all she could, along with the physician she'd fetched from the village, he still remained unconscious. The injuries to his skull had been so severe, the physician feared he may never wake up and if he did, he may not know who he was.

One day Cort offered to take up the watch at Quinn's bedside so Glenna could rest. He felt terrible as he watched the boy's lifeless form. He couldn't be more than fourteen or fifteen, but in his frail condition, he looked even younger.

Why had he said he was sorry when he'd wandered into town? What had he meant? Cort feared the answer, but still held out the hope that Quinn might yet awaken and tell them what had happened.

Cort made a vow that if the boy pulled through this, he would reward his loyalty by seeing to his training as a knight. Most boys started at around eight as pages then moved up through the ranks. But it didn't really matter if Quinn got a late start. He wanted to offer him a position in his military contingent when he came of age.

Leaning back in his chair, he began to doze.

"Sir Cort?"

He shook himself awake and lowered the chair, pleased to see Quinn's eyes wide open and staring at him.

"You're awake!"

"Aye, and thirsty."

Cort handed him a goblet of water and the youth gulped it down then swiped the back of his hand across his mouth. "That bastard couldn't keep me down for long."

"Who did this to you? I'll kill him with my bare hands."

" 'Twas Donovan, that spawn on of the devil. He drew great pleasure beating me every day or so. The time he assigned a guard to do it, I managed to wrest the whip from him and knock him down cold. Thank the saints I managed to escape."

"Through the old air shaft?"

Quinn grinned. "Aye."

"How in God's name did he get a hold of you in the first place? And where's Rhiannon?"

"The day I drove her into town, there was a fire. While everyone was running to put it out, Jamie O'Brien came out of the alley and grabbed her. I tried to save her, but Josette came at me with a huge timber and knocked me unconscious. He hauled both of us to Leathenach Castle."

"*Sacre bleu*, I'm going to throttle that woman." Fury shot through Cort. He wanted to have it out with her right now. But he needed more information. "Where is Rhiannon now?"

"Jamie's got her locked in the tower. He threatened to attack Callinon and kill everyone if she didn't stay with him."

"And in my haste to join King Henry, I took most of my soldiers," he growled. "I left Callinon nearly defenseless."

"You thought the rebels threatened Dublin, my lord. We all did."

"Still, it was reckless. I should have known better."

Quinn winced as he shifted in the bed.

"I'm so sorry this happened, Quinn."

"I'll live.

Cort clenched his fists. "If Jamie's hurt Rhiannon in any way I'll gut him like a fish."

"He hasn't touched her. He wants her looking good and riding at his side when they wage their assault on Dublin Castle. Donovan's got representation from all the clans for his uprising and she'll represent Clan O'Kelly."

"The fools, I can't believe they're still planning to attack King Henry. His soldiers will tear them to ribbons."

"Lady Rhiannon is in grave danger, my lord."

"I know, Quinn. And I know you did your best to try and save her. For that I thank you."

"But I failed."

Cort patted his shoulder. "No you didn't. I'm going after her and I intend to bring her home."

"Sir Cort?"

He turned to see Glenna in the doorway holding little Moran. "What is it?"

"We have visitors. Sir Raoul has returned. He's brought the sheriff with him, as well as two visitors from Normandy."

Cort walked downstairs and out into the bailey with Glenna. A much thinner and paler Raoul and the sheriff stood beside a wagon. A man helped a woman down from her seat and they stood next to the sheriff.

Someone must have hailed the arrival of visitors because Josette came out onto the castle steps along with several other servants.

Cort greeted his friend with a clap on his back, glad to see he'd returned safely. "Raoul, old man. We thought you'd decided to take off for parts unknown."

"You're not so easily rid of me." He looked at Moran chewing on his fists and kicking his chubby legs in Glenna's arms. "Is he yours?"

He nodded. "My son, Moran. Named for his grandfather."

"You don't waste time, do you my friend?" Raoul grinned for a moment then became serious. "I caught a fever nearly the second I stepped foot in Normandy. It took me a while to shake off the malaise and by then the winter had set in. But here I am now."

"What news have you brought us?" Cort noticed Josette creeping toward the castle's double doors.

"First things first." Raoul bounded up the steps, grasped Josette's arm and nodded at the sheriff who came forward and shackled her wrists.

Josette cried with outrage. "How dare you handle me in such a manner? Why are you doing this?"

"You're under arrest," the sheriff said.

"I don't understand," she sputtered.

Raoul led the man and the woman to the castle steps. "I want you to meet Henriette and Remy Toussaint. Fitz's parents."

A collective gasp went up from the gathering. Everyone stared at Josette, their expressions accusatory.

Josette visibly shrank under their harsh perusal and struggled to free herself from the sheriff's grip.

Raoul nodded at her. "Josette posed as the Toussaint's nurse maid, kidnapped their child, and disappeared. They feared they'd never see him again."

Cort's brows rose in amazement. *Fitz isn't my son?* He'd sensed all along something didn't seem right between Josette and the child. Fitz had never seemed to respond properly to her as a child should to its mother.

Josette turned deathly white and her mouth worked open and closed as she thought of what to say. "This is all wrong," she finally snarled. "They're lying."

"We'll let Fitz be the judge of that." Cort took Moran from Glenna. "Would you be so kind as to fetch the child?"

"Gladly." Glenna went inside and returned a few moments later balancing Fitz on her hip. Upon seeing the Toussaints, he began to squeal joyfully and clap his chubby hands. When he reached out toward Henriette, Glenna handed him over.

Tears ran down the Toussaints' cheeks as they hugged their child and spoke lovingly to him.

"Thank you for finding my little Gaston," Henriette said in halting English as tears streamed down her cheeks.

"You are most welcome madam." Cort handed Moran back to Glenna and turned to the sheriff. "Escort Josette to the jail and lock her up."

"But you can't do that." Josette's brow knitted with concern and her voice took on a petulant tone. "My father will not like this one bit."

"I've already discussed this with him." Raoul frowned at her. "He isn't happy about what you've done and fears if people find out about your criminal activities, your family's reputation will be ruined. He met with the Toussaints and together they decided how you should be punished."

"I don't believe this." She strained at her shackles.

"You can spend the rest of your life in prison, or you can enter the convent near your parents' home. Your choice."

"Become a nun?" She wrinkled her nose.

"What do you say?"

Her expression darkened. "I suppose the nunnery it is then."

"Now tell me what you did to Rhiannon," Cort growled at her.

She batted her dark eyelashes in feigned confusion. "Whatever are you talking about?"

"Quinn told me everything. I should have you horse whipped."

"Jamie made me do it," she whined.

"Liar. Tell me the truth."

Her voice took on a petulant tone. "I've been so upset with you lately. I'd have done anything to get you to love me. When Jamie O'Brien came in town to recruit men for the rebellion, I went to him."

"And?"

She looked up at him through lowered eye lashes. "I suggested that he should take Rhiannon with him to represent Clan O'Kelly in the uprising."

"You plotted to have her kidnapped?" He felt like striking her, but would never do such a thing to a woman, no matter how infuriated he became. "How did he take her without anyone seeing?"

"I told him when she'd be in the village. I started a small fire and when everyone was distracted, he made his move."

"Damn you!"

Raoul nodded at the sheriff. "Take her away. I'll come for her when I'm ready to set sail for Normandy."

"Aye." The sheriff dragged a reluctant Josette to the wagon and helped her into the seat. As they drove off, she turned to give Cort one last accusatory stare.

Ignoring her evil look, he met Raoul's gaze. "You are a hero, my friend."

"I don't know about that. But I'm glad you appreciate my efforts."

"Surely everyone's famished from the long journey." Glenna

waved the visitors toward Callinon's entrance. "Come along and I'll have a meal prepared."

"Do you want me to go with you to find Rhiannon?" Raoul studied Cort.

"No. You're worn out from your journey."

"Are you sure?"

"I'll have all the help I need. If it's the last thing I do, I'll bring my wife home."

Cort spent the next hours gathering a company of his best men along with supplies and other provisions for the journey to Leathenach. It wasn't long before they rode from Callinon Castle and headed toward Donovan's nest of rebels.

TWENTY

STANDING ON TIP TOE, RHIANNON TRIED to look out the small window in the room that had been her jail for the last few weeks. The glass panes were secured with wooden shutters, but a crack between the boards allowed her a small view of the sunny courtyard below.

Frustrated at her inability to see more, she pulled away. After all this time, the gloom in her cramped quarters had nearly gotten to her. Fretting about recent events had begun to make her crazy.

When Quinn returned and told everyone she'd gone missing, she imagined Glenna would have Uther send out men to search for her. She knew they'd eventually come to the conclusion that Donovan had taken her, but Cort had left only a handful of men to defend the keep since he'd believed, as everyone else had, that Callinon Castle was no longer a rebel target. She didn't fault him for his strategy. Had she been in a similar situation, she'd have done the same thing.

The fact remained, however, that Uther hadn't been left with enough men to try and rescue her from Leathenach.

With a sigh, she realized, once again, her chances of escape were slim to none. She tried to remain optimistic, but her valiant efforts seemed in vain. As far as she knew, Cort was still in Dublin with

King Henry and had no idea that Jamie had hauled her here. With each passing hour, her hopes diminished. Her situation appeared bleak and desperate.

A familiar ache started at her temples and spread through her brain. She missed little Moran and agonized at not being with him. Each passing day she spent away from her child, the more she died inside. She missed everyone at Callinon, but most of all, she missed Cort.

Only in her dreams now could she feel his reassuring touch and enjoy his magical kisses. Thinking of him made her shiver with longing. In all truth, she may never see him again. As the reality sliced painfully through her, she began to pace.

Do something, a small voice insisted. But what?

Even if she'd been able to escape, she couldn't do it. Jamie had made it clear that if she tried to slip away, he would attack Callinon and kill every living thing that got in his way, including her sister and little Moran.

She would have to take her chances with whatever fate had in store for her when she was caught with Donovan's band of rebels. From what she understood, his army had grown to vast proportions. She still didn't think it strong enough to take on the king's soldiers. Nevertheless, she would be caught in the middle. Because she rode with them, everyone would assume that she, too, had joined their cause.

Slumping onto her makeshift pallet, she cradled her forehead in her hands, feeling the lump where Josette had hit her. Though it had mostly healed, she still suffered daily headaches from the blow. Especially when she became agitated—like now.

Dizziness clawed at her and she felt sick to her stomach. Closing her eyes and breathing carefully in and out, she tried to get a hold of herself.

Hearing someone fumble with the door lock, she looked up in time to see Jamie stride inside, his face full of cocky assurance. Glancing at him from between her fingers, she realized this was only the second time she'd seen him since he'd brought her here. She'd had little company except for the servants who had brought her food and cleared away her chamber pot.

"Good morning love," he offered in a syrupy voice. "How are you feeling today?"

"Like I'd run you through with my sword if I had it. Where's Josette? I want to give her a taste of my blade, too."

He grinned. "You don't need to worry about her. You do need to worry about yourself, you naughty girl. That's no decent greeting for your betrothed."

"You're out of your mind, Jamie." She lowered her hands, fighting back her disgust as she stared at the face she'd once loved. "I'd never wed you now. Fortunately, it's not possible. I'm already married."

"That's right. I heard how your father forced you to marry the Norman." He clicked his tongue. "Such a pity."

She stood and squared her shoulders. "My father didn't *force* me. He simply believed it to be the best for our people and I agreed."

"You don't have to try and save face in front of me, Rhiannon. We shared too much in the past for you hide your true emotions. I know you too well. You must have been devastated when I left. And I'm sure you hated being coerced into marrying that mercenary."

When he tried to pull her into his arms, she pushed him away.

He threw back his head and laughed. "I see you missed my touch."

"Believe me Jamie; I didn't waste any time pining away for you. Traitors and liars have no place in my heart."

"Then why do you stay with the Norman? He's betrayed our people and let the English loose upon our shores."

"He wasn't the one who betrayed us. It was the Pope who bartered us away like a barrel of fish and declared that Ireland belonged to England. No one can defy the Church."

"Which is why we practice Ireland's old religion, not Catholicism. No matter, King Henry won't be around much longer.

We're about to launch a clan war against him. If he's not killed in the conflict, I'm sure he'll run back home whimpering with his tail between his legs."

"Think man! It's foolish to try and attack the English. Do you have any idea of their military strength? King Henry said he brought ten thousand troops with him."

Jamie blinked several times. "He's bluffing. Besides, we have nearly that many clan warriors gathered to fight. And we have the advantage. We know the lay of the land. He doesn't."

Rhiannon shook her head. "How is it you think you can take on the English, when countries all over the world haven't been able to defeat them? You're mad, Jamie. Along with Donovan and the rest. You're going to get a lot of good men killed."

"You've been brainwashed, Rhiannon."

"Hardly. I simply have the common sense you're lacking. Either we make peace with the English or they'll wipe us out entirely."

"Is that what your Norman's trying to do?"

"Aye, he's sworn to represent our best interests. So far, he's done a good job of it. Why don't you let him finish his work?"

"Because he's an outsider. He doesn't belong. This country belongs to us and us alone."

"Don't you see it's too late for the clans to suddenly stand together after centuries of fighting? Ireland has been divided for so long it's become weak. Cort has King Henry's ear and his negotiations with the English are now our only hope of peace."

"Enough of this," he growled. "You're here to represent Clan O'Kelly in our war. Your clan is the only one we've been lacking. Just in case you've forgotten, I'll remind you of my earlier promise. If you don't go along with me, I'll kill everyone near and dear to you."

Even though he held the upper hand, she refused to be intimidated by his threats. "You always were a bully, Jamie. You're mean and vindictive if you don't get your way."

"Once upon a time you thought me brave and fearless."

"I've grown up since then. I see you for the coward you really are. You stand for whatever side will give you the most advantages. You're nothing but a puny excuse for a man."

He seemed to be taking the bait for he clenched his fists and his nostrils flared. "You know nothing of war."

Encouraged by his reaction, she continued goading. "Oh, but I do. When it seemed my father's kingdom had wound up on the losing side, you took your people and went over to Donovan. What did that bastard promise you? Riches? Land? Probably both."

"What do you care?" A muscle ticked in his jaw and he appeared unsettled.

"I don't. It's just a shame how he goaded you into doing so many horrible things for him when he'll probably never come through on his promises. You're just his lap dog, Jamie. He's only using you."

"You're wrong, Rhiannon. He's mentored me. I've learned that the best way to get what you want is to take it by force."

"Someday soon you're going to regret what you've done. Mark my words."

"I doubt it. Now, we've been apart for too long sweetheart. I've missed you." He yanked her into his arms and kissed her harshly.

She jerked loose and slapped him. "You never should have taken me, Jamie. Cort will come. And when he does, he'll kill you."

Placing a hand on his red cheek, Jamie raised a dark brow. "Don't hold your breath, Rhiannon. He's not going to come looking for you. Josette plans to tell him that you went away with me willingly. That you abandoned not only him, but your son."

Fear coiled through her insides. She would not give into it. Holding her head high, she spoke again. "He won't believe her. She's not that good of a liar."

"On the contrary, she is good. Very good. Both in bed and out."

Would Cort believe her? She'd tried to let him know, through the subtle conversation in her letters, that she had strong feelings for him. Would he think she'd been lying?

It had bothered her during her entire captivity that he wouldn't find out the truth of what happened to her and might think she'd betrayed him. To have Jamie remind her of those concerns filled her with distress.

Something inside of her snapped and she lashed out at him again. "Josette's using you too, Jamie. You're such a fool."

"Just as I'm using her." He shrugged. "So what? We all use each other."

"I don't use people."

"Ha. That's not true. You once believed I had much to offer and you told me you loved me. But you love the Norman now, don't you?"

Even as he spoke the words, she knew that at least on that account, he spoke the truth. "Yes, I thought I loved you once. But it wasn't because of what you could offer me. I truly had feelings for you."

"Bah." He waved a dismissive arm. "Women and their feelings. It's ridiculous."

"Love is the glue that holds the world together," Rhiannon said. "But you're right about one thing. Back then I didn't really know what love was. Now I do."

"You love me one minute then you love him the next." His voice filled with a mocking tone. "How easily you switch your loyalties."

"You're just angry because no one will ever truly care about you." She turned her back on him but he grabbed her and wrestled her down to the blankets. His hot breath brushed her skin as he covered her face and neck with wet kisses.

Revulsion coursed through her veins and she scratched his cheek, then drove a knee into his groin.

"Bitch!" He gave a hoarse cry and sat up to rub his groin with one hand and ran a hand over his bleeding face with the other.

At the insistent knock on the door, he swore loudly, then swung a leg over her and went to answer it. A servant girl stood there holding a large basket. Rhiannon immediately recognized Ena—the daughter of Callinon's cook. The girl had disappeared months ago; why was she here?

"I've brought the things you wanted, Jamie." Her eyes widened when she saw Rhiannon.

Grabbing her arm, Jamie pulled Ena inside. To Rhiannon he shouted, "Put these on and be ready to leave in ten minutes."

After he stormed from the room, she walked over to examine the items in the basket. There were leather leggings, boots about her size and a sturdy brown shirt. She also found a hauberk, chausses and gauntlets. Obviously, Jamie wanted her to dress like she had joined the war against King Henry. Though it filled her with loathing, she did so, realizing she had no other choice.

Grunting, she began to put on the clothing and armor. "Your mother's been worried sick about you, Ena."

Ena cast her eyes downward. "I thought I was in love with Jamie so I ran away with him. He treated me like a real lady for a while before I realized he was only trying to get information about Callinon out of me. By then, it was too late. He kept me well guarded and told me if I tried to get away, he'd kill me."

She saw the pain in Ena's eyes and realized she told the truth. Her crime had only been that of being an impressionable girl who had been fooled by sweet words and kisses from a handsome man. Her heart went out to her.

"We all make mistakes, Ena."

"Not like this. I've really made a mess of things. One time Donovan threatened to cut out my tongue if I didn't tell him whether Callinon had a secret passage. I couldn't help it. I told him about the one in the store room."

Irritation washed over Rhiannon, but there was nothing to be done at this point. "Now I know how Donovan was able to get inside and kidnap Ailleen."

"I can never go home now for shame of what I've done." Ena buried her face in her hands and began to sob.

"Ailleen's all right now. We got her back." Rhiannon patted Ena's shoulder. "You and I are going to escape from all of this."

"How?" Ena sent her a look of pure misery.

"I don't know yet. But I'm going try to find a way."

Rhiannon couldn't stomach the idea of giving up. Never in her life had she done so and she wouldn't dream of doing it now. Short of death, nothing would stop her from returning to her son and husband.

Right now, her silent prayer represented the strongest weapon in her arsenal. She needed a miracle.

A second later Jamie stomped into the room. Grabbing Rhiannon and Ena's arms, he hauled them downstairs and out into the bailey. He prodded Ena into a wagon bed and forced her to sit, then tied her to the wooden slats.

He made Rhiannon climb into the front seat where he tied her waist down tightly to keep her from getting away. After taking a seat beside her, he drove through the gate and out into the countryside, which brimmed with a multitude of mounted warriors, foot soldiers, and archers.

The men covered the hills as far as the eye could see and fingers of dread crept up Rhiannon's spine. It had been no small feat to bring all these clan members together. But they were all mad to think they stood a chance against King Henry and his large, disciplined army.

At the sound of hooves, she turned to see Donovan canter toward them. As he pulled up alongside the wagon, he sneered.

"Welcome to our little war party, Princess Rhiannon. I'm so pleased you decided to join us."

He signaled to his ranks and they began to march north.

As Cort and his men rode toward Leathenach Castle, he came up with his plan. Recalling the ambush he'd fallen into the last time they'd approached the same destination; he plotted a better strategy. Deep down, he felt confident his idea would work, though there always existed a shred of reality that it might not.

When they reached Donovan's stronghold, Cort ordered the majority of his men to stay in the woods and to come only if he signaled to them. His plan involved finding out how well the castle had been fortified and where Donovan had placed his men *before* they launched an attack.

Late that night, under the cloak of darkness, he and two men slowly approached the drawbridge, concealing themselves behind trees to avoid detection. The castle seemed strangely silent, but he remained cautious, nonetheless. He signaled to one of the men who waded across the moat, threw a rope over the parapets and climbed up. A short while, he mimicked bird call, indicating he'd taken his place.

Cort and his other man inched forward as the portcullis creaked open just high enough for them to slip through. A guard came at them and Cort hit him over the head. He and the other two of his soldiers dragged Donovan's man outside.

Between the three of them, they hauled the unconscious guard back to camp and dumped him on the ground. After they'd trussed him up, securing his arms and hands, Cort poured water in his face. The man sputtered and shook his head.

Cort hunkered at his side. "Where has Donovan placed his guards inside the castle?"

"Wouldn't you like to know." The guard glared at him.

Cort grabbed a horse whip and cracked it on the ground. "The next one will be on your back unless you tell me."

Trembling, the man finally began to talk. It didn't take him long to give away all the positions.

Encouraged, Cort continued his questions. "Now, where is Donovan?"

"He's not here."

It felt like someone had pulled Cort's insides out with a hook. "What about Princess Rhiannon of Callinon. Have you seen her?"

The guard fell silent, but when Cort coiled the whip around his hand in a threatening manner, he decided to continue his answers.

"She's gone with him, too. She will represent Clan O'Kelly in the attack on Dublin Castle."

Now he realized why Leathenach had seemed devoid of life. The clan uprising had begun. He and King Henry had believed there was no longer a threat and that the fight had gone out of the Irish. They'd been dead wrong.

Cort clenched his jaw and quelled the nausea rising within him. The very idea that Rhiannon might be among the casualties put a sour taste in his mouth.

The guard grinned. "Ireland will finally be rid of King Henry and the English."

"No, Donovan and his men will be killed. They don't have any idea how strong the king's troops are. Those who survive will suffer England's wrath. "

"You're wrong," the guard muttered. "We'll prevail. Clan members have turned out in great numbers to join Donovan. This is the final rebellion."

"It's the final rebellion, all right. By the time King Henry's soldiers finish with your comrades, they won't be so eager to rise up against England again."

Raking a hand through his thick hair, Cort began to pace back and forth, his heart squeezing with fear. Rhiannon would be considered a threat along with the rest of the rebels and would be punished as such. He had to reach her before it was too late.

He turned to the guard again. "When did they leave?"

"Three days ago."

Swearing, he turned to his second in command. "Giles, you and the other troops start for Dublin at first light. I'm leaving right now."

He quickly packed food supplies and a water flask into bags and saddled his stallion. Thinking about nothing but finding his wife, he rode from camp onto the dark road, his heart pounding in his ears.

Rhiannon's beautiful face seemed to float before him, illuminating the way with her tumble of brilliant red hair.

What had she suffered at the hands of Donovan and Jamie? If they'd injured her in any way, he'd see that they both died a slow, agonizing death. He'd never thought he'd ever love a woman like he loved her. To even think that someone would lay a hand on her enraged him.

Cold fury drove him on through the miles. He stopped only to rest himself and the stallion briefly, then resumed his journey. As the horse's hooves pounded the ground, his mind said her name over and over.

Rhiannon, Rhiannon, Rhiannon . . .

TWENTY-ONE

RHIANNON LAY ON A PALLET IN Jamie's tent, wide awake as she listened to his noisy sleeping. In the opposite corner from her, he lay under his blankets, snoring like a hulking bear.

Ever since they'd left Leathenach, he'd insisted she sleep in his tent, giving his troops the appearance that she was his woman. Fortunately, he hadn't forced himself on her. She figured he didn't want to wind up with her knee in his groin again. Mayhap because they'd been close at one time, he didn't rape her at knife point. Whatever the reason, she felt grateful he left her alone.

Donovan's men camped in a secluded valley not far from Dublin Castle. He and Jamie had given orders for the warriors to move out in the starlit darkness before daybreak in order to wage a surprise attack on King Henry's troops.

She knew her countrymen's foolhardy choice to fight the English would cost them their lives. The royal army was far too strong for Irish forces to defeat. She whispered a silent prayer for the souls of those men whose lives would be lost today, as well as herself and Ena. Their presence with the rebels put both of them in grave danger.

Think hard, she told herself as her heart clenched with foreboding. She had to get away before it was too late.

A scuffling noise outside drew her attention. She scooted toward the tent flaps and lifted one. At first, she didn't see anything as her eyes adjusted to the darkness. Then she made out the body of one of the guards lying on the ground. The other one rolled on the ground with his attacker, which the moonlight revealed to be an English soldier. The moonlight also glinted off the steel blade of a dropped broadsword.

Seeing her chance to flee and arm herself, Rhiannon slid on her boots and left the tent, glad she slept in her trousers and shirt. Once outside, she grabbed the weapon and spotted English soldiers crawling throughout the campsite. So much for Donovan's surprise attack. The King's troops had beaten them to it.

Now she just had to find Ena. One of Jamie's captains had claimed her soon after they'd left Leathenach. Believing she remembered which tent belonged to him, she rushed toward it. Her heart hammered as she watched Donovan's men emerge from their tents, only to meet with instant slaughter at the blades of the king's soldiers.

"Ena," she called when she reached her destination. "We've got to go."

Ena appeared at the opening. "What's going on?"

Glad to see Ena wore her shoes, Rhiannon took her arm and dragged her away as the captain shouted hoarsely in the background. By now the entire campsite had become a melee of confusion and they darted between tents, trying to evade the worst fighting. When an English soldier charged toward them, they ran in the opposite direction but he quickly caught up.

As Rhiannon turned and held up her sword, she said, "Halt! I'm Cort Guyot's wife. Jamie O'Brien kidnapped me and forced me to come along with the rebels."

"In a pig's eye," he growled. "You're a traitor along with the rest of 'em."

As alarm rushed through her, she let go of Ena's arm. "Run!"

Ena hesitated, her countenance fearful. "Rhiannon!"

"*Run!*" Rhiannon brought her blade down to clash with the one belonging to the soldier. She hadn't handled a weapon in months and it felt unwieldy in her grip. A cry of dismay escaped her when the soldier knocked the sword from her hand.

She tried to flee, but he grabbed her around the waist and hauled her into the forest where he tied her securely to a tree. Huddled against the bark, she listened to the terrible battle sounds issuing from Donovan's campsite.

The sun had begun to rise over the hills by the time the soldier returned. He released her and jerked her by the ropes toward the periphery of Donovan's campsite where Irish captives had been chained to a sea of wagons. Littered with the bodies of fallen soldiers, Irish and English alike, the campsite and surrounding area reeked of blood and gore.

Sick to her stomach, Rhiannon turned away from the horrific site. God help them all, this had turned out exactly as she had predicted.

"Please, let me go," she pleaded with the soldier. "I'm Cort Guyot's wife! I was forced to come here."

"I'm not so thick that I'd believe the likes of you." Spitting on the ground at her feet, he tied her to the side of a wagon. After climbing into the drivers' seat, he flicked the horses with a whip.

As the wagon rolled forward, she began to walk, her nerves worn to ribbons. When another wagon moved up beside them, she glanced over to see Donovan chained to the slats alongside a group of his men. Meeting her gaze, he threw back his head and laughed.

"So, we meet again, Princess." He leered at her; his grimy face covered in fresh cuts.

"Where's Jamie?"

He shook his head. "O'Brien didn't make it."

A moment of sadness washed over Rhiannon not only for Jamie, but for all the men Donovan had led astray with false promises. She'd had enough of war. Would it never end?

Donovan gave her a dark look. "It seems we're destined to die together, doesn't it?"

Gritting her teeth, she looked ahead and studied the morning sky. He didn't have to tell her that her fate couldn't be a good one. She already knew it.

BY THE TIME CORT REACHED THE battlefield, the clash of forces had ended. Strewn with corpses, the area smelled of death and he recognized bodies of both Irish and English men heaped together. As he rode through the chaotic mess, it was plain to see who had won—the English. There had been no question in his mind that they would, considering they had more disciplined forces.

Though relieved not to find Rhiannon among the fallen, a knife of fresh fear for her safety still sliced through his insides. Had she escaped or had she been taken? Jumping down from his horse, he picked up a stick and stirred the ashes of a smoldering campfire. It hadn't been that long since the skirmish had ended.

Making the assumption that she'd been captured, he swung back on his horse and kneed it away from the site. Picking up his pace, he rode on through the countryside, anxiously watching for any sign of the English. At last, he spotted the king's colors on a banner flying above a company of soldiers. Bloody and bedraggled Irish prisoners plodded resolutely alongside their wagons, chained to the slats.

Searching through the ranks, Cort finally spotted bright red hair lifting in the breeze and his heart lurched excitedly. *Rhiannon!* Her head and shoulders drooped with defeat and exhaustion. A lance of pain went through him and he instinctively knew what she felt.

A lack of hope . . . a lack of faith.

Relieved to see her alive, he wanted to cut through the ranks of men and go to her. He wanted to cut loose her bindings, sweep her off her feet, and ride away. Unfortunately, it wasn't that simple.

Glancing toward the front of the company, he recognized the

commander. He spurred his horse forward and rode up alongside him. "Ho there Broderick."

The man turned toward him. "Guyot. I thought you'd returned home."

"I did, but found my wife missing. I see you've got her, but it's a mistake. She's no rebel. I'm going back to get her."

"Halt," Broderick snarled. "You're wrong. Chadburne said that she-devil came at him with a sword. Are you so certain of her loyalties?"

"I'm positive. She was kidnapped by one of the rebel leaders."

"So you say. I don't know that for sure."

"Sweet *Jesu* Broderick, she's the mother of my child. I know what I know."

"I've got strict orders from King Henry to round up any and all known and suspected rebels."

Anger surged through Cort. "I'm telling you, she's not a rebel! I'll stake my reputation on it."

"What makes you think I'm going to fall for this deception? I saw her with my own two eyes wielding a sword against Chadburne and so did many others. If I don't bring her in, it'll be my head on the chopping block."

"I know my wife. I'm sure she tried to tell him who she was, but he must not have listened and she felt threatened."

"No matter. What's done is done. Did you know the rebels planned to attack Dublin Castle?"

"So I'd heard."

"Fortunately, this final rebellion was put down swiftly. Now King Henry wants to make an example of the prisoners. In all fairness, they'll stand trial. But they can't deny their traitorous affiliation. They'll all be executed. Every last one of them."

Cort winced and frustration rose in his throat, threatening to choke him. "Then let me ride with you. But I'd like to take Rhiannon with me. She looks exhausted—"

"Ha! I know you too well, Guyot. You'd try to trick me. Well, it's not going to happen." Broderick shouted to several of his men-at-arms who surrounded Cort. "Take care of Guyot. He's threatening this operation."

Cort spurred his horse and tried to get away, but the men had closed around him so tightly they forced his mount away from the main company. One of them knocked him from the saddle and he landed painfully in the dirt.

HEARING SHOUTS, RHIANNON LOOKED UP AND turned to watch as two men rolled on the ground, fists flying. She could tell by the armor that one of them was an English soldier. But the other man seemed familiar. Then she realized she knew who he was.

"Cort!" she called out as her wagon passed by the scuffle. Realizing he probably hadn't heard her over the pounding hooves and wagon wheels, she tried again. "Cort!"

He looked at her just as another fist flew at his face. After that, he went still. A cry ripped from her as several English soldiers hefted him to his feet and dragged him off.

A whip cracked close to her head and the man who had captured her shouted, "What are you looking at wench?"

"That's my husband back there. Cort Guyot. I told you I'm his wife."

He laughed uproariously. "Sure. And I'm the Pope. I doubt you're anything more than his bed slave and you've bewitched him with some Irish sorcery."

"No, it's not—"

The whip cracked again, so close to her ear, a few hairs yanked painfully from her scalp.

"Be silent woman!"

She twisted around to look for Cort, but couldn't see him any longer. Hot tears stung the back of her eyes. She would never have believed it possible, but he'd come for her. Obviously by doing so, he'd had put himself in great danger. It couldn't be good for him or his military career to have married someone King Henry now considered a traitor.

All of her hopes had finally been dashed. No one could save her now.

Her heart squeezed with remorse, realizing her time on this earth had nearly come to an end. Why hadn't she ever told Cort how she felt about him? For she knew now, beyond all doubt, she loved him. Her lower lip trembled as she thought of their son, so innocent and sweet, back at Callinon.

At least Cort would be there to raise little Moran. She had that one comfort to cling to.

She thought of Callinon and all the people there, and of Ailleen. Sweet Ailleen. At least her sister would live. She would also be a good influence on her son. And she would tell him about his mother and how much she'd loved him.

The unfairness of it all struck her and her knees went weak. She wanted to spend the rest of her life with Cort and grow old with him. She wanted to see her son grow up. Alas, it couldn't happen now. Despite her inner torment, years of training took hold of her senses. She came from a long line of proud Irish kings and queens. As a true princess of Ireland, she refused to show defeat.

At least she could meet her fate with dignity.

Bzzz . . . Bzzz . . . Bzzz . . .

Cort drew himself from the depths of unconsciousness, irritated at the persistent noise drilling his ears. After opening his aching eyes, he shook his head and a swarm of flies dispersed. He licked his lips and tasted blood. When he winced, the dried substance on his face cracked. No wonder the insects had been so attracted to him. He'd been beaten into a bloody mess.

He tried to move, but discovered his hands and feet were bound. His efforts were met with a bolt of pain down his back and his cramped muscles shouted with agony.

Groaning, he rolled over and took note of his surroundings. After the soldiers had worked him over, they'd dumped in a dry creek bed, leaving him for dead. Well, he was far from it.

Sides of a steep gulch rose around him and as his gaze slid skyward, he saw the sun sinking lower on the horizon.

"Damn it!" He'd been out cold most of the day while the king's soldiers marched Rhiannon and the others toward Dublin where they would be accused of treason and sentenced to death.

Ignoring the throbbing in his body, he managed to sit up. Straining against his bindings, he attempted to work loose the ropes around his wrists. He managed to make some progress, but found the effort excruciating.

"*Sacre bleu!* At this rate it'll take forever to get free."

I don't have forever.

He may not even have days. Ignoring his thirst, his injuries, and the sweat rolling down his body, he began at gnawing at the ropes. Only one thought consumed his mind; getting to Rhiannon before it was too late.

He refused to think of what would happen if he didn't.

DAYS HAD PASSED SINCE RHIANNON HAD languished in her prison cell at Dublin Castle. She barely ate and barely slept. Scenes from her life flashed before her as she paced her tiny cell or rested on her narrow cot during the dark hours. She wondered what other condemned people thought about when they were bound for the executioner. No doubt their minds wandered back to the good times they'd known.

It comforted her to recall her childhood and the happy memories of her mother and father, her brother and Ailleen. They'd been a happy family and the time had passed pleasurably.

Then Donovan had begun to make his presence known, instilling greed into the people and urging kingdoms to rise up and fight against each other for dominion. His sway over the clans had ignited a series of clashes throughout the countryside and the fighting had escalated until everyone lived in fear of their neighbors.

Eventually Seamus had lost his life at Donovan's hand and her father had sought foreign assistance to save his kingdom. Despite

Moran's valiant attempts to protect his family, everything had spiraled into this final eventuality with King Henry exerting his heavy hand over Ireland.

So many of her kinsmen and kinswomen had lost their lives. More still would. She feared there would never be peace among her clansmen—now or ever.

In a brave attempt to rally her spirits, tried to think of the good things—her love for Cort, her son, and her sister's sweet face. They would survive. They would go on to form a new Ireland that would reside under England's rule. Maybe the two countries could eventually learn to live in harmony, though she doubted it.

At least she had her beliefs to comfort her. For in her heart, she knew she would see her loved ones again on the other side.

Early one morning as she once again paced her small confines, she heard voices in the hall and keys rattled. A guard's face appeared in the barred window of the door.

"It's time, my lady."

"Aye. I'm ready." With a weary sigh and a heavy heart, she watched as the door swung open and a priest entered, his long robes rustling. He walked toward her and held up a Bible.

In Latin, he gave her late rites and blessed her. When his kind, gentle eyes met hers, she wanted to cry out for him to save her, but knew he couldn't.

"I'll hear your final confession, my child."

Rhiannon knelt before him and said, "Forgive me father, for I have sinned . . ."

TWENTY-TWO

CORT RODE LIKE A MAN POSSESSED into Dublin and the crowd parted as his horse's hooves clattered down the cobblestone streets. As he approached the castle, he urged the beast to go even faster. He didn't have time to spare.

It seemed like an eternity passed before he'd finally managed to chew his way out of the ropes. Finally free, he'd climbed from the ravine and begun the long walk to the city, cursing every footstep.

Why had he ever left Dublin in the first place? Even though King Henry had released his contingent from duty, he should have remained to make sure everything was in order. In his excitement to see Rhiannon and little Moran, he'd used poor judgment.

Luck finally met him when he found a stream to clean up and drink from. Then he'd come across a farmstead where kindly people had taken him in. Resting only briefly, he'd gathered supplies and borrowed a horse.

At last, after all this time, he'd finally reached his destination. He just hoped his arrival hadn't come too late. If so, he knew he'd be devastated.

He shouted to the guards posted in the gatehouse and they raised the portcullis so he could enter. In the bailey, he galloped through the large crowd gathered to gawk at the platform, outfitted with an executioner's block. Near the platform, seating had been assembled for distinguished guests. Among them sat King Henry, deep in conversation with his advisors.

Turning his attention toward a flurry of activity, he watched as guards exited the castle escorting a group of prisoners. The bedraggled people were led front and center where the crowd jeered and threw rotten food at them.

Still too far away to see if Rhiannon was among them, he pushed forward, tethering his horse on a rail. After jumping down, he shouldered his way through the people. As he watched the scene unfolding, a guard placed black hoods over the condemned's faces, all except for one.

He recognized Donovan instantly; noted his twisted grin and the conceited set of his shoulders. Even to the last, he remained arrogant. His laughter rang out as a guard slipped on his hood.

One of the prisoners wore a dress and had a small, slight build. *Rhiannon.* God, he had to stop this madness!

He shouted at the guards to stop, but they couldn't hear him over the crowd. And even if they could, what made him think they would stop for him?

Nevertheless, he continued to shout frantically as he pushed his way forward. One after the other, the prisoners knelt down and received the executioner's swift justice. By the time Cort arrived, every last one of the prisoners had fallen to the blade.

Horrified, he stared at the woman's lifeless form, thrown like a bag of refuse on the ground. His ears filled with a roar and he realized that the inhuman sound came from him. It seemed as though someone had ripped out his heart and stomped it into the dust at his feet.

He couldn't think, couldn't breathe. Everything around him whirled in a mass of colors and he grabbed his head to try and think straight. The only person he'd ever loved had been cut down. Her life, doused like the flames that bore the color of her hair.

I can't live without her. I'll die of grief . . .

"What's wrong mate? Is the sight of blood too much for ya?"

An elderly man stood at his side, a hand on his shoulder, a questioning look on his face.

Lifeless and numb, he tried to form the words to answer. Finally, his voice came back. "That is . . . was my wife up there. They killed her."

"What was she doing with the likes of them rowdy fellows?" He nodded toward the platform. "They shouldn't have challenged King Henry. It was madness."

"Sh-she was innocent. She'd been kidnapped by one of the rebel leaders."

"May God rest her soul. I'm sorry to hear of your loss." Crossing himself, the man shuffled off.

Cort turned away from the platform. In his mind, he heard Rhiannon's laughter and saw her lovely face. He saw her riding her horse carelessly through the fields of Callinon, her brilliant red hair streaming behind her. Remembering her sweet kisses and soft touch, he thought of how he'd ached to hold her all these months. His knees went weak and he slumped against a post.

He'd never see her again in this lifetime.

She was gone.

Though surrounded by throngs of people, he felt totally alone in his misery.

RHIANNON'S FEET WERE HEAVY AS THE guards marched her and several other prisoners from the castle. Spotting the bodies stacked up beside the platform, she grimaced. Recognizing Donovan's boots on one of the corpses, she felt a twisted sense of satisfaction.

After all of his heinous crimes, he'd finally met a fitting end. He alone was responsible for the loss of many innocent lives over the years. He deserved this.

Her gaze swept across the other bodies and she noticed a small form wearing a dress, crushed beneath the others.

"Ena," she muttered softly, her heart clenching in sadness as she recognized the clothing. All her efforts to free the girl had failed. She hadn't gotten away after all.

Tears slipped down her face as she began to pray. "Hail Mary, full of grace . . ."

When the flash of a familiar face caught her eye, the words in her mouth died away, her heart nearly jumped from her chest. *Saints above.* Cort stood a short distance from the platform and everything about his demeanor told her that he hurt inside. If only she could take away his pain, if only she could tell him how much she truly loved him!

At the very least, she wanted to say good-bye one last time. She only wanted a few quick words with him, perhaps a fleeting kiss to light her way to the other side. Surely her captors wouldn't deny her that one last request.

"Cort, Cort! I'm here! Cort!"

Slowly he looked up and their gazes met, locking with the boundless gaze of lovers in the midst of turmoil.

"Rhiannon!"

He raced toward the platform and hefted himself up. When the guards came at him, he knocked them aside like a raging bull. As they stared at him in disbelief, he pulled her into his strong embrace and crushed her against his chest.

"Cort! I never thought I'd see you again." She drank in his essence, so full of life, so full of vigor. "God's given me one final gift before leaving this world."

Twining his fingers in her hair, he kissed her possessively, pressing his lips against hers. "I'll never let you go again, Rhiannon. *Never.* I love you."

"I love you too," she managed, thrilled beyond belief to see him and hear those words, but saddened to hear them now. "You've got to forget me. Take care of little Moran and Ailleen, but it's over for us."

"What's going on?" One of the guards roughly grabbed Cort's arm.

Cort glared at the guard so hard, Rhiannon found it hard to believe he didn't fall to the ground from the force of it.

"Try that again and you'll find a knife in your ribs," Cort snapped at him.

The man backed off slightly, a scowl on his face. "These are condemned people. You have to leave."

"The hell I will." Cort whistled loudly, garnering everyone's attention and the roar of the crowd died eventually away. Glancing at the risers, he shouted to the king and his advisors. "King Henry, I beseech you. If you have any mercy in your heart, hear me now."

King Henry rose and sent him a confused stare. "Guyot? What is the meaning of this? Have you lost your mind?"

"Mayhap I have. But I insist that you listen to me. Or else you can put me to death with the others."

Murmurs rose from the crowd.

"Cort, no!" Rhiannon clutched his arm. "You can't do this. Stop it!"

"Listen to me for once," he told her firmly, then turned back to the king. "Will you hear me out, sire?"

"Go on. But you'd better not be wasting my time." King Henry folded his arms across his chest, his expression bursting with impatience.

Cort cleared his throat and spoke clearly. "I understand you wish to make an example of these prisoners. But I assure you, my wife is innocent. She was kidnapped and forced to join with the rebels."

"You know what happened?" Rhiannon whispered.

"Quinn told me everything. We can talk about it later."

King Henry's gaze darkened. "Is this a fact?"

"I have it on good authority, your majesty."

After a contemplative moment, the king spoke again. "Take your wife and leave."

Cort added, "But the others—"

"They have no excuse for their misdeeds," he boomed. "Their sentence stands."

When Rhiannon slumped against Cort and began to sob, he pulled her closer, knowing her heart ached for her countrymen who had been deceived by Donovan's greed.

"Consider one more thing, sire," Cort called.

King Henry shook his head. "You're lucky you've proven yourself as one of my most trustworthy commanders, Guyot. Otherwise, we would not suffer this insolence."

"Show mercy on the remaining prisoners," Cort said. "That act alone will draw the undying loyalty of the Irish."

"What? This is madness," King Henry shouted.

"No, on the contrary, it is a solid strategy. The man who led them astray, Tadgh Donovan, has already been executed. He was a traitor to his own people and turned their hearts away from their loyalty to each other. With him gone, I daresay the others will return home to their farms and their families. Since I have married into the O'Kelly clan and can speak as one of their leaders, I guarantee you that if you do this, you'll secure their future allegiance."

"Aye," another prisoner's voice rang out excitedly. "There's been enough bloodshed. I'm the O'Neill clan chief and I pledge our support."

Another prisoner voiced his offer. "The Sullivan clan is with you, too."

"And the O'Reillys," another man added.

As all the clan names were called out, the crowd began to roar with approval and applause rippled through the masses.

"Long live the king!" someone shouted, and everyone joined into the chorus, chanting it over and over.

King Henry looked nonplussed momentarily, then sat back down and conversed with his advisors. Finally, he rose again, and held up his hands. "Silence everyone. *Silence!*"

The voices finally faded away.

"We have decided to pardon the rest of the prisoners. But hear me well; any further disobedience will be met with a similar tragic outcome. There will be no lenience shown again."

Joyous shouts issued from the crowd, along with, "All hail King Henry, a true and merciful overlord!"

As the crowd wandered off and the guards set the prisoners loose, Cort swept Rhiannon off her feet and carried her from the platform. In the shade of an oak tree, he put her down and drew her close for another kiss. Having her in his life and loving her was all he'd ever wanted. The touch of her lips on his was akin to a slice of heaven on earth, her touch, paradise.

To think he'd nearly lost her made him fill with fiery rage. Never again would he allow danger to cross Rhiannon's path. His wife and his family had become his life, and he would die for them.

Withdrawing his mouth from hers, he looked into her flashing green eyes. His heart melted at the sight of her alive and well and cradled in his arms.

"When I returned to Callinon, Josette told me you'd run off with Jamie," Cort said. "I could hardly stand the idea you'd gone to him, but I went looking and found Quinn. He'd nearly been beaten to death by Donovan, but he managed to tell me what happened."

She drew back in shock. "Oh, no is he—"

"He's all right. Glenna's taking care of him. She said he's a sturdy lad."

"Aye, if she's ministering to him, I'm sure he'll survive his injuries."

He smothered her face with kisses again. "God, I thought I'd lost you."

"And I thought I'd lost you," she whispered back, her breath warm and moist on his skin, thrilling him to the core. "I can hardly believe you're here. And that you would actually die for me."

A smile touched his lips. "I couldn't have gone on living without you, *ma cherie*. We belong together. Now and forever."

"Aye," she agreed wholeheartedly. "Until the end of time."

BORN IN PORTLAND, OREGON, CINDY has lived all over the United States and spent five years in Misawa, Japan. She has visited Canada, the Philippines, Samoa, Hawaii, both the western and eastern Caribbean, and New Zealand.

Currently, she lives in Cheyenne, Wyoming, where Cheyenne Frontier Days is held each July. CFD's well-known rodeo is often referred to as the "Daddy of 'em all."

Over the years, she has won or placed in various writing contests. She has also written for and edited numerous newsletters. Her non-fiction magazine articles have been featured in "True West" and "Wild West." She was a book critic for Storyteller Alley and is a freelance writer/editor.

For the last 20 years, she has been a contributing editor and writer for Laramie County School District 1's Public Schools' newspaper titled, "The Chronicle," and now writes for their magazine titled "Elevate," which has a circulation of approximately 46,000 readers.

From baby alligators to glow worms, Cindy has seen a variety of life's wonders.